Southern Spirits

In "A Subtle Breeze" the sex scenes are so sizzling hot you'll want to make sure you have the AC cranked up on high...I really enjoyed getting to know Zeke and Brendon.
~ *Dark Diva Reviews*

"A Subtle Breeze" is a sweet love story with a paranormal twist I didn't expect...Read this and enjoy. ~ *Literary Nymphs Reviews*

A Subtle Breeze is a sweet love story with a bit of a paranormal twist...I really enjoyed the lovemaking scenes, they were very well written and at one point I realized I had my head twisted as far as it would go to the side trying to figure out the mechanics of a position! Very hot and steamy! ~ *Fallen Angel Reviews*

"A Subtle Breeze" is a romance that focuses heavily on love triumphing over evil with hot men and even hotter sex. Add in a handful of interfering women, and you've got an interesting and rather different story. ~ *Rainbow Reviews*

When the Dead Speak by Bailey Bradford is an entertaining mix of mystery, romance, and ghost story...Three dimensional, likable characters and a well developed plot keep the novel moving at an even pace. ~ *Dark Diva Reviews*

When the Dead Speak by Bailey Bradford is a mix between a murder mystery, a hot m/m romance, and a little bit of a supernatural ghost story. Each element alone would have made for an interesting read, but mixing all three together made it not just gripping, but entertaining as well. ~ *Queer Magazine Online*

SOUTHERN SPIRITS
Volume One

A Subtle Breeze

When the Dead Speak

BAILEY BRADFORD

Southern Spirits Volume One
ISBN # 978-0-85715-399-9
©Copyright Bailey Bradford 2010
Cover Art by Lyn Taylor ©Copyright 2010
Interior text design by Claire Siemaszkiewicz
Total-E-Bound Publishing

Published in 2010 by Total-E-Bound Publishing, Think Tank, Ruston Way, Lincoln, LN6 7FL, United Kingdom.

Total-E-Bound Publishing is an imprint of Total-E-Ntwined Limited.

Manufactured in the USA.

A SUBTLE
BREEZE

Dedication

For my sister — your wit, wisdom, and warmth are
incomparable and irreplaceable.
I love you madly, sis.

Chapter One

Ezekiel Matthers stood looking down at his mother's grave. She'd been gone for almost four years now, and he still couldn't get used to the fact that he wasn't going to see her again, at least not in this lifetime. There were mornings when he stumbled into the kitchen bleary-eyed from sleep and swore he could smell her perfume, a soft, sweet scent he had never encountered on anyone else. It always left him with the feeling that he had just missed her, like she had slipped out the door to head to work right before he could hug her.

"Enough," he muttered, kneeling down to place the bouquet of yellow roses he'd brought with him up against the tombstone. "I sure do miss you, Mama. I bet you're having the best birthday yet, dancing with angels on those golden streets." Zeke closed his eyes as a soft breeze caressed his skin, bringing with it a faint fragrance that somehow soothed his soul. The loneliness that was his ever-present companion still gnawed at him, but he pushed it down, as always.

Zeke had all but given up on finding someone to share his life with. When his mama was still alive, he hadn't wanted to risk bringing trouble down on them, on his mother and sisters, by having a relationship out in the open. There had already been too much such trouble once people found out he was gay, and his mama and sisters had been confronted in town on more than one occasion. Ezekiel had, too, but it had never concerned him like it did when it happened to any of his loved ones. On top of that, somewhere in the darkest corner of his heart, Zeke had held out hope that his oldest sister, Eva, would eventually 'come around', as Mama had said she would. That hadn't happened, and when Mama died, the chasm between him and Eva had grown into what he feared was an unbridgeable size. Zeke didn't know if he even had the strength, much less the desire any more, to bother with trying to fix that sad relationship.

That gentle breeze seemed to nudge him, almost chastising him for his melancholy and defeatist thoughts. Zeke shook his head at his fanciful musing, saying a silent prayer for his mama before opening his eyes and standing. He grunted a bit when his right knee popped, something that gave him problems courtesy of a fight—an assault really, though calling it a fight made it somehow seem less personal, less planned. The damage to his knee, caused by a pipe and a few homophobes, was not extensive but it did act up on occasion. All things considered, he figured he was lucky that was the severest injury he had sustained from the encounter. If Elizabeth and Enessa hadn't overheard the men plotting minutes before and rushed to follow them... Well, he had no illusions. Those men had intended to get him out of McKinton, one way or another.

Giving one last glance to his mama's grave, Ezekiel turned and headed for his truck, noting another vehicle pulling in to the cemetery. He squinted, recognising Enessa's little hybrid — that looked way too tiny for the number of people in it. Deciding he didn't feel up to making conversation with whomever she had with her, Zeke waved in her direction and picked up his pace so he could leave before she even stopped her car. He groaned when he realised he wasn't going to make it. Enessa parked and jumped out of her car, running straight for him.

"Zeke! Wait!" Enessa ran full tilt, almost careening into Ezekiel before stopping. He couldn't quite hold back a grin. Nessa was just too sweet to stay irritated with for more than a few seconds. He caught her forearms, preventing her from teetering over courtesy of her sudden stop.

"Thanks, Zeke!" Enessa smiled up at him, eyes lit up like the Fourth of July. "Why were you trying to run off?"

He sighed, wanting only to get back to the ranch where he could keep himself busy with work. "Nessa, I'm really not up to having to play nice with your friends right now, and I have a lot of work waiting for me at the ranch." Zeke tried to ignore the look she gave him, refusing to be guilted into hanging around.

"But, Zeke...I just wanted to visit Mama and my friends were here, and you know Gloria. The other..." Enessa trailed off.

Ezekiel put his arm around her shoulder, using it to steer her in the direction of her car, not paying any particular notice to the two people lingering by the hybrid.

"Nessa, go visit Mama. Take your friends with you, do what you have to, honey, but I am just plain not in any mood to be chatty with your buddies, okay? Not right now." He watched her digest what he said, saw she wasn't going to be hurt by it. "Go on, now. Your friends are waiting for ya." Zeke tipped his head in their general direction, assuming that's what they were doing.

Enessa surprised him with a big hug before she stood on her tiptoes and planted a smacking kiss on his cheek.

"I'm not sure they're waiting on me, but okay. Since you aren't feeling very friendly right now and have so much work to get back to, would it be okay if I invite my friends over for supper? I'm making fried chicken and mashed potatoes, gravy and biscuits and—"

Zeke laughed, shaking his head. One way or another, Nessa was going to make him meet her friends, and there was no reason he could think of not to do so this evening. Not without hurting her feelings, anyway.

"Nessa, if you're going to fix one of your homemade meals for supper, you can bring over the entire college campus for all I care." He hugged his little sister, maybe not so little now at twenty three, but she'd always be little to him, especially as she was a good eight inches shorter than his own six-foot, three-inches.

"I'll see you—and your buddies—at the supper table, okay?" Zeke let her go and headed back over to his truck, pushing aside thoughts of supper and company, already focusing on the tasks waiting for him when he got home. Soon his mind was making lists and shifting around priorities, leaving no room for him to dwell on things like his mama's death or how lonely he was.

* * * *

"Oh, come on, Brendon, you can fit in Nessa's car! I'll crawl in the back." Gloria's voice held the pleading note that Brendon almost always caved in to, but this time he wasn't going down so easily. The little hybrid his cousin Gloria's friend drove might be economical, but there was no way it would be comfortable for his six-foot frame. He'd much rather take his gas-guzzling SUV over to the cemetery where Enessa said her brother would be instead of trying to cram into a tuna can on wheels.

"What is the problem with taking my SUV?" Because he certainly didn't have a problem with taking it, even if it did contribute to ozone decay. That would be a slower death than compression and suffocation in a dinky car.

Gloria and Enessa exchanged looks, leaving Brendon to wonder what they were hiding, and why he had let himself get talked into this whole thing to begin with. He'd visited Gloria over Christmas for a few days, having driven up from UT at Austin before his last semester there. He hadn't seen his cousin in years, since before she had moved to McKinton, and Brendon had looked forward to renewing their friendship.

Now he had his master's in geology, and when Gloria had suggested he come visit her in McKinton again before he decided whether or not to pursue his doctorate, he'd thought it sounded like a nice break. He'd been in college for six years and figured taking the summer off would help him map out his future. Added to that, she mentioned that Enessa, whom he had met over the Christmas break, had a really hot and available older brother...and the whole idea had suddenly become very appealing.

Not that Brendon needed to be hooked up. He was decent looking, though he didn't dwell on it. Still, he knew his face was not a bad one. Attractive, even, with his light brown eyes framed in dark lashes, a straight, narrow nose, a full lower lip—and the dimple in his right cheek when he smiled drew its fair share of compliments. He kept his sandy brown hair short, minimising the amount of time he had to deal with it. Working out and hiking on a regular basis kept his body in good shape, muscles toned and tight. Despite this, Brendon had to admit his sex life had been somewhat…lacking, but that was due more to the amount of time he had spent on his studies than anything else. With his summer free, he could have found someone on his own, but then Gloria had e-mailed him a picture of Enessa standing beside her brother, and Brendon had been sunk.

Ezekiel stared back at him from the photo with eyes such a deep green that Brendon had first assumed the picture had been fixed up, but Gloria assured him it hadn't. She sent a few other pictures, and they all showed the same studious, sexy man staring back at the camera. Brendon's cock had sprung to life as soon as he'd downloaded the first picture, and it seemed he had been walking around with an uncomfortable erection too much of the time ever since.

Zeke Matthers was tall, around six-three or four, broad shouldered and just sexy as fuck. His coffee-coloured hair hung down past his shoulders, framing a face that belonged on a model. Dark brows sat over those wide, slightly uptilted green eyes surrounded with thick lashes. His nose was incredibly sexy, long and narrow, with a slight bump on the bridge where it had been broken at least once. And his lips… Ezekiel had full lips; the bottom one plumper than the top, and Brendon had spent plenty of time thinking about sucking on that lower lip— —right after he ran his tongue through the dimple on the chin below it. All in all, he had it bad. Sunk, just like that.

"Brendon!" Gloria waved her hand in his face and he jerked back, wondering how long she had been flapping around him. "Have you heard anything we said?"

Embarrassed to be caught with his mind teetering very close to the gutter, Brendon shook his head. Gloria harrumphed, something she was quite good at, crossing her arms across her chest and giving him an irritated glare.

"Nessa said it's better to take her car because Zeke will recognise it and probably not leave before we get out. If we go in your SUV, there's a good chance he will just up and run before we can even park." Gloria watched him, waiting to make sure he got it this time.

"Fine, fine. Let's just go, then." Brendon would have asked about the whole Zeke probably not leaving thing, except he knew, thanks to Nessa and Gloria, how hard it was for the other man to come to town. The stories they had shared with Brendon about the harassment Ezekiel experienced in town had turned Brendon's stomach. Having grown up in a much larger and definitely more liberal town himself, he hadn't encountered very much gay bashing. Sure, there had been some name-calling and such, but on a whole, he knew he'd been a pretty lucky man.

Almost perversely, rather than make him afraid to come back to this town without trying to hide his sexual preference, the stories about the hell Ezekiel had been through had only fed Brendon's determination to come stay the summer and be himself. Because, somewhere between the pictures and the stories, Brendon had felt a piece of his heart make room for Ezekiel. He didn't know the man, but he knew of him, and he wanted to see what, if anything, they could have between them. At the very least, he wanted to slake the lust that had been raging in his body every since he'd opened the e-mails from Gloria. If all he and Zeke could have was some really hot sex, going at it until they were both unconscious, that would work. He hoped. But for some reason, whether it was the sharing of information about the man or the pictures or a combination of both, Brendon really wanted something more with Ezekiel. Maybe it was everything, combined with the fact that the man had been so mistreated, so…hurt.

Shaking himself from his thoughts, Brendon folded up into the front seat of the little car, not surprised to find that, once seated, his knees were practically in his armpits. Why did the choice have to be clean air or contortion? He was sure there had to be a third 'c' — compromise — that should be thrown into the whole hybrid craze.

The drive to the cemetery wasn't very long, and even before they pulled in, before Enessa and Gloria pointed and nudged him, Brendon had spotted the lone figure kneeling at one of the graves. The image tugged at his heart. Ezekiel looked so solitary, though not just in the physical sense. Brendon didn't know how to explain it except that he could swear he felt the loneliness rolling off the kneeling man.

He watched the man rise and turn to see who was pulling into the cemetery drive. Brendon noted the moment Ezekiel spotted the passengers in his sister's car; that was when he made a beeline for his truck.

"Better hurry, Nessa, looks like your brother is going to bolt." Not that it would deter Brendon; he would meet the man one way or another.

"Oh no, he isn't!" Nessa declared, stomping on the hybrid's brake pedal. She slapped the gear in park and jumped out, running after her brother. He watched Ezekiel's back stiffen, saw him hesitate as though he were contemplating leaving his sister there, hollering in the graveyard. Of course he didn't. Brendon hadn't thought he would, not after the way Enessa had talked about her brother.

Ezekiel turned around to catch Nessa, who almost smacked right into him. Brendon gasped when he saw the man in person; he couldn't help himself. That man was just so gorgeous, so fine that Brendon felt a quiver of uncertainty as he practically popped out of the little car to stand by Gloria. For once, he worried about his looks, even if it made him feel like a vain fool. He simply didn't know if he was attractive enough to catch Zeke's attention, and that was a fear he'd never had before regarding another man.

Doesn't matter, he thought as he watched the interaction between the siblings. He wanted the man, and would do his damnedest to make it happen. Even though it was obvious from watching Enessa and Ezekiel that he wouldn't have the opportunity just yet. Zeke was shaking his head at Enessa, then paused to hear her out on something, agreeing with whatever it was she said this time.

Never once did he look over and notice the two people waiting by the car, but rather than be offended, Brendon thought it might work in his favour. If the man didn't notice him, then he wouldn't be wary about meeting him. It would all work out; he'd *make* it work out. Determination and hope coursed through him as he stood still, enjoying the gentle breeze that wafted around him. Enessa's grin when she headed back towards them fed that hope, as did her words.

"Zeke's not up to company right now, he has to get back to the ranch, but y'all are invited to supper tonight. With us both." Nessa and Gloria smiled and waggled their brows at Brendon, who couldn't tamp down his own answering grin. He was just glad the girls couldn't see the way his cock had tented his pants, again. Maybe tonight he would find some relief.

Chapter Two

Zeke finished the work he had scheduled for the day, and after stopping to check with his ranch hands, Charlie and Miguel, he managed to slip through the side door of the house. Tired, sore and generally just ready to go to bed, he was wishing he'd never agreed to supper with Nessa and her buddies. A sound caught his attention, and Zeke paused outside the door to his room, recognising Nessa's and her friend Gloria's voices.

It was the darkly sexy masculine voice that froze him in his tracks. That voice smoothed over his cock like a warm tongue. Zeke grew erect so fast he almost felt dizzy. He couldn't make out what was being said, but the sound of laughter soon followed, and suddenly the idea of supper with Enessa's friends, at least one of them, didn't seem so bad — — even if he had to sit through the meal with a hard-on. Zeke listened a few more minutes, then slipped inside his room.

Stripping quickly for his shower, Zeke stared down at his prick, watching it tap against his taut belly, begging for attention. He thought about grabbing it, stroking himself until he came, which wouldn't take much at this point. He hadn't slipped away to Fort Worth for relief since before Mama died and had been taking care of it himself when he couldn't hold off any longer. This, though.... Well, he was flat-out hornier than he could ever remember being, but he didn't want to do anything about it. Not yet, anyway. Not until he had matched a face to the voice that had caused this reaction. Decision made, Zeke turned the hot water off, hoping the cold would blast his cock into submission.

Zeke debated using the blow dryer on his hair, but after spending several minutes combing out the mid-back length mass, he decided that enough time had been spent on grooming. His cock was still semi-erect, and Zeke tried not to think about why it was still in such a state as he slid on a black pair of jeans. He grabbed a tight black tee and put on his socks and boots, then topped it all off with his black Stetson. Good enough, he hoped, for tonight's guest.

It didn't occur to him that the man in the kitchen might be one of the girls' date until he was almost to the kitchen. The very thought caused him to stumble, and accomplished what the cold shower hadn't—his cock went soft with disappointment. Bracing himself in the hall, Zeke took a deep breath and could have sworn he smelled his mother's scent.

He felt his chest tighten with panic, then the sweet smell had the effect it often did. Calmness washed over him, helping him to breathe and focus his thoughts. By the time he pushed away from the wall, Zeke was back to himself, though he didn't regain his erection.

Until he stepped in the kitchen and saw the owner of the voice, or rather the back of the man. And it was a very fine back, broad shouldered and lean muscled, showcased in a white t-shirt, tapering down to a narrow waist and hips, a beautiful firm ass, and long legs that Zeke wanted to feel flung over his shoulders. His cock sprang back to life so fast that Zeke grunted, then immediately moved to take a seat when he realised the man, along with Nessa and Gloria, had heard him.

"Zeke! I thought you were going to stand us up there for a few minutes!" Enessa teased, walking over to him. He started to explain about ranches and constant work, but the words froze in his throat as he finally got a look at the man in the white tee. Zeke managed to snap his mouth shut before he made a bigger fool of himself, but there was no way he could look away from the fire he saw burning in those light brown eyes. Moisture slipped from the head of his dick, enough that he now had the added worry of standing up and revealing a wet spot.

Nessa and Gloria gave each other some look Zeke knew he would never decipher, and didn't really care to as the man with the pretty eyes stepped around the table. He reached out a hand to Zeke, smiling and showing off a dimple that did all kinds of things to Zeke's cock.

"Brendon Shanahan, Gloria's cousin. Nice to finally meet you, Ezekiel. Nessa's told me a lot about you." Brendon winked at him when he added that last bit, and Zeke felt the tips of his ears burn. Somehow, he managed to reach out and shake Brendon's hand, but words were simply beyond him. He nodded, keeping his eyes locked on the other man's even as Zeke started to let go of the guest's hand. Except...Zeke felt Brendon's reluctance to release his hand, felt the gentle caress of fingers as he lowered his hand to the tabletop.

Zeke finally made himself look away, only to find Nessa sliding the plate of fried chicken into the oven. *What's she doing that for?* Gloria had left the kitchen, not that he had noticed when it happened. Brendon pulled up a chair beside Zeke as Enessa walked over and tipped back Zeke's hat. She planted a big, smacking kiss on his forehead, then stepped back, edging to the kitchen door.

"What— Where are you going, Nessa?" Zeke was glad his voice didn't crack, and doubly glad it finally worked.

Nessa looked around a little nervously, smiling first at Brendon then Zeke. "Well, um, we, ah, we didn't think...um. Gloria?" Enessa was almost out the kitchen door when Gloria popped her head in, grinning from ear to ear.

"She means we didn't think about how to exit and leave you two alone. Subterfuge is so not our thing. Bye!" Gloria's head, along with the part of Enessa that was still visible, disappeared as Zeke sat there, stunned and so embarrassed he felt his lungs start to seize up. Breathe, he told himself, closing his eyes to try to battle back the panic he felt welling inside. *Not now, not in front of Brendon, please God.*

"Hey, it's okay, Ezekiel. I can leave if you want." Brendon spoke in a soothing tone.

Zeke kept his eyes shut, all too aware that his breathing was too fast, too irregular. He thought he shook his head slightly, but knew he'd failed when he heard Brendon's chair scrape against the kitchen floor. Zeke's heart kicked into overdrive when a hand touched his shoulder, and another cupped his cheek, turning his head to the side.

"But I'd much rather stay, if that's all right with you." Brendon's breath fluttered against his lips, so close Zeke knew he had only to lean in a little bit. He opened his eyes, surprised to find the other man squatted down beside him, those sweet brown eyes soft with understanding. Zeke lowered his gaze to Brendon's plush lips and his panic start to subside. It couldn't compete with his need to taste the tempting mouth so near his own.

"Stay," he managed to get out before moving in that last little bit and lowering his mouth to Brendon's. Zeke groaned when his tongue met the other man's, the flavour exploding throughout his senses, his cock jerking and releasing more pre-come as he reached out to pull Brendon to him. The hand that cupped his face slid down, across Zeke's shoulder and lower still until it found his nipple, already hard and aching. Zeke moaned his approval as their tongues twined together and Brendon scraped at the nipple with his thumbnail.

Zeke's back arched so fast his hat fell off and he almost slid out of his chair. Grabbing Brendon by the arms, Zeke pulled him up as he stood without breaking their kiss. He steered them to the living room, knowing he'd never make it to the bedroom, never survive the walk. Twisting around, Zeke fell back onto the couch, pulling Brendon on top of him and reaching down to grab his firm ass.

Brendon threw his head back, groaning as he thrust his cock against Zeke's. "Need to…ah, God, Zeke," Brendon panted, pushing himself up on his knees between Zeke's thighs. "Clothes. Get them off." He jerked off his own shirt before reaching down and tugging the hem of Zeke's tee from his waistband. Zeke rose up enough to pull the shirt off over his head, then reached out and stroked Brendon's nipples, pinching the hard buds. Brendon moaned and reached for the snap on his jeans, pushing them and his underwear down his thighs.

The sight of Brendon's cock, the fat crown glistening with moisture, had Zeke's hands stilling on Brendon's nipples. It'd been too long since Zeke had seen another man like this, touched a dick other than his own. He slid his hands quickly down Brendon's hard abs, unable to fully appreciate the firm muscles there when something much more tempting was so close to his fingertips.

"Oh, God, Brendon, you're so thick, so…" Zeke trailed off, eyes wide as he ran his thumb over Brendon's glistening cock head, pressing slightly on the slit. With a low groan, Brendon grabbed his hand, stilling the movement.

"Going to come if you keep doing that, Ezekiel," he explained, then stood to pull off the rest of his clothes. Zeke straightened and reached for the snap on his jeans, but Brendon stopped him and waited until Zeke met his gaze. Only then did he bend down and reach for his jeans. Zeke watched him dig through the pockets and pull out a strip of condoms. He tossed them on the floor beside the couch with one hand while dropping the jeans behind him with the other.

"You had a plan or something, Brendon?" Zeke teased, enjoying the way a bright blush swept over Brendon's body. Nope, he decided it didn't offend him in the least that Brendon had come out here with the idea of seducing him somewhere on his list of things to do. Zeke knew, judging by the hardness of his own erection, *that* particular part of him was really glad about the whole seduction scheme.

"Yes," Brendon admitted, not a trace of humour in his steady gaze. "I've wanted you since…since Gloria showed me your picture weeks ago. Enessa and Gloria thought we'd, uhm, get along."

Well, then, hallelujah and far be it from Zeke to deny either of them this night. He admired the way Brendon didn't flinch or beat around the bush; he'd stood proud and almost daring when he made his proclamation. The man both humbled him and made him want to fuck until they were boneless lumps. Even knowing Gloria and Nessa had been priming Brendon, feeding him information on him, couldn't douse the sheer need Zeke was feeling. He was hot, he was horny, and his cock was so hard he could hammer nails with it.

Zeke was also determined to meet Brendon's honesty tit for tat even if it was embarrassing. "I haven't...been with anyone in over four years," he offered. The effect that statement had on Brendon was immediate and apparent. His whole body vibrated with a level of anticipation Zeke could almost feel.

"Well, then," Brendon drawled, reaching to unbutton Zeke's jeans, "maybe it's time we stopped talking and..." Zeke's cock nearly burst out from its confines as a swift jerk from Brendon freed all the buttons at once. He watched as Brendon paused when he saw how big the cock was that he had just released.

"Damn, Ezekiel, that thing is almost...illegal," he muttered before tracing a prominent vein running down one side. Zeke took Brendon's hand and cupped it around his prick, hips jerking when the man fisted the heavy length.

"It'll fit, you'll fit it just fine, but I want..." Zeke sucked in a breath as Brendon pumped his cock, "I want you to fuck me, Brendon." Brendon's head jerked up, hand stilling on Zeke's dick.

"You sure, Zeke? 'Cause we can...either way, you know?"

He had seen that quick flash of fear in Brendon's eyes, and Zeke didn't view it as a sacrifice to be on the receiving end tonight. It wouldn't be the first time he'd bottomed. Generally, he did prefer to top but he wanted to feel the other man's long, thick cock spearing his ass. Zeke kissed

Brendon, intending for it to be a soft, reassuring kiss, but it quickly became a mashing of lips, nipping teeth and thrusting tongues. When Zeke was finally able to make himself pull away, he was breathing like he'd run a marathon.

"You include lube, baby, in all your planning?" Zeke teased, fighting the desire to cross his fingers in hope. The way Brendon pinked up all over again practically answered the question for him.

"Yeah, yeah, just let me…" Brendon turned back to dig through his pants pockets again, finding the little packets of lube he had brought with him. He turned and bobbled the lube, grabbing the base of his dick and squeezing hard. Zeke had pretty much hoped for such an effect when he'd turned and bent at the waist, forearms braced on the arm of the couch. There was something to be said for the element of surprise, even if Brendon had planned to get in his…pants.

"Holy shit!" Brendon looked so stunned Zeke felt a moment of doubt. Maybe he should have taken a more subtle position, but he did have a reason for this one.

"Brendon," he murmured, voice heavy with need, "I need… I can't, my knee sometimes it acts up and I can't, can't…but I…" *Goddamned bigots and their pipes.* Zeke felt like a bashful teenager fumbling through his first time.

"I know, Zeke, I know. Just, man, you're so damned sexy it sucks the air right outta my lungs." Brendon tore open the packet of lube, coating his fingers and cock with it. He trailed his fingers over Zeke's balls, following the crease above them until he found the tight ring of flesh he sought. Zeke growled, startling himself, as Brendon stroked the sensitive opening, teasing and tormenting with each touch. Zeke thought he was going to go crazy by the time Brendon slowly, steadily, pushed one finger into the tight channel.

Zeke went from growling to groaning as he pushed his ass back, riding Brendon's finger.

"More," he ordered, glaring over his shoulder at Brendon until he complied and pushed a second finger in deep and hard. When those probing fingers lightly rubbed Zeke's prostate, he couldn't stop the hoarse yell that was torn from him. It was bliss and agony, because as great as it felt, his aching dick still needed some friction. Brendon seemed to understand, even without Zeke begging like he wanted to...if his pride would have allowed it. A rough hand slid over Zeke's hip, then snaked around to grab his cock, spreading the leaking pre-come around the flared head. Both of Brendon's hands began moving in synch, stroking Zeke inside and out.

"So fucking hot," Brendon gritted out. The hand fisting Zeke's prick moved faster while Brendon's fingers curled inside him, pegging Zeke's gland again and again. Zeke bucked wildly, hands clawing into the furniture as his cock pulsed and his balls drew up tight, spurting come through Brendon's fingers.

When his vision finally shook off the orgasm-induced haze, Zeke watched as Brendon brought his spunked hand to his lips. Eyes glued to Zeke's, he flicked his tongue out and licked the white gobs from his fingers. *God. Damn.* And the man thought *he* was hot? Brendon had him beat, hands down.

"You taste so good," Brendon ground out, pulling his fingers from Zeke's stretched opening. "Gonna fuck you now."

Zeke groaned and tilted his ass up, reaching back to spread his cheeks while Brendon grabbed the strip of condoms and tore one off. The sound of that package being torn open had Zeke's breath quickening in anticipation.

"Damn!" Brendon muttered the curse as he latched on to Zeke's hip with one hand. Despite being stretched, Zeke grunted as Brendon pushed hard, seating his cock fully into Zeke's snug channel. The pain was brief and quickly blotted out by pleasure, so much so that all he could concentrate on was not coming again immediately. Between watching Brendon lick the come from his fingers and the fullness of the man's cock in his ass, Zeke was having a hell of time trying to hold back.

Doesn't quite seem fair, he thought, so Zeke moved his hips and clamped his inner muscles down tight. Brendon let out a hoarse yell and began surging in and out, one hand still clasping Zeke's hip, the other pressing down on the small of his back. Zeke's orgasm blasted through his body, curling his toes and blowing his mind. His muscles squeezed down hard on Brendon's prick and heard the man bellow as Brendon shoved in as deep as he could get, pumping jets of hot come into the condom.

Brendon's legs wobbled against Zeke's own before the man leaned over him, belly to back, using his weight to push them both over onto the couch. There they lay, panting and shivering until they finally could speak.

"Shit, Zeke, that was...that was... I don't even know how to describe it. I think the top of my head shot off, no joking." Brendon sighed, melting against him. Zeke didn't think it was an exaggeration, either. Hell, it was a huge understatement. Zeke chuckled softly.

"I know, baby, I don't think I am going to be able to move for a while." He groaned, but it wasn't the sexy sound Brendon had drawn from him only minutes ago. "And somehow, I have to find the strength to clean the couch. Damn."

Brendon eased up off of Zeke, his mind spinning with questions now that the blood had returned to his brain. What had happened in the kitchen? He wasn't sure, but it looked to him as though the other man had started to have a panic attack. Enessa had told him she thought her brother suffered from anxiety, but that, well, that was more than just anxiety. Brendon felt an urgent need to help him, a little tweak in his heart when he thought of the man hurting. He felt more for Zeke than he probably should, considering they had only just met. The thing was, since Nessa and Gloria had told him so much about Zeke, had spent the last few weeks telling him everything they could possibly think of about the man, it seemed to Brendon that he had known Zeke for quite a while.

However, he also knew how cautious the man was — and not without good reason — — so he decided it would be best to keep his questions to himself for now. He watched as Zeke stood, favouring his bad knee and grimacing slightly.

"How about you point me to the bathroom and I go grab a couple of cloths for us— —and the couch?" He could, at least, be useful in this one thing.

Zeke turned and looked at him, studying him for a moment before nodding. "Yeah, okay. Down the hall first door to the right."

Brendon left him there, feeling Zeke watching him as he walked away. He was pretty sure the other man had been looking for signs of curiosity over the strange behaviour that had occurred in the kitchen. Hopefully, he had managed to hide it from him. Stepping into the bathroom, Brendon removed the condom and tied it off before throwing it in the trash. He dug around until he found two washcloths and ran warm water over them, wringing them out once they were saturated.

Brendon groaned when he walked back to the living room and saw that Zeke had pulled on his jeans. Zeke's head flew up at the noise, a blank expression on his face.

"Now, why," Brendon asked, handing the other man a cloth, "did you go and do that?"

"Do what?" Zeke asked, washing the drying spunk from his belly. Brendon was sure Zeke knew what he meant and either wasn't ready or didn't know how to answer. From what Enessa had told Brendon, she'd never known her brother to have a lover over or a steady relationship. Chances were good, then, that this whole after-fucking conversation deal was new to Zeke. That thought brought a smile to Brendon's lips. He kind of liked this whole situation being new to Zeke, it might help Brendon to win the man's affection— —something that had, in the last hour or so, become increasingly important. A quick affair no longer appealed to Brendon; he wanted more for the both of them. And no matter how much he would like to be the first man Zeke actually felt something for, the real problem was that he'd rather be the last.

Brendon finished cleaning the couch, enjoying the blush that stained Zeke's cheeks. Ah ha, the man was nervous, and hard, too, which made Brendon's prick harden in response. "I meant," he drawled, watching that blush tint the tips of Zeke's ears, "why'd you cover up that gorgeous cock?" Brendon reached down and stroked his own hard on, feeling its wet head as Zeke watched.

"I, uhn…I," Zeke's eyes were locked, unblinking, on the show Brendon was putting on for him. He hoped like hell he was shorting out Zeke's defences.

He stroked himself the entire time he walked forward, stopping only inches from Ezekiel. Brendon used his other hand to take the second cloth and dropped them both on the floor before stepping between Zeke's spread legs. He stopped stroking his cock, guiding it instead to brush the head across Zeke's slightly parted lips. Brendon almost expected the man to push him away, and nearly fell to his knees when Zeke grasped his hips and engulfed half of Brendon's cock. Brendon's head flew back as a strangled sound was ripped from his throat. Zeke drew back, running his tongue along the underside of Brendon's cock, looking up to meet his stunned gaze. He wasn't so far gone that he didn't catch Zeke's amusement, or the chuckle that vibrated over his dick.

"Ah, fuck, Zeke, fuck," he groaned, curling his hands in his new lover's hair. Brendon's balls drew up, his muscles tingling and tensing. "I'm gonna…need to come," he warned, hands still fisted tight in Zeke's hair, guiding him gently.

Zeke hummed his approval, swirling and sucking and throwing Brendon right into an orgasm that was almost violent in force. He watched as Zeke swallowed the bursts of semen, and shivered as the man swirled his tongue into the slit to suckle out every drop before backing off the now-flaccid cock.

Brendon stumbled backwards, plopping down on the coffee table when the backs of his legs smacked into it. Holy shit, he was pretty sure he'd suffered some brain damage or something. He'd never had a blowjob that intense before. Brendon's hands were shaking so badly he grabbed the edge of the coffee table to hide the trembling. He finally managed to raise his head and look at Zeke, feeling his heart pinch a little at the sweet smile on the man's lips.

"Maybe putting my jeans on was the only way to hold back so I could suck your cock," Zeke whispered. He was so hard he felt breathless. Watching Brendon come, tasting his seed… Zeke groaned softly and reached down to rub his own prick through the denim encasing it.

"I want to fuck you, Brendon." He watched the man's eyes widen with trepidation. Zeke knew he was big, but he also knew Brendon would fit around his cock like a tight velvet glove. He wouldn't push the man, but he would encourage him.

"I want you to ride me, fuck me until I can't breath, can't think, until we are nothing but two bodies burning for release." God, Zeke hoped his words were adequate in explaining what he meant. He never had considered himself an eloquent man, hadn't really worried about it before. Now, though, he wished he had the words to make Brendon understand what he wanted; that blending of two people so completely you couldn't tell where one left off and the other began.

Brendon's mouth opened and shut a few times, and Zeke didn't know if the man couldn't speak or simply didn't know what to say. He waited, watching the doubt and desire flash across Brendon's face. Finally, Brendon nodded, though he still looked unsure.

"It's, ah, it's been a while since I've, you know," he stuttered out, studying the floor. Zeke grinned with delight, because Brendon looked so damn sexy when he was timid and tremulous.

"We'll take it slow, baby, as slow as you want. You'll be in control of how deep and how fast," Zeke promised, standing up and reaching for his lover's hand. "We'll fit, Brendon, and it will be so good, so right, that every fear you've had about it will be forgotten." He studied Brendon, noting the effect the words were having—rapid breathing, pounding pulse, and that lovely cock bobbing with each heartbeat. Oh, yeah, his man wanted this. Zeke drew the shorter man into his arms and took Brendon's mouth, kissing him with enough force their teeth clacked together. The kiss started off full throttle and only burned hotter, tongues thrusting and twisting as each man nipped and ate at the other's mouth.

Moaning as he pulled away, Zeke rested his forehead against Brendon's. A thought that had been buzzing around in his mind finally stilled. "Brendon, is Nessa…"

Brendon nodded. "Yeah, she's staying with Gloria, I'm sure."

Zeke grunted, slitting his eyes at the man. "Just how much of this did y'all plan out? Seems like you went through a lot for one night." Zeke didn't know whether to be relieved or irritated that the three had been discussing his sex life, plotting for him to get laid. Although he couldn't be too irritated. Maybe he should actually send the girls flowers. Or chocolate. Or both. He smiled, trying to assure Brendon he wasn't angry about the whole deal.

"Uh. Well. We didn't really get into specifics. I mean, that would just be too weird with my cousin and your sister." Brendon squirmed a little as Zeke continued to stare at him. "I just, um… One night?"

Zeke laughed at the man's discomfort, finding it oddly endearing. "You just, um, what?" He started to squeeze Brendon a little tighter, then froze when it dawned on him that 'one night' had came back doubtfully. He loosened his hold and leant back to look at the man.

"Yeah, one night, or were you…" Zeke didn't know if he should be hopeful or worried if Brendon was going to be spending a few days in McKinton. If the man stayed here that long, there was no way they would be able to stay away from each other. If he left in the morning… That didn't make him feel any better, either.

"Or were you staying a few days?" Zeke tried to keep his tone neutral, because he honestly couldn't say what he would prefer. Well, he could, but he knew it would be best if this were a one-night thing. Safer for all of them, even if it meant going right back to his lonely existence. The fact that Brendon didn't answer him immediately, instead averted his eyes, had Zeke dropping his arms and stepping away.

"What aren't you telling me, Brendon?" he asked in a soft voice that belied the anger and fear beginning to stir in him.

Brendon heard the warning in Zeke's voice and knew he had a couple of choices. He could play along, tell the man he was only going to be here a few days at the most. That would, possibly, result in a continuation of tonight's fuckfest. Or, he could tell the truth, let Zeke know he wasn't going to be leaving any time soon, and risk alienating him as well as almost certainly bringing the evening to a close.

The fact that he didn't have to debate with himself for long should have frightened him, but the truth of the matter was, he wanted more than tonight, more than a few nights. Brendon wanted a relationship with the magnificent man standing before him. For that reason alone, there would be no lies then. He didn't deceive himself into thinking it would be easy. He would have to fight Zeke and possibly a good number of the townspeople, but he was willing to do it. For whatever reason, he couldn't let Zeke walk away, couldn't walk away himself.

Brendon had never considered himself a coward and wouldn't let the fear of rejection make him one now. Shoulders squared, he stared Zeke straight in the eyes, letting the man see his determination. When he spoke, he made sure to keep his voice equally soft as Zeke had.

"Actually, Zeke, I'm not going to be here for a night, a few days, or even a week," Brendon paused, watching the man pale as he realised what was being said. Showing no mercy, he ploughed on. "Not even for just a month. I'll be here all summer. Possibly longer, if I decide it's worth it."

Zeke shook his head, anger apparent in the gesture as well as in the way his hands clenched into fists. "No, no! You need to leave! There's nothing worth staying here for. Nothing."

Brendon shrugged, unwilling to be intimidated. "I think there is, and I won't let your fear push me away."

"It's not my fear pushing you away, Brendon, it's me. This...what happened between us, it's just fucking," Zeke snarled, flinging a hand through the air. "You're just a body, don't you get it? Any man would have done." He turned and walked to his room, leaving Brendon standing naked and alone.

Chapter Three

Brendon stood in the hallway, trying not to let Zeke's words hurt him. He was pretty sure that Zeke'd said what he did to try to scare him off, but still, shit, that was harsh! No, he couldn't allow himself to be hurt this easily, not if he intended to prove to Zeke that he was serious. Hadn't he just acknowledged that he would have to fight Zeke's fears to build a relationship? If he ran off the first time he got his feelings hurt, then that didn't speak well for his integrity or the feelings he professed, if only to himself, for Zeke.

While Brendon knew he was more emotionally involved than the other man, he fully believed they had a connection between them that could grow into something exceptional. But what should he do, right now? That was the question. He didn't want to be too forceful and freak Zeke out, but something told Brendon he would have to be a bit more forward than he was comfortable with, much as he had every since he'd learned of the man.

A sweet scent permeated the air—right before Brendon felt a faint nudge on his shoulder blade. He jumped, glancing behind him, but nothing was there. Feeling a little silly and a lot creeped out, Brendon walked quickly to Zeke's door. The idea of knocking entered his mind, but that unexplainable nudge had him reaching for the doorknob and twisting it without hesitation. Fuck respecting privacy, he was not going to stand naked out in the hallway a second longer.

Brendon jerked the door open and froze mid-step, his heart breaking at the sight before him. Zeke sat on the floor, back against the bed, arms wrapped around his bent knees. Short, jerky pants were spasming from his lungs. Brendon could see the fear in his eyes, see the struggle Zeke was in the midst of while trying to fight back the panic attack. His lips were tinted a faint blue as his body tried to compensate for the lack of oxygen.

Anger surged through Brendon; he knew without a doubt Zeke had been suffering panic attacks alone, keeping them a secret from everyone. No more, he thought. Ezekiel was not dealing with this alone any more. Brendon rushed over, nearly sliding on his knees as he dropped down on the floor. Zeke didn't seem to see or hear him; he was lost in his own private hell.

Gently, Brendon touched the man's shoulder. "It's okay, Zeke, just concentrate on breathing. Deep breaths in," Brendon inhaled in example, "slow breaths out." He exhaled and repeated the directions, over and over, trying to reach Ezekiel.

More of his heart shattered as tears ran down Zeke's cheeks. Jesus, what could he do to help? He didn't know, but Brendon would be damned if he'd be in such a position of helplessness again. As soon as possible, he would begin researching panic attacks and learn as much as he could. When Zeke's breathing grew even shakier, Brendon wiped at his own tears angrily, struggling for control. Finally, in desperation, he wrapped the man in his arms and started rocking him, uttering whatever soothing nonsense he could manage.

It seemed an eternity before Zeke's breathing started to even out. The gasping noises as air-starved lungs pumped frantically finally became quieter, steadier breaths. Zeke's muscles gradually loosened, unclenching from the rigid state they had been in. Brendon stroked Zeke's back, his arms, chest—anywhere Brendon could reach to try to work the remaining tension from his body. When Zeke finally seemed to be breathing normally with only an occasional shudder, Brendon could not hold back. He gently cupped Zeke's chin and forced his head up from where he was trying to bury it against his knees in embarrassment.

"No," Brendon murmured, taking Zeke's mouth in a tender kiss, a gentle sweep of tongue. "No hiding from me, Zeke. I haven't seen anything I hadn't already figured out."

Zeke tried to pull away but with his body worn from its experience, he couldn't break free. His throat worked twice in an attempt to speak, and Brendon figured he would just cut him off. He was pretty sure he wouldn't like what Zeke was trying to get out. Standing, he gingerly pulled the shaking man to his feet, keeping a hand around Zeke's waist to steady him.

"Not a word, Zeke. Not a one, not right now. You're trembling and probably exhausted after what you just went through. Let's get you stripped and in bed." Brendon sat him down and unbuttoned his jeans. "All right, on your back, buddy." He was fixing to give Zeke a little push when the man suddenly capitulated and flopped back on the bed, raising his hips up so Brendon could pull off the jeans. Brendon was more than a little surprised to find him semi-erect after the panic attack. Maybe it was a side effect, he didn't know, but he would as soon as he could get his hands on his laptop.

Zeke's voice, rough and barely audible, startled him out of his musings. "Why didn't you leave?"

Brendon glanced at him and figured what the hell. He worked part of the covers over Zeke as he spoke.

"Honestly? Because I know there can be something between us, something more than fucking. And I know you know it, too. Yes, you do," he repeated when Zeke shook his head weakly. "I believe you're an honest man, so I have to wonder why you aren't being honest now." Brendon pretended to muse it over as weary green eyes watched him. He grinned at Zeke.

"Got it! You are afraid—for me, for you, probably for everyone." Brendon lay down on the bed beside Zeke, who watched him warily. "This, however," he reached down and stroked Zeke's rapidly growing blanketed cock, "this tells me that you *do* want me. You can shake your head, grumble and deny all you want, but your body tells me the truth." Brendon jerked the blanket off of Zeke, exposing the full erection making a lie of the feeble denials.

"This is the truth, babe," Brendon whispered as he slid down the mattress until his lips brushed against the mushroomed head. Smiling up at Zeke, Brendon ran his tongue over the top of the glistening cock, then down to the sensitive underside of the head. Zeke gasped and jerked his hips, seeking more.

"I know what happened to you." Brendon licked a thick vein that had caught his attention. "I know how you were jumped, how your knee got fucked up." He laved his way across Zeke's balls, suckling one of the orbs as his hand trailed over the wiry hair nestled around the base of the bobbing cock. Zeke moaned, loud and long as Brendon made his way back up to the tip of his lover's prick. He paused, mouth against the rigid length, staring Zeke in the eyes.

"I know what you've been through, and I'm not scared, Zeke. I'm not walking away, and neither are you." Brendon sucked Zeke's cock down until the head bumped his throat, the action pushing aside any response Zeke might have wanted to make. He couldn't speak since he was too busy groaning and thrusting his prick into Brendon's mouth, and somewhere in the back of Brendon's mind, he decided this was a pretty damn good way to shut the man up.

Zeke fisted the sheets, unable to do more than hold on and jerk his hips as Brendon sucked, swirling his tongue along the length of Zeke's engorged cock. He knew he should protest, should pull Brendon off his dick and make the man leave, but damn, the man was right. Zeke wanted him, and not just for tonight. He was so tired of being lonely, of being scared and ashamed.

Brendon trailed his fingers from Zeke's balls to his tight seal and slid two digits in, crooking them slightly to peg his prostate. Stars exploded behind Zeke's eyeballs. He screamed and his body coiled tight, pulsing with the hot jets of spunk shooting from his cock. Brendon purred his approval, sucking and licking and thrusting his fingers until he had wrung out every single bit of pleasure from Zeke. Only then did he withdraw his fingers and release the softening cock from his mouth.

"Damn," was about all Zeke could manage, and even that was elaborate in his opinion, all things considered.

Brendon chuckled softly, scooting up to settle against his side and pulling the covers over them both. Zeke was dimly aware of the swollen shaft pressing against his hip and reached for it feebly only to have his hand slapped away.

"Oh, no, you don't, babe," Brendon whispered in his ear. "That's part of my evil plan to make you cooperate and let me stay with you tonight."

Zeke managed to pry an eye open to look at Brendon, noting the smug smile but feeling too sated to worry about it.

"You're a fair man, albeit an exhausted one. I'm a horny-as-hell man, but willing to wait until you've had some recovery time. I'm sure you wouldn't toss me out without...well, tossing me first, would you?" Brendon punctuated the question by tracing the shell of Zeke's ear with his tongue.

Nodding, Zeke had to agree. He wouldn't want to send the man away unsatisfied, that would just be cruel—especially after the blowjob Brendon had just given him. And if that excuse was lame, at least it allowed Zeke to stave off the loneliness, to hold Brendon and sleep with him for a little while during the night.

Zeke woke early, years of working the ranch ensuring he was up before dawn. It would be great if he could stay in bed and just enjoy the warmth of Brendon's body curled up against him for a while before waking the man up properly, but there were chores that couldn't wait. Stifling a sigh, he eased out from underneath Brendon's limbs and stood at the side of the bed, looking down at the sexy as hell man sprawled on his bed. Brendon was all long legs and lean muscles, with a tight ass that almost broke Zeke's determination to leave the man in peace. He couldn't recall ever having seen such a breathtaking sight. Forcing himself to turn away, Zeke grabbed some clothes and slipped out of the room, heading for the guest shower so as not to disturb Brendon.

* * * *

"Morning, Zeke." Charlie, one of the two ranch hands Zeke had found who was willing to work for him, was waiting out by the barn.

"Morning, Charlie." Zeke tipped his head at the man. "Is Miguel already out with the herd?"

Charlie nodded, following Zeke into the barn. "Need some supplies, boss. Thought maybe I could run into town and pick them up, if that's okay."

Zeke looked back at him. Charlie knew that it wasn't safe for him to go into McKinton, not as long as he worked at the ranch. Zeke had made it clear that he ordered all supplies from Fort Worth or Dallas—anywhere but locally. He wouldn't risk his men being harassed or worse because of him, nor would he contribute financially to the town any more than he had to. Still, occasionally, Charlie would push the issue.

"You know better, Charlie. If you don't want to drive into Fort Worth for whatever it is we need, and it can't be delivered, then I can send Miguel or pick it up myself." Zeke was not budging on this.

Charlie shook his head. "Ya know, boss, it ain't ever gonna change if ya don't make it. You keep punishing everyone in that town for what a few people did—"

"Enough!" Zeke snapped. "We've been over this before, so quit pushing me, Goddamn it!" He stormed over to Charlie, shaking with anger. Brendon was on him, his cowhand was on him —his own conscience was on him. Zeke was ready to hurt someone, even though that was the very thing he was trying to prevent. That realisation had his temper evaporating. What the hell was wrong with him that he flew off the handle so easily? He took his hat off and ran shaky fingers through his hair as he took a deep breath.

"I'm sorry, Charlie." Zeke looked at Charlie, expecting to see anger, condemnation, some type of justified judgment. What he saw instead was understanding tinged with compassion, which made him feel like an even bigger asshole. Charlie reached out and patted him on the shoulder.

"It's okay, boss. I shouldn't have, well… It's a nice day for a drive, and if you don't need me here, I reckon I'll head on in to Fort Worth, 'kay?"

Zeke murmured an agreement, slapped his hat back on and turned to his chores, forcing everything out of his mind except what needed to be done. Thoughts of Brendon, soft lips and hard cock, threatened to distract him. What he offered Zeke—a relationship, something more than he'd ever had with another man before— tempted him sorely, and he wondered if there was some truth to Charlie's words. After being jumped a couple of times in town, being harassed and called names, Zeke had let fear slowly creep in and take over his life. No, he hadn't exactly *let* it take over, he just hadn't known it was happening, and when he realised it, hadn't known how to stop it. Added to that was the damned panic attacks which had only gotten worse since his mother's death.

So, what should he do? Throw Brendon out, leave him to spend the summer at Gloria's? Zeke believed the man when he said he was staying for the summer—at least. No doubt Brendon wouldn't bother trying to hide his sexuality, and while it wasn't like he was anywhere even close to flaming, the rumours would start once he turned down a couple of dates with some of the town's beauties. Zeke knew what would happen then, and wasn't that a good enough reason there for him to keep Brendon close?

Cursing soundly, he finished up and headed back to the house, confusion and desire swirling around in his head. Well, he might not know what to do about the confusion, but for the other, he was going to slip back into bed beside Brendon and lose himself in the depths of the man's body.

Zeke's dick filled with blood and pressed hard against the seam of his jeans. He reached for the back door and caught a whiff of something…bacon? His stomach growled, reminding him that supper had gone forgotten last night, and breakfast hadn't occurred to him. Was Enessa back, then? Disappointment surged through Zeke as he slipped into the house. He had hoped for a little more time with—

Brendon stood in the kitchen, wearing nothing but jeans, flipping bacon as it sizzled in a cast iron skillet. Pancakes were stacked on a platter, kept warm by the heat of the stove. Zeke felt a rush of relief at seeing the man, so much so that it actually felt like his heart grew lighter in his chest. He knew he had to have the silliest grin ever on his face, but he just couldn't help it.

"Morning," Zeke said, not wanting to startle Brendon as he was scooping the bacon out of the skillet. Brendon grinned at him over his shoulder.

"Morning, Zeke. Heard you come in the back door, but I wasn't sure…" Brendon trailed off, grin faltering as he looked away, and Zeke felt like pure shit. He walked over to Brendon and pressed up against the shorter man's back, wrapping him in a tight hug. Zeke closed his eyes and buried his face against Brendon's neck, soaking in the scent of him.

"I thought you'd still be asleep, babe." He nibbled on the strong column of Brendon's neck, tonguing the artery that pulsed beneath his lips. The spicy taste sent a bolt of fire zinging straight to Zeke's cock, snuggled tight against the crack of the firm ass he'd been thinking of filling.

"Mmm, needed food," Brendon answered, pushing against Zeke's prick. "And you need to eat, too." He waved the plate of bacon in one hand and grabbed the platter of pancakes with the other. "Wouldn't want all my hard work to go to waste, would you?"

Zeke grunted and stepped back enough to let Brendon turn in his arms, then startled the man with a hungry kiss.

"You know, that's really not fair when I have my hands full," Brendon pointed out, trying not to tip either of the plates he was holding and feeling a little breathless from the affection. He'd really expected to be kept at a distance this morning, not held snug, not licked and kissed senseless.

"I think it's perfectly fair," Zeke argued playfully, "because all I've thought about since waking up is getting my hands—and a few other parts—on you." He gave Brendon's ass a firm squeeze before releasing him. Zeke swiped the bacon and placed it on the table. Plates and utensils had already been set out, so Zeke poured them each a glass of milk before he sat. A comfortable silence filled the kitchen, broken only by the occasional sound of the men enjoying their meal. They were almost through with breakfast when Brendon's phone rang displaying Gloria's number on the caller ID. He thought about excusing himself from the table but discarded the idea. He didn't want Zeke to sneak off on him.

"Hey, Gloria, what's up?" Brendon watched Zeke, noting the stillness that came over the man. Was he expecting trouble? Or was he always this paranoid? Not that he didn't have his reasons, but Brendon found it sad all the same.

"Oh, nothing much, just wanted to make sure everything was okay?" Gloria's cheery voice could be heard across the kitchen, so he knew Zeke heard every word, though the man didn't relax. Brendon got up and walked over to stand behind him, placing a hand on Zeke's tense shoulder, massaging as best he could.

"Everything here is just fine, Gloria. You and Nessa heading over?" God, he hoped not. He needed some time with Zeke to show the man what they could have together.

"Actually, Bren, if it's okay with you and Zeke, we thought we'd head over to the Dallas-Fort Worth area for a few days. Sort of take a mini-vacation and, you know, give you two a chance to get to know each other. Um, if… ah, y'all haven't already?"

Brendon was glad he was standing behind Zeke so the man couldn't see the grin splitting his face. No way was he going to answer the question Gloria was hinting at, though, it just wasn't her business. Besides, what he and Zeke had shared was too new and fragile to pull out and pass around for examination.

"That's fine with me." Better than, really. "Zeke? You okay with it?" And there, didn't Gloria just get an answer to her earlier question? Damn it, he would have smacked himself on the forehead but he didn't want to stop touching Zeke. Brendon watched Zeke's head bob hesitantly up and down. *Yes!* "He's good with it. Y'all stopping by here first?" He crossed his fingers. *Please; please, let them just go.*

Gloria laughed, loud enough that Brendon jerked the phone away from his ear. "Don't sound so thrilled with the idea, Bren! And, no, Nessa has clothes with her, plus we plan on having a shopping spree or three. You two have fun—and lots of it!" Her laughter boomed through the phone again, causing Brendon to hold the phone at arm's length as he finished the call then tucked the phone into his pocket.

He could still feel the tension in Zeke's shoulders, so he began working at the knotted muscles with both hands. Brendon leant down, placing his lips against Zeke's ear. "Hey, it'll be okay, all right?" He straightened, massaging the tense flesh under his hands until he finally felt the man relax. Zeke reached up and grabbed one of Brendon's hands, bringing it to his cheek. The tenderness of the gesture hit Brendon so strongly he felt his eyes prick with tears. Not the time to be a damn puss, he thought.

"I hope so, Brendon, I really do." Zeke twisted in his chair and, using the hand he had captured to pull Brendon around, settled him on his lap. He stared at Brendon, not bothering to hide his fear or his desire. "I want... I just don't know if I can believe it. If we'll be safe," Zeke said wearily. He closed his eyes briefly and sighed.

Brendon wasn't going to let the man doubt it. "It will be, babe. I'm not saying it will be easy, or always a barrel of monkeys, but sometime you have to start trying to live, Zeke. You can't just avoid life." He waited for the backlash, denial and anger, but Zeke only nodded.

"Charlie, my ranch hand and friend, pretty much said the same thing to me this morning," he admitted. "I wanted to rip his damn head off," Zeke said ruefully. "He's tried before to get his point across, but this time, something snapped. Besides my temper."

"Well, I think that maybe our first step should be for you to drive me over to Gloria's to get my clothes and SUV. If it's okay that I stay here, with you," Brendon used 'our' deliberately, wanting to see Zeke's reaction. He held his breath, wondering if there would be acceptance or rejection, knowing he was pushing past his lover's comfort zone. Hell, he was blowing the whole zone to bits. Brendon watched as Zeke took a steadying breath, and that was when he noticed it.

The sweet scent was back, the one he'd caught a whiff of right before he'd felt that…nudge last night. The one he'd tried to forget, because it was just a little too scary to think about.

Still… "Do you smell it, too?" Brendon didn't know if he wanted the scent to be real or not.

Zeke jerked his chin up so fast their heads almost smacked together. He stared into Brendon's eyes, searching for long seconds before answering. "Sweet, subtle, like it's carried through on a breeze?" he asked.

"Yeah, exactly like that, except last night…" Brendon suddenly had second thoughts about continuing that sentence. He didn't want to sound like some spooked kid, but it was obvious Zeke wasn't going to let it go. He bounced his legs, jostling Brendon.

"Last night, what?"

Brendon groaned, trying not to roll his eyes. He needed to learn to bite his tongue, but he hadn't, and now here was the consequence.

"Last night, when you walked off and left me in the hall, bare-assed naked, I might add." He couldn't resist teasing Zeke, drawing a smile from his sexy lips.

"I'm sorry about that," Zeke murmured, his gaze flickering away before returning to Brendon's. "I was a complete asshole last night to say what I did." Zeke tightened his arms around Brendon, the action as much of an apology as the words. "But, you really do need to quit distracting me and finish telling me what happened."

"I wasn't distracting you. I was just pointing out... Okay, okay. Anyway, I was trying to figure out whether I should just give in and concede defeat, or go after what I wanted — you. So, there I stood, confused as hell, when that scent just appeared, and then...uhm." Brendon glanced down at the floor as he considered whether or not he wanted to admit to what happened in the hallway last night. This was the hard part to confess, because if Zeke laughed at him, Brendon didn't know what he'd do.

Zeke stroked a finger along Brendon's cheek, down below his chin. He pushed gently, forcing Brendon's head up, looking him in the eyes. "Whatever it is that you're so worried about telling me, just stop worrying. You came in and found me last night; you know how you found me. You didn't laugh, didn't tease; instead, you helped me. Why would I laugh at anything that upset you?"

And just like that, with the sincerity shining at him in those beautiful green eyes, Brendon felt the rest of his heart tumble straight into Zeke's hands. Sunk, for certain. He was terrified and elated... and Zeke was waiting for an answer. Brendon cleared his throat, trying to work out the tightness that had suddenly seized his vocal cords.

"You, ah, you wouldn't, I suppose. It's just kinda...heebeejeebee-ish, creepy. I was standing there confused and such, like I said, then there was the smell, and then there was a, uhm, a nudge. On my back, like, pushing me towards your room, that kind of nudge. Now do you understand why I wasn't real eager to explain it?" Brendon twiddled his fingers together, feeling like an idiot despite Zeke's assurances.

"No feeling foolish," Zeke ordered. "I don't feel foolish, and I've felt a nudge, a push, even a caress sometimes when that scent hits. And it always comes when I seem to need it. I needed help last night, Brendon," he whispered, melting Brendon with his gaze. "I needed you, and that nudge, that scent—you really are going to think I'm crazy, Brendon, but it's the scent my mama always wore, and the way she would nudge and push to get me to do what she knew was right. She always knew what was right, babe."

Strangely enough, that explanation didn't freak Brendon out. Well, maybe he was a little uncomfortable at the idea of his man's mama—in any form whatsoever—seeing him bare assed, among other bare parts, but he liked the idea that love could live on. Or linger, or whatever it was that was happening.

"Actually, I think it is pretty cool, you know? Except for the being naked part, I'd rather not, not your mom, you know, not in any, uh…" Shit! Here was a perfect example of another time when he should have bitten his tongue!

Zeke burst out laughing and squeezed Brendon tight enough he thought his eyes bulged out a little. "I can't blame you there; I wouldn't care to have either of our mamas seeing me buck naked. But look at the bright side, at least my mama didn't slap you on the ass."

Brendon snorted at that and stood. "If she had, we wouldn't be having this discussion. My naked ass would have been out the door and calling for a ride home last night."

Standing, Zeke chuckled. "Nah. I doubt she'd have let you out the door, not if she wanted you here." The chuckle grew into laughter once again as Brendon spluttered, more than a little disturbed by his lover's statement.

"You…you think she'd do that? Make me stay if I didn't want to?" Brendon didn't want to leave, but the idea of being forced to stay, by a ghost at that, was just wrong on too many levels to contemplate.

Zeke looked at Brendon and stopped his teasing, tossing an arm over his shoulders. "Trust me, Mama wasn't the sort of person who would kidnap someone when she was alive. I don't think even, ah, passing away, would change that, you know? Now, let's get your clothes and vehicle before I lose my nerve."

Brendon nodded and hoped like hell this trip to town was uneventful. He knew it was a big step for Zeke, for them both, really. One thing he was certain of, if anyone dared to so much as look at this man wrong, Brendon was going to go off. Zeke was going to learn that he didn't have to fight his battles alone any more, nor did he have to hide away from them. Brendon wasn't afraid to fight Zeke's battles or his own, and he would see to it that everyone, including the man he was falling hard for, knew it.

Chapter Four

Zeke couldn't make himself relax no matter how hard he tried as he drove through McKinton with Brendon. He knew, logically, that it was ridiculous to be so self-conscious about it. He wasn't the only man to drive through the town with another man in his truck. But, he was the only gay man — that anyone knew of, anyways, and that made all the difference. Zeke couldn't help but feel like everyone was looking, judging and getting ready to gossip and cast that first stone. Hell, they may already be gathering a mob. His chest constricted at his morose humour and he worked hard to keep his breathing normal.

"Are you okay?" Brendon's voice held such understanding that Zeke almost reached for his hand. He caught himself, tightening his grip on the steering wheel as he glanced at his passenger. Seeing the compassion in those soft brown eyes helped ease the rest of the tension in Zeke's chest.

"I reckon I'm okay enough for now, all things considered," he answered. It had been years since he had ridden into town for anything other than a trip to his mama's grave. It had been all too easy to remain tucked away in the relative safety of his home. He hadn't seen his sister Elizabeth since she had moved away three years ago, and the last time he had seen his oldest sister Eva...

Speak of the devil and he — or in this case, she — shall appear, Zeke thought as Brendon pointed at the pissed off woman in the car beside him at the stoplight.

"Who is that miserable looking bitch, Zeke?" Brendon glared right back out his window, not looking the least bit intimidated by the hatred pouring off the dark-haired woman.

Zeke couldn't bring himself to turn his head fully and look. He knew what he would see, and frankly, coming into town was already trying enough for him. Glancing out of the corner of his eye, he saw Eva, still full of anger and hate. Some day, he hoped his sister would find peace instead of the poisonous emotions that seemed to fill her, but he wasn't keeping his fingers crossed.

One thing was certain, seeing the way Eva was glaring at Brendon, her mouth spewing silent words of hatred reinforced Zeke's decision to keep the other man close. There was no chance that Eva wouldn't be gunning for Brendon now after having seen them together, even in such an innocent setting.

"That," he gave the truck a little gas, trying not to appear eager to flee, "is Eva, my oldest sister."

Brendon whipped his head around so fast Zeke was surprised the man didn't get whiplash. "That is the bi... That is the sister who went all batshit when you came out to your family? That one?"

Zeke could feel the anger pouring off of Brendon. He didn't bother to ask how the other man knew about Eva. He was sure Gloria and Enessa had been feeding Brendon information about him for some time.

"Yeah, she would be that one. When I told my mama, she didn't freak out or start lecturing me on the Bible or anything, even though she was a faithful church-goer. No, she just said that I was exactly the way God meant me to be; He didn't make mistakes." And how had he forgotten that? Zeke checked his mirrors and switched lanes, watching his sister's face twist with fury in his rearview. "She helped me tell my sisters. Elizabeth, the second oldest, just nodded and went back to her room to study. Enessa, well, she has always been a loving soul. She gave me a great, big hug and told me she loved me." He smiled at the memory, letting it warm him all over again.

"Nessa is a wonderful person, Zeke," Brendon agreed. "But that one behind us, she has some serious issues." He turned to glare out the back window of the truck. "She also just turned right a block back."

Zeke nodded. "Probably heading home to prepare for a holy war. You know, I can't ever recall her being particularly happy; she was always just so angry and judgmental. Even before I came out, Eva would nag and preach and just fly off in rages sometimes, but she never viewed her own behaviour as wrong. She seemed to think she was the only righteous person in town, other than her then-fiancé John. Since he was our preacher's son, he was automatically elevated up the holier-than-thou ladder in her book."

Brendon flopped back in his seat and crossed his arms over his chest. "Well, she just sounds like a pure treasure to me. Someone ought to bury her and slap an invisible 'x' over the spot, then burn the damn treasure map."

Laughter burst out of Zeke before he could help it. Brendon in a snit fit was just too cute, and it felt damned good to have someone indignant on his behalf. "As good as that sounds at times, she's still my sister. And I'm pretty sure the devil wouldn't want her any closer to hell than she already is, too much competition, so burying her probably wouldn't work."

Grumbling, Brendon shifted in his seat. "Nessa said that Eva went off in front of them, calling you an abomination and such. She said even your mama couldn't get her to shut up."

"Yeah," Zeke nodded, "she lost it. Said I was ruining the family name, that John wouldn't want to marry into our perverted family, lots of things like that. Mama couldn't get her to calm down, and when Eva started physically threatening me, Mama told her to leave. I tried to talk to Mama about it, but she said she wasn't having that kind of hatred in her house no matter how much she loved Eva. So, my sister packed a couple of bags and left, ran crying to the preacher about all of us sinners, which pretty much put an end to Mama's going to church. Eva got her husband, her place in the church, and she has all those bitter feelings to keep her occupied, but she tossed aside her family. Didn't even come to her own mother's funeral. You can't tell me that is what Jesus would do."

Brendon snorted. "Baby, I don't think you should use her name and Jesus' in the same paragraph, hour, day or week, just to be safe. So, Eva left, but she would verbally assault you every chance she got in town, and Enessa thinks her constant spewing about how evil gays are is what fuelled those idiots to attack you."

Zeke pulled into Gloria's driveway, shutting the truck off as he faced Brendon. "I never told Nessa, don't want her to know, but Eva did very deliberately work those guys up to come after me. She told me so herself, when she stopped by the hospital to tell me how much she wished I had died like I should have. Like she wanted me to." Why that still hurt so much, he didn't know. He'd had plenty of time to get past his sister's hatred of him, but couldn't.

Brendon sat motionless on the bench seat for so long that Zeke was starting to worry. He was seriously considering reaching over and shaking the man or something when Brendon finally nodded before getting out of the truck. Zeke slid out and followed him silently to the house, wondering what the hell was going on in the other man's mind. He found out as soon as they stepped inside and Brendon shut the door.

"Look, I know that Eva is your sister, but what she did, it's all just beyond fucked up. She's beyond fucked up." Brendon shook his head when Zeke would have spoken. "No. No excuses. I don't know your other sister Elizabeth, but I know you and Enessa, and neither one of you are anything like Eva. In fact, y'all are two of the best people I know. I think that, like so many people feel they are born gay, others are born evil, mean or good. Trying to murder your brother—that's just evil, you know it is. She of all people should know that, being married to a preacher's son. I mean, what, did she just conveniently forget the whole Cain and Abel story in the Bible? And you may be all chivalrous about never hitting a woman, but I will rip that bitch's head off if she ever tries to hurt you again."

Zeke didn't know what to say, but when Brendon put it like that, even calling his sister a bitch couldn't irritate him. Before he could decide what he did feel about that speech, Brendon grabbed his hand and tugged him down the hall into the guest room. Zeke assumed he was going to have to help the man pack and was totally unprepared for the shove in the middle of his back that sent him tumbling onto the bed.

"What the fu—" His voice stuck in his throat when he rolled onto his back. Brendon was stripping, throwing his clothes off in a frenzy and kicking off his shoes. Zeke rose up on his elbows to watch, his own cock filling hard and fast at the sight of the beautiful, bare, male flesh before him. Brendon reached into one of the bags sitting on the dresser and pulled out a tube of lube and a condom.

"Scoot up to the middle of the bed," he ordered as he approached the bed. Zeke's mouth dried up as he took in the look on Brendon's face. Erotic, determined and wanting, his expression sent sparks of heat zinging through Zeke. He moved to the centre of the mattress, his erection uncomfortable against the denim jeans. When he reached down to unbutton them, Brendon snarled at him, which, he realised perversely, made his cock throb.

"I'll do that," Brendon insisted as he crawled on all fours across the bed until he could straddle Zeke's thighs. Setting the lube and condom down, he reached for the button he had just warned Zeke away from and, with a sharp tug, had the denim parted. Brendon grabbed a handful of the jeans on each side and pulled them down to Zeke's thighs.

"Good enough," Brendon grunted, picking up the condom and laying it on Zeke's chest. He grabbed the lube and coated his fingers then passed the tube to Zeke. "Get your cock ready for me."

"Sweet fuck, babe." Zeke picked up the package and thought he was going to shoot before he even got the condom on his dick. Watching Brendon reach back as he leant down, knowing he was stretching that snug little opening with his own fingers, Zeke groaned. He managed to rub the lube on quickly, so absorbed with the way

Brendon was moaning and pushing back against his own fingers that he couldn't look away. How many was he using? God, he'd love to watch Brendon stretch himself, almost as much as he was going to love fucking that tight ass. Zeke leant down and caught the next moan with his mouth, latching on to Brendon's lips like a desperate man.

Brendon sat up suddenly, and Zeke realised his lover had finished stretching himself. He watched as a strong, tanned hand grasped his cock, pressing it against the lubed hole that was, hopefully, ready for him. Brendon leant forward again and reached for Ezekiel's hands, clasping them in his as he sank his hips down, taking in Zeke's cock inch by torturous inch.

Zeke watched Brendon's face closely, looking for pain or discomfort. He saw each a time or two, but Brendon just bit his lower lip and kept sliding his ass down, slow and steady, until he was finally, blissfully, fully seated.

"Ah, Brendon, babe, shit," Zeke panted, wanting to thrust so bad he was shaking. As though sensing his need, Brendon began moving, up slow, down hard and fast. The feel of that sleek, satiny channel squeezing his cock was going to toss Zeke right over the edge in no time and he knew it. He reached for Brendon's bouncing prick, using the pre-come on the swollen head as lube, and started tugging. He faltered as his balls jerked tight, muscles tensed and bowed with his rapidly spiralling orgasm.

"B...Brendon, God, oh God!" Zeke was pretty sure he screamed it out, barely aware at first of Brendon's hand covering his own where it had stilled on his lover's cock. The touch helped Zeke to focus enough so he resumed stroking, spinning Brendon into his own climax. Heat shot over Zeke's belly and hand, onto his chest as Brendon's inner muscles clamped down like a vice, dragging another yell from Zeke. He slapped one arm over Brendon's thighs, holding him down hard as Zeke's balls emptied out deep inside his lover's ass.

Zeke pulled Brendon down on top of him, needing to taste his lips, needing…*more,* though he didn't know what that could be after what he'd just experienced. The tender feeling seeping through him had Zeke parting Brendon's lips with his tongue, entering into his mouth with all the gentleness their fucking hadn't had. Brendon moaned softly, opening in acceptance, and Zeke felt something inside himself melt. He wasn't sure what this man was doing to him, didn't know if he wanted to analyze it just then, but he did know he didn't want it to stop.

Brendon looked down at Zeke, wondering at the way the man had kissed him, caressed him. Afraid to read too much into it, he started to pull away, only to be wrapped in two strong arms.

"Where're you going?" Zeke grumbled, watching him through slitted lids. Brendon just shook his head, not trusting himself to speak, not yet. He'd had to bite his cheek to keep quiet while they were making love, afraid if he let out any sound, he'd be yelling out how much he loved Zeke, and he was pretty sure the man wasn't ready for that yet. For that matter, he didn't know if he was ready for it, but it was true, he did. Now Brendon was worried he'd blow it all to hell by blurting it out, and Zeke's sweet kisses were not helping him keep quiet, not at all.

"Hey, what's wrong, babe? Did I do…something?" Oh shit. Now Zeke sounded worried, which wasn't Brendon's intention. The last thing he wanted was for Zeke to feel any more guilt. Brendon shook his head as much as he could, which wasn't much at all as he was pressed tight against Zeke's chest.

"No," he managed to scrape out, "Don't ever think that, Zeke. I just…it was just…" *Just what? Just me trying not to blurt out something that would send you running for the hills?* Somehow, he was pretty sure that was not the answer he needed to give right now. Brendon was feeling his own bout of panic coming on, not wanting to lie to his man but knowing he couldn't very well tell the truth, either. Zeke hugged him harder and nudged Brendon's head with his chin.

"It was what, babe? Please, talk to me." The soft pleading tone made Brendon squeeze his eyes shut tight against tears. He was so screwed. Zeke's body twitched as he inhaled. "Brendon? Babe?"

Brendon kept his eyes scrunched shut, nose pressed into the smattering of hair on Zeke's chest.

"Breathe, babe. Can't you…" Zeke drew in another deep breath. Brendon popped an eye open, catching the sweet scent that had assailed him before. It penetrated his brain. That was the same one Zeke said his mama wore—

Brendon squeaked and jerked out of Zeke's arms, almost falling off the man and wounding them both. He reached for an edge of the blanket, trying to cover himself, eyes darting around the room. The sound of Zeke's laughter reached him, and Brendon glared at him.

"That's just not right, Ezekiel," he huffed, feeling his cheeks burn. Zeke rolled to his side, facing Brendon, not bothering to cover himself.

"What's not right, babe?" His green eyes glinting with laughter, Zeke looked so young and carefree Brendon had a hard time holding onto his pique. A really hard time, but he managed.

"That…that…not when we're still, you know. That's just not right, man." Brendon was aware that he sounded ridiculous, but then again, having your lover's mother's…

spirit?…make an appearance when your man was still buried deep inside your ass… Naked was bad enough, but this, this was just a whole 'nother level of wrong. His eyes swept around the room again, coming to rest on Zeke, looking so beautiful Brendon felt like someone had punched him in the stomach. He felt a soft breeze ruffle his hair and almost closed his eyes to enjoy it before he caught himself. Letting out a startled yelp, Brendon dove for the bathroom, slamming the door hard enough to rattle the pictures hanging on the bedroom wall.

Zeke chuckled, reaching down to remove the condom and put his parts back in his jeans. *Really, Mumu, that was just…* His thoughts trailed off as he felt that breeze wrap around him. He didn't fight it, tried to open himself up to it, even. No one would ever be able to convince him that it wasn't his mama, finding a way to comfort him. And one thing Zeke knew for sure about the woman, she wouldn't have ever deliberately upset the man he thought he might be falling in love with. Zeke nodded to himself; yeah, he could admit that much. He wasn't too far off from falling ass over teakettle for Brendon, but something had been bothering the man. He'd been quiet throughout their frantic fucking, and unwilling to talk after, too. Zeke's brow knitted in confusion. What the hell had happened? Whatever it was, it had been a strong enough emotion that it drew the comforting—well, usually comforting—spirit to them.

"Huh," he grunted. Every time he'd had an encounter with, well, Mama, it had been when he was hurting, or confused—some kind of emotional duress. Zeke had no doubt that something had happened to offset this encounter, too, and he'd bet it centred on Brendon. This was twice in as many days that the man's distress had called out for...what? Backup? No, guidance, maybe, or reassurance. So what could have upset Brendon today?

Zeke rolled the question around in his mind as he disposed of the condom and checked the room, gathering anything he thought was Brendon's. He'd pile it on the bed for now. There were only a few items, anyway — some clothes, a laptop, a thumb-worn novel released a couple of years ago. Zeke listened to the shower, imagining Brendon naked and soapy, rubbing a washcloth all over his body...

He didn't need a nudge. Zeke stripped in the bedroom, tossing his clothes on the little pile of stuff on the bed. Anticipation skittered up his spine as he opened the bathroom door, cock already tapping against his belly as he took in the sight before him. Brendon had his head tipped back, rinsing his hair, and Zeke's mouth watered as he admired the slick, glistening corded muscles. Damn, the man was just fine. He watched a little patch of bubbles slide between Brendon's shoulder blades, straight down his spine to the top of his crack. Zeke groaned then, he couldn't help it. His hand slid over his prick as Brendon turned towards him, one hand still in his hair.

"Zeke?" Brendon's cock was half erect, and Zeke watched as it filled and grew with each step he took toward his lover. By the time he reached the shower door, that pretty prick was swollen, extended to its full length. He tore his eyes away from it long enough to meet Brendon's gaze as he opened the shower and stepped in, then Zeke was taking his lover's mouth in a kiss that scorched his soul.

Groans mingled with the sound of the shower. Zeke didn't know which of them was groaning or if it was both of them, and he didn't care. He lifted his head and spun Brendon away, bending him slightly at the waist and guiding his palms to the shower wall. Zeke nudged Brendon's legs open, giving him the access he wanted.

"Don't move, Brendon," he ordered, staring at the man spread out for him. The long lines of muscles from Brendon's arms to his shoulders, tapering down to a narrow waist and a perfect bubble ass—perfect didn't even begin to describe it. Zeke felt the warmth of pre-come on his cock head and grabbed the base, squeezing hard.

"Zeke, I..." Brendon's voice trembled as a shiver rippled over his body. He turned his head to look at Zeke, eyes wide with excitement and nerves. That look let Zeke know that, yeah, his man was enjoying his submissive role. Zeke shook his head, grabbed one firm cheek and squeezed hard, drawing a moan from Brendon.

"Not a word, babe," he ground out, kneading the flesh in his hand. Brendon gave a slight nod, his head still turned so he could watch Zeke. Zeke slid his hand over into the suds-slicked crease. His fingertips trailed over the pink hole still plump from his cock. Brendon arched his back and pushed against the fingers. Zeke jerked his hand back and grabbed the man's hip.

"I said don't move, Brendon, and I meant it." Zeke waited until Brendon met his eyes, held his stare. His lover nodded, then turned his head, dropping it forward enough to brace his forehead on the shower wall. Excitement arched between them, so thick Zeke was almost surprised he couldn't actually see it. He stepped up and pressed his hips against Brendon's ass, wedging his cock into the slick crack and placing his palm over the length. Leaning over, he nipped at Brendon's neck and began thrusting, his hand pressing his prick between those taut ass cheeks. Zeke turned the water off with his other hand and grabbed Brendon's cock, sucking harder on the man's neck as he felt Brendon tremble beneath him. Brendon was panting now, and Zeke wanted to see his face, see what he was doing to his lover. Lifting his mouth from the purple bruise he had sucked up, Zeke straightened as he brushed the tip of his thumb over the slit of Brendon's cock.

"Turn your head towards me." Zeke heard his lover's stuttering breath, and when Brendon obeyed him and turned his head, Zeke felt his own breath, and heart, stutter in response. His man was flushed with pleasure, eyes hazy with it, and bit at his bottom lip to keep quiet. Fuck, he had never seen anything so sexy in his life. Zeke's hips thrust harder of their own accord as he stroked Brendon's cock faster, knowing they were both ready to come.

"Come for me, babe, so I can shoot on your back and this pretty ass."

Brendon arched beneath him, a whimper slipping from his mouth as he bit down hard on that full lower lip. Heat splashed between Zeke's fingers, the scent hitting him as his body tightened in preparation of his own orgasm, pushing hard and fast against Brendon. He watched even as he yelled, watched his cock spurt thick, pearly ropes of semen on that strong back beneath him, watched and yelled again as he drew his cock back and shot more seed at the top of Brendon's seam.

He pulled Brendon upright against him, rubbing the come between them both. Some part of him wondered a little at his behaviour, but Zeke had never had more than a one-night stand. He figured it was probably some territorial caveman-type instinct that Brendon roused in him. Whatever it was, it was working for them both. Brendon was melting against him like warmed butter, rubbing and making the sexiest little moaning sounds as Zeke petted him.

"Mine." Zeke startled himself with the proclamation, but Brendon only nodded. It was right, they were right. Zeke knew it and he was pretty sure Brendon knew it, too. What they were building might not work out, but with that one word, Zeke had let his lover know he wanted it to, wanted something more. He nipped at the hickey on Brendon's neck. "Say it, babe. Tell me."

Brendon reached his arms behind him, holding Zeke as close as he could, letting his head fall back against Zeke's shoulder with a smile. "Yeah, Zeke, yours. All yours."

Zeke couldn't stop the grin that split his face any more than he could stop the ass over teakettle effect he'd felt coming on. "It works both ways, Brendon. I'm all yours, too." He felt Brendon still in his arms, saw the questioning look on his face. "What is it, baby?"

"Does this... Do you, you know." Brendon shifted, turned to face him. "You want me to stay?" The uncertain tremor in his voice made Zeke's heart do a little flop in his chest.

"Yes, I want you to stay. I want you, here, with me. Even though it scares me, even though it's selfish." Zeke knew it wasn't the most romantic speech, that it didn't say everything he wanted to say. For now, though, it was the best he could manage. Brendon knew that it could be dangerous here — probably would be dangerous — and was willing to stay. Zeke respected the man's choice, and it meshed so perfectly with what he wanted as well.

For once, Zeke was going to face his fear rather than hide away from it. The idea that Brendon might be hurt terrified him, but Zeke would do his damnedest to make certain his man was safe. Right now, that meant keeping the man close, which pleased Zeke so much it rattled him.

How someone he'd met such a short time ago could come to mean so much, so quickly...but it was what it was. Other people had proclaimed to have experienced love at first sight, so why should he question what was growing between the two of them?

Brendon let loose a shaky breath. "Okay. Okay, that's what I want, too. Just...maybe we can get your...mom...to stay away during, um, certain times?"

Ezekiel laughed, relief and joy shooting through him. "I have a theory about that, you know. I think stuff like that only happens when there's something like emotional duress going on. Think about it."

"Uh, yeah, maybe. So, what's the solution? No getting upset while nude? Or when we're fucking?" Brendon's smile took the sting from his words. Still, Zeke wondered if he didn't have a good idea there.

"I don't think she sees us, exactly. I think it's more like...she feels us, emotionally, maybe, ya know?" Zeke tipped Brendon's chin up, studying his lover's brown eyes. "Is that what happened earlier? You thinking too much while we were fucking? If so, I was doing something wrong."

Brendon tried to avert his eyes to no avail. "It was after. Just...lots of things on my mind, okay?" He gave Zeke a grin, that pretty dimple popping up and causing all sorts of distractions for Zeke as his lover continued talking. "I'm gonna go with your assessment there, Zeke, because it takes a lot of the humiliation aspect away from two of the encounters I've had."

Zeke laughed as he turned on the shower again. "I completely understand, and really, it's the only way I can deal with the whole issue. If I thought my mama could see what we were doing..." Just the thought made him shudder, melting the semi erection he'd had. God, he hoped to hell he was right about that, or he might never have sex again.

Chapter Five

Zeke stepped out onto his back porch, sipping his coffee and enjoying the cool morning air. By noon, it would be hotter than hell, and by four or five in the afternoon, hell would be a respite from the Texas heat. He planned to be finished with work well before then, if he could just keep his mind from drifting back to the image of a very nude Brendon sleeping in their bed. Zeke shook his head, trying to dispel the vision of Brendon lying spread open, cock resting softly against his thigh. His mouth watered as he fantasised about taking that soft length into his mouth, working it into a thick erection as he lapped at the head —

"Damn it," Zeke muttered, feeling his own prick straining against the seam of his jeans. Looked like it was going to be a long day no matter what he did. He swallowed the last bit of his coffee and was fixing to walk down the steps when he noticed the old ranch truck hauling ass from the south trail. Squinting, he could just make out two figures in the cab. Charlie must have Miguel with him. The speed they were coming in at had a sense of urgency kicking into Ezekiel's gut—something was wrong. It was too early in the morning for the men to be heading back to the main house. He stepped off the porch, glancing back when he heard the screen door squeak open and bounce closed. Brendon stood on the porch, barefoot, in jeans and a black tank. He winked at Zeke, then brought one hand over his brow to watch the progress of the truck.

"Something wrong?" Brendon kept his eyes on the truck, and Zeke was distracted for a moment by the display of masculine beauty. He turned back, watching as Charlie and Miguel drew nearer.

"Must be, they wouldn't be coming in if there wasn't. They'd be out working the cattle and such," he answered.

"Huh." Brendon moved closer to him. Apparently the man wasn't concerned with getting his feet dirty. Zeke grinned; he'd have fun helping his lover get cleaned up later. Brendon stopped when he reached Zeke, giving him a worried glance.

"Is it gonna be okay that I'm out here with you, or you want me to go back in?" Brendon frowned when he said it, but Zeke knew he'd go back in whether he wanted to or not if it made Zeke more comfortable. Hurting Brendon wouldn't make him comfortable at all, though. Zeke had no intention of making his lover hide away. He placed a hand on the small of Brendon's back, rubbing in small circles. The relief he saw on the man's face had Zeke leaning in to give him a chaste kiss on the lips.

"That answer your question, baby?"

Brendon's eyes crinkled as he smiled, that dimple that fascinated Zeke burrowing deep into Brendon's cheek.

"Yeah, yeah it does." He turned to watch as the truck pulled in the yard. Zeke felt a hand slide behind him, a finger knuckling through the belt loop in the centre of his jeans. It felt so good to be standing here, with his man. Even the worry over what bad news Charlie and Miguel were bringing him couldn't push aside the rightness of having Brendon beside him. He tensed a little as he watched Charlie and Miguel scramble out of the truck, anger flushing their faces. Brendon started to pull his hand away. Zeke growled and shook his head.

"It's not about us, those looks they're wearing; neither is me getting all tight, okay?" Brendon nodded but still didn't relax. Well, Zeke couldn't blame him at all. Charlie reached him first, Miguel hot on his heels. Zeke could see the curiosity battling with anger on his ranch hands' faces. Charlie even had his lips tilted up on one side in a smile. Well, good, then. He nodded to Brendon.

"Charlie, Miguel, this is Brendon." He didn't offer an explanation. Both of his hands knew full well that Zeke was introducing his lover to them. Charlie and Miguel smiled, taking turns shaking Brendon's hand and welcoming him to the ranch.

"Glad you're here, Brendon," Charlie told him. "Ah, Zeke, there's some shit happening in the south pasture. Got about sixty head down, looks real bad, too."

"Down, how? And how bad is 'real bad'? You call Doc Michaels yet?" Zeke tried to push back the anger and worry that threatened to break free. There was no reason for his cattle to be sick. Vaccinations were current on all head, and he had helped clear away every last bit of the toxic plant life in the pastures and along the trails — and inspected the areas where Charlie and Miguel had handled that task without him. No cattleman wanted to risk losing stock because he was careless about pigweed or any of the other number of deadly plants in the prairie region of Texas. The water tanks were checked regularly as well, which meant...

"Down like they ate something they shouldn't have, Zeke, and I know damn well we cleared the pasture. We got dead and dying cattle all over, and yeah, we called Doc before we headed back here, should be here any time now," Charlie answered. As if on cue, the sound of an engine roaring down the long dirt drive reached them. Zeke looked up, verifying it was Doc Michaels coming to the ranch. He looked back at Charlie and Miguel.

"You move the rest of the stock?" He knew they had — these men were good hands — but he had to ask. Miguel nodded.

"Yes, sir. We moved them out right away. We called the house but, ah..." Miguel looked down at his boots.

"Fuck," Zeke bit out. They had turned the ringer down on the phone and the volume down on the answering machine last night. Eva had called once, and after the first hateful word left her mouth, Brendon had jerked the phone away from Zeke and slammed it down. When it rang again immediately, they'd decided to cut off her fun by silencing the phone. Which was the same reason Zeke'd turned off his cell phone. Damn it, he knew better than to be out of reach!

"Shit, Zeke, I'm sorry, I shouldn't have suggested—" Brendon looked so upset Zeke couldn't stop himself from giving the man a one-armed hug.

"It's not your fault, babe, not at all," he told Brendon. Facing Charlie and Miguel, he explained to them what had happened, from the drive through town to the calls from Eva — omitting, of course, what had transpired between them in Gloria's house. Charlie spat on the ground in disgust as Doc Michaels finally pulled up.

"Zeke, I know that woman is your sister and all, but she is just a..." Miguel smacked Charlie on the back hard enough to make the man stumble slightly. "Uh, she is just a mean, vindictive person," Charlie finished and glared at Miguel, who shrugged in return.

"Charlie," Zeke waited until the man looked at him, "I know what Eva is, believe me, she made sure I had no illusions about her. But this isn't about her—" he hoped— "so tell me what the hell happened."

Doc Michaels walked over to the group. He glanced at Zeke and Brendon, greeting them as though seeing the men together was an everyday occurrence. Zeke didn't quite know what to make of it. He'd expected some sort of censure.

"So what is going on? Miguel said you got about sixty head, at least, that he is pretty sure you're going to lose?" Doc Michaels glanced back at Miguel for confirmation then turned back to Zeke.

"Seems the cattle got into something in the south pasture. I haven't made it out there yet, but Charlie and Miguel said it's bad. Pasture was cleared, and the tank... Miguel, did you check the tank yet?" Zeke knew Miguel had been busy, but there was always a chance.

"Yes, sir. Everything seemed fine, but I don't know if that means anything, Doc?"

Doc Michaels shook his head. "Have to send a sample off for testing. Let's get going." He took a step, then turned back to Zeke and Brendon, thrusting out a hand as he smiled. "I'm Doc Michaels, by the way, since someone didn't bother with introductions," he teased, laughing when Zeke felt his checks warm with embarrassment. Damn it, he'd been thinking about cattle and Eva and everything but manners.

Brendon grinned as he took the man's hand. "It's a pleasure to meet you, Doc Michaels. I'm Brendon Shanahan, and I'm sure Zeke just has too much on his plate to think about introductions right now."

Zeke grunted, feeling all kinds of a fool. The cattle were important, sure, but not more important than the man at his side.

"I'm just teasing you, Zeke; you have every right to be rattled." Doc Michaels patted Zeke's shoulder. Zeke wondered how he had never noticed the kindness in Doc's eyes before. It shamed him to realise he'd only been seeing what he expected to. How many other people had he judged in such a way? And didn't that make him as bad as Eva? It was something he would have to think about once this was taken care of.

Brendon squeezed his hand, pulling Zeke out of his self-recriminations. "If it's okay, I'd like to throw on my boots and come along. Maybe I can help somehow."

Zeke wasn't sure he wanted Brendon to see a bunch of sick and dying animals, but those determined brown eyes met his, and any thought at arguing died in Zeke's throat.

"All right, but it's going to be bad, Brendon." Worse than bad, he was sure.

Brendon nodded, squeezing his hand once more before heading into the house. Zeke turned back to the three men waiting in the yard, watching him with various expressions of amusement. He felt the tips of his ears burn.

"We, ah, can take three vehicles, if you all want. Otherwise, Charlie and Miguel, you two will be bouncing along in the truck bed." And that would knock those smirks right off their faces.

"They can ride with me, if you don't mind, Zeke," Doc Michaels offered. "Doubt I will be leaving before them anyways."

Brendon dashed out the screen door, long-sleeved shirt dangling over one arm and one pant leg tucked into his boot in his hurry to get ready. Zeke thought about pointing it out, but the man looked like such a hot mess he decided to let it be.

He nodded at his ranch hands, indicating they should load up with Doc and led Brendon to the ranch truck. Once inside, Zeke reached over and stroked Brendon's cheek.

"You sure you want to do this? No one is going to think less of you if you don't." And he really didn't want his man seeing the horror he feared was waiting for them. Brendon reached up and cupped Zeke's hand, holding it to his cheek.

"I would think less of me, Zeke," he murmured. "No matter how bad it is, I'll be there." Brendon turned his face and placed a kiss on Zeke's palm before letting it go. Zeke nodded, too touched to say anything right then. Brendon hadn't been talking about just this, just the cattle. He'd meant so much more, and that more soothed a lonely broken place deep down in Zeke's soul.

* * * *

Brendon felt his stomach churn and clenched his muscles tight, grinding his teeth together in an attempt not to hurl. His intention to spend the day researching panic attacks had been pushed aside for a chorus of 'I will not throw up, I will not throw up' looping over and over in his head. The sight of bloody, dying cattle was only a little less upsetting than the sounds the creatures made, which was still not as bad as the smell. He'd been out in the heat — which only made everything worse — helping Zeke in any way he could.

Maybe he should have been offended that his helping had been confined mostly to running back and forth with information between the other four men, or going back to the house and getting drinks, but damn, he knew he couldn't have handled much more.

Zeke, Doc, Charlie and Miguel — those men were covered in a mixture of manure, blood, saliva and God only knew what else. Still, watching Zeke take charge, sure of himself and doing what needed to be done… Well, Brendon hadn't seen anything so damn magnificent in a long time. Looking at the man right now, no one would ever know he had a moment's doubt about himself, or that he'd lived in fear for so many years. And there was no way anyone would ever think this calm, assured man had been tormented with panic attacks. It amazed Brendon to think how much more there was to a person than what people let show. He was so proud to be the person Zeke trusted enough to share himself with.

As though he felt Brendon's gaze on him, Zeke turned, exhaustion and worry fading a bit as he gave Brendon a slight smile and gestured him over. Brendon knew the man was beat, emotionally and physically. He'd just have to do his best to push this from Zeke's mind when they got back to the house.

"We're about ready to head back," Zeke told him, and Brendon didn't think he'd ever heard someone sound so weary. "Charlie's calling for removal of the bodies, scheduling some of them for necropsies and all of them for incineration. I… Fuck, Brendon. Someone poisoned them, and I just…" Zeke shook his head, all his earlier confidence fleeing. Brendon couldn't stand to see the pain flickering in his eyes. He wrapped Zeke in a hug, not giving a good Goddamn what anyone else thought or worrying about what he was getting all over himself.

"I know, Zeke. I'm so sorry, honey, I am, but it'll be okay. We'll make it okay, despite this." Despite the fact that Brendon was pretty sure that he knew who did this. There was only one person he could think of who would want to hurt Zeke, and if he got the chance, Brendon was going to set that bitch straight. Someone needed to, for God's sake. He enjoyed the feel of Zeke pressed against him, though he tried not to inhale much. Wouldn't do for him to heave on the man he was trying to comfort.

"Got everything scheduled, Zeke." Charlie strolled over, Miguel and Doc not far behind him. Brendon and Zeke parted reluctantly, turning to face the three men.

"All right, thank you, Charlie, Miguel. And thank you, Doc Michaels.," Zeke reached out to shake the man's hand. "You think it'll be long before you get the lab results back?"

Doc shrugged. "Doubt it. I have a friend or two who owe me a couple of favours up at the lab. I'll see if I can get them to kick this up on their to-do list."

"Ah, I wouldn't want you to use up your favours for me, Doc." Zeke looked a little uncomfortable, but Doc waved a hand through the air, cutting him off.

"I don't want to hear it, Ezekiel Matthers, not when there are sixty-three dead head of cattle laying here, almost half of which we had to put down because they were convulsing like…well. You saw it; and I have no doubt it was a deliberate poisoning. I didn't find a thing in this pasture that would have caused this. Goddamn it, I will call in whatever favour I have to, you hear me?" Doc had worked himself into an impressive tizzy. Zeke looked properly chastised while Charlie and Miguel tried to hide behind him. Personally, Brendon wanted to slap a high-five on the doctor. Someone needed to let Zeke know he deserved help; that he was worth it. Well, someone besides him.

"Yes, sir." Zeke's mouth twitched, fighting a smile. "I appreciate it, Doc."

Doc Michaels huffed out an irritated breath, jerking a hand through his hair. "I don't mean to snap, Zeke, it's just... Damn, man, you have to let people help you sometimes. Not everyone in McKinton is a backwards homophobe. Most of us aren't, for that matter." He stared at Zeke until he got a nod. Brendon winked at Doc before turning and leading his man back to the truck.

"What do you say we head back to the house, take a long, hot shower, then I'll massage out all that tension running through you? Right before I swallow your cock?" Brendon was counting on shock value to knock Zeke out of his Doc-induced musing, and it worked like a charm. Zeke's head whipped around, mouth opened in a sexy-as-hell 'o'. Oh yeah, his man liked that blowjob offer, sure enough. Brendon could see Zeke's cock trying to burst free from the confines of his jeans. He let his knuckles 'accidentally' brush Zeke's erection as he walked by, winking at the man as he slid into the passenger seat.

"Of course, if you'd rather, we could just go to sleep I reckon," Brendon teased as Zeke started the truck. Zeke reached over and cupped Brendon's cock, squeezing with enough force to make him groan with need. Geez, he'd thought he was doing so good teasing Zeke into a horny state, but the man had it all over him on making someone hot. Steering the truck onto the dirt road with one hand, Zeke continued to stroke Brendon's cock using light fluttering touches that gradually became firmer and insistent, making his hips buck up into the touch.

"I don't think sleep is gonna be happening for a while, babe." Zeke popped open a few buttons and slid his hand into Brendon's jeans. Rough fingertips teased his wet cock head, and Brendon found himself running an embarrassing risk of creaming his jeans like a kid.

"Ah, fuck, fuck, Zeke…" He really *was* going to come with that hand stroking his cock and the bumpy ride. "Stop, I don't wanna come yet," he panted, reaching for Zeke's hand. Brendon pulled back quickly when Zeke squeezed his prick, hard, sending a bolt of pleasure-pain to his balls.

"Shoulda thought of that before you started teasing, babe." Zeke caressed the head of Brendon's cock, pressing his thumbnail into the slit. Oh, damn, that was it. Brendon's entire body clenched, head flinging back as thick, white spunk pulsed from his prick. He gasped for a minute straight, trying to stop the shivers that raced through his body.

"Holy fuck, Zeke," he muttered "Uhn…" He was pretty sure something had just shorted out in his brain. Zeke shot him an evil grin, the weight of today's events vanishing entirely from his expression for a brief moment.

"I can think of better things for you to do with that mouth other than just grunt, ya know." Those green eyes glowed at Brendon, stoking the fire inside of him all over again.

Brendon grinned back, finally able to form a coherent thought or two. "Doubt you'd want me to blow you while we're bouncing around the cab of this truck, could be dangerous," he pointed out.

Zeke nodded. "Yeah, but as soon as I get you home, babe…" He looked down and seemed only then to notice the mess he was wearing. The sight of the blood and other evidence of the dead cattle took the teasing right out of

Zeke. Brendon watched the man go from happy to restrained in a snap, not that he could blame him. He reached out and petted Zeke's thigh, squeezing it lightly, getting a little smile back from his man.

"Reckon I need to shower first, huh? Been a bitch of a day."

A ball of fear formed in Brendon's stomach at the emotionless tone of Zeke's voice. What had happened to his teasing lover of moments before? Why did it feel as though he was suddenly freezing Brendon out? He looked at Zeke, willing the man to meet his gaze, but Zeke kept his eyes on the bumpy road. They pulled into the yard and parked in the shade. Zeke slid out from under Brendon's touch and practically bolted out of the cab of the truck.

Brendon watched Zeke walk toward the house without even glancing back. What the fuck? No way was the man going to escape him that easily. He jumped out of the truck and ran after his stubborn lover.

Zeke felt like a total asshole, but he didn't know what to do. He'd been letting go of some of the sheer horror of the day, teasing and laughing with Brendon, just feeling lighter inside. When he'd looked down and realised he was coated in graphic reminders of the attack on his cattle, he'd had one thought—what if, next time, Brendon was hurt? Or, God forbid, killed?

The tight band squeezing his chest at those thoughts had nothing to do with a damned panic attack. If something were to happen to Brendon, Zeke didn't know if he would survive it—

Zeke was so lost in his thoughts he didn't heard the pounding of Brendon's boots as the man chased him across the yard. A hard hand grabbed Zeke's shoulder and spun him around right before he reached the porch steps. Angry brown eyes clashed with Zeke's startled green ones as Brendon stepped close, almost bumping their chests together in a show of force. Zeke reached behind himself and grabbed a porch rail to keep from toppling onto his ass on the steps.

"What the fuck is your problem?" Brendon bit out, hurt seeping through each word. "One minute, we're better than fine, and the next, you just turn cold as ice and walk—no, run—off like you can't stand the sight of me? Is that how you're going to handle it when something scares you, by pushing me away?"

Zeke felt his own temper spike, guilt from hurting Brendon, worry about the man's safety, frustration and fear boiling up and over. Letting go of the railing, Zeke grabbed a double handful of Brendon's shirt, pulling his lover up to his toes.

"Maybe you should fuckin' leave if you can't deal with it, Brendon. Just pack your things and get gone." It didn't matter that even saying the words broke something inside of him; Zeke couldn't seem to stop himself. He felt like he was wound so tight he was ready to shatter, but he'd handle it if only Brendon would be safe. Which meant the man needed to be away from here, from Zeke...from this cruel little town.

Brendon's hands came up to clasp Zeke's, holding them in place. Zeke blinked in surprise; he'd expected Brendon to try to pry his shirt free. Instead, his thumbs were gently caressing the tops of Zeke's fisted hands. He blinked as he realised his lover's eyes weren't shooting out angry sparks any more, but were soft and warm in a way that touched something deep inside of Zeke.

That didn't bode well for his hastily derived plan to get Brendon to leave at all. Yesterday, he had been almost certain he could keep the man safe with him, here on the ranch. Today, now, with someone trespassing onto his property and perpetrating a violent attack on his herd, Zeke just didn't feel as assured of his protective skills any more. Zeke tried to pull his hands free, but Brendon grabbed both of his wrists, holding them in a surprisingly strong grasp.

"Is that what you want, Zeke, for me to leave?"

No, no, it wasn't what he wanted, but it was what would be best for Brendon, and that was more important. Zeke shrugged, trying his best to look bored with the whole conversation.

"I know what I don't want, and that's to put up with this kind of shit So maybe you should just leave, run on back to Austin." Somehow, Zeke found the strength to get the words out, even made them sound convincing, he hoped.

Brendon kept his grip on Zeke's wrists, studying him so closely Zeke feared the man could see into his soul. Brendon's lips twitched, tipping up slightly at the corners. Zeke felt his heart sink even as he tamped down the joy trying to spring up at the sight of that beautifully curving mouth.

Shaking his head, Brendon pressed forward, forcing Zeke to stumble backwards up a step. Brendon just kept on moving, walking until he had Zeke pressed up against the door.

"You don't want me to go. You're just afraid—for me. Admit it, lover."

Zeke shook his head, some line about protesting too much flying around in his conscience.

"No. You can go, you can stay; it doesn't matter to me. You choose to hang around, don't expect me to be touching you or—" Zeke's protest was cut off by Brendon's laughter.

"I don't think so, Zeke. You can't even say those words like you mean them." Brendon pressed harder into Zeke, finally removing his hands from Zeke's wrists, only to slide them up and around his neck.

"You suck at lying, babe, and you're not going to run me off just because you're afraid. I've told you that before. I get that today has hit you hard, but I'm here, and I'm staying, and you want me here." Brendon brought his lips up to Zeke's, stopping short of touching. Zeke couldn't hide the way his body reacted to the other man. His cock was hard and throbbing, and he couldn't tear his eyes away from Brendon's pretty mouth. It was so fucking close...

Brendon chuckled softly, rubbing his own hard cock against Zeke, stealing his strength and determination with that one move. Zeke's eyelids sliding down, too heavy to hold open when all he could think about was stripping this man naked and burying his cock so deep inside Brendon that his lover would feel it for days. That thought drew a groan from Zeke's throat before he could stop it. Brendon's smile grew bigger as he thrust his cock again.

"I'm not going anywhere, unless it's to your room, Zeke. And I can guarantee that you won't be able to not touch me. Guarantee it." Brendon grabbed the back of Zeke's head and pulled him down the little bit that was needed to bring their lips together. Teeth nipped his lower lip, sending a jolt of fire straight to Zeke's balls. He groaned again as he opened for Brendon's kiss, letting the man dominate and control the melding of their mouths.

When the kiss ended, Zeke rested his forehead on Brendon's, trying to catch his breath. When he could manage it, Zeke met his lover's gaze. Maybe he was just imagining the bit of hurt he saw there, but he doubted it, and his conscience wouldn't let him ignore it.

"I'm sorry, babe. I just...I don't want you to be hurt, and yet I turned around and hurt you myself. I'm so sorry, Brendon."

Brendon nodded, hurt replaced by something that caused his eyes to glisten with tears. "I knew, within minutes, what you were doing, Zeke. Doesn't mean it didn't hurt, so don't ever pull that shit again, you understand me?" Brendon hugged Zeke tight as he spoke, burying his face against the side of Zeke's neck.

"I won't, Brendon," Zeke promised. "Not like that, though I won't vow not to ask you to leave if I'm worried about your safety." He gave into the need and wrapped Brendon in his arms.

"You can ask all you want. Just remember to respect my decision when I turn you down flat. Every time." Soft lips nibbled against Zeke's neck, making his cock leak even as his heart swelled with happiness. They'd figure this out, somehow, and he would keep Brendon safe at the same time. Right now, though, it was time for the make-up sex Zeke had heard so much about. Well, if it was supposed to be more explosive than non-make-up sex, he and Brendon just might end up killing each other—in the best way possible.

Grinning, Zeke pulled Brendon off of him. "Time to shower, babe."

Chapter Six

Zeke took Brendon's hand and waited until he had stepped under the water before following. "You are so fucking sexy, baby, all wet and slick. Makes me want, need."

Hearing those words had Brendon whimpering and leaning into Zeke, feeling the burn of his own pressing need. Zeke held Brendon tight, belly-to-belly and cock-to-cock, rubbing them together in slow, scintillating circles. When his lover stepped back, breathing hard, and tapped Brendon's nose with a fingertip, Brendon was more than a little disappointed.

"I have plans for these." Zeke touched their cocks, a quick stroke that had them both gasping. "We need to get done with this shower, fast before I toss my plans to hell."

The wicked look he gave Brendon made his prick thump against his belly with anticipation. *Wait. Zeke had plans?*

"You know, babe, I had plans, too," he informed Zeke, trying to figure out when, exactly, he'd let those plans go.

Probably sometime in the truck, or during their little spat on the porch. Well, Brendon had to admit there was a lot to be said for spontaneity.

Zeke grinned, eyes burning hot. "I bet our plans work just fine together, but for now," he reached out and pinched Brendon on the ass, making him yelp, "for now, let's hurry up and wash so we can…merge our plans."

Brendon rolled his eyes at that, which in turn got him another pinch. Reaching for the soap, he lathered up a cloth before tossing the soap to Zeke.

"Race ya," he taunted, knowing Zeke wouldn't be able to refuse the challenge; judging from the way his cock jerked and pulsed, that man was every bit as eager to get out of this shower as Brendon was.

Rinsing the last traces of shampoo from his hair, Brendon pushed the shower door open and reached for a towel. Zeke batted his hand away, wrapped an arm around his waist and lifted him out of the shower. Before Brendon could say a word, Zeke's mouth was on his, tongue plunging in and fucking his mouth as Zeke guided Brendon to the countertop. Withdrawing his tongue, Zeke bit Brendon's bottom lip, then spun him around so he faced the mirror over the sink. Brendon's heart stuttered as he watched their reflections, Zeke's hand clasping Brendon's shoulder and pushing him forward so he was bent at the waist and braced his forearms on either side of the sink. His eyes began to drift closed as Zeke stroked his shoulder, then started trailing his fingers down Brendon's spine.

"No," Zeke growled out, "watch me, watch us."

Brendon forced his eyes open, meeting Zeke's gaze in the mirror as both hands now stroked down Brendon's lower back, stopping and cupping his ass cheeks firmly. Zeke leaned over Brendon, licking and nipping at his neck, using that sexy mouth to follow the path his hands had taken. He heard Zeke's knee creak when his lover knelt behind him and started to say something, tell him not to put a strain on the injury. Opening his mouth to speak, he instead let out a whimper when his ass cheeks were spread open, exposing his anus for a kiss.

"Ah, fuck, Zeke!" Brendon moaned, pushing his ass against Zeke's face as his lover nibbled and sucked on the sensitive opening. He thought he heard a grumble in response, then Zeke laved his hole with the flat of his tongue and Brendon couldn't hear anything but the buzz of pleasure that exploded from his balls to his brain and threatened to blow out his eardrums.

At some point, it registered to Brendon that he was panting and making a sound that was awfully close to a whine. He was certain that would emasculate him in any other circumstance, but he right now, didn't care. He'd give Zeke everything, including his pride, and not regret it. His cock was so hard with the need to come that it hurt, each thrust of that tongue in his ass making his balls throb with the need for release.

"Zeke...please," Brendon moaned, breaking down and reaching for his cock. Zeke ran his tongue over Brendon's hole one last time then rose, reaching beside Brendon to open a drawer and pull out a condom and a tube of lube.

"Stop, babe." Zeke watched, waiting until Brendon took his hand away from his cock and resumed his position. Zeke ripped open the condom package and had his dick sheathed in seconds. He uncapped the lube and coated his dick, gaze burning into Brendon's the whole time. Zeke stepped back behind Brendon, spreading his cheeks wide once again and pressing two fingers into his saliva-slicked hole.

It wasn't enough. Brendon needed Zeke, needed his lover inside and filling him until he thought he would burst from the pleasure of it. "Please," he whispered, voice breaking with need.

Zeke scissored his fingers once, twice, then pulled out and slid his cock in, thrusting hard until he was buried to the hilt in Brendon's clasping channel. His groan blended with Brendon's, eyes locking on each other in the mirror. Zeke smiled and rocked his hips before pulling back, one hand coming around to grab Brendon's prick, the other reaching for his balls. Zeke slammed back into the depths of Brendon's ass, tugging at his balls while stroking his prick.

Bending his knees slightly, Zeke began thrusting short and hard, hands moving in time with his hips, drawing groans from Brendon as pleasure hit him from every direction. Brendon jerked his hips back to meet Zeke's thrusts, forward to fuck the hand around his cock. A hoarse sound was torn from Brendon's throat as his spine tingled, pleasure racing through him as his inner muscles clamped down on Zeke's dick.

When the first drop of spunk hit Zeke's hand, he let go of Brendon's balls and pulled him upright, watching in the mirror as come shot onto Brendon's body. Zeke locked his arm tight and buried his cock so deep in his ass that Brendon came up on his toes and reached back to clasp Zeke's hips for support.

Brendon couldn't take his eyes off the sight they made in the mirror—Zeke's strong arm around his waist, Brendon's own arms extended back to clasp his lover, his head tipped back on Zeke's shoulder. And Zeke, so gorgeous, so fucking perfect, teeth clenched as he tossed his head back and filled the latex in Brendon's ass with pounding jets of spunk. Just looking at the tendons standing out in his lover's neck as his orgasm ripped through him had Brendon's cock twitching all over again.

"Fuck, baby," Zeke groaned, resting his chin on Brendon's shoulder once their climaxes were complete. "Just, holy fuck."

Brendon turned his head and tipped it back, kissing Zeke as they both trembled and struggled to breath.

"I know, Zeke, I think we are in serious danger of fucking to death." Brendon figured if they had many more sessions like this one, his heart might just burst, or stop, or something. But, still…

Zeke opened one eye and looked at Brendon's reflection. "I can think of many worse ways to go. As a matter of fact," he brought his lips to Brendon's neck, sucked hard and brought up another mark, "any way is a worse way to go."

Laughing, Brendon couldn't do anything but agree.

* * * *

Zeke jerked upright in bed, eyes flying open in the darkness as he gasped for air. A sheen of sweat coated his body, soaking the sheets. Just a nightmare, he knew, but his heart felt like it was going to beat right out of his chest, and he couldn't get enough oxygen. Fuck, he felt like he was dying.

Through the fog of panic gripping him, Zeke heard a voice calling his name. "Breathe," it said, and damn it, wasn't he trying to do that with each short, jerky gasp? Hands gripped his shoulders, smoothing and working at the tensed muscles.

"Zeke!" Brendon, it was Brendon who was reaching out to him.

Zeke latched onto that voice like a lifeline, struggling to focus on the sound of his lover's words even if they weren't making sense yet. He felt something press up against his back, felt the warmth of Brendon's breath against his ear. Zeke tried to remember what Brendon had told him last time this had happened. If he could just focus, convince his body it didn't need to ratchet up the fight-or-flight instinct just now… The pressure of his lover's warm thighs bracketing his own helped push against the fear throbbing through his veins. Breathe, relax — that's what he needed to do.

"Long, deep breaths, love," Brendon murmured against his ear.

Zeke tried to suck in a slow, deep breath, but the adrenaline and panic had him gasping as his lungs seemed to clench tight. Hands fluttered over his chest, down to his belly as Brendon continued chanting to Zeke, encouraging him to relax and try again. He tried again, and this time when it felt as though his airway was going to close off, Zeke pushed harder, willing himself to fill his lungs with air. The next breath was slightly easier, as was each that followed until finally, he lay back against Brendon, who had somehow managed to wedge himself between Zeke and the headboard. Brendon massaged Zeke's trembling muscles, murmuring soothing words of reassurance even after Zeke's body settled, relaxed in his lover's warmth.

"Tell me," Brendon asked, and there was no way Zeke could, or would, deny the man. Zeke wanted the intimacy with him, wanted Brendon to know all of him, good and bad. He wanted, he realised, for Brendon to accept him and love him, just as Zeke accepted and loved him. He clutched at Brendon's, twining their fingers together and pressing them against his chest. Jesus, he loved this man so much it made his heart ache.

"You know that I was jumped years back. Sometimes it's that, sometimes it's just about going into town itself, some things that happened there, I guess. Maybe it's a mix, you know? Tonight, it was about being…assaulted. Probably from all the death and suffering here at the ranch today, so it just sort of sent me back." Zeke kept his eyes shut as he spoke, but felt Brendon's answering nod. "Well, by the time I was jumped, I was already staying away from town for the most part; too many times I'd come in and Eva would catch me somewhere and start going on about how I was going to burn in hell. Walking away wasn't always successful as many a time she would grab at me or follow me so she could keep up her spiel."

Brendon growled. "Didn't anyone ever step in and tell her to shut the fuck up?"

Zeke couldn't not grin, not when he was listening to his man get all snarly for him. Made him feel plumb special. "Most people just looked the other way, unless it was Mama or Enessa. Sometimes Elizabeth, but she tends to live in her own little world. The afternoon I was attacked, it was me, Elizabeth and Nessa in town. I'd gone into the feed store while the girls went to the café. That's where they overheard a group of men talking about what they were going to do when they caught me out alone." Zeke fought back a shudder, trying to concentrate on just telling it rather than reliving the whole thing. He was aware Brendon was holding himself perfectly still, as though the man was afraid any movement might stop Zeke from continuing.

"Anyway, when I walked out from the feed store, I was pulled around to the side of the building. Had enough time to count four men with bandanas tied over part of their faces before they started in on me. It was mostly fists, I thought, until I saw that pipe swinging down low, felt it hit me. That sound, metal cracking bone…sometimes I still hear it." Zeke shook his head, his stomach clenching. Remembering that sound alone was enough to give him nightmares sometimes.

Brendon didn't offer him any platitudes or stilted sympathetic words, for which Zeke was grateful. Instead, his lover just held him, petting him with hands that conveyed more than any words possibly could. Zeke closed his eyes for a moment, just letting himself be soothed by the loving touches, finding some sense of peace before he continued.

"It was right after that, right after I went down, that Nessa and Elizabeth came screaming across the street, scared those four men off and saved my life."

It was a cleaner, easier version of what had happened, but it was the best he could do, because delving too deeply into that memory caused more pain than he could handle. And it wasn't as if there were words to describe what it felt like to be beaten and reviled by four cowards who didn't even have the balls to show their faces.

"So they got away, after what they did to you. Just took off and never had to pay for it." Brendon's soft voice didn't fool Zeke. The man was furious on his behalf.

"Yeah, they did, but I fully believe they'll answer for it one way or another. I have to believe there's some sort of justice in this world."

"You may be right, Zeke, but I'd much rather bigoted assholes like that face the consequences of their actions pretty swiftly. Why didn't anyone in this town do anything about it? Why didn't they do something about your sister harassing you?" Brendon's arms tightened around Zeke, anger making them constrict more than was comfortable. Zeke tapped at his lover's arms, fearing if the man got any angrier, he'd soon be squeezed breathless.

"I'm sorry, sorry." Brendon loosened his grip but didn't release Zeke from his arms. "It's just...that they got away with it, your sister included, Zeke. It just drives me crazy. I don't understand it."

Zeke understood. It was a small-town mentality thing, probably hard for people who grew up in big cities to comprehend. "Brendon, it's just...different in a town like this, where everyone knows everyone. I wouldn't press charges for the assault; I've already explained why. Remember, this was ten years ago and laws have changed since then, but regardless, this is still a small town, probably slower to change than a big city. As for what happened with Eva... Well, it was more like a family dispute, I guess, and people didn't want to interfere. Then there was the fact, *is* the fact, that she's married to the son of a preacher at one of the churches here. Add to that the point that she's a woman and I'm a man—a gay man at that—and it tended to have people turning their heads the other way."

"That's shit, Zeke, all of those reasons. Laws are laws regardless of who is breaking them." Brendon tugged a hand free from Zeke's, bringing it up to turn his lover's head, forcing their gazes to meet. "Is that why you didn't notify the sheriff about the poisoning? You figure he will just blow it off?" Those brown eyes burned hot with anger, which, predictably, Zeke thought, had his cock growing hard. He was beginning to feel a bit twisted about the way Brendon's anger turned him on, but it was a good kind of twisted. In this case, his kink was okay.

"No proof yet, but even so, Doc Michaels was going to stop by and talk to the sheriff. I won't file charges, though; not if it's my sister."

Brendon cursed loudly and started to slide out of the bed. Zeke turned and grabbed him, pushing him down and pinning him to the mattress.

"Goddamn it, Ezekiel! What is wrong with filing charges? You can't just let people do this to you, you just can't." Brendon's anger was something to behold. The man was bristling and glaring, so pissed he was trembling with it. Zeke rocked his hips against Brendon's, moaning at the feel of his lover's prick responding so beautifully.

Brendon let out a frustrated groan of his own. "Zeke, stop trying to distract me...ahhh! God..." Brendon's complaint tapered off as Zeke slid a hand between them, squishing their cocks together in his grasp. He squeezed and stroked, loving the way his man's mouth dropped open just the smallest bit as he panted. No way could Zeke resist that open mouth. He licked the full lower lip then sucked at it, nipping lightly when Brendon's hands grasped his hair. Zeke let go of their cocks and pushed up to his knees, sliding over to his lover's side.

"On your side," he muttered over Brendon's protest, turning him until his back was to Zeke. Grabbing the lube and a condom from the top of the nightstand, Zeke quickly had his cock covered. He snapped the cap open on the lube and poured some in his hand, closing the lid and tossing the bottle somewhere on the bed before coating his cock and fingers.

"Fuck, yes!" Brendon groaned as Zeke pushed two fingers into his man's ass, testing for readiness. Still stretched from their last round of fucking, Brendon's hole took the fingers easily. Zeke inserted a third, twisting his wrist so he rubbed against the gland in his lover's tight heat. Brendon bucked and yelled, reaching for his own prick as pre-come leaked onto the sheets. Zeke cock's grew wet and he knew he couldn't wait any longer.

Pulling his fingers out, Zeke grabbed his prick and pressed it to the winking hole. He reached an arm down and slid it under Brendon's thigh, lifting it to spread him open. Sliding his other hand under Brendon's body until he clasped him firmly around the chest, Zeke thrust hard and buried himself balls deep in Brendon. Sparks shot out behind Zeke's eyes, making his vision waver as pleasure zipped from his cock to every point in his body.

"Ah, shit! Fuck me, Zeke. Hard!" Brendon's arching back emphasised his order, and Zeke could do nothing but comply. He pulled Brendon's thigh up higher and started pounding into his ass in a savage way Zeke knew Brendon would feel tomorrow. His lover pushed as hard into Zeke's thrusts as he could, feeding Zeke unintelligible sexy-as-fuck sounds that made his hips drive harder.

"Guhn..." Brendon whimpered, pumping his prick just before spunk shot out onto his belly, with more spurts hitting his chest and Zeke's arm. The sight alone was enough to have Zeke's balls scrunching up against his body, but when the tangy scent filled his nostrils, along with the almost painful clamping down of his lover's inner muscles, Zeke lost it. He moaned as buried his cock in Brendon, the hand on Brendon's thigh clenching down tight as Zeke pumped his come into his lover.

Releasing Brendon's leg, Zeke pulled his cock out and rolled to his back, carefully removing the condom and dropping it in the trash bin beside the bed. He tugged on his man until Brendon was snuggled up with his head resting on Zeke's shoulder. Holding his lover in his arms, Zeke felt his eyelids grow heavy even though he wanted to stay awake and enjoy this moment and the feelings that were spinning around in his head and heart. He looked at Brendon, smiling when he realised the other man was already asleep, mouth slightly parted and so pretty Zeke couldn't resist a soft kiss before he, too, gave in and slept.

* * * *

Zeke came out of the barn as soon as he heard a car pulling down the drive. When he saw the sheriff's car approaching, his brows flew up almost to his hairline. What the hell? He walked over to wait by the porch, trying to figure out why the sheriff would be here. While he'd told Doc he could mention yesterday's events to the sheriff if he had to, Zeke had also been clear on the fact he wouldn't file a complaint or press charges. If it was his sister, he didn't want her in jail, and if it wasn't... Well, he already had enough enemies in town. He nodded at Sheriff Stenley as the tall, lean man got out of his car.

Sheriff Stenley walked up, frowning as his grey eyes pinned Zeke with an angry glare. Zeke didn't know the man; he'd only been sheriff here for a year, but he damn sure wasn't intimidated by Stenley. He arched a brow, giving the man what Zeke hoped was his best un-intimidated look. He wasn't sure it was successful considering that the sheriff stalked right up to him, invading his personal space and leaning down—just how tall was the man anyway?—until their noses were just an inch or two apart. Zeke stood straight, dropping the aloof air to glare right back. Fuck this; he wasn't going to cower for anyone.

The back door squeaked as Brendon ran out and down the porch, papers that Zeke guessed had to do with panic attacks, as that was what Brendon had been researching only a few minutes ago, fluttering in his hand. "Is there a problem, uh, Sheriff?"

Stenley didn't turn away from Zeke as he acknowledged the other man. "I do have a problem with crimes going unreported in my county, yeah. It tends to piss me off a bit."

Zeke smirked at that, because there wasn't a damned thing the sheriff could do about what had happened here yesterday, at least not until they got the test results back from the lab. Something he was going to enjoy pointing out to the man.

"Don't know that there was a crime committed, Sheriff. Weeds get missed, cattle die, happens all the time." Zeke looked at Brendon, noted the worried look on his face as he folded up those papers he had brought out with him and shoved them in his back pocket. He reached out and pulled Brendon to his side as Sheriff Stenley stepped back a few inches.

"So, if there is a crime, you gonna file a complaint and press charges this time? Even if it's your sister who's the perpetrator?" Stenley's eyes were hard and cold as his voice mocked the very idea of Zeke following his suggestions.

Zeke had what he could only describe as an 'oh, fuck!' moment when he realised what the sheriff meant by 'this time'. The man hadn't been around when Zeke had been assaulted but he apparently knew about it; the old sheriff had let the whole thing drop when Zeke refused to press charges and claimed he couldn't remember anything about his attackers—which wasn't exactly a lie. The men had covered their faces but Zeke thought he knew who one or two of them were regardless. By the time the former sheriff had gotten to the hospital, Eva had already been by to get her digs in about how she had managed to turn the town against him, and to let him know she wasn't exactly pleased he was alive.

"Breathe," Brendon murmured in his ear, apparently having felt the tightening of his body. Zeke gave a curt nod and, following his lover's advice, took a calming breath.

"Would you want to put your own sister away, Sheriff? Could you do that?" Zeke watched the man, expecting a glimmer of understanding. What he got was nowhere even close to it.

"Damn right I would. If she'd tried to kill me and then wiped out a chunk of my livelihood, yeah. Add to that, if there was someone I cared about," Stenley drawled out as he cut his gaze to Brendon, "and my sister posed a threat to that person...hell, yeah."

Goddamn it, that was what Zeke worried about—something happening to Brendon. His lover squeezed his hand, locking their fingers together before facing the sheriff.

"Don't be a dumbass, Sheriff Stenley," Brendon demanded, causing the sheriff to jerk like someone had slapped him. "I can take care of myself, and I am pretty sure you know Zeke doesn't care to come into town much anymore thanks to the horrible job your predecessor did, so back off. It doesn't take a genius to figure out the approach you're taking here is the wrong one."

Zeke thought the slight eye roll his lover threw in was a little melodramatic, but damned if the sheriff didn't actually almost grin at the man.

"I really would put my sister in jail," Stenley directed at Brendon. "She used to tattle all the time when we were kids." He looked back at Zeke, any trace of humour vanishing.

"Your man has a point, Ezekiel. Sheriff Rawlins messed up several times from what I understand. There were numerous complaints made against your sister, got a whole file of them, dated back to about a decade ago. The man never did a damned thing about them. But I'm not him."

Zeke was only dimly aware of the sheriff's glare. He was still stuck on the fact that people had complained about his sister's behaviour, even before the attack on him. For so many years, he'd thought the people in McKinton just didn't care, but now it seemed that some had. It was just that the former sheriff hadn't given a rat's ass. It was a bit much to wrap his mind around after so many years of feeling like an outcast.

"Anything else I ought to know?" Zeke grumbled, wanting the sheriff to leave so he could have some time to think and fuck Brendon. Or fuck Brendon then think. Yeah, that sounded better.

"Yeah. You're going to file a report, and if the lab tests come back proving that the cattle weren't deliberately killed, then we will drop it. If it was intentional, then you're going to press forward." Zeke started to protest, but the sheriff cut him off. "There are other people, Ezekiel Matthers, in this town, who are gay. What kind of example would we be setting for them if we just rolled over?"

Brendon gasped in his ear, and Zeke was hard pressed not to do the same. We? Sheriff Stenley was…what? Or did he mean it as in we, the people who could possibly affect some changes? And who were the other people? What would his sister, and people like her, do to them?

He knew he must have looked dumbfounded, but Zeke honestly didn't know what to say. He'd never heard a word about the new sheriff's sexual preferences. Certainly the man wouldn't be able to let on about them, but Zeke was definitely getting the feeling the man was trying to tell him something without saying anything specific.

"What if, Ezekiel, the next person who gets the shit beat out of them in an alley doesn't have a couple of worried siblings who come looking for him or her? What happens then?" Sheriff Stenley's voice had dropped so low Zeke could hardly hear him, yet the words he spoke seemed to come screaming into Zeke's head.

Brendon wrapped him in a tight hug when he flinched at the realisation of the extent of his self-centredness. He'd been worried about himself, his family, and now Brendon, but what about people other than his loved ones? Why had he never even considered there might be others like him in town? Not that he thought there was going to be any Gay Pride parades through downtown McKinton any time soon, but still. Everyone in town knew he was gay and knew what had happened to him—and how he had reacted. Hadn't he, through his inaction, given the okay for other bigots to go after anyone different?

"Fuck," he muttered. It was a lot to take in, and his brain felt scrambled in confusion. A sweet scent floated in on a breeze, ruffling his hair as Brendon's arms tightened around him.

"Zeke?" Brendon's voice trembled slightly. He raised his eyes to Zeke's, the emotions swirling in their depths almost dropping Zeke to his knees. "Whatever you decide, Zeke, it's okay. I'm with you."

Straightening his spine, Zeke looked at Sheriff Stenley, studying the man's intent expression. Zeke dipped his chin in agreement. "All right, Stenley, we'll file a complaint about the attack on my ranch yesterday—and I'm pretty certain that's just what it was." He turned and led the way into the house, Brendon at his side and Sheriff Stenley at his heels, and hoped he was doing the right thing.

Chapter Seven

Brendon listened as Zeke finished up the call to Enessa, glad she and Gloria had finally agreed to stay in the Dallas-Fort Worth area for a few more days. His lover had argued and pleaded with the women after telling them about Eva and the attack on the ranch. Having them stay out of the area was one less thing for Zeke to worry about, which was exactly what he had texted Gloria while Enessa had been arguing with her brother on his phone. Luckily, Gloria had passed the text on to her friend, and the girls realised that at this particular point in time, Zeke needed to know they were safe more than he needed the comfort of his family. A united front was good, sure, but in Zeke's mind, it was also a bigger target.

Brendon knew from the information he had printed off on panic attacks right before Sheriff Stenley had arrived that Zeke needed less stress. He'd also learned about managing the panic attacks with biofeedback, relaxation exercises, and of course, therapy, which he knew Zeke would never agree to. But all in all, he would rather just help Zeke prevent them. Watching his man suffer through one tore him up inside.

Zeke dropped his head down into his hands, looking so beat that Brendon felt his heart pinch. Walking over to him, he plastered his chest to Zeke's back, wrapping him in a fierce hug. After a few seconds, Zeke reached down and covered Brendon's hands with his own as he sighed heavily.

"Is that a relieved sigh or a frustrated sigh?" Brendon thought he knew, but sometimes it was best to ask.

"Relieved, I think. At least we won't have to worry about them being bothered for a few more days." Zeke turned in Brendon's arms and placed a lingering kiss on his lips. Brendon's cock perked up as soon as their lips touched, almost to the point of pain when he felt Zeke's own thick length rubbing against him. He was still a little sore from Zeke pounding into his ass last night and this morning, but damned if he wouldn't try again, if he didn't suspect his man was trying to stall him.

"Nah ah, buddy, we don't have time. We're supposed to meet with Doc Michaels in twenty minutes to get the lab results and then take them to Stenley," Brendon reminded him. He'd been impressed with the sheriff — well, once he got over the man trying to bully his lover around. Stenley seemed very efficient and determined, asking a multitude of questions and taking even more notes as well as photographing the crime scene. And it was a crime scene, as the lab results attested. Someone had poisoned the stock tank and the pasture. All in all, Zeke was lucky he'd only lost the number of cattle he had. It could have easily been every head in the south pasture. More, if the other tanks had been contaminated, which thankfully they hadn't been. This time.

Grumbling, Zeke released Brendon and reached for his Stetson. "All right, let's go, then."

Brendon smiled at the way his lover sounded like a petulant child. It was cute coming from such an alpha. Of course, he couldn't let it continue, so he figured a distraction of his own was in order.

"So," he mused, walking to the truck, "what do you think Stenley meant by that cryptic comment he made? You know, about being resigned to being alone? He's a nice-looking guy," Brendon bit his lip to keep from grinning when Zeke growled at that. "Seems a shame for him to spend the rest of his life alone." The sheriff had dropped that bombshell seemingly out of the blue, right before he'd gotten in his vehicle and left. There'd been something close to envy in the man's expression as he'd looked at Brendon and Zeke, their arms around each other's shoulders.

It wasn't anything like the way Zeke was looking right now. Brendon met Zeke's angry glare, cock twitching at the look in his lover's eyes as the man stormed over to him. Huh, looked like his Zeke had a little jealous streak. Strong hands gripped his biceps as Zeke leaned in so close to Brendon that his vision blurred.

"I don't give a good Goddamn what he meant, baby," he ground out before taking Brendon's mouth in a brutal kiss.

Oh, just damn. Brendon had never particularly cared for possessiveness, but this kiss almost singed his balls, it was so hot. Maybe he'd just never had the right man want to go all caveman on him before, or maybe it was the fact that he loved the hell out of Zeke. Whichever, it made him so horny he didn't know how he was going to keep from peeling his clothes off.

Zeke bit Brendon's bottom lip hard enough to send a zing of pain through him, then sucked and licked the little wound until Brendon thought he'd come in his jeans. He actually stumbled back a step when Zeke released him, smacking into the passenger side door of the truck. That hot gaze raked Brendon from head to toe, stripping him and letting him know Zeke intended to ensure Brendon didn't notice the sheriff, or any other man, as soon as he got the chance. A little shiver of trepidation crawled up his spine, chased away by desire. He'd have to think about provoking Zeke a little more before he ever did it again, maybe. Or not. The man got so sexy when he was jealous that it was insane.

Zeke gave him a curt nod and walked over to his own door and got in. Brendon had to take a couple of breaths and steady himself to keep from telling the man they should just head back inside. He reached down and adjusted his cock, not wanting to cause himself any pain when he sat. Damn, no two ways about it, this was just going to be a painful ride.

* * * *

What the hell was wrong with him? Zeke fumed. He'd never been so jealous and possessive before. Then again, he hadn't had anything more than fuck-and-flees before, either. He glanced at Brendon, soaking up the sight of the man as he read the reports they'd picked up from Doc Michaels. Zeke had been worried, once he got over his alpha fit, that Brendon would be pissed for the manhandling. Instead, Zeke had been very aware of the heated glances sent his way, and he'd swear he could feel his lover's anticipation building steadily. Maybe it was just his own, he didn't know any more. It seemed he was so mixed up with Brendon, so tuned into him, that Zeke wasn't sure who felt what. Didn't particularly bother him any, either.

Brendon looked up, caught Zeke's sideways glance and winked. Zeke felt a smile tugging at his lips and realised he had driven through town to the sheriff's office without even a twinge of fear. He'd been so preoccupied with thoughts of his lover he hadn't cared about whether people were watching. Parking the truck, he reached for Brendon's hand and waited until the man looked at him.

"No ogling Stenley," he ordered, but knew the smile dancing across his face took any real heat out of his words. Brendon laughed, running his thumb over Zeke's knuckles.

"I haven't ogled the man to begin with, Zeke. I'm too busy ogling you."

They walked into the sheriff's office and were greeted by Doreen, who'd been the receptionist there for as long as Zeke could remember.

"Ezekiel Matthers, look at you! What a handsome man you've become." She beamed at him, and he ducked his head, just flat-out embarrassed. She wasn't treating him like some kind of misfit. First Doc, now Doreen—how many other people had he been wrong about? Brendon's snicker had Zeke casting a slitted look his way. No doubt he was enjoying the blush that had crawled all over Zeke at the woman's words.

"And who is your handsome friend, hm?" Ha, now it was Brendon's turn to blush, except he handled it much better than Zeke had. Brendon stepped forward and reached out a hand, uncaring of his pinked cheeks as he flashed his dimple for the receptionist.

"Brendon Shanahan, ma'am. Pleased to meet you."

Doreen took his hand and seemed genuinely happy to meet him. Zeke was saved from having to make any attempt at conversation by Sheriff Stenley, who stepped out of his office just as the handshake ended. His steady gaze took in everything, and a little uptilt to one side of his mouth showed his amusement. Zeke looked the older man over. Yeah, well, maybe he wasn't bad looking, but Zeke wouldn't call him handsome—and Brendon damn sure better not.

"Doreen, you done flirting with those two?" Stenley winked at Doreen as he said it, surprising Zeke that the man had a sense of humour. He looked at Brendon only to find that his lover was looking right back at him.

"Greeting two nice-looking young men is hardly flirting, Sheriff." Doreen waved the men on back to Stenley's office, adding teasingly as they passed, "Though, really, who could blame me?" Stenley arched a brow at her and she arched one right back, a clear dare for him to make another comment. Zeke wanted to laugh when the big man backed down—a wise decision, if Doreen was the same terrier she'd always been.

Sheriff Stenley shut the door behind them and gestured for Zeke and Brendon to sit as he plopped down behind his desk. Zeke took the papers from Brendon and almost tossed them toward Stenley before he caught himself. Not that his lover nudging his foot had anything to do with his decision. Zeke knew Brendon wasn't interested in the other man, so he needed to stop wanting to growl at him. Stenley picked up the reports and read over them carefully. The man was pretty good at hiding what he was feeling, but Zeke noted the tightening around the sheriff's eyes and mouth, little telltale signs of anger. Those eyes were hard and cold when he looked up at them, then focused on Zeke.

"You realise that oleander isn't native, though it is naturalised in parts of Texas, and that it's highly toxic to just about every living creature, including humans?"

"Yeah, actually, I do. I also know it doesn't grow wild in pastures. Which means someone dumped some in the water as well as tossed leaves in the pasture." Zeke tapped the reports with his finger. "The lab was able to find some bits and pieces in a couple of the necropsies they did. Water was contaminated with it." Because someone wanted to do as much damage as possible, so they had poisoned both resources.

Sheriff Stenley leant back, steepling his fingers under his chin as he kept that narrowed gaze on Zeke.

"Why do you think someone used oleander instead of something that wouldn't point so obviously to a criminal act, say, something like buttercup or pigweed? Those would have been harder to prove as intentional. Coulda just said you and your crew missed some weeds."

Zeke knew, and he knew Stenley knew. He didn't like being treated like an idiot, even if he was slow to take action. Brendon took Zeke's hand and answered before he could.

"You know, Stenley, am I gonna have to call you a dumbass every time we meet? Because that's going to get old fast. Zeke isn't stupid. He's more than aware that whoever did this—and it is still whoever, because it's not like you have proof otherwise—figured he wouldn't report it. So, they made a huge mistake. He's reporting it, filing charges, all the things that need to be done. Stop giving him a hard time already; you haven't been through what he has." Brendon glared at the sheriff, looking about ready to fly over the desk and tackle the man. Zeke couldn't help but grin; guess he wasn't the only one who could growl.

Stenley's cheeks turned ruddy, but he gave a curt nod, then all the piss and vinegar seemed to seep out of him. He turned his head for a minute before looking back at Zeke and Brendon.

"Sorry. It isn't you I'm pissed at. Something should have been done years ago, even before you were assaulted. Nothing was, but at least this time..." Stenley trailed off and looked down at his hands for a brief moment before he raised his head back up.

"You ought to know that I spoke to your sister this morning."

The words hit Zeke like a bucket of ice water. A grunt from Brendon made him realise he was squeezing the hell out of the man's hand. Letting up on his grip, Zeke glared across the desk at the sheriff.

"Why the hell did you do that? You don't have any proof—"

"I have proof, Ezekiel, of her calling you and threatening you—and Brendon. You didn't listen to the answering machine tapes you gave me yesterday. Those alone can take her down for making a terroristic threat, and the damage they would do to her in the eyes of the public, the church congregation..." Sheriff Stenley was nodding, almost as though he was thinking to himself out loud. "Eva knows that she committed a criminal act by leaving those threats. She is fully aware that the only reason I didn't arrest her on them is because, one, you didn't know about them and therefore hadn't filed charges yet. Two, they are a part of the investigation into the attack on your ranch, and as much as I would love to throw her in jail, I want to make sure that everything is done properly. She won't be getting away with this because I made a hasty mistake."

Stenley paused, letting the silence give weight to his words before continuing. "Eva also knows that I am going to take her down. Hard."

Zeke's stomach twisted in a knot, not over what the sheriff promised to do to Eva, but over the tapes Zeke foolishly hadn't bothered to listen to. All that mattered, all that really hit Zeke was that she had threatened Brendon. Visions of his lover beaten and broken, or worse, swam before his eyes. Fury pulsed through him, over him, trembling in his muscles.

"Nothing, no one, is going to hurt Brendon." Zeke rose out of his chair. He wasn't sure what he was going to do, but he had a vague notion of finding Eva and doing...something. Brendon jumped up to stop him as Sheriff Stenley bolted from behind the desk. Neither of them were what made him stop in his tracks, though. No, it was the scent that assailed him, right before he smacked into an invisible force. The impact was hard enough that he bounced backwards into Brendon, knocking him into Stenley in turn. Three grunts hit the air as arms flailed with men trying to keep upright.

"Goddamn it!" Zeke shouted, frustrated and...trapped. It wasn't something he enjoyed at all.

"Zeke." Brendon reached for him, grabbed his arm and pulled him around, holding on tight.

Zeke's eyes met Stenley's over Brendon's shoulder. The man looked a little spooked and a lot confused.

"What the fuck," Stenley grunted out, "just happened?" He and Zeke glared at each other, pissed and ready to burst with it. "And what is up with that smell again?"

Sheriff Stenley narrowed his eyes at Zeke, as though he were somehow responsible for this. The fact that he was, in a way, took some of the air out of Zeke's sails. All the years of hurt and anger had finally boiled to the surface, putting Zeke in a dangerous mood. Suddenly he was very glad his mama had smacked some sense into him. He took a deep breath to steady himself, then actually managed to smile at Stenley.

That smile grew bigger the narrower Stenley's eyes got. "Well," Zeke placed a kiss on Brendon's neck, watching the Sheriff the whole time, "how do you feel about spirits, Sheriff Stenley?"

Chapter Eight

Brendon managed to wait until Zeke put the truck in park behind the house before he reached for his man. They stumbled through the door, wrapped around each other, bucking and pulling their clothes off as they made their way down the hall. When they finally reached the bedroom, Brendon found himself pinned to the closed door, Zeke pressed up hard against him, devouring his mouth in an almost violent kiss. Brendon locked his arms around Zeke's shoulders and his legs around his lover's waist, grinding their cocks together. The friction had him groaning into the kiss, everything inside him burning with the need for release.

Pulling his lips away, Zeke latched onto Brendon's neck, to the purple bruise already there, sucking and biting at the sensitive skin. Brendon's head fell back, thumping against the door hard enough to make him see stars, or maybe it was from the pleasure shooting throughout his body. Zeke's hands were everywhere — stomach, cock, ass, back—Brendon couldn't keep up and didn't even try, the lips tugging at the skin on his neck taking the last of his senses. All he could think about was how good it felt, and how much he needed Zeke inside him.

"Ah, fuck, Zeke, need you in me now!" Brendon needed so badly he was trying to seat himself on Zeke's prick, lube and a condom the last things on his mind. Zeke's arms clamped around him, stopping Brendon from accomplishing his goal. "Goddamn it! Zeke!"

Zeke just grunted as he started walking, Brendon wrapped around him. Zeke fumbled for the lube on the nightstand, bringing it to his mouth to flip the cap open, and Brendon finally found a measure of relief as two big lubed fingers pushed into his hole, burying deep and bringing a burn of pleasure-pain.

"So fucking tight." Zeke added a third finger and brushed against Brendon's prostate. Brendon howled and jerked his hips. "More, baby?" Zeke asked through gritted teeth, lowering them both to the bed before he removed his fingers from Brendon's tight channel.

"Zeke, yes. Please." Brendon reached for his lover as Zeke pushed himself back up and stepped away. A firm shake of Zeke's head had Brendon dropping his arms back down by his sides. He watched impatiently as his lover dug a foil package out of the nightstand drawer. The package was ripped open and the condom rolled down Zeke's enticing length in a quick, smooth stroke. A coating of lube followed, then Zeke was moving back towards Brendon.

"Legs on my shoulders," Zeke ordered, sliding his hands under Brendon's ass, tilting his hips. Zeke lined his cock up with Brendon's snug pucker and clasped his big hands around Brendon's wrists. With two quick, hard thrusts, he buried his prick to the hilt, groaning as a tremor worked over him. Brendon felt his cock leak, the fullness in his ass and the look on his lover's face drawing his balls tight. He tried to move his hips, needing Zeke to thrust.

"Stop. Lock your legs around my neck, baby, trust me." Green eyes burned, watching until Brendon nodded. Legs locked, Brendon found himself being dragged off the bed as Zeke stood, still clasping his wrists, holding him suspended at a downward angle. Gently, Zeke lowered Brendon's shoulders and head to the floor while widening his stance so his prick was still buried fully inside Brendon. Zeke nodded at Brendon, then released his wrists.

Brendon braced his weight on his elbows and forearms, shoulders and neck as Zeke gripped his hips firmly, locking them together. Slowly, he began moving, barely thrusting, watching Brendon's face intently. Zeke's cock stroked his gland with each thrust, and Brendon's vision blurred with sheer ecstasy. Damn, Zeke was going to kill him like this. He groaned as Zeke started moving faster, harder, jarring thrusts that had Brendon's elbows and shoulders sliding across the floor. Zeke clamped an arm down across the tops of Brendon's thighs, keeping him from slipping away as Zeke pumped into his ass with a ferocity that Brendon thought might have scared him, if it hadn't felt so damned good. His eyes rolled back as the strokes on his gland continued; Brendon had never been fucked like this, and wasn't sure how much more of the pleasure he could take.

"Guh...gonna..." He gave up on being coherent when Zeke wrapped his other hand around Brendon's dripping prick and tugged.

"Ah! Godddd!" Brendon shouted, back arching and vision blackening as his orgasm ripped him inside out, hot come hitting his cheek and God only knew where else.

Zeke cursed and released Brendon's cock as his own orgasm hit, ramming his dick in deep and biting the inside of Brendon's leg as hot jets of come filled the latex. Zeke pumped his hips over and over, groaning and grinding through his climax.

"Shit," Zeke muttered once he'd stopped trembling, bracing Brendon's legs as he pulled out from Brendon's hole. He held on, sliding Brendon's hips down until they rested on the floor, then Zeke reached down and helped Brendon to stand. Grabbing him by the back of the head, Zeke leaned in and kissed Brendon, a sweet, heart-melting kiss that brought tears to his eyes. Jesus, this man had him, Brendon knew it. Zeke was it for him, and that was pretty much that. He watched his lover's gaze heat up as their kiss became harder, needier.

Brendon nipped, then pulled back just enough to whisper "I love you," across Zeke's lips. Part of him was really afraid to share that information with his lover, but his heart just wouldn't let him hold those words in any longer.

Zeke paused, froze actually. All except for his eyes, because something in them seemed to just melt, going happy and soft, and Brendon knew it was fine. He saw the words there, swimming in those gem-coloured eyes, before Zeke ever said them back.

"I love you, too, baby," Zeke murmured, pulling Brendon closer, "and I'm gonna show you just how much."

* * * *

He had to wake up, now. The urgency pounded in his head, sure and strong, as his mama's subtle scent enveloped him. Beside him, Zeke felt Brendon wake, knew his man's eyes had just flown open with the same sudden awareness. Zeke felt a nudge on his bare shoulder, and judging from Brendon's jerk beside him, Zeke figured his lover had received the same warning.

"We need to get up, now." Zeke rolled quietly from the bed, felt Brendon sit up and press against his back. Hands linked, they rose, letting go of each other only long enough to slide on their jeans, all the while being gently battered by the invisible force. Zeke picked up his cell phone with his free hand and passed it to Brendon. Leading them stealthily into the bathroom, Zeke locked the door and pulled his lover behind him as Brendon sent off a text to Sheriff Stenley before calling him. Stenley's voice was rough with sleep but loud over the cell phone, giving both Brendon and Zeke a moment of worry.

"Get here now," Brendon whispered, then disconnected and set the phone to silent. An eerie silence fell over the house. Zeke felt his heart slam in his chest, the tell-tale signs of a panic attack setting in as his breathing started to come in spastic little jerks. Not now, he couldn't have this happen now. Brendon wrapped his arms around Zeke, head resting on his shoulder.

"Breathe, baby, breathe with me." The words, so soft, spoken into Zeke's ear as hands caressed his chest, soothing and loving. Brendon drew in deeply, urging Zeke to follow his example. "Concentrate on me, Ezekiel," he pleaded softly.

Zeke forced his muscles to relax, refusing to let the panic take over. Air reached his lungs, filling them so he no longer felt like he was suffocating. Breath for breath, he followed Brendon, trusting that his man was right; he could do this. The creak of the bedroom door sounded loudly in Zeke's ears, causing his breath to hitch for a second before resuming. That sound finished what

Brendon had set out to do—the panic attack vanished and fury took its place.

Enough. He'd had enough of being afraid, of feeling hunted and hated. It was time for this to end. Zeke started to step forward, only to find he was caught tight in Brendon's grip. He turned to glare at his lover, meeting his eyes.

"No, Zeke. If she has a weapon, a gun, we could both be killed. Both of us." Brendon's eyes bored into his just as the words he spoke almost stopped Zeke's heart.

He hadn't thought of that, of Brendon being hurt, possibly...worse, even. What kind of idiot was he? Zeke's chin dropped to his chest just as a loud thump came from the bedroom. Guess his sister hadn't seen the footlocker he kept at the base of the bed. That thought had his lips tilting up despite their precarious situation. The sound of muted footsteps approaching the door knocked the amusement right out of him. Another sound sent a chill through Zeke—a second set of footsteps. The significance of those unexpected sounds had Zeke pushing Brendon tight behind him up against the bathroom cabinet. Brendon wasn't happy about it, judging by the squirming the man was doing, but he was wise enough to know he couldn't do much about his situation without letting the intruders know exactly where they were. Zeke knew, however, that the bruising grip Brendon had on his upper arm was a promise of retaliation for later. That was fine with him; he'd be pretty pissed if their positions were reversed.

The quiet turning of the doorknob almost caused Zeke's heart to stop. For one frightening moment, Zeke thought maybe he hadn't locked the door even, though he knew he had. He shook his head to push away the irrational doubt and fear. There would be no giving in to it, or to panic, not now. When the knob stopped turning, proving the door was locked to everyone on both sides of it, Zeke heard what he thought were muffled voices coming from his room. *Yes,* he thought, *now you know that we know you're out there, fuckers.* He stood perfectly still, not willing to chance Brendon being shot or injured in any way. The assault he was expecting on the door didn't come, though. Instead, there were slight thuds that eventually filtered through his brain as sounds of retreat.

Zeke dove for the door, intending to put an end to this harassment. He wanted it over and done with so he and Brendon could get on with their lives. Brendon's hand, still clamped around Zeke's upper arm, prevented him from grabbing the doorknob and following the intruders. He tried to spin around and break Brendon's grip, but the man was surprisingly strong, locking both arms around Zeke to hold him in place.

"I don't think so, love." Brendon's voice carried a hint of anger. "Not until we get the all-clear from Sheriff Stenley. I know you heard two sets of footsteps, just like I did. It could be a trap—lead us out, jump us, and since neither one of us can outrun a bullet, we both wait right here. You better understand something, Zeke. Where you go, I go. We stay together."

"Damn it, Brendon." Zeke slumped against his lover, knowing he was right. "I wasn't going to confront them, just slip out and try to determine for sure who it was." He wouldn't endanger Brendon any more than he already had by forcing a confrontation. Opening the bathroom door and giving chase when he didn't even know how many intruders there were—what if there were more than the two they'd heard? Added to that, he and Brendon had no way of knowing what manner of weapons were waiting for them through that door. Zeke did know

Brendon was right—again. Trying to follow whoever was in the house was every bit as foolish as confronting them. He would have to stop letting his temper overrule his common sense.

"Fine. Fine, you're right. I won't touch the damned doorknob." Brendon muttered a few choice words Zeke felt him relax his hold. Stepping back, he pulled the cell phone out of his pocket and fired off a text message, no doubt to Stenley, giving the Sheriff an update. That done, he stepped back up to Zeke and poked him in the chest, hard enough that Zeke slapped a hand over the stinging spot right above his heart. He opened his mouth to sound off but Brendon beat him to it.

"If. You. Ever." Brendon stabbed his finger into Zeke's chest, punctuating each word with a jab, startling and pissing him off at the same time. "Pin. Me." Zeke caught the finger before it could stab at him again.

"Stop with the whole finger thing, babe." Because really, it was stoking his temper something fierce, and Zeke didn't want to snap at his man—much. Brendon jerked his finger back out of Zeke's grasp. Instead of poking, he leaned in close to Zeke. The scent of Brendon, all man and anger, filled Zeke's senses. Everything was blotted out except that smell, which flowed through Zeke and had his cock filling with need. God, Brendon could turn him inside out in a heartbeat. Zeke's lips quirked and he sincerely hoped his lover wouldn't see them in the dark bathroom.

"Don't ever do that again, Ezekiel, or I will kick your ass. You can stand beside me, but not in front of me, got it?"

Zeke could have argued that Brendon would have done the same thing, but he was aware that his lover was talking about their relationship as a whole, not just this one instance. In that context, Brendon was right. He'd do his best to make sure and remember that.

"All right, babe, but you know it's natural to want to protect the ones we love. It doesn't mean I think you are any less capable than me; it just means that I would rather die than have you hurt." Zeke might have said more, but Brendon grabbed his head and pulled him down for a searing kiss.

"Same goes, Zeke, same goes."

* * * *

Brendon sighed as they pulled into the parking lot of the sheriff's office. At this rate, they would be assigned their own parking slot. After the early morning break-in and Sheriff Stenley's subsequent interviews and inspection of the premises, there hadn't been time to go back to sleep. Frankly, he felt like cold shit and knew Zeke couldn't feel much better. Glancing over at the man he loved, Brendon noted the dark smudges under Zeke's eyes, the pronounced lines around his tightened lips. He reached across the seat and took Zeke's hand.

"Hey," he waited until Zeke looked at him, "at least nothing was damaged at the ranch, including us, Zeke." In fact, the only damage had been the jimmying of the front door lock and a lamp that had been knocked over. Sheriff Stenley was quick to point out it could have been much worse; and next time, it might very well be. The fact Brendon and Zeke had heard two intruders was extremely troubling. Some partial footprints the sheriff had found also backed it up. Stenley, along with Zeke and Brendon, was determined to bring this insanity to a swift end before someone got hurt.

Watching the emotion swirling around in Zeke's eyes, Brendon had to fight his instinct to slide across the bench seat and hold the man in his arms. While they hadn't had a problem the few times they had come into town, it wouldn't do to give anyone a chance to raise a ruckus. The inability to show his lover affection out in public was the only thing Brendon regretted about being gay. Not that he would change who he was. No, the change needed to be on the part of society as a whole, and that was a long way off. Certainly too far off to do him any good right now.

Zeke gave Brendon's hand a slight squeeze, then turned back to look over the parking lot. "Doesn't look like Stenley's cruiser is here. Must have gotten an emergency call."

Brendon glanced around and realised that the Sheriff's cruiser was, indeed, gone. Well, hell, maybe the man would be back soon. It wasn't like there was a lot of crime out in this area...unless it was directed at Zeke and himself.

"You want to wait around for a few minutes?" Brendon shifted in his seat. The Texas heat was already kicking in, obliterating the idling truck's ability to keep the cab cool. Sweat beaded up on his brow and back, tickling a little trail down his spine.

Shaking his head, Zeke let go of Brendon's hand and put the truck in park. "I'd like to go to Virginia's café, maybe get a slice of pie and a cold drink, if..." He trailed off, looking down at the floorboard. Brendon's heart skipped a beat as he realised what Zeke was saying. It was a huge step for the man, walking the few blocks through town and sitting in the local diner, right across the street from where he'd been assaulted.

Giving the area a quick scan, Brendon figured it was safe and gave in to the need to hug Zeke. It was only a brief hug, a mere few seconds, but it seemed to give Zeke the strength he needed. Brendon grinned as his lover shut off the truck and got out, shoulders back and head held up high. Who would have thought Zeke would come so far so fast? Well, he knew the man was special, had from the first time Gloria had shown him Zeke's picture.

He met Zeke at the tailgate and they began walking the short distance to the cafe. Later, Brendon would think that if he hadn't been so distracted with thoughts of how proud he was of Zeke, feeling a little smug himself at the changes in the man, he might have noticed the danger. Might have even been able to spare his lover the pain, and himself the guilt caused by his few moments of revelry. As it was, he barely registered the roar of an engine before Zeke yelled out "Brendon!" and shoved him hard enough to bounce him off the big glass window of the café.

Brendon didn't feel the pain of smacking into the café's window. No, he was too busy screaming, running as he watched the front bumper of Eva's car hit Zeke. A sickening *crack* filled the air. Brakes screeched as Zeke careened over the hood and into the windshield. A spider web of cracks appeared at the impact before Zeke's body slid off the side of the hood onto the sidewalk.

Brendon was kneeling at Zeke's side as soon as he landed, heart breaking at the image of his lover lying broken and bleeding. He could hear shouting in the background—a woman's voice high-pitched and venomous, other people yelling and angry—but nothing penetrated other than Zeke. Brendon felt frantically for a pulse, watching for Zeke's chest to rise and fall, and went boneless with relief when he found both, weak as they were.

Blood covered Zeke's face, pouring from gashes caused by the impact with the windshield. It was hard to tell what were cuts and what was just blood-soaked. He knew tears were streaming down his cheeks, landing on Zeke's battered face, but he could not back away, couldn't stop himself from lifting Zeke's head into his lap and holding him to his chest.

"You'll be okay, Zeke, you will," Brendon murmured, trying to reassure himself as well as his lover. "Help will be here soon, baby, I promise."

Still, he jumped when strong hands landed on his shoulders, squeezing before someone knelt down beside him. Brendon tore his gaze from Zeke long enough to meet the sympathetic gaze of a dark-haired man wearing a paramedic uniform.

"You need to let us help him," the man said calmly, waiting for Brendon to step back. Letting go of Zeke and moving away was the hardest thing Brendon had ever done, but he knew the paramedics had to take over. He scooted back and was helped to his feet by a pair of men who held him up when he would have stumbled. Brendon looked out over the gathering crowd, then at the men who were helping him remain upright. What he saw astounded him—looks of concern and regret, even tears, on the faces of those surrounding him and Zeke. He felt humbled and terrified all at once, his head spinning as he tried to take it all in.

"Brendon." The voice behind him startled him out of his confusion as he turned to face the speaker. Sheriff Stenley stood behind him, shoulders slumped and anger vibrating off him. Brendon stepped away from the men beside him and walked over to the sheriff, giving him a curt nod.

Stenley looked down at the ground as though fascinated by the pavement, then met Brendon's gaze. A tic in the sheriff's jaw caught Brendon's attention as he waited to hear what the man had to say. God help him, if they let that bitch get away, someone was going down. Stanley must have read the look on Brendon's face, because he shook his head and pointed his thumb at his cruiser.

"She's in the back, Brendon, cuffed and waiting to go for attempted murder, and tack on a list of hate crimes with the shit she was spewing."

Brendon nodded, waiting for the rest, though it was all he could do not to go to the sheriff's cruiser and rip Eva's head off. Stanley cleared his throat before continuing.

"You should know that Eva's husband John was in the car with her, giving orders if what that woman is saying is true. That damned preacher tried to run, but a group of our good citizens, including some from his own congregation, tackled him and held him for me."

"Goddamn it!" Brendon felt like a scared, angry, hurting fool. Why hadn't any of them thought about John Calencia being one of the intruders last night? It made sense. The man was aware of Eva's behaviour, had never censored it. Hell, the fucker most likely encouraged it!

He turned back and watched the paramedics working on Zeke, saw the stretcher being rolled up.

"Is there anything else, Stanley?" Brendon couldn't keep the bitterness from his voice, even though it wasn't the sheriff he was furious with. It was Eva and her evil spouse.

"I'm sorry. Brendon, that's what I want to say. I'm sorry." Sheriff Stanley's eyes glittered with moisture and guilt as he apologised.

Brendon nodded—he'd talk to Stanley later. He didn't blame the Sheriff for Eva being an insane bitch any more than he blamed the man for Eva's husband being the spawn of Satan. Right now, though, his focus was on Zeke. He turned and followed the paramedics as they began wheeling the stretcher to the ambulance. When they loaded Zeke inside, the dark-haired man who had spoken to Brendon earlier turned and placed a hand on Brendon's arm.

"We can't let you ride back here with him." Those understanding eyes had Brendon's own overflowing with tears again. "But, if it's okay with you, my brother, Nick," the paramedic gestured to someone in the crowd, calling him over, "will give you a ride right behind us to the hospital."

Brendon looked at the man's brother, Nick, finding the same understanding in the man's eyes.

"All right, okay. Thank you." The brothers nodded at Brendon before Nick grabbed his elbow and led him to the truck. Nick clicked a button and unlocked the automatic doors, climbing in once he saw Brendon seated.

"Brendon, right?" Nick asked, following the ambulance onto the street. Brendon nodded, not caring if the man saw or not. He felt like he was going to shatter any second now. All he could think about, all he could see was Zeke, flying into that windshield over and over. The first sob tore out of him before he could stifle it, ripping through him and turning him inside out. Brendon tried to stop, but his body wouldn't—couldn't—cooperate. He didn't care if he was making a fool of himself in front of this stranger, or if he was making the man uncomfortable. All he wanted was to have Zeke safe in his arms, unhurt and un-traumatised by this new attack.

Brendon wasn't even aware of the truck coming to a halt until his door opened and Nick reached in to pull him out. He felt the man hesitate for a second before Nick hugged him, hard, uncaring of Zeke's blood on Brendon's clothes. He slapped Brendon on the back a few times before letting go. Brendon looked at the man, confused as hell.

Nick grinned and took Brendon's elbow once again. "I'm not gay, buddy, but you can't tell me you didn't need a hug. And I'm secure enough to give you one. Went to school with Ezekiel, you know."

"No, I didn't know. He, uh, doesn't talk about the past much." Brendon figured that was as much of an explanation as he could offer right now. Forming coherent sentences was struggle enough.

"Yeah, well, maybe you could let him know that he still has friends. Some of us miss him like hell, ya know." Nick nodded at Brendon's surprised look. If they had missed Zeke, why hadn't they visited? Called? Broken Eva's kneecaps? The other man must have seen the doubt in Brendon's face, known where his thoughts were at—mostly.

"We tried, you know. He wouldn't let us in when we came over. Hell, most of the time, he wouldn't even answer the door, or take our calls—nothing. I don't know if it was because he was protecting himself from more rejection, or if he didn't trust us not to…well, act like some of the other people in town. But the fact is we wanted to be there for him. I wanted my friend, and I wasn't the only one. So, just let him know, will ya, that he has friends, okay?" The serious look in Nick's eyes as they walked through the hospital doors told Brendon what he needed to know.

"All right, yeah, I'll tell him. Thanks." Brendon nodded at Nick then headed over to the nurses' station, everything forgotten except Zeke.

* * * *

Jesus, fuck, he hurt like a mother. Why'd he feel like this? Oh. Yeah. He was pretty sure he would never forget again. The vision of his insane sister steering her big old car, loving husband at her side, right towards him and Brendon— Brendon! Zeke tried to crack an eye open, failed and tried again, biting back a groan as light battered his poor eyeball. He blinked a few times until his vision cleared, panicking until he spotted Brendon dozing in a chair pulled up to the bed. Zeke studied his lover closely, trying to pry his other eye open, settling for the one when he couldn't. Other than the bruising under his eyes from lack of sleep, Zeke was guessing, Brendon looked fine. Rumpled, stubbly, and exhausted, but still fine as hell.

He told himself to push aside his selfish need for comfort and go back to sleep, but figured some part of him somewhere must have disagreed, or else Brendon had some built-in lover-alert radar, because that man's eyes shot open—oh. Zeke could smell it now, just barely. Seemed like his mama wanted to make sure Brendon woke up. His lips twitched in a grin as Brendon gasped and leant forward, holding Zeke's hand for dear life.

"Zeke?" Brendon's voice was quiet, and Zeke could hear the tears and strain buried in there. He looked into Brendon's soft brown eyes and felt his heart melt all over again. Jesus, what would he have done if he'd lost Brendon?

"S'okay, babe," Zeke tried to reassure him. Brendon's tears were breaking Zeke's heart; he couldn't stand to see his lover hurting in any way. How bad did he look himself, and how much was Brendon hurting for him?

"Come here," Zeke hoped Brendon knew what he meant, because his strength was fading fast. When he felt Brendon gently place his head on his chest, Zeke finally allowed himself to rest again.

After letting the nurses know Zeke had come around, Brendon sat back and watched him sleep, feeling a little better now Zeke had woke up, even for a few brief minutes. Looking at the damage done, Brendon knew Zeke was lucky to be alive. His knee was torn to hell, femur snapped like a twig, and his hip had been banged up. That was just the lower half. For that, Zeke had plates and pins, a rod in his thigh for the shattered femur. Above the belt, Zeke had bruised ribs, bruising to his spleen and liver, and cuts and stitches a few places on his face, including one by his eye which had resulted in a great deal of swelling.

The concussion Zeke had sustained had been more worrisome; he'd been unconscious for two days. Even though doctor's tests had shown that there shouldn't be any long-term damage from Zeke's head injury, Brendon had worried about him regaining consciousness. As for the stitches in his lover's face, Brendon didn't care. He didn't think he had ever seen a more beautiful sight than when Zeke had finally come to.

He heard the door open and glanced up to see Enessa and another woman poking their heads in. Guess the nurses passed the information on. He gave the women a tired smile and nodded for them to come in. Enessa's face was lined with worry; she'd stayed up at the hospital with Brendon almost the entire time they had been waiting for Zeke to wake up, only leaving to shower and grab clean clothes. The other woman, though... Brendon narrowed his eyes at her. The resemblance between her and Enessa was clear. She approached Brendon and offered her hand.

"I'm Elizabeth. Uh, nice to meet you?" Her voice was timid and her introduction came across more as a question than anything else. Brendon considered ignoring her outstretched hand. After all, where the hell had she been for the past few years? In the end, the sadness in her big green eyes, so like Zeke's, had him caving. He reached for her hand, figuring he could wait until he heard from Elizabeth herself why she'd pretty much abandoned her brother before passing judgment. Sort of. He'd try his best, anyway.

"Brendon, and maybe under other circumstances, I'd agree." Well, that was as nice as he could get right now. Elizabeth pulled her hand back as if she'd been burned then turned to study her brother.

"Oh. Oh, God," she murmured. When she started to reach for Zeke, she hesitated, and Brendon felt himself soften just a bit towards her

"It's okay." He nodded. Whatever had driven her away, it seemed to Brendon that it had hurt her, too. Elizabeth touched Zeke's shoulder, gently caressing her way to his cheek. Her quiet sob as she leaned in to place a soft kiss on Zeke's cheek had Brendon's eyes tearing up again.

"I'm sorry, baby brother, I'm so sorry," Elizabeth seemed stricken by the sight of Zeke bruised and battered, and Brendon knew just how she felt

"Elizabeth?" Zeke's voice was barely a whisper. Brendon started to speak, but Enessa caught his eye and shook her head. Okay, he could do that. He could sit back and allow Zeke and Elizabeth a few minutes together. But, swear to God, if she did anything to hurt Zeke, Brendon was going to have her tossed out, sister or no.

Epilogue

Zeke felt like an idiot as he made his way into his house with the assistance of Brendon, and of all people, freaking Sheriff 'Just-call-me-Laine' Stenley. *What, the man feels guilty and now we're buddies?* Zeke didn't blame the sher — Laine, and wished the man didn't blame himself, either. There was plenty of fault to go around, most of it belonging to Zeke, Eva, and John Calencia. Him for not taking action years ago, and them just for being evil...people.

Elizabeth opened the door for him, her bright smile never letting on that she'd suffered both physical and psychological abuse at the hand of Eva when they were growing up. When Elizabeth had told them why she had left and stayed away — it was the only way she thought she could escape her abuser and tormentor, her sister — Zeke had been hard pressed not to go to the jail and confront Eva. Not that he could have, any way. He'd been a little too busted up. Every time he thought about

Elizabeth having to share a room with Eva throughout her childhood, it just about brought him to tears. He understood now why Elizabeth had retreated into her head, why she had finally fled from McKinton. From Eva, really.

"Welcome home, little brother," Elizabeth teased, rising up on her toes to give him a kiss. She pulled the door open wider, and Zeke made his way in — and froze. What the hell? Brendon nudged him from behind, moving him further into the living room. There were flowers everywhere, cards, fruit baskets... *fruit baskets*?

Zeke became aware of the fact that his mouth was hanging open and snapped it shut. He turned to Brendon, choosing to ignore Sheriff Stenley's snicker at his befuddlement. It would serve Laine right if Zeke just accidentally crutched the man in the crotch.

"What's that evil grin for, babe? 'Cause it's causing my ba —" Brendon cut himself off with a guilty glance at Gloria and at Zeke's sisters. The girls started laughing; Brendon turned pink and Zeke thought his lover was just the sexiest damn thing ever.

Brendon glared back at Laine, who was almost doubled over laughing. "Shut up, you dumbass." He turned his attention back to Zeke. "All this...stuff...is from different people in town. You know, 'hoping you get better', 'sorry your sister is a psycho' — whoops, well, the oldest one, ladies. That kinda stuff. Probably a healthy dose of 'we're sorry we didn't intervene years ago' in there, too."

Oh. Oh hell. Zeke felt the water works wanting to start up. He looked away and blinked a few times, then turned back and faced Brendon. The love he saw reflected back in those warm brown eyes settled into Zeke, filling him with peace. So, he'd been a little wrong about the people in town. Zeke figured he could live with that. He'd rather be wrong and feel happy than right and afraid.

Zeke leant down carefully, not wanting to topple himself or his lover, and took Brendon's mouth in a sweet kiss. Here at home, surrounded by his family, his partner and, though he'd rather not admit it out loud, his new friend, Zeke felt so overflowing with love, he thought it must surely be pouring out of him. Ending the kiss, he buried his face in Brendon's neck, holding his lover with one arm as Brendon held on tight in return.

"Thank you, babe, for everything. All of this, all of this good, it's because of you." Zeke pulled back to look in Brendon's eyes, wanting him to know how much he meant it, that every word was true. Brendon's smile could have melted the coldest heart, but he shook his head at Zeke.

"No, love. It's because of us, our family and friends. And we can't forget..." Brendon closed his eyes, drew in a deep breath. Zeke did the same, and heard a muttered curse from Laine. Yes, Brendon was right; they couldn't forget. As he felt the nudge on his shoulder, watched Brendon's eyes open big as saucers, heard another resounding curse from Laine and squeals from the girls, Zeke burst out laughing. Yeah, like any of them could ever forget Mama.

WHEN THE
DEAD SPEAK

Dedication

For AMK, because I love you and a million other
reasons as well.

Chapter One

"I'm losing my God damned mind." Sheriff Laine Stenley ran his fingers through his hair, tugging at the dark strands until his scalp tingled with pain. A frustrated sigh slipped from his lips as he stared at the spinning tin star that denoted his position of sheriff, lying on the sidewalk because it had once again popped off. He released the grip on his hair and slapped the Stetson back on his head. Laine bent and picked up the star, grumbling as he pinned it back on, *again.* If he had one more run in with the dead, he might just pop an artery.

"Morning, Sheriff."

The voice came from behind him and nearly gave Laine a heart attack. *That would be one way to be done with this mess.* He managed not to jump—barely—but he just knew the man behind him had to be able to hear his heart slamming against his ribs. *And it is all that particular man's fault!*

Laine turned slowly and glared at Ezekiel Mathers. If Mathers hadn't unwittingly given Laine his introduction into the paranormal... But that wasn't fair, and Laine knew it. It wasn't Zeke's fault his mama had decided to...hang around, so to speak, after she died. Not really.

Zeke's lips were tipped up in a smirk, and that just made Laine scowl even more. Beside Zeke, Brendon was giving Laine a scowl of his own. Brendon's soft brown eyes were usually alight with laughter, and a softer emotion would gleam in them when he looked at his lover. The man was easygoing and kind, for the most part, but he never hesitated to call Laine—

"Don't be a dumbass, Laine." Brendon rolled his eyes and bumped his shoulder against his lover's. "Zeke didn't mean to startle you. It isn't his fault you were daydreaming and didn't hear us walking up behind you."

Zeke's lips spread into a shit-eating grin and he arched one brow at Laine. Laine pushed down the urge to snarl at the man; he was pretty sure that's what Zeke wanted. Not that he and Zeke hated each other or anything. They just had a competitive friendship...that often seemed to border on combative. Laine wasn't in the mood to trade insults today, though, so he just shook his head and glanced away from the teasing he saw in Zeke's green eyes. He felt too old, too worn out and aching inside, to play their usual games right now.

"Morning." Laine mumbled it, not looking at Zeke or Brendon as he stepped into the street to walk around them. He might be screwed up in the head, but he still was aware of the fact that Zeke was recovering from an attempt on his life. The cane the man had to use was another weight on Laine's shoulders, a reminder that Laine hadn't acted quick enough, hadn't been smart enough, to keep Zeke safe. It was a burden Laine felt shoving him down beneath the surface every time he tried to catch his breath.

As he walked back towards his office, Laine couldn't help but wonder how much more he could take before he broke. God willing, he wouldn't ever get an answer to that.

Brendon watched the sheriff walk off, studying the defeated droop of his shoulders. Laine might seem fine to everyone else, but there were little tells, small nuances that one had to know to look for. Beside him, a low growl slipped from Zeke's lips. Brendon, turned on and irritated at the same time, started to set his lover straight but stopped when he saw the teasing grin on Zeke's face. He wasn't quite able to bring himself to smile back, instead darting another worried glance at Laine's retreating figure.

"Something's wrong with him." Brendon pushed at the small of Zeke's back.

"I've been saying that since we met him, babe, but you refused to see it." Zeke tossed in a look that all but said 'Duh!'

Brendon fought against a smile; he was not going to encourage Zeke. Not for this, anyway. He applied a little more pressure to Zeke's back and looked up at him through his lashes. Sometimes that worked. "Go talk to him, please?"

Zeke snorted and shook his head. "I know that look, and I don't *want* to go talk to Stenley. What the hell am I gonna say to him? Let's have an Oprah moment?"

Brendon tried to cover his chuckle with a cough, not that he thought his lover was buying it. *Time to try a different tack.* "Then I guess I can go talk to him and you can hang around at the cafe or something so he doesn't feel like we're ganging up on him. Hopefully, it won't take long."

Zeke studied him. Brendon knew what he was looking for, but he wouldn't find it. Brendon wasn't attracted to

Laine — nor was Laine attracted to him. They were friends, plain and simple, and he'd really like for his lover and his friend to get along. Somehow, Brendon doubted Laine had many close friends.

He knew the second Zeke gave in by the way his brilliant green eyes seemed to turn a darker shade — and the resigned sigh that pushed from his lover's lungs was a dead giveaway, too. "All right, I'll go talk to the man, but why you think he'd tell me anything…" Zeke shook his head and gave Brendon's hand a quick squeeze. "I'm only doing this because I love you."

Brendon wanted nothing more than to throw his arms around Zeke and kiss him until they were both breathless, but the small town of McKinton, Texas was not that tolerant. At least, he didn't think the folks here were, and wasn't willing to bet their lives on it. He settled for letting his hand trail down Zeke's arm, brushing the hand on the cane with his fingertips.

"Thank you. I love you too." Then Brendon couldn't help himself; he leant over and whispered into his lover's ear. "But you *know* you're worried about him, too."

Zeke opened his mouth for what Brendon assumed was a denial. He didn't know which of them were more stunned with what actually came out.

"Yeah, I am." Zeke snapped his mouth shut and turned to follow Laine.

Zeke managed to get the door open without bobbling his cane, something he seemed to have trouble with for some reason. He glanced up at Doreen's excited squeal, the sound nearly puncturing his eardrums. Doreen never squealed, not that he'd ever heard before. It wasn't a pleasant sound, even if it did warm his insides. He was still trying to wrap his mind around the fact that not everyone in this small town hated him.

"Ezekiel Mathers! It's about time you stopped in to say hi!" Doreen was up and had an arm around his waist before Zeke could protest that he didn't need the help. When her other arm came around him and Zeke realised that Doreen was hugging him rather than trying to help him limp along, he was glad he hadn't snapped at her.

"I'm so glad to see you!" Doreen leant back as Zeke patted her awkwardly on the back. "You look pretty good, Zeke." She grinned and waggled her eyebrows at him and Zeke thought he'd stepped into an alternate universe. Doreen was a lot of things — tough, determined, *female* — but he surely couldn't remember her being this much of a flirt. Then again, hadn't he learnt that he didn't know the people of this small town as well as he thought he did?

"You're looking good yourself." Zeke winked at her and immediately felt himself blushing. He cleared his throat and took a steadying breath. "Is Sheriff Stenley busy?" Suddenly, the idea of talking to Laine didn't seem as intimidating as staying out here with Doreen.

Doreen laughed and released him, mostly. She held on to his free hand and tugged him along behind her. "Sure, Sheriff Stenley is available. He's probably not doing anything other than sitting in his office brooding." Doreen glanced back at him, a troubled look on her face as she stopped walking. "You know," she shot a glance at the sheriff's closed door, her voice dropping to a whisper, "he feels responsible for what happened to you. I think it's been eating at him."

Zeke felt sucker punched, and not a little confused. He'd had no idea Laine felt that way. "Why should he feel responsible? He wasn't driving that car. For that matter, if I'd filed charges on Eva sooner, she wouldn't have been out on the loose and I wouldn't be standing here holding a cane." That was a truth he had to live with, his own bundle of anger and guilt that Brendon refused to let him get bogged down in. *But who did Laine have to help him?*

Shaking her head, Doreen clucked her tongue. "It wasn't neither of you boys' fault." Zeke wasn't even going to protest being called a boy. Doreen would ream him a new one if he did. "The only one at fault was that sister of yours. Not to offend, but Eva was never quite right in the head, Zeke."

Considering Eva had tried to have him murdered, had poisoned a good chunk of his cattle, threatened his lover, then run Zeke down with her car, nearly killing him—and that was the abbreviated list of what she'd done—Zeke had to agree. He realised Doreen was looking at him, waiting for something. A light clicked on in his head.

"I'll make sure he knows I don't hold him responsible. Neither does Brendon." Zeke's skin grew warm when he mentioned his lover. He was still very cautious, wary about how people would react, having been a victim of hate crimes more than once. But Doreen knew, and she hadn't judged. Her smile was toothy but genuine and it eased a knot of tension coiled inside Zeke.

"I'd appreciate it, Zeke. He's a good man, and so are you." Doreen turned and hurried to Stenley's door, tapping firmly on the wooden frame. She opened it and poked her head in when Laine called out. "Got a visitor."

Zeke stepped up behind her and grinned. The fact Laine didn't groan, didn't glare or make any cutting remark, joking or otherwise, wiped the grin away. Brendon was right, and maybe Doreen was, too, but that flat grey stare Laine gave Zeke told him that there was more going on than Laine feeling guilty. It told Zeke that Laine was balanced on an edge, and close to tipping over the side. Zeke stepped into the room, murmuring his thanks to

Doreen before she skittered off, and locked the door behind him.

Laine watched Zeke make his way over to the chair across from his desk and didn't even try to squelch down the guilt he felt as he studied the other man's stiff movements. Zeke had come a long way in the months following Eva's attempt to murder him, but he'd always have scars—more on the inside than the outside, Laine would bet.

Zeke sat and leant his cane against the side of the chair. Laine forced himself to meet Zeke's eyes, something he hadn't been able to do for longer than a handful of seconds earlier. If he had, then they wouldn't have been having this little tête-à-tête, forced on them both by Brendon. Laine knew Zeke wouldn't have come in here without some serious *encouragement* from his lover. God only knew what Brendon had to threaten...or promise.

The silence was uncomfortable, but Laine didn't know what to say. He'd used silence before when questioning suspects and wouldn't have ever thought to be bothered by it, yet it took all of his willpower not to squirm in his seat under Zeke's penetrating gaze. He couldn't see a trace of the sarcasm Zeke usually wore like a second skin, at least when it came to Laine, but Laine was waiting for it. It was the way things always were between them. When Zeke finally let loose with his opening volley, Laine's eyes shot wide with surprise.

"You wanna tell me what's wrong?" Zeke's voice was soft and gravelly, a hint of embarrassment evident in the tone. Laine wanted the floor to open up and swallow him; he didn't feel a *hint* of embarrassment, he felt a damn *dump truck* load of it.

"Christ," Laine muttered, dipping his head down and rubbing his forehead with both hands. He immediately regretted the action, knowing it showed Zeke more than Laine wanted him to see. He peeked around one of his wrists and saw Zeke frowning at him. Laine looked longingly at his door, then his radio. What he wouldn't give for there to be an emergency call right now, nothing major, even a cat stuck in a tree would get him out of this farce of a heart-to-heart chat. Maybe the phone would ring...

"I think you're stuck with me." Zeke's amused voice had Laine shutting his eyes against a newly erupting pounding in his temple. He dropped one hand down on top of the desk, wishing he didn't always keep the surface so neat so he'd have something to fiddle with. Laine rubbed at the throbbing pain in his head with the other, giving Zeke a measuring glance.

"No, not really. You can just head on back and tell Brendon that I'm fine." Laine held his breath, waiting for Zeke's answer.

"I don't think so, Laine." Zeke shook his head slowly, once, twice, then pinned Laine with a sharp look. "I'm not going to lie to my lover for you."

Laine let out the pent up breath, irritation taking place of his normally cool disposition. "Fine. Then tell him I *said* I'm fine!" That way, it'd be Laine telling the lie, because he so was *not* fine. He watched Zeke work past anger and cringed when he saw sympathy in the man's expression.

Zeke leant forward. "Laine..."

"Zeke?" Laine managed, just barely, to keep from snarling. He didn't need this man in particular or anyone else in general feeling sorry for him. "You can leave." It wasn't an offer, more of an order, and about as polite as Laine could get it out.

Zeke wasn't intimidated at all. Laine wondered why he even bothered to try to get the other man to back down. It hadn't been successful before, had it? Brendon would call him a dumbass again, if he were in here.

No, instead, Zeke leant closer, elbows braced on the desk and couching his chin in his hands, framing his face with long, tanned fingers.

Laine slumped back in his chair, the fight going out of him in the blink of an eye. "What do you want, Zeke? What do you want me to say?"

Zeke shrugged, jostling his head. "How would I know? I don't know anything about this male bonding crap."

Lips twitching despite his surly mood, Laine brought his other hand to the desktop. "Then if I say there's nothing to say..." Maybe there was a chance to get out of this yet.

A snort was Zeke's immediate reply, then he added, "I guess I'll have to sit here till you *do* have something to say. I'm not an idiot, Laine. And..." Zeke sat up straight, looking a little flustered, his gaze darting around the dull grey walls of the room before finally settling back on Laine. "Brendon's not the only one worried, okay? He didn't even have to bribe me." Zeke seemed as mortified at the admission as Laine felt.

Shit, he must look pretty bad if even Zeke was worried. But what could he say? Laine was scared that if he said one thing, admitted to one problem, everything would come tumbling out—and his pride could not survive that. But, he rationalised, there was something he could admit to Zeke. He owed the man, didn't he?

Laine sat up straight and lifted his chin. "I'm sorry. I should have done more to keep you safe. This," Laine gestured with his hand at Zeke's cane, "shouldn't have happened. I made a mistake by not putting Eva in jail for making threats against you and Brendon." That was one weight off his shoulders, but it didn't take the guilt away.

"You think that would have stopped her? Seriously?" Zeke slapped the desktop. "You don't think she would have posted bail and been back out on the street immediately? Or that her freaking holy husband wouldn't have tried to kill me anyway? Because he was in that car, too, Laine, don't you forget that."

"How could I?" Laine wanted to shout, to strike out and hit something, but there was no reason for that something to be the man in front of him. Laine struggled to keep his voice low, calm. "If I'd have done my job right, they'd both have been in jail."

"Bullshit. That's bullshit and you know it. If, if, if! If I'd filed charges on any of the numerous occasions Eva had threatened me or assaulted me; if your predecessor, Sheriff Rawlins, had been a half-assed decent sheriff! You don't get to carry that by yourself, you don't. So tell me, why are you wallowing in it, Laine? Or are you?" Zeke narrowed his eyes and Laine would have sworn those eyes could see into his soul. "What's really eating at you?"

Laine wouldn't answer, couldn't. Besides, wasn't that bit he'd shared enough? He knew Zeke was right to an extent, but it was Laine's job to take care of everyone, keep the people of McKinton safe, and he'd failed spectacularly where Zeke was concerned. Whether or not he'd screwed up by not tossing Eva in jail, he'd failed to keep Zeke from harm.

It wasn't the first time he'd let someone down. At least this time, he'd been aware of the problem and someone he cared about—though he thought *that* might just be stretching it— hadn't died regardless. A slight ruffling of his hair had Laine closing his eyes in defeat. What was it with him drawing the dead now? Was it even happening, or was he just fucking losing it, bit by bit? If it was real... But if it wasn't, that was surely worse, right? His hair was carded again, a soft caress. It firmed a lump of rigid fear in his belly even as he almost enjoyed the otherworldly—or imaginary—touch. Words slipped out, pushed up by a need to know what, exactly, was reality. "Zeke, can't you tell your mama that now isn't the best time?"

Silence cloaked the room for minutes. *That's it, I'm hallucinating or something, and now, Zeke knows I'm losing it. Christ. And I'm still feeling imaginary fingers in my hair... That's it, I am fucked.* It took several deep breaths before Laine finally had the nerve to open his eyes. Zeke had gone pale as the proverbial ghost, and was staring at Laine with startled eyes.

"I don't know who that is, Laine." Zeke shook his head and Laine didn't miss the fine trembling in Zeke's hands as he reached for Laine's hands on the desk. "But I swear to you, that isn't my mama's spirit playing with your hair."

"Shit." Irritation warred with relief. After all, if Zeke saw it, too, then Laine wasn't making it up. Relief was stomped down quickly as those ghostly fingers tugged smartly. Laine had had about enough of this. He stood and grabbed his Stetson, pushing it down on his head. It didn't surprise him in the least when his hat was batted to the ground, his hair once again carded by whatever determined spirit had decided to show up.

Zeke, on the other hand, looked like he was on the verge of a meltdown. He was reaching blindly for his cane, his gaze never wavering from Laine's head. Laine stooped down, picked up his hat and hurried to Zeke's side before the man could hurt himself trying to get up.

"Cut it out already." Laine wasn't sure if he meant the grabby ghost or Zeke, who had knocked his cane to the floor and was trying to get up and, no doubt, out of the office immediately. Laine reached for the cane and handed it to Zeke, placing his arm around Zeke's waist and making sure the man had a steady grasp on the cane before Laine let go. He kept close to Zeke as they skirted around another chair and made their way out of the office.

Doreen was on the phone, chatting away to some friend or relative, and waved to them as they left the building. Laine was grateful for that bit of luck. Neither he nor Zeke was fit to hold a conversation with Doreen just yet. They stepped out into the hot Texas day and just stood there, letting the sun chase away the spooked feeling. Well, Laine wasn't so spooked any more. It was sad to say that he was kind of getting immune to being creeped out by ghosts, or spirits, whatever they were called. At least now he knew it was all real. He found himself actually grinning as he glanced over and saw Zeke's shaken expression.

"The hell are you smiling for? That was creepy as all get out!" Zeke was looking at him like he was crazy, but Laine wasn't, was he? That little encounter in his office just proved it. He slapped Zeke on the back, careful not to knock the man on his butt since he still seemed unsteady. Laine felt his grin blossom into an unfamiliar, wide-lipped smile.

"Zeke, I thought I was going crazy, but you saw it, too." Laine couldn't hold back a relieved chuckle. "You don't know what a relief that is. I was ready to set up appointments for some MRIs or something."

The expression on Zeke's face made it clear he thought Laine had blown past crazy and into stark raving insane territory. "That makes you feel better? Because I saw it? Maybe you should still have your head checked."

Laine looked at him and raised both eyebrows. "You saying you didn't see it now?" Laine *knew* he did!

"Oh, I saw it all right," Zeke shook his head, frowning. "But how can you feel better knowing you have some...unknown spirit...hanging around you? At least there's probably some medicine around to clear up hallucinations, but that, back there?" Zeke shook his head again. "I don't know what the fuck you can take to make that go away. Unless..." Laine nearly jumped when Zeke reached out and placed his hand on Laine's shoulder. Zeke was never that friendly with him, that familiar. "Do you know who that was? In your office?"

"Nope. Not a clue." Laine mulled over what Zeke had said about medicine curing hallucinations and decided that, given the choice, he'd rather actually believe in ghosts than be hallucinating, which worked out well since that was exactly what was happening. "Don't know if that's the same one that's been hanging around, or if there's more than one, either," he added as an afterthought. He hadn't really been checking for any sort of familiarity when the odd visits occurred.

"More than one?" Zeke's voice sounded strained, and Laine had to fight down another grin. "There's more?"

"I don't know. Guess it could be the same ghost. I usually just have a silent meltdown when it happens." Seeing the unsteady sway of Zeke's body, Laine slipped his arm back around Zeke's waist. He felt a little unsteady himself now, knowing the spirit, or spirits, popping up around him were real—and he couldn't help but wonder, would Conner...*could* Conner be one of them? It was too painful to dwell on, and Laine shoved those thoughts aside. "I don't know why this is freaking you out so much. Your mama has been visiting you since she passed." Laine turned them with a slight pressure to Zeke's hip and began leading Zeke towards the café. "Shouldn't surprise you that she isn't the only one around."

"But you said you don't know these, ah, spirits, right?"

Laine nodded. It was mostly true; he hadn't been interested in finding out who or what was messing with him. Better to ignore it and drive himself crazy with worry. Now that he knew they were real, he just might start naming them. Or numbering them, if there was more than one, but that could get hinky if the number got too high…

"So why are they, or it, coming to you then? It makes sense, Mama visiting me, but that, back in your office?" A shudder worked through Zeke's body.

"I don't have an answer for that, except to tell you it started not too long after, ah, I met your mama." Laine had thought about it a lot; there had to be some correlation. "All I can figure, now that I know I'm not going crazy, is somehow, meeting one spirit, seeing it or *accepting* it, I guess, opened up something inside of me that made me receptive to… Well, now I sound like some new age guru, don't I?" Laine laughed, *laughed*, for the first time in a long while. He felt Zeke's tension drain away under his arm.

Zeke shook his head and laughed as well, raising his free arm and slipping it over Laine's shoulder, surprising them both. "You sure sound like something, Laine, you surely do."

Chapter Two

"Your boyfriend already cheating on you?"

Brendon looked at the waitress standing beside his table, her pinched face lit with malicious glee. He must have looked as confused as he felt by the comment, because she thrust a thumb over her shoulder and snickered. Brendon leant back and looked out the window, smiling when he saw Zeke and Laine walking down the sidewalk. His smile started to slip when he saw Laine's hand around Zeke's waist and Zeke's arm over Laine's shoulders, but not for the reason the waitress implied. Didn't they realise it wasn't safe to walk out in town like that?

But it should be; they're just friends... Hopefully, they've become friends, anyways. Neither man should be ostracised for that. Brendon firmed his smile back up and batted his lashes at the waitress.

"You're just seeing gay people everywhere, aren't you? Sheriff Stenley isn't gay," Brendon didn't feel guilty for the lie, not when it could keep Laine from losing his job, or worse, his life. He let his smile drop away, all teasing cast aside. "But he's obviously secure enough to be able to help out someone who is and not worry about it. I'd think even you wouldn't begrudge an injured man some help." He flicked a borderline bitchy look over her, debating whether or not he'd be risking something nasty in his food if he said anything else. A voice from the table behind his took the risk for him.

"What's the matter, honey, he turn you down, so he must be gay?"

Brendon turned and looked at the man sitting behind him. How'd he miss this guy when he walked in?

"Not that I'd blame him," the stranger intoned. Brendon grinned. The man already had his food; he could be a smartass and not worry about it too much.

The waitress glared and walked off, muttering some very politically incorrect words that made Brendon want to break the cardinal don't-hit-a-woman rule. Instead, he flicked a glance at Zeke and Laine as they made their way closer then turned in his seat, as much as he was able, and looked at the man who'd spoken.

Definitely attractive, definitely not his type, either. Zeke was exactly his type. This man had large, startling pale green eyes that were offset by the soft brown colour of his skin and Brendon had no problem admitting the contrast between skin and eyes was stunning. He winked one of those gorgeous eyes at Brendon and grinned.

"So, is he?"

Brendon felt one of his eyebrows winging up his forehead. "Is which he what?"

The man's laugh almost sounded musical. "Let's go with is he running around on you?" The man laughed again, but his eyes seemed to be asking the other question. Brendon shook his head. He wouldn't discuss Laine's sexuality with anyone other than the man himself—and Zeke, of course.

"Why would he give this up? The man's not stupid." Brendon stood and stepped over to the other man's table, offering his hand. "I'm Brendon Shanahan, and the man with the cane is my partner, Zeke. I'll introduce you when he gets here."

The man slid from his seat and Brendon hoped he didn't look as surprised as he felt; the guy was smaller than he'd seemed with his deep voice and big personality. Maybe only five-six or seven.

"Severo Adulio Robledo," he said, shaking Brendon's hand firmly. "Everyone here so friendly?" His gaze flickered over the sneering waitress standing at the register before finding Brendon's as their handshake ended.

"I'm still trying to sort out who is and who isn't, but there's been some history of hate crimes." Brendon turned when the bell fastened to the door tinkled and watched as his lover and Laine made their way into the café.

"Is that what happened to your partner?" Severo's voice was a low rumble. Brendon looked back at him and watched the man finger a silver necklace that had been hidden by his collar. Severo wasn't looking at Brendon as he spoke, and if Brendon wasn't mistaken, he wasn't looking at Zeke, either.

"Something like that," Brendon murmured, trying to gauge Severo's line of sight. It was, he mused, latched onto one very big sheriff. *Interesting. This should be fun.*

Except it wasn't, because Severo was tossing some bills down on his table and striding past Brendon.

"Another time, perhaps," Severo offered with a faint smile and a subtle glance at Laine, then the smaller man made his way to the register. *Very interesting, indeed.* Zeke and Laine made their way over to Brendon and Severo slipped out the door with a tinkle of the bell.

* * * *

Severo had to press a hand to his chest, his heart was beating so rapidly. He risked a quick peek over his shoulder and saw the sheriff taking a seat with Brendon and his partner. What the hell was wrong with him, getting all fluttery and flustered like some chittering virgin? Severo's shoulder smacked into a lamppost and he turned back to watch where he was going before he did some serious damage to himself. *Geez. At least the big, sexy sheriff hadn't seen that.* Severo would prefer not to come across as a klutz in front of the man.

Not that it should matter. He wouldn't *let* it matter; he hadn't come here looking for a fuck. Severo didn't know why he had come here, except that he'd been told to, nagged until he'd packed his things and taken the bus to this dinky Texas town. Now, here he was with no idea why he was here, not a single clue, and the only thing that stirred him, spoke to him, was the tall, lean man who'd been helping Brendon's partner — *Zeke, that's his name, and he has a guardian. Maybe he's why I'm here?* It didn't feel right; Severo was sure the reason he'd been led here didn't have anything to do with Zeke or Brendon. Who, or what, then?

Zeke disappeared from Severo's mind as the image of the sheriff rushed to the forefront. He'd tried his best not to stare, and had ended up devouring the man with his eyes. First as he had spotted the man helping Zeke to the café, then as he stood talking to Brendon, and yet again, as Severo paid his bill.

He couldn't *not* look at the man. The sheriff was long and built just right, not too muscular but definitely ripped, at least a foot taller than Severo—not his usual type at all. He'd never cared to feel smaller than he already was, or like his lovers could easily overpower him. The sheriff could, of that Severo had no doubt, but as he'd taken in the man's sexy body, the sharp angles of his cheeks and the quicksilver flash of his eyes, it wasn't the sheriff's physical strength had had scared the crap out of Severo. No, it had been the fact that Sev sensed something wounded about the man; the strength and intelligence mingled with pain that called to Severo, that whispered into his ear *this man can shatter you.*

Severo didn't want to be shattered, didn't want to risk any kind of emotional pain. For this reason, he had always kept his affairs brief and light-hearted, a mutual understanding of *hey, this is fun and it feels good, that's all it's gonna be.* He didn't doubt that sex with the man would be phenomenal, though he didn't think it would be something as trite and shallow as *fun.* Nothing that simple.

There was a reason he didn't play around with men like the sheriff. They were too intense and wanted too much from a lover. They didn't *play.* Men like that, they demanded everything from a lover, and sometimes, they even gave as much as they took. It was too deep, too dangerous, and too permanent for someone who went from place to place whenever the whim hit him. Or whenever he was nagged to go. And Severo couldn't imagine someone like the sheriff understanding what drove a man like Sev. *Yes, Sheriff, I commune with the dead...* He'd probably end up locked away in the little jail if the sheriff found out what he did.

Then again, the sheriff would, Sev suspected, check him out. He just seemed like the protective and suspicious sort. The man would want to know who Sev was and why he was in McKinton. Maybe it would be best to get their introduction over with — though not under the prying eyes of that waitress. And, damn it, for some reason, the sheriff stirred up all sorts of lustful feelings in him. It was weird, a little intimidating, and Sev would have sworn he'd felt the man checking him out with more than a hint of interest. Not gay, Brendon had said. Sev didn't think so, not at all. Turning, Sev walked around the block, avoiding the front of the café, and made his way back to the Sheriff's Department.

Sev pushed open the door to the Sheriff's Department and stepped inside. A woman sat at a desk off to the side, talking away on the phone. She nodded at Sev and held up a finger. Sev smiled and nodded back, then wandered over to a row of uncomfortable looking chairs. He sat and crossed his legs at the ankle, one arm flung across the back of the chair beside him. The place wasn't too bad, he decided, with unfinished wood panelling and bright lighting keeping the windowless room from being dark and oppressive. Well, Sev thought, it might be oppressive regardless if one was here under different circumstances. He was trying to figure out whether the Ficus trees were real or not when the lady at the desk hung up the phone.

"Can I help you?"

Sev looked at her and knew right off the bat she was a shrewd lady. She wasn't studying him unkindly, but she wasn't smiling, either. He smiled and stood, smoothing the front of his shirt down as he approached her desk and offered his hand.

"Hi. I'm Severo Adulio Robledo." His hand was shaken briskly then released. "I wanted to talk to the sheriff when he gets back from lunch, if that's okay."

"I'm Doreen." She raked him with an intimidating gaze while she tapped her fingernails together. "Is there a problem, Mr. Robledo? Something specific you need to speak to Sheriff Stenley about?"

Here's where it gets tricky. Sev didn't want to come across as a weirdo. His cheeks heated and he shrugged self-consciously. "I'm new here in McKinton, and thought it might be a good idea to introduce myself."

Doreen stared at him for a moment or two then blinked, as though processing and filing her thoughts with that single movement. "Really. Is that something you do often?"

"Actually, yes, I do." Sev held up a hand when Doreen frowned. "Not to, like, check in for parole or anything! Just... Sometimes, I've been asked to assist with cases here and there, that's all." And he wasn't going to explain how.

"Hm." Doreen's brows scrunched together, her forehead wrinkling as she considered him. "I can't think of any cases we have open, and I know Sheriff Stenley hasn't requested any help. So why are you here again?"

Sev tucked his hands in the front pockets of his jeans. "No, I'm not here in that capacity." *I don't think, anyway.* "But I know small towns, and I saw the sheriff at the café earlier and had the distinct impression that he was the sort of guy who'd check out anyone new to town. Figured I'd help him along."

He felt like Doreen was peering into his brain, and it was borderline creepy. Sev willed himself not to blush again, sure the woman would scent out the attraction he felt for the other man.

"Why didn't you just introduce yourself there?"

Damn. "Ah, he was fixing to eat with his friends—and there was this waitress there who was tossing out some homophobic crap." Sev stopped himself from shrugging again, barely. "Since she was making suggestions about the sheriff, and since I'm definitely, uh... " Okay, maybe that wasn't the smartest thing to say. Sev bit his bottom lip and gave up on not blushing. "He was already getting sh— The waitress was already saying stuff about him hanging out with 'the town queers', and I figured throwing another one in the mix might just make it worse." God, his cheeks and the tips of his ears were burning! He dared to glance at Doreen, afraid of what he'd see in her expression. She looked pissed. *Oh shit.* "Hey, look, I—"

Doreen stood and marched around the desk, the heels of her shoes tapping loudly on the ceramic tiles. Sev turned to meet her, figuring his ass was fixing to get chewed.

"It was that bitchy niece of Virginia's, wasn't it?"

"Huh?"

"The waitress. It was Irma, wasn't it?" Doreen nodded before he could answer. "I am going to give that girl a piece of my mind, messing with the sheriff and my boys." Doreen turned and headed for the door as Sev stood stunned, rooted in place. "You watch the place while I go beat her with Zeke's cane," Doreen ordered as she went out the door.

Sev wondered what in the world had just happened. "Yeah, I'll just...do that." Otherwise, he was pretty sure Doreen would beat *him* with whatever was handy next time she saw him.

* * * *

"So, what'd you think of Severo?"

152

Brendon's tone was light, but Laine wasn't fooled. The man was watching him closely, alert to any nuance that might give him a clue as to what Laine really thought of the small man who'd slipped out the café door. Laine hadn't turned to look, but he had been aware of…Severo as soon as he and Zeke had entered the café.

"I think he's trouble." That, at least, was the truth. Laine couldn't deny he'd seen the man, though he had tried not to stare, not to make it obvious that he was checking Severo out. Which was stupid, because as sheriff, Laine always checked out newcomers, a quick sweep to form a judgement as to whether or not he needed to keep an eye on them. It shouldn't have been any different this time around, but it was, and if the look on Brendon's face was anything to go by, Laine had given something away by varying from his usual behaviour. He couldn't explain why this particular stranger seemed dangerous to him, why he couldn't risk turning around and studying the man. It was ridiculous, but Laine had felt exposed as soon as he'd caught a glimpse of the man's light brown skin, the sharp angle of his chin, as if, in seeing the man, Laine was risking everyone else seeing *him*.

Brendon scoffed at Laine's proclamation. "Please. He's all of five-six and a hundred and thirty pounds dripping wet. How much trouble could he be?"

Zeke saved Laine from answering. "That little dark-haired guy? Babe, it's always the little ones you have to watch out for. They have that whole Napoleon complex going on." Zeke winked at Brendon and opened his menu. "He was a cute little guy, though."

"And gay," Brendon pointed out, still watching Laine, who decided a grunt was the only answer to that statement. "And he has balls —"

"Well, I'd think so," Zeke cut in, grinning. Laine was relieved to see Zeke had gotten past his nervous discomfort. The man's hands were steady as he opened his menu.

"Smart ass." Brendon flicked a glance at the waitress, Irma, who was watching them with a petulant look on her face. "It seems our waitress thought there might be more to you accepting a helping hand from Laine than there really was. She wanted to know if you were already cheating on me."

The blood in Laine's veins iced over. He grabbed Zeke's forearm when he started to rise and pulled the man back down, frowning at Irma as Zeke's muscles tightened under his hand.

"No need to get in a tizzy," Laine said as he let go of Zeke, still pinning Irma with a glare.

Fear and anger warred in Laine. He didn't need people stirring up rumours about his sexual preference. *If I have to hide it, maybe I shouldn't be here. But where else can I go? And am I willing to lie to keep my job?* Laine didn't have any answers for those questions, but it didn't stop him from tipping his head at Irma. She came to their table, her lip curled in disgust.

"What do you want?" Irma didn't even bother trying to sound polite, so neither did Laine.

"An explanation." Laine hadn't had a problem with Irma before, not in the three years he'd lived here. She'd flirted, he'd avoided, and apparently that was a good move whether he was gay or straight. The woman had a sneer that could cause a man's balls to drop off.

"I'm not the one who needs to explain why he was walking around all lovey-dovey with a queer." Irma spat the words out, her knuckles going white on the pen she was gripping.

Anger burst and spread through Laine, an explosion so forceful he saw spots dance before his eyes. He was on his feet before he knew it, Zeke and Brendon flanking him. He heard the kitchen doors swing open, and the sound of scuttling footsteps helped him rein in his temper. It wouldn't do any good to blast Irma; he needed to stay calm.

"Is there a problem here?" Virginia, who'd owned the café for decades, looked from Laine and his friends to Irma, then back again. "Sheriff?"

Laine was so disgusted he didn't know what to say, but Irma didn't have the same problem. She turned to Virginia, her shoulders rigid and her voice shrill.

"I was just pointing out that our good sheriff seemed to be awfully friendly with the town queers." Irma glanced back at Laine and smirked before facing Virginia again. "He had his arm wrapped around that one." Her hand flopped behind her in Zeke's direction. "Looked all too friendly. Makes me wonder, you know, since there ain't a woman around here who he's ever dated."

"Well, if you're anything like the female options here, it's no wonder."

Laine didn't know whether he wanted to high five Brendon or deck him. He settled for ignoring him. An angry flush had covered Irma's face, and she looked ready to attack Brendon. Laine's common sense kicked in. This situation needed to be defused, but Virginia's jaw had dropped down and she was looking at Irma like the waitress was the antichrist.

"Irma Jean!" Virginia sputtered and snapped her mouth shut. "You know better than to start rumours and gossip like that! You owe these men an apology, right now."

"But, Aunt Virginia—" Irma wheedled, her head dropping down low.

Virginia wasn't having it. "I mean it, Irma Jean. You apologise, then you clock out and gather your things. Go home and think about how much trouble running your mouth is going to get you in." Virginia reached out and tipped Irma's head up, forcing Irma to look her in the eyes. "Because, I promise you, if I hear one whiff of rumour, one innuendo or one more hateful remark from you, I'll fire you and send you back to live with your mama." Virginia waited until Irma nodded then dropped her hand back to her side.

"Sorry," Irma muttered, not sounding sorry at all in Laine's opinion.

"Irma…" Virginia must not have thought it a sincere apology at all either, as she reached out to grab Irma's wrist as the waitress spun around and walked away.

"Let her go, Virginia. It's not worth the trouble." Laine turned to Zeke and Brendon. "Ya'll good with eating here still?"

"Reckon so. It isn't Virginia's fault Irma decided to get, uh, snarky." Zeke slid back into his seat and rested his cane against his knee. Brendon nodded and sat beside him. "Besides, it's not like we can pick our family, can we?"

Virginia shook her head as Laine took his seat. "No, we sure can't, and I'm sorry for that, believe me." Virginia looked at them and gave them a half-hearted smile. "That girl's my flesh and blood, and she's had a hard life, but that don't excuse her behaviour. I am sorry, Sheriff. I apologise to all of y'all."

"Wasn't your fault, Virginia." Laine wanted to say more. He'd like to know what was running through Virginia's head about Irma's accusations, but it was better to let it drop.

"I own the place, I put that girl to work here, so it is my fault, in a way." Virginia patted Laine's shoulder. "I know you were helping a friend, and there ain't a thing wrong with that. Nothing wrong if you don't find girls appealing, either," Laine's heart skipped a beat, "but that ain't no one's business but your own, and I don't know anything one way or the other — except you three eat free today."

Laine nodded and concentrated on breathing past the lump of fear in his throat. The door to the café opened, bells tinkling. Doreen stormed through the doorway and immediately found Laine. She pointed at him.

"You need to have Virginia pack up your lunch and head back to the office." Doreen's tone brooked no argument. Laine felt like a kid being sent to his room by his mother. It got his hackles up, something that, if he wasn't careful, would get his butt chewed unless he handled it carefully. He glared at Zeke and Brendon, who were both snickering at him across the booth, then faced Doreen.

"Doreen, I'm not ten."

Doreen actually snorted at him, which resulted in more snickering from his two *friends*. "No, but you have someone waiting there to talk to you, and I don't need you here witnessing me. Irma Jean!"

Irma came out of the kitchen carrying her purse and froze, looking more than a little scared. Doreen nodded at Laine. "You get your food and go, and I promise not to break any laws." Irma bolted for the kitchen, only to be dragged back out by Virginia, one hand locked around Irma's forearm, the other carrying a to-go box.

"Here you go, Sheriff." Virginia waved the box at him when Irma dug in her heels and refused to take another step closer. "Take it and go. I won't let anything happen."

Laine scooted out of the booth, keeping Doreen in sight. Obviously, she'd heard about Irma's accusations — and there'd only been one other person here when Irma had started her ranting, which meant... Laine's stomach quivered with nervousness as he took the box from Virginia. He couldn't decide whether he was excited or terrified by the prospect of talking to the man who'd been here earlier, and couldn't figure out why he'd be either.

"Look, Doreen, don't...don't do anything rash. I'd hate to have to lock you up."

Doreen laughed and shook her head. "You won't have to — this time. Now, you need to get back."

"Yes ma'am." Laine felt reassured by the fact Doreen had never assaulted anyone before — that he knew of. God knew, it would have taken a stronger man than him to report it if she had. He glanced at Zeke and Brendon as he pushed the door open. *What's with those smirks?* Laine left and tapped the glass beside his friends' booth as he walked past, wishing he could reach through and thump those looks off their faces.

Once he was sure he was out of their sight, he sped up, just stopping himself from jogging. *Guess that answers one question. I wouldn't be in such a hurry if I was terrified, now, would I?*

Taking a moment to try to calm his racing heart, Laine stopped a few feet from the door. He took several deep breaths before he felt ready to face the man — Severo Adulio Robledo, per Brendon — inside. Well, as ready as he was going to be. Laine opened the door and stepped inside, the Styrofoam box in his hand making a crunching noise as he unconsciously clenched it. He thought his eyes might just bulge out of his head when he saw the figure sitting in Doreen's chair, arms up and hands behind his head, feet propped up on Doreen's desk.

"You'd better thank God it was me instead of Doreen who walked in."

The man smiled and Laine's heart sped up and his cock twitched at the way that smile lit the guy up, making an attractive face dropdead gorgeous, those pale eyes gleaming.

"She left me in charge when she ran off to play white knight." Severo lowered his feet and hands, then stood, that bright smile still in place. "Figured since I wasn't getting paid, I might as well get comfortable. Those chairs over there suck."

Laine tried to keep his gaze on Severo's face, but damn, the little guy had some broad shoulders! "Yeah, well, small town budget and all. Come on back—" Or maybe his office was a bad idea. His step faltered and he was about to tell Severo that they were going to stay in the front instead, when the man's smile widened.

"Scared?"

Oh, hell no! Laine met Severo's gaze and swallowed his sarcastic reply. The man was trying to goad him, and Laine wasn't going to play. He didn't even glare—much. Laine opened the door to his office and headed for his desk, aware of Severo behind him. He'd swear he could feel the man scoping him out…scoping his ass out, mostly.

"Have a seat." Laine set his lunch on the desk and sat, pointing at Severo. "But keep your damned feet off my desk."

"Yessir." Severo plopped into one of the two chairs in front of Laine's desk, tossing Laine a lazy salute. Instead of irritating him, it made Laine want to smile, though he didn't. Not even when Severo gave him a wink.

"Why are you here, Severo?" Laine might not have smiled, but his prick had perked up and it wasn't going to soften any time soon. Best to get the man out of here as soon as possible.

Severo grinned and winked again. "Brendon tell you my name? Guess he must have." He shrugged and leisurely swept Laine with a heated gaze. "I figured you're gonna run a check on me, be the big, bad protective sheriff and all that. Plus, I think you're hot." The *and gay* went unspoken, but Laine could see the knowledge in Severo's eyes. The need to keep his sexuality secret kicked in as Laine worked to hide his panic.

"No. I don't think so." And that was as much as he was going to protest. "And I meant, why are you here, as in, why are you in McKinton?"

"I felt like I needed to be here, Sheriff. Make of that what you will, though when you pull a report on me — you were still going to do that, right?"

What did that mean? "Of course." And he would not feel bad about it, either. Laine opened a drawer and took out a notepad and a pen, pushing them across the desk. "You can give me a head start by writing out your full name, birth date, license number, and social."

"I don't have a license, but the rest, sure. Anything else you want? Need?" The man had the audacity to lick his lower lip and look up flirtatiously at Laine through thick lashes. "You just let me know."

Laine refused to shift despite how uncomfortably hard he was. Why was he reacting this way to this man, for Christ's sake? "That should be more than enough to get me started."

"Okay." Severo stood and walked around the desk, handing the paper to Laine, his thighs brushing against the arm of Laine's chair. Laine couldn't look away from the desire burning in those pale green eyes, couldn't stop himself from inhaling deeply, taking in Severo's scent. The mix of soap, sweat and a faint lingering cologne had Laine's prick leaking, and he realised too late that Severo was now in a position to see just what effect he was having on Laine. His words confirmed that he had, indeed, noticed.

"I could help you finish, too. No strings attached. I don't do strings."

"Shit," Laine muttered before he caught himself, heat spreading throughout his body. It'd been so long since he'd gotten laid, not since Conner. So long that even the thought of Conner didn't dampen his desire, a fact that confused Laine more than it unsettled him. "I'm not... I don't." *No strings?* Could he do that? He never had before, unable to shake the thought that one-night stands were just sleazy.

That he was even considering it was a testament to how hard up—pun intended—he was. He couldn't do it, of course, but he couldn't quite bring himself to lie, not while he was pinned by those eyes, his cock obviously hard and wanting what he was denying it. "No. I'm not interested, sorry. Not my thing." Severo could interpret that however he wanted to.

"Okay." Severo's lips tipped up just the slightest bit as he stepped back. "It must be pretty difficult, being in your position."

Laine refused to comment, a confirmation would be an admission he wasn't yet prepared to make, and he'd already decided he didn't want to lie.

"You'll probably have questions once you run that," Severo tipped his chin towards the paper in Laine's hand. "I'm right down the road at the hotel, room one-fifteen if you have any questions or if you need anything." He turned and left Laine's office without looking back, leaving Laine to wonder what, exactly, Severo meant with that last statement.

* * * *

Once Doreen was gone for the day, Laine seated himself at her desk and tapped at the keyboard until he opened the programme he wanted. He didn't question why he hadn't asked Doreen to run a search on one Severo Adulio Robledo. Laine wanted to do the search, as though he could keep the man to himself. Something about that impish face and those thick-lashed barely-green eyes had stirred feelings in Laine he didn't dare think about.

Laine drummed his fingers on the desk and waited for the printer to spit out the information on Severo, trying to sort out just what it was that he was feeling. Nervous... and horny, damn it.

"No way. Not now, not still!" Maybe if he said it enough, it would be true. "No fucking way!" The man wasn't even his type, nowhere close to it. Laine's type — when he'd *had* a type — tended to be tall and rangy, much like himself, not small and damn near delicate looking despite the broad shoulders. Not someone pretty enough to catch your eye and keep it. Not someone who didn't do anything other than fun fucks. Maybe this was simply a case of an available lay; maybe if he drove over to Fort Worth, hit up one of the bars he'd heard about from Zeke and Brendon — but no. The very idea of doing that made him cold, while thinking of Severo damn near burnt him alive. *Why?*

The printer spurted and sputtered out the papers on Severo. Laine pushed and rolled the chair over to the printer, not trusting his legs to hold him up just yet. He picked the papers up between his thumb and forefinger, like they might be evidence and he was risking contaminating them. He rolled back over to the desk and put the papers down and started reading, shaking his head and feeling a sense of panic welling up. The man wasn't a criminal by any means, though he was familiar with more than one police department. Laine leant back after reading the last page and tried to think. The papers on the desk fluttered and Laine glanced up to watch them rise in the air and swirl around, his own miniature tornado courtesy of whatever Casper was hanging around right now.

"Christ." Laine reached out and started grabbing at the papers. It wouldn't do for them to be scattered all over and have Doreen find any of them. He caught all of them except for one that kept just ahead of his trailing fingers, teasing and taunting him every time he thought he had the paper in his grip.

"Cut it out already!" Laine's temper snapped. "I've had a bitch enough of a day as it is, so just stop!" The paper dropped to the floor, every evidence of the 'breeze' that had toyed with it gone in an instant. Laine picked the paper up and told himself he did not feel like a bully for running off the playful spirit. The last thing he needed was more guilt, and it was plumb stupid to feel bad about hurting a dead person's feelings, wasn't it?

Laine stuffed the information on Severo into his desk drawer and steeled himself. He needed to make a call, one years past due probably, and it would take all of his courage to pick up the phone and plunge himself into his past.

* * * *

He watched Richard Montoya as the detective talked on the phone, laughing occasionally at something the deep voice rumbled over the line. Pretending to read reports, he noticed Montoya taking notes, heard him promise to 'check into him' for the man who'd called. It was all he could do not to walk over to Montoya's desk and read what he'd written. Excitement and anticipation tingled inside him; he'd waited over three years for this. He'd always known he'd get another chance, and this was it. Soon, he'd have the man who'd slipped through his fingers years ago.

Montoya hung up the phone and grinned, looking over at him. "Damn. Guess who that was?"

He kept his voice disinterested as he shrugged. "No idea." But he *knew.*

Montoya laughed and shook his head. "That was Laine Stenley, my old partner. You remember him, kid?"

Oh, yes, more than you'll ever know. "Vaguely. Tall guy, dark-haired? The one whose, ah, friend, was… " He let his voice trail off, hoping there was enough insinuation in his words to keep Montoya talking.

Montoya cast a mean look his way. "Yeah, his *friend.* Anyone who says anything else will answer to me." Montoya gathered up the paper he'd written on and tossed his sport coat over his arm, then slammed his chair against the desk.

Fuck! He's still protective of Laine! I fucked up, but I can fix it. "Hey, man, I didn't mean anything by it. I was just trying to make sure I had the right guy."

"Yeah, well, it didn't sound that way to me." Montoya glared at him one last time then left the room.

That fucker needs to learn a lesson. Maybe I'll teach him what happens to people who talk to me like that – after I finish what I started years ago. Grinning despite his anger with

Montoya — because the man would pay for his snotty attitude — he walked over to Montoya's desk and picked up the note pad Montoya had written on while talking to Laine. Sure enough, he could see the deep pen strokes left on the paper beneath the one Montoya had torn off. He pocketed the whole note pad and strolled out, ready to get home and plan his next move.

Chapter Three

Laine hesitated, his hand curled into a loose fist as it hovered over the number on the hotel room's door. Why was he doing this? No, why was he hesitating? This inner battle that had him wanting to pound on the door and run away at the same time had to stop.

"Yeah, yeah, whatever." Laine tapped the door three times, trying to organise his thoughts. When no response followed, he rapped his knuckles harder against the door. He'd come early — it was just a few minutes past seven in the morning right now — hoping to catch Severo off guard. Laine had a feeling this particular man posed a risk to him and felt it would be best to keep Severo off balance.

When the door finally opened, Laine realised the error of his thinking. *He* was thrown completely off balance, off his guard, damn near off his feet by the sight of the bed-warmed skin and tousled hair, the soft, heady look of sleep still showing in Severo's heavy-lidded eyes. Even the pillow impressions creased into Severo's cheek looked sexy and called to Laine with a promise of smooth sheets and even smoother skin.

What the hell was he thinking? Laine watched Severo blink the sleep-induced haze away and willed himself not to let his gaze drop down to the tempting expanse of golden brown skin on display. *Damn. Who'd have thought the little guy was so built?* Severo was shirtless, Laine had noticed that the second the man opened the door, and the promise of a visual feast was making it difficult for Laine to keep himself focused on Severo's startling eyes.

"Can I help you, Sheriff?" Severo's voice was soft and slightly slurred, as though his tongue hadn't yet woken up with the rest of his body. It was the sexiest thing Laine had heard in a long time.

"Yeah." Laine wondered when his voice had gotten so low, so hard. "You want to tell me again what brings you to McKinton?"

Severo rubbed his eyes and the gesture seemed to chase away whatever sleepiness had remained. He looked up at Laine with clear, pale green eyes and pursed his lips while fingering a silver chain. Laine felt his control slipping again, glancing down to watch long, surprisingly elegant fingers rub a thin silver necklace. The contrast between Severo's skin and that silver chain was fascinating, scintillating even. Laine's gaze dipped lower, to Severo's well-defined chest, still surprised at the amount of muscle the small man had packed onto his frame. Two small, dark copper coloured nipples rested on firm pecs, a slight smattering of black hair between them leading down to bisect abs that put Laine's six-pack to shame.

"I don't know if I should invite you in, or lock the door and protect my...virtue." Severo's teasing words had Laine snapping his gaze back up where it should have been all along.

"Your virtue," Laine didn't bother biting back his sarcasm, "is not at risk." *Hell, the guy's virtue had probably not been in danger for years, not with a body and face like that.*

Mouth twisted in a wry grin, Severo stepped back and gestured Laine in. "Since you're the sheriff, I'll take your word for it about my virtue. For now."

Laine pulled up short and glared at Severo. "What do you mean by that?"

The look Severo sent him was one that called Laine on his bullshit; it told him Severo knew Laine had more than liked what he saw.

"Don't worry, Sheriff Stenley, I'm not gonna go telling everyone in town you're gay."

Back to that. Laine rocked back on his heels and tried to keep his expression impassive. He closed his eyes, needing an escape from Severo's penetrating stare. He couldn't deny it again, not after he'd visually mauled the man without a single thought to the repercussions. At this rate, he wouldn't have to worry about Irma or anyone else outing him, he'd do it just fine on his own, at the worst possible time, no doubt. He'd be lucky if he wasn't killed. Zeke being gay was one thing. He was born and raised here, and even so, the man had been assaulted numerous times. The townsfolk were, for the most part, decent about it now, and treated Brendon better than Laine had expected since he was Zeke's lover. But for their sheriff to be gay?

No, that wouldn't do at all, and it hadn't been a problem in the past since Laine never intended to take another lover while in office, but one small—well, maybe not small, exactly—man was threatening it all.

Shame washed over him, which was stupid, in his opinion. There was no need for him to tell anyone he was gay, not when, no matter how appealing he found *any* man, he wasn't going to act on it…maybe. If he could summon up enough willpower.

Laine flinched when he felt a warm hand on his forearm. He opened his eyes and looked at Severo's hand resting there, the man's skin only a shade or two darker than Laine's tanned forearm.

"I won't tell anyone." Severo squeezed quickly then stepped away. Laine felt the loss of the man's warmth immediately and, in his opinion, inappropriately. *It was just a God damned hand!*

Laine nodded and spoke before he could think about it. "If people find out, I'll have to leave. Then I can't watch over them." Laine looked at Severo and told himself he was glad the man had put on a t-shirt. "I can't protect Zeke and Brendon if I'm not the Sheriff here."

Zeke and Brendon… Those two men had wormed their way past Laine's defences, past his promises to keep everyone at a distance, and he was determined that no one would ever hurt them again. Zeke was the one who'd been physically injured, but Brendon had suffered along with him to the point that Laine had worried what would happen to him if Zeke didn't pull through. It had been a harrowing and eye-opening discovery to learn that he could still care about other people so much. And if he could save either man from going through what he had…

"I understand." Severo leant down, rifled through his open suitcase and grabbed some clothes. "Do you mind if I brush my teeth and freshen up, for lack of a better term, before you grill me on my reasons for being here?" His cheeks darkened and Laine didn't fight a grin. Poor guy probably had to pee so bad that his eyes were watering. God knew Laine usually had to stumble to the bathroom first thing in the morning or his bladder would burst.

"No problem. I'll just..." Laine spotted the cheap table and chairs by the hotel window. Ugly floral drapes were pulled shut, blocking out any curious stares. "I'll just have a seat." He pulled the report he'd printed out on Severo yesterday from his pocket, ignoring Severo's frown and sitting.

"That's it?"

Laine looked at the smaller man. "Yup."

Severo's frown deepened, wrinkles appearing on his forehead as his eyebrows scrunched together. "And does it tell you that I..."

"Go do what you have to do, Severo, and we'll talk when you get out." Laine turned back to the papers.

"But—" Severo started to protest, walking over to Laine.

"Go on. A few minutes isn't going to make a difference, is it? This information will still be here and so will I."

Severo exhaled a much-put-upon sounding sigh. "Fine. You haven't laughed at me so far or tried to run me off yet, so I don't guess a few more minutes will change that."

Once Severo turned away, Laine let himself look at the man. Dark, softly curling hair came down to rest on the top of Severo's back. His shoulders were broad and muscular for his small frame, and even through the t-shirt, Laine could tell Severo was defined and stacked in a manner that would have been imposing if the man were a foot taller. *Hell, who am I kidding? It's imposing regardless of whether he's six-six or five-six.* Laine's eyes drifted down to a beautifully rounded ass just before Severo slipped into the bathroom and shut the door. That quick glimpse of the man's tight ass was enough to firm up the semi-erection that had started to fill Laine's jeans. He groaned and slapped his palms against his forehead. What was it about Severo that went straight to his dick?

Severo had to piss so bad he was hopping in place as he brushed his teeth. The fact that he was doing what his nieces and nephews referred to as the potty dance wasn't lost on him. It was ridiculous at his age. He would have laughed, but his bladder was cramping and his prick wasn't softening fast enough to take care of the matter. He spat and rinsed out his mouth, then splashed cold water on his face. By the time he'd wet his hair down, he had his unruly dick under control and was finally able to relieve himself. Severo washed his hands and dried them off, then quickly got dressed, irritated with himself for anticipating the next few minutes spent with Laine...make that Sheriff Stenley. The man appealed to him in a way that frightened Severo and fascinated him. He had the feeling there were so many layers to Stenley, and Severo wanted nothing more than to peel each layer back and bury himself in the man.

Well, I'd rather him be buried in me, as deep and hard as possible...as often as possible. Severo's fingers fumbled on the button of his jeans. *Oh, no. No, no, no, no! What am I thinking? That man is too scared to take what I offered him anyway — and I don't do as often as possible; that implies a relationship.* That freaked Severo more than anything, because he wanted Stenley more than he could remember ever wanting a man before, but Stenley didn't seem to be the one-night stand type, and Severo didn't know how to be anything else.

Then again, he mused, *the sheriff felt the need to keep the closet door shut tight, so maybe there's more than one reason for today's visit. The man probably hadn't been laid in a while. He might be open to the suggestion of a one nighter after all. Surely Sev could keep his heart safe for a night?* He'd been able to bury everything except his attraction to Stenley yesterday in the man's office; Sev had come dangerously close to begging the guy to fuck him. All those feelings of doom and gloom and shattered…whatever had just been his hyperactive imagination, right? He'd never been at any emotional risk before when he'd had a quick fuck, so this wouldn't be any different. Once they'd gotten each other out of their systems, they could walk away happy—and a lot less horny. The more he thought about it, the better the idea sounded. Now, if he could just convince the sheriff to go along with it…

Severo stepped out of the bathroom wearing his most seductive smile, which quickly slipped away as the fine hairs on the back of his neck stood up, as it always did when the dead made their presence known. He'd have sworn his stomach dropped to his ankles as the realisation that the man in his room was, most likely, the reason Sev had been led here.

Sheriff Stenley was muttering and glaring at a piece of paper lying on the floor by his feet. He bent down to pick up the paper, only to end up cursing soundly when the sheet fluttered a few feet away before dropping back to the floor.

"Oh, come on, now! That's enough!" Stenley threw his hands up in the air and froze as he spotted Severo. Sev watched with fascination as a pink flush crawled over Stenley's neck and face, his grey eyes widening in a way that should have been funny but instead shot a bolt of need straight to Sev's prick. *Damn, the man is freakin' sexy!*

Stenley's mouth opened and closed twice before he cleared his throat and shook his head. "Think maybe he— or she, I don't know what the hell it is—will let *you* grab that?" Stenley pointed at the paper.

"Well. No wonder you didn't laugh at me once you read that report."

The sheriff's blush deepened. "I'd be hard-pressed not to believe you can speak to the dead, not when you've consulted on several investigations and helped solve so many of them." He sighed, his shoulders slumping slightly. "And not when I've got this character giving me shit all the time."

Sev sucked the air back into his lungs—he'd forgotten to breathe apparently, fascinated by the deep colour marking Stenley's skin—but couldn't look away from the sheriff's silvery gaze. The paper whipped up into the air and started spinning, snapping Sev out of his stupor. He lunged for the paper at the same time Stenley did, crashing into the bigger man. Laine's big hands gripped Sev's shoulders, jerking him forward just as his heels rocked back. He collided with Stenley's hard body, the impact knocking the breath from his lungs. Heat surged through Sev, his prick swelling painfully fast, the friction of Stenley's thigh as the man sought to keep Sev upright drawing a groan from Sev's lips—and he wasn't alone in his arousal. Stenley's cock felt thick and scorching against Sev's stomach.

Every reason for him not to get involved with the sheriff fled and the only thought remaining in Sev's mind was the knowledge that he planned to offer this man his body. Sev's head felt heavy despite the fact that all the blood in his body seemed to have shot down south. He looked up at the sheriff and felt seared by those molten silver eyes. Sev pushed aside the nervousness that threatened to bubble up and over. *This*, seduction and sex, he knew how to do.

"Laine." Sev didn't know if it was a prayer or a protest. He licked his lips and ground his prick against the thick thigh, whimpering as jolts of pleasure spread throughout his body. A look of torment dimmed Laine's pretty eyes even as the man ground his cock against Sev's abs.

"I can't do this..." The anguish in Laine's voice was impossible to miss, but his body was telling Sev a different tale.

"You can." Sev tugged on Laine's shirt, jerking the tails from Laine's waistband. He shoved his hands underneath the starched material and the cotton shirt as well, shuddering when he felt the smooth, hard planes of Laine's stomach. "Who's gonna know but you and me? And I promise not to tell." Sev dragged his nails over the taut muscles, just hard enough to push the spark between them into a fury of flames.

Laine rocked against Sev, his hands tightening on Sev's shoulders. "I can't, I shouldn't—"

Sev found Laine's nipples, tight and pebbled, just waiting for Sev's touch. He flicked them once, then pinched. Laine's back arched and he growled, and Sev had more than a fleeting thought that he might be in trouble after all, because that was a sound he wanted to hear again and again, a sound he'd never grow tired of.

"I ca—" Laine's grip started to loosen.

Sev scraped his nails over Laine's nipples, then his world was spinning, twirling in a dizzying kaleidoscope of confusion that had Sev scrabbling for a hold on Laine's chest. Sev's back hit the bed then his body was covered by one lean, sexy sheriff. Eyes slitted narrowly, Laine lowered his head until his lips hovered a breath away from Sev's.

"I shouldn't..." Whatever had held Laine back before flitted across his features then was gone. Sev opened his mouth to protest, because he was going to curl up and cry if he didn't get to come some way or another with this man. Laine cut him off before he could speak.

"But I'm gonna." Laine's lips brushed against Sev's softly, setting off sparks in every nerve in his body, then those same nerves seemed to burst with pleasure as Sev's mouth was devoured, Laine's tongue sweeping in, learning every ridge and groove. The taste of Laine flooded Sev's senses, mint and coffee blending together with a unique flavour that pulled a strangled sound from Sev. Teeth and lips mashed together, pricks ground against each other's bodies. Laine pushed up with one arm, then Sev felt Laine's other hand grappling for the button on his jeans.

Sev reached down to help Laine and their fingers fumbled and fought to open Sev's pants. Another of those sexy growls passed Laine's lips, the vibrations rumbling into Sev's mouth as Laine plundered it again. Sev's balls drew close to his body and he groaned. He wanted to feel Laine's hand on his cock before he came. Laine lifted his lips from Sev's and pushed himself upright until he was straddling Sev's thighs. Sev knew a moment's panic, sure that Laine was going to crawl off the bed and leave him wanting, but the need in Laine's eyes reassured him that wasn't going to happen. Instead, Laine grabbed the waistband of Sev's jeans and popped the button open. His hands were steady until he had Sev's zipper down, then with trembling fingers, he pulled at the elastic of Sev's underwear, groaning as the glistening head of Sev's cock appeared.

"Damn, that's pretty." Laine's voice was only a hair less shaky than his hands as he ran a finger over Sev's leaking slit. The shudder that rippled through Sev bordered on painful as his muscles clenched.

"God, Laine...please!" Sev tried to thrust against Laine's hand and whimpered when Laine's weight on his thighs kept him from finding the friction he needed. Sev reached for his prick, desperate to come, but Laine batted his hand away.

"Just a sec…" Laine fisted Sev's cock at the base, squeezing with just the right amount of pressure. His other hand worked the button of his jeans. The zipper slid down and Sev's eyes widened at the thick red cock head peeking from the waistband of Laine's boxers. Sev pushed himself up on his elbows, his mouth watering at the amount of precome that slicked the crown of Laine's dick.

Laine shoved his boxers down far enough to grip his heavy length, and before Sev could speak, before he could tell Laine that *he* wanted that thick slab of meat in his ass, Laine started stroking them both, a prick in each hand, with a grip that was better than anything Sev had ever managed on himself. His arms gave and Sev's head hit the pillow, his eyes closing no matter how hard he tried to keep them open as pleasure swamped his body. Laine's strokes became faster, his breath coming out in heavy grunts. Laine's legs trembled, but the man's hand never faltered. Skin tingling with warmth as his body flushed, Sev's back bowed as he dug his fingers into the mattress.

Something that sounded like a mix between a whimper and a yell was torn from him as he came, spraying spunk onto his belly and chest. Sev gasped and struggled for air, then forced his eyes open as he felt Laine's knees shift. Laine let go of Sev's cock and dropped down until he was kneeling over Sev, head flung back, one arm planted by Sev's shoulders as he jacked his prick and groaned as bursts of thick, hot come hit Sev's chest. Sev forgot to breathe, he was so stunned by the erotic vision of Laine in orgasm. The man's face almost glowed with the intensity of his climax. His cock pulsed out one last jet of come, then his head dropped, hanging low enough that his hair tickled Sev's forehead. Deep shudders rocked Laine and jerky breaths sounded harsh in the small hotel room.

Sev pried his fingers loose from their grip on the mattress and slipped his hands inside Laine's shirt again. Laine hummed in approval as Sev caressed his sides, nothing overtly sexual in the touch, just the two of them enjoying the feel of each other's flesh.

Later, once Sev had spent hours dwelling on his stupidity, he would believe that if his brain hadn't been melted into a sloppy grey liquid he might not have opened his mouth and screwed up. *If* he'd been thinking, Sev knew, he would have been cautious, would have waited until he and Laine had touched and kissed and stroked to their heart's — *No!* Their *body's* — content.

But no, he had to be a dipshit and forget everything he knew about spirits. The nagging presence that had pushed and annoyed Sev until he'd given in and come to McKinton was whispering along Sev's senses again, buzzing in his brain, pleasantly happy instead of insistently harping as it had done before. Sev was relaxed and felt safe in a way he hadn't before. Laine knew about Sev's ability to speak with the dead; it was there in that report, had to be, and he hadn't mocked him… Well, Laine hadn't really gotten the chance to, either, since they'd gone at each other in a spectacular frenzy of need. Still, Sev had seen and heard Laine speaking with the spirit, so it didn't seem like a bad thing at the time to ask him.

"Who's Conner Sutherland?"

No, it hadn't seemed like a big deal at the time, but as Sev sat alone in his hotel room, the evidence of their climaxes drying on his skin, the desolation he felt served to remind him just how much of a fool he'd been.

* * * *

The smell of Severo's come mixed with his own haunted Laine on the drive back to his house. He'd barely parked the truck and got the door open before he dropped to his knees and threw up.

Who's Conner Sutherland?

The question echoed repeatedly in Laine's head, his body heaving and rocking with fear and adrenaline. Had the pesky ghost been the man Laine loved? It had to be. Severo wouldn't have asked otherwise, would he? But how could he not have known, not have felt something…familiar about the presence? Conner had been dead for over three years, but Laine still thought of him, still missed him when he went to bed at night, lying awake and aching until his exhausted body finally shut down.

How could he not have known? Another violent shudder racked Laine's body, the force of which set his teeth to chattering as his stomach clenched again. The wind kicked up and sent a bolt of panic through Laine until he realised there was nothing supernatural to it, just Mother Nature doing her thing. He forced himself to stand and felt his knees tremble when the image of Severo, looking completely debauched and sexy as sin hit him. The expression on the man's face when Laine had left him tore at Laine.

He would have sworn Severo meant it when he'd said he was more of a fuck-and fun-type of guy, but when Severo asked about Conner — and not just anyone named Conner, but Conner Sutherland, so there was no doubt — Laine had felt as though someone was ripping his heart out. He'd leapt from the bed and hauled ass out of there so fast, he'd been lucky to remember to tuck his prick back in and zip up. Laine had spared a seething glance at Severo, and the hurt he'd seen there was almost as bad as the pain Laine felt when the other man had brought up Conner.

Letting the scene play out behind his eyes, Laine realised he hadn't spoken a word, not one, after Severo had asked that question. He'd run off like a coward, not giving a second thought to the man laying on the bed covered with milky white spunk, tangy proof of their attraction.

Had Conner seen them? Been aware of what they had done?

"Oh God." Laine dragged his hands down his face and headed to the front door. *Too much, this is too freakin' much for me to comprehend!* His fingers trembled and he had to try several times before he got the key in the lock. Once inside, he made a quick call to Doreen and told her he was running late. Standing in front of the bathroom mirror, Laine was startled by his appearance. He looked desolate and more than half wild, his eyes reminding himself of a hyped-up suspect, guilt and a frenetic look bordering on crazy clear in his gaze.

Laine understood both of those things. He'd felt a searing sense of desolation since Conner had been murdered, tied and tortured, in his bed. The things that had been done to Laine's lover were unimaginable. Never in all of his years on the police force had Laine encountered a level of twisted viciousness such as he'd had to face when he'd found Conner. Seeing his lover cut open like that had killed something inside Laine as well, leaving him raw and hurting, anger and guilt riding him until, at times, he felt no different than a wild and wounded thing, ready and needing to strike out at any and everybody.

Conner's death was compounded by the fact that neither of them had been out; that made it impossible for Laine to grieve openly. Conner had deserved that grief, but instead, Laine had kept it tucked deep inside, where it festered with the guilt he felt, not only for not being able to protect Conner, but for not being brave enough, not loving the man enough to step out of the closet. Conner had been as deeply secretive about their affair as Laine had, but it didn't matter. Laine was the one left behind.

What made it worse, so much more unbearable, was the fact that the sick fucker who'd murdered Conner hadn't been caught. The police had never even had a suspect, and the knowledge that Conner's death was still unsolved, his murderer unpunished, could put Laine in a black mood for days, even weeks. At times like that, Laine tried to seclude himself, but it wouldn't be possible today.

He turned on the shower and stepped under the lukewarm water, trying to get his shit together. Severo's wounded eyes kept haunting him, and he wondered if, were the spirit really Conner, what had happened between Laine and Severo had vanished Conner forever.

His thoughts of Conner combined with the cruelty Laine had inflicted on Severo back in the hotel room was nearly enough to crush him. Somehow, he had to find a way to deal with it all. Conner deserved to rest in peace, his killer rotting away on death row, and, though Laine wasn't quite sure how he would manage to do it, there was a certain man who deserved an apology as well as an explanation.

Do what you know is right, in everything, Laine told himself. That was his grandmother's advice, and Laine had tried to live by it every day. It was good advice, and he would continue to follow it. The doubts that niggled away at him about whether or not it was right to keep his sexuality a secret, he ignored. Laine shut off the shower and reached for a towel. He couldn't let himself fall apart again. Laine dried himself off quickly and hung the towel on the towel bar. He turned and walked to his bedroom to get dressed without seeing the gentle flutter of the towel in the small, closed bathroom.

* * * *

Okay, Sev thought to himself, he could understand Laine completely shutting down on him that morning. It was understandable, once Sev had shaken himself out of his funk and gotten busy on his laptop. The articles he had pulled up on Conner Sutherland had been heartbreakingly brutal, and from Laine's reaction to the name, not to mention the loving vibes Sev felt coming from Conner's spirit, Conner had been more than just a friend to Laine. Sev made himself look at the picture of a smiling, blond man in the archived news article he'd clicked on.

Conner Sutherland had been a clean-cut, wholesome looking guy. The picture was a little blurry but Sev would swear he could see a mischievous sparkle in the man's dark eyes. Not exactly plain but not classically handsome, there had been something about Conner that seemed to shine. Sev would be willing to bet it would show through in every picture of the man, though he wasn't at all certain he wanted to test that theory. That look of agony on Laine's face when Sev had spoken Conner's name... Laine had loved the man, probably still did. With a dull ache in his heart, Sev read the report, dated April 19th, 2007, on Conner's death again.

Houston Fireman Brutally Tortured and Murdered

Conner Sutherland, 31, was found dead in his apartment by a Houston police detective. Laine Stenley, a detective with Houston PD, became concerned when Sutherland did not answer his phone. After several attempts to reach Sutherland by phone, Stenley drove to Sutherland's apartment. When

Sutherland did not answer the door, Stenley tried the door and found it unlocked. Inside, he discovered Sutherland bound to his bed and brutally murdered. Police aren't releasing many details, though an inside source has confirmed that it appeared Conner Sutherland was tortured over a period of hours early in the morning. Police are declining to speculate on a motive for the murder, and they have no immediate suspects.

Sutherland was a Houston native and had been a member of the Houston Fire Department for nine years. Updates to follow.

Sev found Conner's obituary next. The picture was clear, Conner in his fireman's uniform, broad shoulders back and what would have been a solemn look on his face except for the slightest quirk of his lips on one side and that gleeful look in the man's eye. No mention of a partner, which Sev could understand, he guessed, given the two men's chosen careers. No surviving family members, as Conner's parents had passed on some time before him.

Those sparkling eyes kept drawing Sev back to them. It was hard to picture Laine with a man who appeared to be full of mischief; the sheriff was such a serious, lone man.

Except for when his eyes tipped into that molten silver colour brought on by need, then Laine was everything sexual and potent. Sev rubbed at his semi-erect prick and groaned.

"Definitely not the right time," Sev muttered, clicking on the link for the next article. Not the right man, either, and he knew it. It was apparent that Laine had loved — *still* loved — Conner Sutherland, and Sev was as different from the big blond man as he could be. *And why should I even be thinking about that?* He wasn't looking for Mr. Right, he *wasn't!*

The next couple of articles didn't offer up any new information on Conner's murder, and Sev had just about given up hope on learning anything more about the man when what he was reading stopped him cold. The story contained more information leaked from an anonymous insider, and as he read the details surrounding exactly how Conner was tortured and killed, the room grew unnaturally chilly and his senses picked up a presence. This particular spirit was stronger than it had been previously, the power emanating off of it calling to Sev in such a way that he couldn't block it out if he tried. Sev slowly turned from the laptop and scanned the room.

"Conner?" The temperature continued to drop, sending goose bumps traipsing over Sev's skin. He stopped himself from rubbing his arms and willed the spirit in the room to speak to him. "Conner...please. You need to tell me what's going on. Why are you here?"

A form seemed to coalesce across the room, a barely discernible shape Sev could only define as the very air thickening, growing dense until a definite outline of a man was apparent.

"What the fu—" Sev tried to stand up and scoot back as the shape approached...floated. "This is... You can't... Shit!" Sev spun around the small table and tripped over the other chair, landing flat on his butt. He'd never seen a ghost, not like this, not in the form of a person, and he didn't care for it. Felt them as an almost electric tingle, sure; heard them, of course, but this? He wasn't prepared for this at all. In fact, his heart was beating so fast he was dizzy and black dots kept dancing in front of his eyes— but there weren't enough dots to block out the image of that dense, see-through spirit as it got closer. The form stopped inches from Sev's feet and seemed to be studying him.

The cold temperature was way past uncomfortable. Sev darted a glance at his fingers and saw the purplish-blue tinge to his skin, could see his breath slip from his lips in smoky white puffs. Not even the bolt of fear-fuelled adrenaline that shot through him when the spirit sank down until it was sitting directly in front of Sev did anything to warm his freezing flesh.

"What… How can you do this?" Sev's voice sounded way too squeaky even to his own ears, and when he finally worked up the nerve to look up into the spirit's 'face,' he would have sworn his heart actually stopped. Though no features were visible, Sev got that same feeling he'd gotten as he'd studied the gleam in a certain pair of dark eyes over the past few hours.

"Conner S-Sutherland?"

Please, God, if You're real, let it be Conner! As scared and cold as Sev was, he didn't think it was safe to jump to conclusions, but he didn't have any other brilliant ideas. A familiar buzzing sound filled Sev's head, a voice he'd heard before, and the fear and cold ceased to matter as the urgency coming from the spirit filled Sev. He nodded slowly and closed his eyes.

"Okay, Conner. Tell me what you need to tell me." Sev leant back against one of the table legs and let that otherworldly voice speak to him.

Chapter Four

Skin tingling, prickling with an awareness he didn't understand, Laine stood in front of Sev's hotel door for the second time that day.

"Just nerves," Laine tried to assure himself as he shivered. He raised his hand to knock but stopped as a wave of chills swept over him. Laine braced his hand on the door to steady himself and jerked it back with a startled hiss.

"What the hell?" He touched the door with shaky fingers, then pressed his palm flat. *Cold as ice.* Laine pressed his other hand against the door and felt fingers of unnatural cold creep over his skin, spreading from his palms up to his forearms. *What is going on?* Laine made his fingers slide down the door instead of pulling his hands away. He gripped the doorknob with both hands and twisted, shoving hard against the door when Sev's slurred voice seeped through the steel door.

The knob didn't turn, and Laine's fingers were cramping from the cold. The hot Texas sun was damn near searing his back while his front felt like he'd be suffering from frostbite within minutes. Laine clamped his jaw tight to keep his teeth from chattering and leant into the door once again, bringing his ear to the chilly surface. Sev's voice was nearly unintelligible, the words so slurred now Laine was afraid the man was in serious danger of freezing to death.

"Severo! Open this damned door!" Laine pounded on the door, the impact shooting shards of pain up his cold hand. "Severo! *Now!*"

Laine banged on the door again and paused, listening and trying to discern if Severo was conscious. He heard the smaller man's voice faintly, could make out 'cold', and then a name that had Laine shoving away from the door, eyes wide with shock. *Conner? Conner is doing this?*

"Can't be you," Laine whispered. "You wouldn't...you wouldn't have done someone the way whatever... whoever is in there's doing Severo." Laine took a faltering step backwards then turned and ran to the hotel office. He needed a key before something bad happened to Severo.

"I need the key to room one-fifteen, now!" Laine yelled at the hotel clerk. The poor guy looked shocked but Laine had to give him credit, the man was efficient and level-headed. He had the key in Laine's hand before Laine drew his next breath. "Call an ambulance and send them over there."

The door was still as cold as it had been moments ago. Laine was afraid, but not for himself. He couldn't think of anything other than the small, sexy man inside. *How long?* Laine shoved the key in the lock and twisted. *How long has he been in this God damned meat locker?* He got the door opened and nearly dropped the key. There was…something, Laine couldn't describe it right now if his life depended on it, but it was in front of Severo – and the room temperature was dangerously, impossibly low. Severo's eyes had a glazed look to them, his lips an unnatural colour that spurred Laine into action.

"Get the fuck out!" Figuring it was futile, but not knowing what else to do, Laine charged at the form. "What are you doing to him? Get out!" He swung at the figure and felt his breath lock up in his lungs when the shape seemed to shift around. Laine caught a glimpse of something familiar, and as his arm passed through what he guessed would be the head of the spirit, an odd sense of warmth burst over him. The sensation was so startling that he yelled and stumbled back. He'd expected a blast of the icy cold that was emanating from the thing, and to experience the opposite threw him.

Laine caught himself on the edge of the bed before he tumbled backwards. He stared transfixed at the approaching shape with equal parts hope and fear. A low groan from Severo brought Laine out of his thrall.

"Conner?" Laine pushed down his embarrassment; he was *not* hallucinating. He remembered that build, the broad shoulders and the faint outline of thick arms and thighs. "Conner, you need to stop. Can't you see what you're doing to him?" Laine swallowed against the thick knot of guilt in his throat and shook his head slowly. "You're hurting him, baby. You wouldn't have ever done something like that before…before."

The shape hesitated, hovering as if unsure or trying to comprehend Laine's words.

"Look at him, Conner. Look." Laine glanced at Severo, noted his slow breathing. "The man I knew wouldn't have done that, Conner, and I can't believe you would –" Praying he was wrong, Laine continued, "I can't believe you would hurt someone because I had, we had... Jesus! I'm the one who jumped him! Why would you do this?"

The figure seemed to vibrate, head swinging violently from side to side in an attempt, Laine hoped, to negate his accusations. An eerie moan rose and resonated inside Laine's head, then stopped so suddenly Laine blinked in surprise. It—Conner—vanished in the split second Laine had blinked his eyes. Laine's legs gave out and he scrambled across the floor to the too-still man he'd stormed out on hours ago. He'd barely reached Severo and found his pulse when the paramedics came through the door.

* * * *

He was dying. Sev knew it, and he was too frightened to open his eyes. The way his body was being rocked with painful spasms, the pricks of fire that shot up from his fingers and toes, and the damned ghosts that were pounding at his brain and trying to make him listen... Yep, he was dying and already spiralling down to Hell— feet first, if the agonising heat in them was any indication. He'd always been terrified that he'd lose the ability to block out the ghosts when he needed or wanted to, much like when he'd first developed his ability. That had been a terrifying and humiliating point in his adolescence. Now it was happening again and Sev felt like his head was going to burst with the pressure from dozens of supernatural voices screaming for his attention.

A ghostly voice screeched in his head, the equivalent of nails digging into his temples and Sev screamed, trying to push himself up, stop his fall. The pain and need to flee from the tormenting voices spurred him to pry his eyes open. Sev realised dimly that he was in a hospital. Panic speared through him and he tried to sit up. Big, warm hands pressed him down, and even though his vision was blurry and his senses disoriented, Sev was aware enough to know who was touching him. Laine's voice was as warm as his hands, and Sev wished he could make out the words the man was uttering.

If he could just get the damned voices of the dead out of his head… Sev tried to concentrate on pushing the voices out, visualising a burst of wind carrying them away. He pictured building a wall to block them, grey cinderblocks stacked tightly, keeping his mind safe. The whole thing only took minutes, but Sev hadn't had to resort to such basic measures for years and doing so now taxed him and left him feeling drained.

Unsure of how long his cinderblock fortress would hold, Sev looked at Laine and resorted to pleading. "Get me out of here. I can't be here!" Sev tried to get his arms to move and clumsily grabbed at Laine.

Laine's dark eyebrows knitted together and his mouth tipped down. "Severo, you damn near froze to death. I don't know why…" Laine swallowed audibly, pain dulling his eyes. "Are you sure that was Conner?"

Sev knew it without a doubt, but he needed away from this place full of misery and death. Hands clinging to the sheriff's arms, Sev tried to pull himself up, fingers digging in to Laine's flesh as another shudder racked Sev's body. "Laine, do you realise how many people have died here? How many voices there are trying to…trying to make me listen? I can't be here!"

"Shit." Laine's eyes widened with shock. "I didn't think about that. I haven't felt anything at all."

Sev clenched his jaw and tried to keep his teeth from chattering. "B-because they a-are a-a-ll swarming me! Look, Laine. *Really* look!"

In an instant, Laine stiffened and paled. His eyes darted around the room nervously and a startled sound slipped past his lips. "Jesus Christ, how come I didn't feel them like—like before?"

"They weren't trying to get your attention, but they might now that you've acknowledged them. Laine, please." Sev's eyes were burning with tears he wouldn't shed; it was bad enough that he was begging. Tears would make his humiliation complete.

Laine's hat started to slip from the chair where he'd set it. He pulled away from Sev and grabbed his Stetson, cursing soundly. "Let's get your clothes."

"No, can't we just go? I don't care if I moon everybody in this freaking hospital!" Sev was already pushing himself from the bed, hoping his trembling legs would hold him. A nurse rushed in, clucking like a hen, glaring at Sev and then Laine.

"What do you think you're doing, Sheriff?" She reached for Sev before he could set his feet on the cold tile floor. "And you, you need to lay back and rest!"

"Lynn, let him go," Laine said in a tone that brooked no argument. "He can't stay here. Got a phobia of hospitals."

Sev dropped all pretences and let the desperation he was feeling show clearly.

Nurse Lynn wasn't satisfied. "Well then, I can have Dr. Hunter give him a little something—"

"No!" Sev twisted away from the nurse and swung his legs over the side. His knees refused to lock and he started forward, trying to bring his arms around to stop his fall. Laine caught him before Sev could tip more than a few inches, holding him steady much as the man had done this morning. That made Sev think of what followed right after, and he didn't bother to censor the desire he felt as he met Laine's steady gaze. The need he saw in those cool grey eyes calmed something inside of Sev.

"See? He can't even stand up, much less walk out of here!" Nurse Lynn shook her finger at Laine. "You need to leave him here!"

Laine helped Sev to the chair and pushed him down gently before turning to the nurse. "No, *you* need to get the man a wheelchair before I decide to carry him out of here. You can't make him stay, so get me a damned wheelchair for him."

"Well, I have never—" Nurse Lynn's face was red, anger bringing an unpleasant flush to her already mottled skin. A voice behind her had Sev snapping his head around.

"Sheriff Stenley is correct, Lynn. We can't make the man stay, and he isn't in any danger, really." A thin, older woman approached Sev. "Go get the wheelchair like the sheriff asked—and bring me Mr. Robledo's release forms as well." Dismissing her, the woman smiled at Sev. "I'm Dr. Hunter. You seem determined to leave." Her sharp brown eyes studied Sev closely.

"I can't stay here. I'm sorry." What was he apologising for? Maybe he'd lost a couple of his much needed brain cells.

Dr. Hunter nodded. "It's not really necessary; you seem to have come around just fine. Though if you could explain to me how you nearly froze to death in a hotel room...?"

Sev glanced away from her and tried to think of something believable. Nothing came to mind, and a swell of panic rose. A big hand on his shoulder helped the panic abate.

"I'm checking into it, Dr. Hunter," Laine sounded so calm, so sure. "We don't rightly know how it happened, but the only explanation for it, has to be a freak accident involving the AC unit malfunctioning."

Dr. Hunter chuckled and shook her head. "I've never heard of an AC getting cold enough to cause hypothermia—and I've never stayed in a hotel in Texas with air conditioning that even did a half-decent job of keeping the room cool."

Sev spoke up before Laine could, feeling the man's tension by the way his grip tightened on Sev's shoulder. "Then how would you explain it, Dr. Hunter? Because I don't remember touching the AC. All I remember was a bit of a chill entering the room, a sense of disorientation, then being so cold I thought I'd never be warm again." Pretty much the truth, minus the interacting with the dead guy. *No, not just 'the dead guy,' but Conner, Laine's former lover.*

"Hmm. It is indeed a puzzle, and please don't take this wrong, Mr. Robledo, but if the paramedics hadn't recorded the room temperature, I might have thought you were crazy."

Sev couldn't stop himself from stiffening under Dr. Hunter's gaze any more than he could stop the fear that threatened to choke him. He'd already been down the thought-you-were-crazy route and was in no hurry to ever repeat it.

"But, everyone was cold, every *thing* was cold. Yes, a puzzle that will drive me nuts until something else takes its place."

Sev was saved from the Dr.'s intense study by Nurse Lynn.

"Here's the release forms, and here—" the nurse gave the wheelchair a pat, "is your ride out of here."

Lynn took the signed release forms and left. Dr. Hunter smiled and shook her head.

"Lynn's usually a much more pleasant person than that. I don't know what her problem is today." Dr. Hunter extended a hand to Laine and then to Sev. "It was interesting, that's for certain, gentlemen. Sheriff, if you find out what happened, would you mind filling me in?"

Laine nodded once and took the papers the doctor held out to him. "I don't think we will ever figure it out, one of those freak accidents like I said. Thank you, Dr. Hunter."

"Read over those, and if there are any problems, don't hesitate to bring Mr. Robledo back." Dr. Hunter turned to leave then stopped at the door and grinned over her shoulder. "Oh, and you might want to consider seeing to it the Mr. Robledo gets a different hotel room." Chuckling, she left the room.

"I don't think she believes the AC story," Sev mused as he leant forward in the chair to push himself up. Laine was there, strong hands reaching out to lift Sev.

"Grab your gown." Laine's lips were so close to Sev's ear he could feel the heat coming from the bigger man, the moist breath sending a different type of shiver down Sev's spine.

"Afraid you won't be able to resist me if you see my cute ass, Sheriff?" Sev couldn't help but tease, even though he knew it was a petty attempt to combat the butterflies he seemed to get in his stomach any time Laine was around. Laine plunked Sev down not ungently in the wheelchair. Bracing his hands on the wheelchair's arms, Laine leant in until he was almost nose-to-nose with Sev. Laine's eyes seemed to shift, the colour deepening in a way that Sev felt ensnared by.

"I don't know if I could, but I'm damned sure I wouldn't even want to try."

Sev felt that trickle of fear, the sure knowledge that this man could consume him, body and soul. He couldn't think of a single joke or a smart-assed reply to save his life and so he found himself held by Laine's gaze. There was nothing humorous in the dawning knowledge spearing Sev. Somehow, this man had managed to get to him. Sev finally tipped his head down and studied his own shaking hands.

"Can we go now?" Sev cringed at the tremulous note in his voice—it sounded like a dead giveaway to him, but hopefully Laine would put it down to exhaustion and sheer terror. *Anything,* Sev thought, *but that I am vulnerable to him.* It was easier to think of himself as vulnerable. Not that Sev cared for it, but it was better than admitting that his emotions were already tangled up over this tall, serious man. He reached up to finger his chain, the familiar feel of the links his one source of comfort, and flinched when he only found bare skin.

"Where's my—" Sev tugged at the neck of the gown as he looked at Laine. The sheriff reached into his shirt pocket and pulled the silver necklace out before moving behind Sev and fastening it in place. Sev was fingering the chain before the clasp was closed, but it was the stroke of roughened fingertips gliding down the back of his neck that had him shivering, breath stuttering.

"That chain means a lot to you?" Laine's fingers stroked over Sev's nape again before slipping under the necklace and rubbing gently.

"It... uh." *God, I can't think when he's doing that!* Sev rolled the chain between his finger and thumb, searching for the calm the motion brought him. "It's just... It was my Grandmother's." Sev tried to make himself shut up, but his nerves were jangling, which set his mouth to running. "She was the only person who believed me when, as a child, I tried to explain that I could hear the dead speak. If she hadn't been able to convince my parents not to follow the psychiatrist's suggestion, I would have spent my teenage years, at the very least, in a psychiatric facility. Fortunately, Grandma was intimidating, and the fact that she held the purse strings didn't hurt, either." God, he just couldn't shut the hell up. "She was good to me, believed me about all this." Sev gestured with his other hand, finger twirling circles in the air.

"Was she the only one?"

Sev didn't want to go there, but he didn't want to argue, either—and he wanted to get out of the hospital. "Of the adults, yeah, but she was enough, she really was. My brothers and sisters don't treat me like a freak." Mostly.

A grunt was the only reply he got, along with a last, lingering brush of fingers against his skin. Those touches had chased away the residual chill from his body, though he still felt somewhat shaky.

Laine grabbed the bag with Sev's clothes in it. He put on his Stetson and tossed the bag to Sev. "We're out of here, Severo."

"Sev." He turned and winked at Laine. "I mean, all things considered, I think you can call me Sev, huh?"

Laine's laugh was a barely audible huff. "Sure, Sev."

* * * *

The more distance Laine put between them and the hospital, the more Sev seemed to relax. By the time they were on the outskirts of McKinton, the smaller man was sleeping, his head tipped down and thick, dark lashes resting on his cheek. Laine had bitten his cheek in the hospital to keep from asking Sev about his childhood. There'd been a reluctance in the smaller man's countenance, despite his nervous ramblings, that had intrigued Laine. That intrigue had been quickly quashed;

there was no reason for him to delve into Sev's history, was there?

Laine pulled into his driveway and left the truck running, hoping the rumble of the engine would let Sev continue sleeping while Laine studied the man. With his head down and those thick, dark lashes resting against his cheek, Sev looked incredibly sexy and innocent. Laine had no problem acknowledging the first, but the second he'd have to be a fool to believe. Everything about Sev seemed to scream fun and sex, and Laine had a feeling Sev was a firm believer in both.

This posed a problem for Laine, as he found himself inexplicably drawn to Sev, and Laine wasn't exactly a sunshine and good time type of guy. He'd never indulged in one-night stands. In fact, what had happened between him and Sev this morning was, for Laine, out of character enough as to have him questioning his sanity all over again. And yet, he hadn't hesitated to bring this tempting man home —

Sev grunted and blinked his eyes open, giving a slight start when he saw Laine. Sitting up straight, Sev looked around, stiffening somewhat when he saw the house. "Where am I, Sheriff?"

Laine tapped the steering wheel with his fingertips and hoped for the best, though he wasn't sure if that would be Sev agreeing to stay or demanding to leave. "Brought you to my place." He shrugged when Sev whipped his head around, mouth dropped open in shock. "Didn't know what to do with you. I couldn't take you back to the hotel, and leaving you with Brendon and Zeke is out, so… "

Sev looked at him like he was crazy. "And you don't think this…" he waved his hand at Laine's house, "is a bad idea *at all?* Jesus, you gotta be worried about what people will say."

Laine bit down on his temper. Yes, he'd thought about what people would say, but when it came down to it, the fact was he wanted Sev here. He wasn't going to examine the reasons why. "Are you planning on packing up and leaving?"

"No, I..." Sev cleared his throat and looked away. "I have to be here. Conner—"

"Then you're staying here. The only people I would trust are Brendon and Zeke, and I won't put them at risk of being frozen to death." Laine's heart clenched at the thought of Conner hurting anyone, but he'd *seen* it, hadn't he? Had felt Sev's icy skin. And he'd felt the awareness, the presence of Conner as surely as if the man had been standing there in the flesh. "Are you sure that was Conner? He wasn't a cruel man, not at all. I don't understand how dying would make him into something he wasn't."

Sev reached for Laine's hand where it gripped the steering wheel, knuckles white with the force of his hold. "It was Conner, and I'll explain it, but... Laine, you could lose your job, maybe even worse if I stay here, you know that, right?"

Nodding, Laine couldn't bring himself to look at Sev. He was too afraid Sev would see that Laine was more concerned with the immediate risk of losing his heart to a man who wouldn't be sticking around.

"Are you sure you want to take that risk? *Why* would you take that risk? I don't understand it." Sev's confusion permeated his voice.

"It's my job to take care of everyone, keep them safe. I can't see as how leaving you alone somewhere to be turned into a Popsicle is doing my job—" Laine's explanation stuttered to a halt as Sev slid his hand up

Laine's arm and cupped Laine's cheek. He tugged until Laine was forced to turn and look at the smaller man.

"What else, Sheriff Laine Stenley?" Sev studied him with those eyes Laine found so fascinating. "I don't think you're being honest here, and it's screwing with my image of the honorable small-town sheriff I've always fantasised about."

Laine took a deep, shaky breath, blew it out and did it again. He hadn't counted on Sev calling his bluff, but then again, he didn't really know the man, did he? Laine didn't know how to play games, how to tease and flirt, whether harmlessly or intently, and he couldn't see himself starting now—but he *wanted* Sev, with a pressing, aching need he hadn't felt before, ever. He was trying to put it down to not being laid in years, but lying to himself wasn't something he'd done much of and he was finding he wasn't good at it, either. Best to just lay it out there, he figured.

"I want you." *Shit.* That came out belligerent and defensive and more than a little snarly.

Sev's laughter rang out in the truck cab, easily drowning out the noisy diesel engine and replacing it with a rich, musical sound. Laine felt his cheeks heat with embarrassment and tried to turn away but Sev's hand tightened on his jaw.

"Oh come on, now, Laine!" Sev snickered then let his humour drop away. "You sound so unhappy about it, it was either laugh or get pissed. Am I supposed to be flattered that wanting me seems so distasteful to you?"

Laine could see the hurt in Sev's eyes and closed his own on a wave of guilt. "I didn't... That's not it. I just, I've never... Damn!" Laine thumped the steering wheel and shook his head.

Sev pulled his hand back and spoke so softly Laine had to strain to hear him. "You just what? I don't get what you're trying to tell me, here."

His sigh sounding like that of an old, tired man to his own ears, Laine opened his eyes and faced Sev. "I've never done casual sex, okay? I don't know if I can, and you don't seem to be —" Sev's hurt look shut Laine up. Sev nodded and reached for the door handle.

"Yeah, I get it, and maybe I would have agreed with you yesterday, or even before you knocked on my door this morning — probably right up until you hauled ass out of my room earlier." Sev opened the door and stood on the ground. He paused with his hand resting on the handle, then turned to Laine. "I know I said no strings, but I thought... maybe there was something more here, you know? It scares me, sure, that this feels different, that I don't want to pack up and run, and I kind of thought that was mutual. What do I know, though? Other than that I want you again, want you in ways I'd never thought about. But somehow, hearing you cast me as a good time slut..." Sev shrugged. "It just reminds me of why I've never tried, I guess."

Laine cringed. He hadn't meant to do that, but he'd been sure that Sev wasn't interested in an actual relationship.

He shrugged again and clutched at the back of his gown as he turned away from Laine. "Can we get inside so I can maybe shower and put on some real clothes?"

Feeling like the biggest asshole in the world, Laine shut the truck off and got out. He grabbed Sev's bag as well as the man's luggage he'd had one of his deputies get from Sev's room. "Sure. Look, Sev —"

"Forget it. I'm sure you were right." Sev hurried to the front porch. "So I guess we can't fuck since you don't do casual and I don't do anything but that, right? This should be fun."

Laine didn't miss the bitterness in Sev's words, even though the man tried to make the whole thing sound like a joke. He'd have to be an idiot to miss it, though right now, Laine figured being an idiot would be a step up from where he was. All he could do was try again. "Will you just let me explain?"

"Nope, I don't think my heart can take it." Sev never even turned around, denying Laine the opportunity to judge the exact meaning of that statement. "Can you open the door or do you want to hand me the key?"

* * * *

Fresh from the shower, Laine was still trying to figure out how to make things right, or at the very least, bearable, when Sev stepped out of the guest room, having taken advantage of the extra bathroom there. His dark hair wet and slicked back, the smaller man was looking irresistible in a tight pair of faded jeans and a white tank top. Laine looked, not caring if it was rude, letting his gaze linger on the growing bulge he'd had his hands wrapped around earlier, then swept down the length of Sev's legs and found himself growing achingly hard as he studied Sev's narrow, elegant feet.

You got it bad, he thought, *getting turned on by the man's bare feet; better get your act together.* He watched as Sev brought his fingers to the silver necklace, fidgeting with it as he did when he was nervous. It was endearing, seeing that bit of fragility exposed unconsciously.

"Are you feeling better?" Laine forced himself to walk to the kitchen and started rummaging through the cupboard.

"I'm warm finally, if that's what you mean." The sound of a chair scraping against the floor told Laine Sev was making himself comfortable at the table.

"I guess that's a start." Laine pulled down a jar of sauce then placed a bag of pasta beside it. "You good with spaghetti? It's quick and I'm starved."

"Yeah, that's fine. Do you have any beer?"

Shows how often I have company. I didn't even offer the guy a drink. "Got some Shiner in the fridge. Hang on and I'll get it." Laine found the pans he was digging around for and set them on the stove. When he turned, he nearly ran into Sev, who had walked over to the refrigerator. Just being near the man had Laine's prick swelling again, and when Sev opened the refrigerator door and leant over, Laine thought he was going to come on the spot. God, he wanted to touch Sev, lick his warm brown skin and just lose himself in that compact body.

Sev looked over his shoulder, the grin he'd been wearing slipping. He stood slowly and clutched his bottle of beer to his chest. "We...we need to talk about earlier."

Laine nodded and took a step forward. "I think so." Sev stepped sideways and shut the refrigerator, eyes locked with Laine's. The bit of fear in those beautiful eyes made Laine's chest ache. He took another step towards Sev, grimacing when Sev tried to sidestep again. "Where are you going, Sev? I didn't mean to hurt you earlier. I just really suck with words, trying to explain something I don't really understand myself." Laine reached out and trailed a finger from the top of Sev's shoulder, down and across his collarbone, up to the top of the other shoulder.

"Laine." Sev closed his eyes and groaned. "We have to talk about *Conner*."

If Sev hoped bringing up Conner's name would kill off Laine's desire, he was wrong. Laine's fingers stroked a series of small circles on Sev's shoulder, but he nodded. "Okay. But first we're gonna—" Laine pulled Sev close, ignoring the cold beer between them, and slid his hands to Sev's butt. Sev's mouth opened, on a protest or on a plea, Laine didn't wait to find out. He lifted Sev and spun around, pinning the smaller man to the refrigerator and thought, *finally!* Laine lowered his lips to Sev's and took the kiss he'd needed.

Chapter Five

Sev's squeak was swallowed by Laine's mouth. More than just the sound, it seemed as if Laine was devouring Sev, each stroke of the man's tongue, each shift of his lips pulling apart the walls Sev had kept up to protect himself. Sev swept his tongue across the roof of Laine's mouth and shook when Laine moaned. Hard hands gripped and kneaded Sev's butt, pulling him closer as Laine ground his prick against Sev's. The beer bottle was making a dent in Sev's chest, his hands clenching it, pinned between them. Sev nipped at Laine's lip, then laved the small sting with the tip of his tongue. He squirmed and tried to work one of his hands free but Laine's weight held Sev immobile.

Frustration had Sev jerking his head to the side, but it was hard to speak when Laine moved his lips down Sev's jaw then began a series of nibbling bites and licks down his neck. Sev's shudder had nothing to do with cold and everything to do with the fiery explosion of heat that spread from his belly to his balls, disbursing to the rest of his body. Stunned by the force of the lust surging through him, Sev was reduced to gasping as he tried to speak. The feel of sharp teeth biting, of lips latching on and sucking, had Sev's head snapping back against the refrigerator.

"God… Laine!" *Is he marking me?* Sev was torn. It felt erotic, painfully good, but he'd never let any man put a mark on him before. The fact Laine was, hadn't even asked, nearly sent Sev into a panic. The sharp tug of pressure against his skin as Laine suckled, hard, sent the panic skittering away as Sev's balls drew up tight and his cock pulsed. It felt good, too good, and if he wasn't so damned horny, he would have protested. As it was, he arched his neck, giving Laine more skin to torture. Another stinging, sucking kiss on the sensitive skin below his ear had Sev crying out, his body trying to arch into the pleasure. He felt Laine's moist tongue lave the newest mark, then Laine lifted his head, his liquid silver eyes flaring with need.

Carefully, Laine lowered Sev's feet to the floor. One hand came around and took the beer from Sev's numb fingers. The beer was set on the counter, then Laine was taking Sev's hand and leading him into the bedroom.

"You have what we need?" Laine's voice was rough and deep, and sent another one of those pulsing aches to Sev's balls.

Sev nodded, his eyes on the firm, round denim covered ass in front of him.

"Sev? Do you?"

"Oh." Sev had been so distracted by Laine's ass that he hadn't even thought about the fact that Laine couldn't see him nod. "Yeah, in…in my suitcase."

Laine jerked Sev around and kissed him until Sev's head spun, then he stepped back and gave Sev a nudge.

"Go in my room and strip. I want you spread out on that bed by the time I get back." Laine veered to the room on the left. Sev looked at that big, lean body, the rangy muscles that flexed and rolled with each step Laine took, and decided that feeling Laine inside him was worth any risk. Every cell in his body screamed out for the man's touch, for the feel of Laine's thick cock pressing into him. Sev turned and sprinted for the bed, jerking his clothes off and tossing them in whichever direction was convenient.

He paused long enough to pull back the dark blue blanket and sheet, then crawled into the middle of the bed, determined to make Laine as crazy for him as possible. Sev spread his legs wide and cupped his balls, not bothering to bite back the moan as he did. With his other hand, he began slowly working the length of his cock, and when Laine stepped in the room and froze, gaze locked on to Sev's prick, Sev knew he'd succeeded in stoking Laine's need up as high as he could. The man stood stock still and barely breathed, his muscles trembling.

"Fuck, Sev." Laine got one trembling hand on the buttons of his jeans. "You... I can't describe it. You're fucking perfect."

Sev thought Laine did a pretty good job describing it, so he stroked his prick faster, letting his eyes close as his hips thrust up and another moan left his lips. There was a flurry of sounds that didn't really register, then the bed dipped down and Sev's eyes flew open as his arms were yanked up above his head.

"That's enough of a show." Laine's lips hovered above Sev's and he kept Sev's hands pinned at the wrist.

"Laine, let me touch you, please!" All that beautiful, lightly tanned skin, firm muscles still quivering underneath, and Sev couldn't touch it. He bucked his hips and hissed as his prick slid along Laine's.

"You touch me and this'll be over before it gets much farther. Been a long time, this morning aside." Laine lowered his hips and rubbed his leaking prick on Sev's stomach, letting him feel the intensity of his desire. "I need inside you."

Sev nodded and wiggled his hips. "Yes, God yes!"

Laine kissed him, claiming his mouth all over again, then lifted his head. "Keep your hands up, or grab the sheets. I'll let you touch all you want next time...or maybe the time after that."

This time, Sev's moan had nothing to do with the hands that were stroking his chest. Laine's words, more than words, a promise that there would be more of *this,* more than a one-night stand, sent a trickle of fear through Sev that was quickly blotted out by something warm and soft and *right.* For the first time, Sev wanted something more, wanted it badly enough to ignore his own fears and attempts at self-preservation.

Sev opened his eyes enough to watch Laine tear open the condom and slide it down his thick meat, but watching Laine coat his prick with lube was sheer torture, because Sev wanted nothing more than to touch that steely length. Then Laine's fingers found his hole, and Sev decided that he did want something more than to get his hands on Laine's dick. A thick, slick finger pressed in and Sev ached with need. A whimper slipped from his lips as he tried to get more, then a second finger filled him, twisting and pumping, stretching Sev in an erotic way that left him gasping in a manner too close to a sob.

"Laine, please!" Sev broke off as a knuckle pressed against his prostate. His hips bucked and he bit his lip to keep from screaming. Another deep thrust then he was empty, groaning in protest until he felt Laine push his legs up, feet braced against Laine's chest, and that heavy cock he needed began pressing into him.

Their moans mingled and filled the air as Laine pushed in until his balls pressed against Sev's ass. The burning stretch of his inner muscles sent a chorus of pleasure-tinged pain from Sev's channel to his balls, then Laine was moving, thrusting in deep and hard, filling Sev over and over. He felt Laine shift, then Sev screamed, back bowing hard as Laine's cock zeroed in on Sev's gland. Sev's balls sucked up against his body and his prick throbbed as come burst free onto his chest. Laine's harsh breaths seemed to burrow in Sev's ears as that hard cock pounded into him, rhythm gone, nothing but need and frenzied lust fuelling the grinding fucking. Laine shoved in deep, his hips swivelling as though to bury his cock so far inside of Sev that neither of them would ever be free. Sev watched in awe as Laine flung his head back and yelled, his hands gripping Sev's thighs bruisingly, muscles clenching and veins protruding as Laine pumped his release into the condom.

Laine's head dropped forward, chin on his chest, as he struggled to breath. Sev felt as though something had been permanently altered inside himself, his world tipped and thrown off balance. Laine's hands loosened and began rubbing Sev's bruised flesh with a touch so gentle he found himself having to fight to stay awake.

"Jesus, Sev." Laine chuckled softly, and Sev wanted to look at the man but his eyelids were too heavy. "That was…"

"I know," Sev mumbled, hoping he'd actually spoken the words but unsure since his body felt like it was floating on a cloud of satiated bliss. He quit trying to fight it and let himself doze off, unable to deny his body and mind the rest they needed.

Laine stood in the bathroom doorway and tossed the damp cloth he'd used to wipe his lover clean over his shoulder in the general direction of the sink, unwilling to turn away from Sev's sleeping figure long enough to be sure of his shot. Maybe he shouldn't have jumped the man so soon, but he hadn't been able to turn away from the hurt he'd put in those beautiful eyes. Laine snorted softly and rolled his eyes. Who was he trying to kid? Yeah, he wanted to take that pain away, but he'd also wanted to bury his cock so deep in Sev that he'd never feel the need to leave, never want another man inside him. He'd planned to seduce Sev, take his time and make love, stretch it out for hours and show Sev how good it could be between the two of them. Instead, he'd ploughed into that tight, silky heat like a horny teenager. Well, he had a bit more finesse than a horny teenager, but still.

And now that he'd had Sev, Laine was very much afraid he'd been ruined for other men. Sure, he hadn't ever intended to take another lover any time in the near future, but he hadn't intended to die a lonely old man, either. Now, there, lying in his bed, was someone Laine realised he not only wanted but needed, and it scared him as much as it thrilled him. He didn't know if he could convince Sev to stay—then again, once the people of McKinton found out that their sheriff was gay, staying *here* was probably not going to be an option. It pained his heart to think of leaving his job and his friends—the only two people he would really call his friends—behind.

But as Laine took one last long, lingering look at the warm, sexy man sleeping in his bed, he knew he'd do whatever he had to in order to keep one Severo Adulio Robledo.

* * * *

The sauce had been simmering on the stove long enough that the scent of oregano and basil filled the house. Laine slid the garlic bread in the oven then went to the refrigerator, his prick swelling as he thought about the way Sev's body had felt against his, those soft, wide lips moving under his and the sweet taste of the man's skin. He would never be able to open that damn refrigerator again without popping wood. Laine opened the door and grabbed what he needed then heard the muted shuffle of feet behind him. He turned and found Sev standing in the doorway, sleep rumpled and so sexy it made Laine ache.

"Are you feeling okay?"

Sev yawned and nodded, padding over to the table and pulling out a chair. "Can I do anything to help?"

Laine thought it would be enough for Sev to sit there looking gorgeous, but he set the makings for the salad on the table.

"You think you can take care of this? And—" Laine walked back to the refrigerator and took out a beer. "I reckon you might want this now."

Sev chuckled. "Yeah, I'm past ready for it. You have something for me to put this in, and maybe you could tell me where a knife is? And a cutting board? Unless you don't mind your table getting a few nicks in it."

No wonder Brendon called him a dumbass on a regular basis. Laine opened the beer and passed it to Sev before finding a large bowl, a suitable knife and the cutting board. Placing them on the table, he couldn't resist leaning down and placing a chaste kiss on Sev's smiling lips, pulling back before he lost control and ended up spreading Sev out on the table.

"You feel up to explaining what happened earlier now, or do you want to eat first?"

"That depends," Sev looked up from the tomato he had started to slice. "How long until the food's ready?"

"All's that's left is the pasta and the salad, so maybe fifteen minutes." Laine turned a knob on the stove to start the water boiling.

"How about after, then? It's going to take longer than fifteen minutes, and I really want to eat first. It smells good." Sev winked at Laine's nod and went back to preparing the salad.

They worked in a comfortable silence for a few minutes. Once Sev had the salad put together, he let his gaze roam over the kitchen. Like every other room he'd seen in Laine's house, it was undecorated, the white walls bare. The whole place lacked adornment, as though this wasn't a home, merely somewhere Laine existed in.

"How long have you lived here?"

Laine looked up from stirring the pasta, one eyebrow arched. "About three years now, I guess. Why?"

Sev glanced at the bland room, white everywhere— appliances, the tiled floor, even the countertops were a pale grey, close enough to colourless that they blended in rather than standing out. *At least the damn pot on the stove is copper-bottomed!*

"It just looks so, I dunno." He shifted slightly in his chair, trying to decide how to say what he wanted to without being rude. "Bare, maybe? Like there isn't really anything of yourself here."

Laine blinked, then looked around the kitchen as though seeing it for the first time. "Well, yeah, I guess there's really not. I'm not the kind of guy who gives much thought to decorating, but you do have a point. This place has less character than your hotel room."

Leaning back in his chair, Sev thought about that statement. "Not necessarily. I mean, at least your couch and chair are dark blue... and so are your sheets and blanket—and the curtains. Kind of fond of that colour, Laine?"

Laine's grin was sheepish, his cheeks tinting as he chuckled. "Well, yeah, it was my favourite colour."

"Was? You got a new one?"

The flush on Laine's cheeks darkened, spread up to his forehead and the tips of his ears, but his gaze held steady with Sev's. "I'm thinking that I've discovered a new colour I like even better." He walked to the table, bending until his nose was almost touching Sev's. His pupils dilated, the black centers chasing away the silver irises until only a thin ring of that fascinating colour remained.

"And w-what..." Sev stuttered as he fought his body's impulse to shiver under the pressing need that coursed through him. "What colour would that be?"

Laine's slow smile demolished Sev's control, his body quaking inside and out. "I'm not sure what it's called, really, but it's...fascinating, this pale green." Laine's index finger traced the line of Sev's jaw. "This close, I can see just the slightest streaks of grey in there, too. What colour is that, Sev? You tell me, 'cause I don't have a word for it."

Melting, he was melting inside. "My grandmother said it was celadon." Sev's breath hitched, his chest squeezing tight. "I always figured that was a big word for 'dull green', you know?"

"Sev," Laine's warm breath teased Sev's lips, "there isn't a dull thing about you." Before Sev could utter a protest, Laine's hand cupped his jaw and Laine's lips were covering his, mastering Sev's mouth with a kiss that threatened to make him come where he sat. The stove timer went off and Laine ended the kiss, saving Sev from losing his dignity along with his load. He was still trying to recover when Laine sat a plate piled high with spaghetti and garlic bread in front of him.

Garlic bread… "You do realise that no amount of brushing is going to get rid of the garlic, right?"

Laine nodded, his lips quirking as he picked up his piece of bread. "Yup, so I reckon we better both eat it. Kind of cancel each other out, you know?"

That warmed Sev all over, and he hummed in agreement as he reached for his fork. Neither felt the need to speak as they ate quickly, casting occasional heated glances across the table. The food was good—well, Sev thought it was probably good. He was too distracted by Laine to really pay much attention to anything else. And he was nervous, having to constantly stop himself from reaching up to finger the necklace that always seemed to calm him. Before long, their plates and salad bowls were empty. Sev leant back in his chair and rubbed his stomach, trying to get his brain into gear. "Tasted better than it smelled."

Laine's embarrassed grin was fleeting, his urgency to find out what had happened with Conner palpable. He started to speak, but Sev cut him off with a hand gesture.

"First thing you should know, Conner didn't do it on purpose."

Laine looked at Sev like he was crazy, which made Sev bite his lip against the laughter bubbling up inside him. "How do you—or how does a ghost—*accidentally* nearly freeze someone?"

"Inexperience, lack of control…" Sev met and held Laine's gaze, all traces of humour gone. "An urgency to get a message across. Look, Laine, today is the first time I've ever *seen* a ghost. Sure, I've heard them since I was a kid, and damn near ended up locked away in a psych ward for life because of it, but seeing one coalesce? That's a new one for me, and I doubt it would have happened had Conner not felt desperate."

Laine sat back, arms crossed over his chest. "You gonna explain that, about nearly ending up in a psych ward?"

Sev glanced away, his lips tightening to a thin line. "I thought this was about Conner?"

"We'll get to that in a minute." Laine leant forward, elbows on the table. "That's twice today that you've mention that you were almost shut up in a mental hospital. I think maybe you want to talk about that."

Did he? Was that why he'd brought up something he never talked about? Well, he'd already blurted it out *twice*, so what the hell? Sev stared at a spot over Laine's shoulder. "Would you believe your kid if he or she told you ghosts were speaking to them? Or would you drag the kid to a psychiatrist, then another and another? Listen to them when they told you your kid was showing signs of juvenile onset schizophrenia and needed to be medicated and regulated and—"

"Sev."

Sev closed his eyes, squeezing his lids tight against images popping up in his head. "They put me there, you know, after the medications didn't help. You'd think I would have learned, would have shut up instead of trying to convince them. Even when I would tell them things that could be proven, things I shouldn't have known, they wouldn't listen. Or maybe they did, and they were afraid of what I was, what I could do, so they stuck me away—"

Strong arms lifted him, pulling him into Laine's embrace, but Sev couldn't stop. "If my grandmother hadn't found out, I might still be locked away, my brain scrambled from whatever treatments the psychiatrists felt were necessary."

Laine's arms tightened around him. "But your grandma, she got you out of there quick, right?"

Sev shuddered, the memories threatening to overwhelm him. The state hospital was underfunded and understaffed; the number of patients grossly out of proportion to the workers on hand. Some of the things he'd seen there, experienced, would haunt him always. "Five weeks. Not so quick, but at least she got me out."

"Damn." The word was whispered, Laine's breath tickling Sev's ear. "I'm sorry, Sev, sorry it happened and that you were there for so long. I can't imagine a kid... How old were you, can you tell me?"

Sev's stomach roiled, but he reached around Laine, clinging with something bordering on desperation as he held on to the one man who made him feel safe. "I was twelve. Not the youngest kid there, either. It was like a nightmare, something that couldn't possibly happen in real life, but it did. When my grandmother found out, she threatened to disown my parents unless they got me released, then she took care of me."

Laine didn't speak, just began rocking gently, his hands smoothing over Sev's back until Sev stopped shivering, the tension seeping out of him slowly. He thought he should be embarrassed, but he couldn't manage it, not when he felt so soothed and protected, his head resting on Laine's chest, the steady *thumpthumpthump* of the man's heartbeat lulling Sev into a peaceful sense of belonging. A niggling worry kept him from giving himself over completely to the experience, though. There was a message he needed to pass along, an explanation Laine needed to hear for his own peace of mind. Sev forced his eyes open and tipped his head up to find Laine's steady silver gaze on him.

"We really need to talk about Conner."

Laine studied the man in his arms, trying to discern if Sev was evading any more questions about his past. God knew Laine felt torn open from learning about Sev's past. Hooking his ankle around the leg of a chair to manoeuvre it closer, he sat, pulling Sev down onto his lap.

"Okay, let's do that." Then Laine was going to take Sev to bed and fuck away all those shadows lingering in his *celadon* eyes. "So, what's the message, Sev? What was so God damned important that he nearly killed you? You don't think, that all things considered, his timing was a little suspicious?" Because it sure seemed so to Laine.

Sev smiled, just a faint echo of his usual breath-stealing smile. "Let me ask you this, was Conner a liar when he was alive? Was he a cruel, vengeful person? Or was he a truly decent person who maybe, sometimes, acted rashly, didn't consider the consequences of his actions, but never intended harm? Because what he was in life, he still is even in death. The things that make us, us, the core centre of our personality—death doesn't change that, it can't. It doesn't work that way."

Laine didn't even have to think about it. "Conner was… He was excitable, that's how I always thought of him. Energetic and eager, just bursting with life. Not a cruel bone in the man's body, either. He could be impetuous, but only because he was so enthusiastic…"

He was surprised that it didn't hurt to do this, to share Conner with someone else, or to remember the man. "The police thought that might have been what got the attention of the bastard who killed Conner. He was just… He had this shine, I don't know how to describe it."

Sev stiffened in his arms, pushing at Laine's chest. "There you go then, Sheriff—"

Laine's head snapped up and he pinned Sev with an angry look. "Sheriff? I had by dick buried in your ass not more than two hours ago. How did I go from being Laine in that bed to Sheriff right now?"

Sev's only answer was a shrug, but Laine wasn't letting it go so easily. "Explain that to me."

"He wanted you to know that you're in danger. Someone is coming for you. Soon."

"Duly noted. Probably someone like Irma." Laine stood, keeping Sev in his arms. "You didn't answer my question, Sev. Explain to me why I'm back to being Sheriff."

Laine could see the anger flash in Sev's eyes, his lips tightening and his jaw clenching. "Fine! Laine, then. Conner—"

"I know what he told you; I got the message—someone wants me dead," Laine shrugged the statement away and lifted Sev until their lips were almost touching. "But I think maybe you're not getting mine."

Laine closed the distance between their lips, brushing across Sev's once before pressing in and teasing Sev's tongue. Sev tensed then melted against him, the implied trust making Laine's knees weak and his heart pound. Laine kept it gentle, sharing instead of taking, giving Sev the tenderness Laine doubted the man had much experience with. Sev opened for him beautifully, and Laine poured as much as he could into each stroke of his tongue, each press of his lips. He couldn't tell Sev how he felt, the need he had to protect and comfort the smaller man, but he could damn sure show him. Judging by the startled gasp that flowed from Sev into Laine, he must have gotten the message. Laine pushed away the flicker of hurt, unsurprised when Sev turned his head and broke the kiss.

"We should...we should clean up the kitchen." The panic in Sev's big eyes broke Laine's heart. His lover was so afraid of trusting, and now Laine knew why. He wasn't going to give the man time to think. Laine dipped his head and began kissing a line down Sev's jaw, down to the sweet spot right by his ear. "And I didn't finish telling you what happened. We...we..." Sev groaned and tipped his head back. "I can't...can't think when you're doing that!"

Laine laughed softly and continued sucking, scraping his teeth on sensitive skin, not letting up until Sev's protests died away and the man was writhing against him. When Sev's legs gave out, Laine took advantage and encouraged Sev to wrap them around Laine's waist. He carried Sev into the bedroom, only letting go of him long enough to set Sev down and strip his clothes off. This time, he was going to show Sev there was more to sex than just getting off.

Sev felt heavy with lust, so much so that he couldn't even express surprise when he found himself lying on the bed, the long, hard stretch of Laine's body pinning him down, and still, Laine's lips never left Sev's body. He tried to help when Laine began removing his clothes only to have his hands shoved away. Sev was naked and aching, his very existence narrowed down to *feeling*. Then Laine's hot mouth swallowed Sev's cock, a slow, tight slide of wet suction that caused pinpricks of colour to burst behind Sev's lids. Moaning, he drove his fingers into Laine's hair, gripping the silky strands, not guiding or encouraging, just holding on to the one thing, the one person who had suddenly become his entire world.

Laine kept his movements slow and languorous, his tongue sweeping almost lazily over the length of Sev's cock. One hand rolled Sev's balls, while the other slicked up his body to tease his nipples. Sev was going insane with the pleasure, his breaths released in a stream of whimpers. The tip of Laine's tongue dove into the slit of Sev's prick and Sev felt his balls pull up. Another quick flick of tongue across his cock head, a twist of his nipple, and Sev's fingers clasped spastically in the dark strands of hair. His stomach and thighs clenched, muscles quivering as he came in Laine's mouth, that talented tongue pushing and caressing, swiping as Laine sucked down every drop of spunk.

Laine let Sev's cock slip from his mouth and scooted down, dislodging Sev's fingers from his hair. Those strong hands smoothed their way to Sev's ass, thumbs sliding in the dark cleft to open him up to Laine's seeking tongue. Sev barely had the chance to breathe without moaning when Laine's tongue laved over his hole, then Laine suckled and nipped at Sev's opening, working the tight muscle until finally his tongue slipped in.

It was an intimacy Sev hadn't often experienced, yet he could deny Laine nothing—and denying himself this sensual torment was out of the question. As Laine's tongue fucked him, twirling and curling around the rim of his entrance, Sev's inner muscles rippled, his prick responding by filling in a dizzying rush. Laine worked Sev's ring until Sev was near mindless, a babbling and incoherent pile of burning need. He might have begged, pleaded even, but Sev didn't care, and when Laine finally rose up and pulled off his own clothes, the grateful sob that slipped past Sev's lips didn't embarrass him at all.

Sev gripped the backs of his thighs and pulled his legs to his chest, then Laine was rolling a condom down his thick dick. A smearing of lube followed before Laine dropped down over Sev and lined his prick up to Sev's hole. Another strangled sound burst free, telling of Sev's aching need, as Laine began to fill him. Laine took his time, working his length in so slowly Sev wanted to shout in frustration—except, it felt too good to change it.

Once he was fully buried inside Sev, Laine brought a hand to Sev's cheek and forced Sev to meet his molten gaze.

"You need to understand something, Sev." Laine's eyes seemed to see into Sev's soul, and he couldn't stop the shudder that worked through him. "I think you believe that I still love Conner—ah, not a word. I will always love him, that's true, but Conner is dead. I know that, I accepted it a long time ago. But you—"

Laine moved his hips, small movements from side to side that completely stole Sev's ability to speak.

"You are right here, right now, and I want you more than I have ever wanted anybody. Anybody, Sev." Laine's eyes seemed to flash, something showing in them that Sev couldn't comprehend, then it was gone and Laine began pounding into him. He pushed Sev's hands away and held his thighs, leaving Sev to scramble for something to grasp.

Laine's forearms bulged with restrained strength, and Sev gripped them, holding on as the force of Laine's thrusts increased. Sev's orgasm slammed into him, the intensity of it whiting out his vision as bursts of semen hit his stomach and chest. Laine groaned then roared, the sound exploding in the room as he rammed his prick home, filling Sev as he filled the condom.

The sounds of completion—heavy breaths and sweat-slick bodies pressing against each other—seemed amplified to Sev, but not nearly as loud as his heartbeat drumming in his ears. As his vision cleared, so did Sev's mind, and he knew that he'd just been claimed, his body owned and tamed by this one man. No one else would ever make him feel what this man could. Sev didn't even want to consider letting anyone else try—and that scared the pleasurably sated feeling right out of him.

* * * *

Darkness had long fallen over McKinton by the time he pulled his car around the back of an abandoned gas station at the edge of town. Not that anyone was out and about, but he'd learned over the years that paranoia paid off. *Good thing none of the toys ever figured that out, though it would make the game so much more interesting.* Interesting was fine and good, but Laine Stenley's three-year disappearing act, that was unforgivable.

Not that he'd been worried. He'd never doubted that Laine's escape would be anything other than a brief respite for the man. Actively looking for Laine had been a risk he hadn't been willing to take. Besides, he *knew* Laine was his, had never doubted that someday Laine would find a way back to him. His patience had paid off, and now he was eager to claim what belonged to him.

As he opened the door and slid out of his car, the dome light disabled because he wasn't a careless idiot, he thought about all the ways he would make Laine pay for breaking the rules of the game.

Chapter Six

Laine was still fretting over that look he'd seen flit across Sev's face last night when he walked through the door of the Sheriff's Department. As usual, Doreen was already at her desk, phone pressed to her ear. Laine tipped his head in greeting and started to walk past her, stopping at the side of her desk when he heard Doreen's part of the conversation.

"Edward, you know how smalltown gossips are. Rumours are the life's blood of places like McKinton!" Doreen's face pinched in disapproval over whatever the voice on the other side of the line was saying and Laine's stomach took a sharp dive. Edward could only be Mayor Edward Jeffries, Laine's boss. The man also happened to be Doreen's brother-in-law, having been married to Doreen's sister Mona for several years now. Doreen's link to the mayor had benefited Laine at times when he and Edward didn't see eye to eye. Doreen had always staunchly supported him, but whether that was because Laine was her boss or her friend, he didn't know.

"No, you will *not* jump to any conclusions based on innuendo! I don't care who contributes to your campaign or how much they contribute, if you do something rash…" Doreen's eyes took on an evil gleam. "Did you know Mona used to date Chad Easton, the news anchor for channel six in Dallas before she married you? I bet a story on smalltown bigotry would get a lot of coverage—"

Laine felt frozen in place, though his legs seemed curiously gelatinous. He'd known the risks when he decided to take Sev home with him, but the reality of his fears coming to fruition, and in less than twenty-four hours, was still a shock.

Doreen jerked the phone away from her ear at the mayor's retort then hung the phone up. She turned to Laine and shook her head. "My sister married an idiot."

"Doreen…"

"Now, now, Sheriff, why don't you go sit down and I'll bring you a cup of coffee and then we'll talk." Doreen was already stepping away from her desk when she spun around and grabbed a stack of pink messages. "Oh! You might want to go through these, but this one, the one on top, it's from a Detective Montoya out of Houston PD. He called early this morning, said it wasn't urgent, but since we've never gotten a call from Houston PD, I kind of wondered, you know? Isn't that where you came to us from?"

Laine managed a nod and forced his legs to carry him to his office. He heard the front door opening, and a few seconds later, Deputy Matt Nixon stepped into Laine's office.

"Morning, Sheriff, everything okay?" Nixon's eyes were serious, his normally jovial demeanour absent as he studied Laine.

"I guess so, Matt, why?" Laine stopped himself from tapping his fingers on the desk, his nerves spiking the longer Nixon kept up his inspection.

"Well, there seems to be some talk." He shrugged and gave Laine a slight grin, a bare tip of his lips. "I just thought that, I don't know, you should know there are people who support you whether the rumours flying around are true or not. You're a great sheriff." The last sentence came out gruff and tinted Nixon's cheeks pink. Laine let out a breath he hadn't known he was holding.

"Thank you, Matt. That...that means a lot." Laine felt his own cheeks heat. The resulting awkward silence was broken by Doreen's entrance, two steaming mugs of coffee in her hands.

"All right, boys, here's your coffee." Doreen sat Laine's on his desk then turned back to hand Nixon his cup of coffee. "Don't you have somewhere to be?"

Nixon was used to Doreen's blunt nature. He smiled, bringing up dimples on his cheeks, and winked at her. "Well, I had to hang around here to see you first, now, didn't I, Doreen?"

Doreen snorted and swatted at him. "Go on and take your flirting butt off. See if you can find someone that stuff works on!"

"Now, Doreen—"

"Now, Deputy Nixon! Go uphold the law before I take your coffee away!"

Nixon laughed and gave Doreen a mock salute. "Yes ma'am. Sheriff, if there's anything I can do..."

"I'll let you know. Thanks again, Matt." The knowledge that one of his deputies had his back made Laine feel a little better, until Doreen returned from shutting the door and pulled the chair closer to Laine's desk. A quiver of fear spread through him at the serious look on Doreen's face.

"You know that was Edward."

It wasn't a question, but Laine nodded anyway.

"Well, I guess there are rumours going around that you took some man home with you last night—"

Laine put up his hand to stop her. "Those aren't rumours, Doreen. I did bring Severo Robledo to my place last night, but I didn't know what else to do with him." This was partially true; Laine hadn't thought leaving Sev at the hotel was a good idea, and he didn't want to endanger anyone else. Doreen didn't need to know that Laine had wanted the man more than his next breath.

"He's the man who was attacked at the hotel? I thought that was who it might be." Doreen studied her nails for a moment before she looked up again. "He told me yesterday that he's gay. Just tossed it right out there. You think that has anything to do with what happened to him?"

Sev had told Doreen? *Oh. Probably when he was telling on Irma. Least I hope that's why.* "We don't know what happened at the hotel, which is why I couldn't let him go back there, and the only friends I have are Zeke and Brendon. I wasn't going to ask them to put up someone who might bring trouble to them. They've had more than enough trouble as it is."

Doreen clucked her tongue at him and leant over the desk to pat his hand. "Sheriff, you don't realise just how many friends you have, do you?"

Well, he thought he did, but Doreen was intimating he was wrong.

"Laine, there's more people in this town who'd help you out than not, and that's something I am going to make sure Edward is aware of. That man's a fool, and *if* there was any other reason for you taking that man home, it isn't anybody's business but yours and his."

The kindness showing in Doreen's eyes was his undoing. Laine slumped in his chair and placed his hands in his lap, studying his fingers intently. "I don't think... I don't think I'd have many supporters if people found out I'm gay, Doreen."

Laine heard Doreen's chair slide back and figured he'd just lost one of said supporters, but instead, she came to his side and squatted down, her hands reaching into his lap to hold his trembling ones.

"Look at me, Laine." She waited until Laine met her gaze. "You think people haven't talked before? Haven't suspected, especially with how close you are to Zeke and Brendon?" Doreen shushed him when he opened his mouth to speak. "Now, I ain't saying a straight man can't have gay friends, but this is McKinton, and sure, Zeke and Brendon have more friends than they'd ever thought, but no one as close as you. There ain't anyone who would defend them two like you would and everyone knows it, and most people accept it. Just because you haven't said the words doesn't mean a lot of people don't know, whether they've admitted it or not."

Doreen's words and the sincerity with which she spoke them eased some of the tension coiling Laine's body. He squeezed her hands briefly, an unspoken thank you, then Doreen let go of him and rose.

"You deserve to be happy, Sheriff. I think you can do that and keep your job, though I won't tell you there won't be problems. People like me and Nixon, and of course

Zeke and Brendon, along with a whole passel of other folks, will do everything we can to help you out."

Laine felt the bizarre urge to laugh at the choice of words as Doreen left his office. He had the feeling people were going to help him out in more ways than one.

The note from Detective Montoya fluttered across Laine's desk at the same moment he felt the presence in the room. Feeling a little foolish, Laine glanced around then watched the paper swishing back and forth in the air right in front of his face.

"Is that you, Conner? You trying to tell me something? I really don't think I need the information on Sev that I asked Montoya for, ya know."

The pink slip started spinning furiously, a mind-boggling sight at one time but Laine was not as thrown by it as he had been at first.

"All right, then." Laine stuck out his hand, palm up. "Let me have it." The paper floated down into his hand and a silly thought struck him. "You know, if I could just get you to bring me coffee when I need it, now… "

His hat was tipped off backwards and his hair ruffled, then Laine was left alone. He wondered briefly at the sudden departure then reached for the phone. He had one quick, he hoped, call to make then he would tell Montoya he knew what he needed to about Severo Robledo.

"Good morning, Sherry. Can you put me through to Mayor Jeffries?" Laine tapped the desktop as he waited for the mayor to pick up the call. No matter what, he was determined not to lose his temper with the man.

"Stanley? What's with these rumours I've been hearing about you…you being, *you know*?"

Laine felt his lip curl at the mayor's tone, and his apparent inability to say the word 'gay.' Far be it from him to help the fool out. "No, I don't know, Mayor Jeffries, but—"

"Like your friends! Zeke Mathers and his, uh, partner." The relief at finding a suitably unsexual word was evident in the Mayor's gleeful tone. Something about that tone had a feeling of calm filling Laine. He leant back in his chair and propped his booted feet up on the desk, crossing his legs at the ankles.

"Well, now, I don't see as how anything about my personal life is your business, Jeffries, and if I were to listen to the town gossips about you, I *might* think you're screwing around on your wife with one of the waitresses at Virginia's. Lotta gossip about that, rumours and such, but my momma raised me better than that, you know?" It wasn't a threat; it also wasn't a rumour that Laine had paid particular attention to, but he *had* heard it. The fact that Doreen hadn't gone after Jeffries meant either she hadn't heard the rumour, or she knew Jeffries was innocent. If the mayor wanted to keep his privates intact, he'd best be innocent.

Indignant sputtering was the only reply Laine got before Jeffries got off the phone. He couldn't help smirking a bit. Let the man see what it felt like to have someone pry into his private life. At least what Laine and Sev were doing wasn't going to hurt anyone else. Laine had no other lovers, and he was certain that Sev wasn't in a relationship, either.

The matter settled for now, Laine dropped his feet back to the floor and stretched his arms, arching his back to work out the kinks. As comfortable as he was going to get for now, Laine went ahead and called his former partner at the Houston PD. He didn't know whether to be relieved or not when he got Rich's voicemail.

* * * *

Warm sheets and a comfortable mattress were all the encouragement Sev needed to stay in bed, dozing off shortly after Laine left for work. His body pleasantly sore, Sev pushed away thoughts and worries over what was happening between him and the sheriff, choosing instead to replay numerous erotic memories of their shared loving. Images of Laine's big dick, glistening beads of precome coating the bulbous head, had Sev's prick hard and straining for relief. He'd just reached down and fisted his prick when the buzzing started in his head, the plea for him to listen.

If he didn't know better, he'd swear Conner was deliberately interrupting. But he'd learnt through the years that ghosts couldn't see, not physically. They seemed to exist on an emotional plane, reacting to deep-rooted emotions and needs. But it sure had seemed like Conner had been *looking* at him yesterday, and Sev had never known a ghost to take on a form like Conner had, either. Not to mention the whole freeze-Sev's-balls-off incident. Maybe he didn't know quite as much about ghosts as he'd thought. Then again, since they were so responsive to strong emotions, maybe that was why Conner was making such intense appearances. Sev and Laine had to have been sending out some decidedly strong and horny emotions, at the hotel and here in this house.

The buzzing intensified and Sev let down his guard enough that Conner could 'speak' to him. Ignoring him wasn't an option, not after nearly freezing to death yesterday. Sev had no doubt it was an accident, but the urgency he sensed in Conner at this moment was tantamount to what it had been in the motel room. There was no sense in risking a desperate bid for attention from an impetuous ghost.

"What is it, Conner?" Sev started to sit up in the bed only to find himself held down by an invisible force. Panic kicked in and Sev began to struggle. "What the hell? What are you doing?" A prickle of cold brushed across his forehead and Sev stilled, closing his eyes and reaching out with his senses. The warning from Conner slammed into his mind, clear and stark. *Danger. He's here — outside!*

With a sudden clarity, Sev knew who 'he' was. The man who'd come for Laine wasn't some ex-con with a grudge — he was the same man who had killed Conner. Terror unlike anything he had known filled Sev. He damn sure didn't want to die, and especially not like that. Even more so, though, he didn't want Laine to ever have to experience such a thing again. Finding his new lover dead and butchered would surely push the man over the edge.

"What do I do? Help me, Conner, please, don't let this happen to Laine again!" Sev's hair was pushed off his forehead then he felt a nudge. A quick glance informed him that the curtains over the window were drawn, but there was an inch or so where the material gaped open, certainly enough for someone to see into the room. Sev scooted to the edge of the bed, never looking away from that gap until he quietly tumbled to the floor.

Uncaring of his nudity, he crawled to the door and, with one last look backward, turned the knob and hurried into the hallway. Back braced against the wall and his knees pulled up to his chest, Sev considered his options. The guest room was almost directly across from him, but were the curtains pulled? Would he open that door only to find a sociopath peering in at him? Sev shuddered at the thought, sure his heart would just up and stop right then if that happened. There was another door that Sev suspected was a linen closet; not a good spot for him to hide. A tug on his hair had him looking up, and Sev spied a panel in the ceiling. *Of course Conner would suggest the attic, but there's no way that wouldn't make a lot of noise!*

A soft 'snick' sounded from Laine's bedroom followed by a scraping noise. Sev knew it for what it was, had slid his own bedroom window open dozens of times as a teen and slipped out into the night. Terror spurred him into action; Laine's home was outside of town, secluded by cactus, mesquite and scrub—no one would hear him if he screamed. The urge to run was strong, but Sev squelched it, hoping to keep his steps silent as he edged towards the kitchen. There was a door there that opened to the side of the house; if he could just make it to that door, maybe he'd have a chance.

* * * *

Laine was headed out on a call for vandalism when the temperature in his vehicle dropped from hellaciously hot to chill inducing. *Sev!* He couldn't say how he knew it, but the man was in danger. Whoever Conner had tried to warn them about was here... *No,* Laine thought, *he's there, in my house, and so is my lover.*

Flipping on the lights and sirens, he jerked the steering wheel around as hard as he dared, trying to remain calm against the fear that threatened to cripple him. He was only about fifteen minutes away from home—less if he really laid on the gas. Laine had a second's debate about whether he should call for backup, but he had sent Deputy Nixon to a rustling call that was a good forty-five minutes out.

Hand shaking, he flipped open his cell phone. There was only one number he could think to call for help. Laine needed to warn them. He'd asked them earlier to stop by and check on Sev, but now he was torn between hoping Zeke and Brendon were still safe on the ranch and hoping they could rescue Sev if Laine wasn't fast enough.

* * * *

Goosebumps covered Sev's skin as an angry snarl came from Laine's bedroom. It had to be obvious that Laine had been fucking his lover hours before; the scent of sex had lingered in the room, and condom wrappers and lube were easily found. And if that man touched the bed, he'd feel the warm spot Sev had just vacated…

The utter silence seemed to confirm Sev's worst fear as he reached for the kitchen door. *Please don't let it squeak!* The knob turned quietly, the door opening with ease. Sev squeezed through as soon as the door was open enough and carefully closed it behind him. He ran full tilt towards the mesquites, one hand cupping his genitals — there were just some places he was *not* going to risk getting scratched — nearly stumbling with each step as his feet landed on rocks and mesquite thorns.

As he lunged through the scrub and prickly pear, skin stinging with each encounter of the spiky stuff, Sev could just make out the sounds of sirens in the distance. Relief was doused by fear. If Laine went into that house while the intruder was still there… Sev knew Laine was the real goal, had been all along. Conner had just been a convenient way for the sick fucker to torment Laine. How angry would that psycho be that his target eluded him for years?

The sound of an engine competed with the noise from the sirens; Sev peeked out from behind the cactus he was using for cover. A big, black Dodge pulled into the drive, dust and gravel spitting out from beneath its wheels. He squinted and thought he recognised the men in the cab. The sound of sirens grew closer as the two men threw open the truck doors, the bigger man—Zeke, he remembered—grabbing a shotgun from the gun rack. Sev stood and whistled, not wanting them to go any closer to the house and the mad man inside. When Zeke rounded on him with that rifle pointing at his chest, Sev nearly pissed himself.

"Hey! That's Severo!" Brendon pushed Zeke's rifle aside and ran to Sev. Zeke was slower in moving, his cane nowhere to be seen. Brendon's eyes widened as he took in Sev's naked state. "Why are you naked? Jesus, you're all scratched to hell!"

Still cupping his privates, Sev tried to explain, but he stuttered to a stop as a masked figure shot out the back of the house and took off running. Zeke and Brendon turned to see what he was staring at. Zeke brought the rifle up and fired, the sound of the shot temporarily blotting out the wail of the sirens.

"Fuck!" Zeke handed the rifle to Brendon then turned to Sev. "You look like shit. Here." Zeke pulled off his t-shirt and handed it to Sev as Laine roared to a stop a few feet away. Sev tugged the shirt on, only mildly surprised to find Laine in front of him when his head popped through the hole of the tee. Before he could even blink, strong arms were pulling, lifting and crushing him against Laine's chest.

The feel of those arms holding him was worth every bit of discomfort that skittered over Sev's abraded skin. Sev wrapped his arms around Laine's neck and held on for dear life.

"He was here," Sev finally managed to murmur. "I don't think he knew I was there at first. Laine, he wants you—"

Laine's embrace tightened and cut off Sev's explanation, then he was gently lowered to his feet. Pain shot up from the soles of Sev's feet and he hissed before he could stop himself. In a split second, his world tipped, and Sev found himself, much to his embarrassment, being held in Laine's arms, carried like a child.

"Put me down!" He squirmed and then gasped when Laine popped him on the butt.

"You just keep still or I'll toss you over my shoulder — that'd be quite a show for Brendon and Zeke, huh?"

Feeling like a fool, Sev grabbed a handful of the t-shirt and made sure his parts stayed as covered as possible while he was carried to Zeke's truck. He tried to ignore the snickers he heard coming from the two other men, but really, this was humiliating on too many levels.

Brendon pulled open the truck door so Laine could set Sev down. He picked up Sev's feet one at a time, scowling at the damage to them.

"You're feet are all torn up, baby. Going to have to dig out a few thorns." Laine glanced over his shoulder and tipped his chin. Zeke leant down and shook his head.

"Buddy, you are a mess — and Laine hasn't even seen all the scratches that shirt's hiding." At that, Laine grabbed the edge of the shirt, intentions clear. Sev smacked at his hand, unwilling to take any more hits to his ego.

"Stop it! I am not taking this off and sitting here bare-ass naked!"

Brendon laughed. "We already saw everything pretty much anyway when we got here — what are you glaring at, Laine? Whose shirt do you think he's wearing? I'll give you a hint — it belongs to the sexy guy *without* a shirt on."

"I don't give a rat's ass what you saw when you pulled up! This is staying on my body until I can have some privacy!"

Laine leant forward until his nose was almost touching Sev's. "I've got news for you, Sev, it's only staying on your body until *I* take it off, understand?"

Sev wanted to thump his stupid prick for liking that dominating tone. He started to snarl a reply when Zeke intervened.

"Okay, I just want to point out that some nutbag was in your house, Laine. And I missed the fucker when he ran out the back door. Maybe we should deal with that before you two decide how Severo gets naked again."

Laine knew Zeke was right, but leaving Sev was one of the hardest things he'd ever done.

"All right, why don't you and Brendon take Sev back to your place and—" The other three men immediately protested that idea, with Sev pointing out that Laine had just told him he couldn't take off the damned shirt without Laine present.

"Fine! You can take off the shirt, then!" Laine flung his hands up in the air and let them flop back at his sides. "If it will get you somewhere safe, then you can parade around butt-naked!"

"Laine, why don't I take Sev back and you and Zeke check out your place? You have to call this in or write up a report, right? And while I am not in a big hurry to leave Zeke here, he is a much better shot than I am."

Zeke rolled his eyes and popped Brendon's hip. "Apparently not today. I didn't even nick that bastard, but Brendon's right."

Laine didn't like it, but Sev needed tending to and it was better that somebody stay here with Laine. He nodded, a sharp jerk of his head showing his unhappiness with the whole situation, then he did what he'd been needing to do since he'd got up for work. Laine leant back into the truck and kissed Sev, stealing the man's surprised gasp.

"I'm so glad that bastard didn't hurt you, baby."

Sev's eyes seemed to melt at the words, or maybe it was the kiss, Laine didn't know. He brushed his thumb over his lover's bottom lip then stepped back. "We'll be there as soon as we can be."

"Be careful, please. I meant what I said, Conner… He told me when he showed up to warn me that I was in danger. That man wants you, Laine."

Laine put on a smile he wasn't feeling. "Well, he can't have me, and he isn't going to take you from me, either. You ready, Zeke?"

"Let me get my cane out of the truck. I won't do you any good if I fall flat on my ass while some weirdo is trying to nail you."

"Here—" Brendon jogged around to the driver's side and got Zeke's cane, handing it over to his lover along with a kiss. "You two take care of each other, and only shoot the bad guy. I will be one angry man if I lose either of you."

"I'll bring him back in one piece, Brendon, though I think I'll toss one of my shirts on him first. I don't want to have to keep looking at that flabby body." Laine grinned and ducked back from the swing of Zeke's cane.

"You only wished you looked this good, old man. Now, quit drooling over my abs and let's get this done."

Sparing Sev one last glance, Laine drew his weapon and led Zeke to the house. Once the truck was headed away, Laine worked his way around the outside of the house. When he found his bedroom window pried open, icy fingers of fear trailed down his spine. If Sev had been asleep… But he had been, hadn't he, or close to it. And Conner had warned him. Laine closed his eyes and leant against the side of the house, ignoring Zeke's questions about whether he was okay.

On a shaky breath, Laine murmured his gratitude. "Thank you, Conner. You saved more than just his life, you know. I'll get this son of a bitch, I promise." The only reply forthcoming was a soft breeze that swept across Laine's cheek.

Chapter Seven

Between Brendon's worried looks and knowing smirks, Sev wasn't sure what to expect from the man. Then there was the fact that he felt ridiculous sitting in the truck wearing Zeke's shirt and nothing else…

"So who's Conner?"

He hadn't expected *that*. "Uh. I don't know if it's really my place to say…"

"Why not? Is he a ghost or something? Zeke told me Laine was worried he was going crazy because he's been having some paranormal fun. I know the first time I had a run in with Zeke's mama, I nearly had a heart attack." Brendon laughed and shook his head. "There I was, standing naked as the day I was born in the hallway outside of Zeke's room. We'd just…uh." Brendon's whole face turned red.

"I think I can figure it out, you being naked and all, but why were you out in the hall?" There was a story there, if Sev could draw it out.

"Well," Brendon flashed a grin at Sev, a dimple in one cheek winking, "what can I say? Zeke's sister Enessa and my cousin Gloria had been priming me to meet Zeke for weeks, sending me pictures, telling me about this gorgeous man. By the time I actually met him, my inner slut took over. Worked out great, though. But, he wasn't thrilled with the idea of me hanging around McKinton. He'd been assaulted years before and had numerous run-ins with his bitch of a sister—not Enessa, his older sister Eva. Anyway, he kind of got upset when I told him I was staying for the summer at the very least, and stomped off to his room, all self-righteous and snarly. It was kind of cute…" Brendon paused, thinking it over. "Okay, maybe not right then. So I was trying to figure out what to do when this scent appeared, then something nudged my shoulder. I couldn't get into Zeke's room soon enough, let me tell you!"

Sev gave Brendon a minute to make sure he was done talking. When nothing else was said, he figured it was safe to speak.

"So you and Zeke don't have a problem believing in ghosts, then?"

Brendon laughed so hard he had to wipe his eyes. "I wouldn't say we have a problem believing in them at all, but I sure have a problem with when his mama pops in, like when I'm in the buff or when we're…you know."

Sev felt his eyebrows creeping up his forehead. "When you're… You mean she's been there when you two…when you have sex?" Suddenly, Sev's mortification at being carried and wearing only a t-shirt didn't seem half so bad. The idea of anyone's mom popping in while he was fucking was enough to make him swear off sex. Almost.

"We'd just finished, actually, but were still, uhm, engaged, if you will."

"Shit! I can just hear them, you know, like a buzzing in my head at first unless I push them out. I can't imagine what my lover's mom would have to say if…" The very thought had him shaking off the hinky feeling. "God, that's messed up."

Brendon turned down a dirt road and winked at Sev. "Yeah. I didn't handle it well, but you hear them? That I couldn't handle at all."

"You learn to cope, build up a wall in your mind to keep them out for the most part. Some are too insistent; if that's the case, you need to listen. When the dead speak, whether you want to or not, you need to hear what they have to say — again, if they won't leave you alone. It's almost always something of major importance, a message that needs to be passed along or something like that." Listening to the dead had become Sev's livelihood, a point that wasn't lost on him.

What Sev had mistaken for a dirt road was actually a very long driveway that lead to the home Brendon shared with his lover. The wraparound porch had a pair of rocking chairs on it, and Sev could just picture him and Laine sitting on a similar porch at the end of the day, sharing details of their jobs and teasing each other. That fantasy snapped Sev back to reality. He had no right to expect anything permanent from Laine, and even less of a right thinking of himself as someone who could stay around. He'd never tried to stay in one place, but then again, he reasoned, he'd never had any incentive to, either. Laine Stenley was one hell of an incentive.

"So, this is home sweet home." Brendon's dimple flashed as he got out of the truck. Sev groaned, dreading the moment when his feet would hit the ground. Brendon was standing in front of him, arms out.

"I'll walk, thanks." A man had to have some pride, didn't he?

"Yeah, because pushing whatever's stuck in your feet in deeper is *so* much better than swallowing your pride. Think of how much worse it's gonna hurt when I have to dig around with the tweezers…"

"God damn it." Pride was overrated sometimes, anyway, and Sev wasn't a pain slut. In fact, he knew there was a good chance he might scream if Brendon had to jab him too much. "Fine. Whatever."

To Brendon's credit and Sev's unspoken gratitude, Brendon didn't laugh or so much as smirk as he swept Sev into his arms.

"Huh." Brendon grunted as he carried Sev up the porch steps. "You're heavier than you look. I would have put you at one thirty-at the most."

"One forty, the extra ten pounds is—" Sev gasped as Brendon let him drop a couple of inches. "I was *going* to say it was all muscle! Perv."

"And I bet I know just which muscle you were going to claim it was." They looked at each other and laughed, which Sev really appreciated later, when he was sitting on the bathroom countertop getting thorns plucked out of his feet. He hadn't yelled yet, but there had been some groaning and a lot of sweating.

"Geez, man, aren't you done yet?"

"Well, if you'd have thought to grab some shoes after the mysterious Conner tipped you off, we wouldn't be doing this, would we?" The tweezers pinched and Sev nearly kicked Brendon in the head. On accident, he claimed, though the look Brendon shot him very clearly showed his disbelief.

"There ya go, all debris free from what I can tell. You need to let me check again after you take a bath." Brendon stood and sauntered over to the bathtub, turning the taps on. "You want it hot, cold, or just right?"

"Hot. Hot would be just right." Sev wasn't sure the cold he felt was a physical thing. Every time he thought about Laine being hunted by some sick bastard, another layer of ice seemed to coat Sev's veins. Brendon made the appropriate adjustments and came back to Sev.

"Okay, off with the clothes—or shirt, rather." Brendon waggled his eyebrows and leered, looking so goofy Sev couldn't hold back his laughter.

"I can undress myself and get to the bathtub. My feet don't hurt as bad as they did when stuff was still buried in them. Unless..." Sev dipped his head down a little and looked up at Brendon through his lashes, "you just want to see my hot bod again."

"Now you're trying to get my ass whooped, though you do have a hot little body. Poor Zeke was trying to sneak a look when he thought I wasn't watching."

Sev felt the tips of his ears grow warm even as he grinned. "What? You can look but he can't?"

"Nah, he can look. I just like him to *think* he can't. Come on, off with it." Brendon reached for the t-shirt and Sev let him. "Shit, you are scratched all over, Severo. We're going to have to play doctor again once you get clean—and when the water hits those spots, oh man, I am glad I'm not you."

"Sev, please. Despite all the damage, I'm glad you're not me, too," Sev muttered as the shirt came off. He would put up with scratches and a little discomfort for Laine.He'd put up with a lot of things for the man. The realisation nearly sent him into a panic. Sev looked up to find Brendon studying him intently.

Sev reached up and fingered his silver necklace. He fought against the urge to look away from Brendon's brown gaze, fought his fear of commitment and fear of exposure with one overpowering thought—he wanted Laine. Period. And why was Brendon staring at him like that?

"What?" He sounded defensive, a little angry and wished he'd thought before he'd spoken.

Brendon didn't so much as blink at Sev's tone. "What's going on in there?" He tapped Sev's temple with a finger.

"Nothing I feel like sharing." Sev smiled to take the sting out of his words. "I have a lot to think about, that's all."

"Like what's going on between you and Laine?"

Sev groaned and rolled his eyes. "God, you are one of those guys who likes to share, aren't you?"

Brendon snorted and shook his head. "Not particularly into sharing, but I am worried about my friend."

That told Sev where he stood with Brendon, didn't it? "I'm worried about him, too, Brendon. Someone wants to hurt him, and that isn't me." That was as much as he'd offer about...whatever it was that was going on between him and Laine.

Brendon's mouth tightened, and for a minute, Sev thought the man was going to tear into him, but he didn't. Instead, he took Sev's arm and guided him to the bathtub. "Okay. Let me just say that, while you might not want to hurt him, he's very... He's a special guy." Brendon huffed out a breath. "I don't know what I'm trying to say, but I can tell I'm pissing you off, and that wasn't my intention. Let's get you in the tub."

Sev let it drop for now, sure that Brendon would circle back around to it again soon. Maybe when he did, Sev would have a better idea how to answer. He didn't know himself how he felt, except that he wanted Laine. What that meant, where it would go, was a question he couldn't answer.

Sev lifted one foot and yelped when he stuck it under water. Brendon held on to him, not letting him back away.

"Nope, get in there, Sev. I would advise you do it as quickly as possible, get it over with. You seem to be a tough li—ah, a brave guy."

Why not, Sev thought, glaring at Brendon. He'd already emasculated himself with that damned yelp, and he knew good and well what Brendon had stopped himself from saying. And if Brendon made any more remarks about him being a brave little man, he'd find his nosy butt taking an involuntary dunk in the tub.

* * * *

The need to see Severo, to ensure himself that his lover was okay then fuck the man until they were both unconscious had been building in Laine ever since he'd learnt Sev was in danger. By the time Zeke pulled up to the house he and Brendon shared, Laine was ready to snap from the tension inside him. He figured it was a good thing Zeke, after a hushed phone call from Brendon earlier, had insisted Laine and Sev stay with them until Laine caught the bastard who'd broken into his home. Laine would have argued Sev into agreeing if he'd had to, but luckily Sev hadn't protested at all when Laine had spoken to him about staying with the other two men. Laine certainly wasn't too proud to accept the help or the safety it offered, not when it could mean saving Sev's life. Right now, however, he just needed to get inside—first the house, then the man.

Zeke put the truck in park and Laine was out of the vehicle and halfway up the porch before he remembered

Zeke's injury. He started to turn, but Zeke's firm "Go ahead" had Laine knocking on the door with a trembling fist. Barely sparing Brendon a glance when the door was opened, Laine found himself instead brushing by his friend and zeroing in on the man sitting on the couch, who looked at Laine with the same need, the same *ache* that was pounding in him.

His intent must have been obvious, because Sev pushed himself up from the couch and stood in his sock-covered feet. A pair of soft grey sweats—Laine was betting they were Enessa's since they didn't swamp Sev—hugged his lover's lean hips, clinging just enough to his package to make Laine's cock fill in response. A thin, faded t-shirt moulded to Sev's body, the muscular proof of his abs and chest emphasised. He was vaguely aware of Brendon asking either him or Zeke questions about what they'd found, but Laine blocked out the background noise.

Stopping inches away from Sev, Laine studied him, looking for hints that the man was injured worse than he'd seemed earlier. What he found was the same wild need he felt reflected in the depths of his lover's eyes. The smaller man stepped forward, bridging the gap between them, and reached up to wrap his arms around Laine's neck. Warm fingers entwined in his hair, tugging his head down even as Laine wound his arms around Sev's waist. He slid his hands down to the sweet, firm ass he was becoming addicted to and lifted Sev until his feet left the floor. The kiss was nearly brutal, not the tender, caring kiss Laine had thought to give.

As soon as their lips touched, something sparked between them and the result was a mashing of teeth and dueling of tongues, teeth nipping ungently and hands gripping, fingers digging bruisingly into neck and ass. When it ended on a gasp for air, only then did Laine remember there were two other people in the room. He'd never been one for public displays, and the realisation that they had an audience set Laine's cheeks on fire. Judging by the way Sev buried his face in Laine's neck, he figured his lover was embarrassed, too.

Steeling himself, he turned his head and found that Brendon and Zeke had left the room. Or combusted from the heat, but he wasn't going to take the time to look for ashes. "Can you walk okay?"

Sev looked up at him through thick lashes. "The bedroom Brendon put us up in isn't far, but you should probably keep an arm around me. Just to be safe."

"I'm all for being safe." Though what he felt for this man in his arms didn't feel safe at all. It felt hot and dangerous, overpowering, something that could surely leave him bleeding from a thousand wounds—and he wasn't going to walk away from the risk.

In the bedroom, Laine held Sev still with a hand splayed over his hip. He traced the shape of Sev's lip with a finger, watching the man's eyes flash with desire. He tipped Sev's chin up and, keeping his gaze locked with Sev's, lowered his mouth and gave a tender, searing kiss to his lover. When his tongue slicked over the roof of Sev's mouth, Sev grabbed Laine's shoulders and moaned. The sound and vibration of it worked through Laine's body and threatened to snap his control, forcing him to pull back before he took Sev right then and there. He wanted more than that tonight.

Licking Sev's lips as the kiss ended, Laine stepped back and reached for the hem of his lover's shirt. Sev raised his arms, and Laine thought to enjoy the leisurely stripping of that compact, muscled body—until he saw the number of scratches on the chiseled torso. Breath slipping out in a hiss, Laine tossed the shirt to the floor and quickly pushed down Sev's sweats. More stinging damage to that sweet skin had Laine cursing, vision blurring with the force of his anger.

"They're just scratches—" Sev's breath stuttered at the look Laine gave him. "Mostly."

"Yeah? You look like someone held you down and tried to flay your hide. C'mon."

Laine led Sev to the bed and nudged him until he sat. He stripped off his own clothes, his pants and boxers puddling in a pile on top of his boots and socks, his shirt landing…somewhere. After kneeling between Sev's knees, Laine sat back on his heels and picked up one of Sev's feet and carefully pulled off the thick sock, almost afraid of what he would find. It wasn't good, but it was nowhere near the mangled mess he'd imagined. There were a few nicks and some obvious spots where hard and sharp objects had penetrated soft and smooth flesh. Laine stroked over the damaged sole with the barest of touches, relieved when Sev didn't jerk back in ticklish response.

"Jesus, Laine, please." Sev's voice quavered, filled with longing. His eyes widened as though the depth of need in his tone startled him. That pitch slithered over Laine's cock so that it throbbed, and he wondered if he could come from Sev's voice alone

The other foot was treated to the same tender inspection, then Laine reached up and pushed at Sev's chest, encouraging him to lay back. Once Sev complied, sort of— he propped himself up on his elbows so he could watch— Laine picked up Sev's foot and began kissing each spot of ripped flesh. A shudder racked Sev and his breath became a series of moans and whimpers as Laine's tongue gently licked the less grievous wounds. The other foot received equal care, then Laine began working his way up, nibbling and kissing, nuzzling and licking, wanting to take away each ache and replace it with pleasure.

Long licks up the outside of Sev's thighs had him reaching to bury his fingers in Laine's hair, and when Laine repeated the move, adding nips and sucking as he tasted the skin on the insides of Sev's thighs, those hands tightened and tugged until Laine's eyes watered. Scalp stinging in a way he found made his balls ache with the need for release, Laine sucked hard, bringing a deep purple mark up on the tender skin of Sev's inner thigh. The keening noise it drew from his lover had Laine tugging at his balls, trying to stave off the need to come. He sucked and brought up a matching mark on the sweet, soft skin of the other thigh, then buried his nose in Sev's balls and inhaled, taking in the man's musky scent. Sev moaned and rocked his hips, hard enough that Laine worried one of them would end up hurt. Laine stood and slid his hands under Sev's arms, sliding him farther up on the bed. His plans to work his way over Sev's torso, to kiss and soothe each scrape as he had his lower body, were shot to hell when Sev thrust his hips up, humping the air as his hands reached down to spread his ass cheeks.

"Please, Laine. Need you so much." The words sounded as if they were ripped from somewhere deep inside of Sev, as though he hadn't wanted to let them out at all.

Laine couldn't look away from the erotic vision of Sev's cock, hard and leaking copious amounts of precome, his balls already snugging up against his body, the wrinkled skin of his dusky pucker stretched taut by Sev's own hands. His fingers were gripping so tightly into those firm ass cheeks that the tips were sunk at least two inches into the flesh, and Laine's desire to soothe his lover was replaced with the need to sate instead.

Crawling halfway up Sev's body, Laine swallowed Sev's cock, tongue swiping over the proffered precome before swirling down the steely length. Sev's back bowed, his hips trying to bury his prick in Laine's throat. He slipped two fingers into Sev's gasping mouth, moaning around Sev's prick as the man's lips closed tight and he began to suck Laine's fingers, his tongue working to spread saliva between them. Laine sucked and started bobbing his head, his tongue working the thick vein that pulsed along the length of Sev's prick. When he reached the crown, Laine locked his lips firmly under the rim and dipped the tip of his tongue into the wide slit on the head.

Sev's mouth popped open on a gasping breath, and Laine brought his fingers to the place where he longed to bury his cock. Fingertips placed against the clenching ring of muscle, Laine shoved and buried both fingers in Sev's ass as he sucked Sev's prick down, swallowing as his fingers rubbed across Sev's prostate.

The reaction to Laine's dual sensual assault had Sev's entire body jerking, Laine's name flying from his lips in a broken groan, his hands dropping to the mattress to fist the sheets as his prick released a load of come down Laine's throat. Laine's fingers were held immobile in the clutch of Sev's body, the heat and squeeze of his inner muscles almost painful as Laine suckled the softening length in his mouth.

Laine let Sev's prick slip from his lips and carefully slid his fingers free. He pushed off the bed and found his pants, digging through the pocket until he felt the crinkle of foil and the cold plastic tube of lube. His fingers trembled as he tried to open the condom, so he ripped the package open with his teeth. As he worked the rubber down his cock, Laine looked at Sev and felt his balls hitch up at the sight. Sev was sprawled, looking boneless and willing, and the heavy rise and fall of his chest as he struggled to get his breath back had Laine gripping the base of his cock to push back his orgasm.

Sev made a 'come here' gesture with his hand and Laine shook his head. If he let Sev rub the lube on him, he was afraid he'd come before the first stroke was finished. Laine slicked his cock and started to straddle Sev, but his lover showed a sudden burst of energy and flipped over, knees tucking up under him and ass lifted in the air. When Sev reached back and pulled his cheeks apart again, Laine's moan felt like it started from his toes and worked its way up, scorching every nerve ending along the way. Sev opened himself wider, stretching his hole until the skin went almost white and that tempting pucker clenched.

Laine lined his cock up, wishing he had a little more restraint. He wanted to tease, to rub the thick head over Sev's hole until he begged, but since Laine was biting his lower lip hard enough to draw blood to keep himself from coming, it wasn't going to happen, not this time. Canting his hips, Laine tried to ease his way in, but the gripping heat around the crown of his dick stole his ability to go slow. Laine splayed his thighs wide, surrounding Sev, and dropped down onto his elbows, covering the smaller man. He wedged his arms underneath his lover, gripping Sev's shoulders from the front as he thrust his cock into the hot, pulsing channel, burying himself to the hilt in Sev's silky sheath. Laine battled back the tingling trying to spread from the base of his spine to his balls, needing this to be more than just a quick fuck — needing *Sev* to know it was more than that. He rose, spreading his thighs just a bit more, pulling Sev's back against his chest. This way, he could touch Sev, run his palms over the sweat-slicked planes of his stomach and chest —

Sev groaned, a deep rumble that vibrated all the way through to Laine's cock. Laine licked the side of Sev's neck, from below his ear to his shoulder, and began slowly pumping his hips, the movements so small but they felt so damn good. His fingers found Sev's nipples, fluttering softly over the tight buds first, then pinching them with thumbs and forefingers.

The feel of Sev's hands grappling for a hold, finally clasping on to Laine's forearms, those surprisingly strong fingers digging into his trembling muscles told Laine what his lover needed. He began thrusting harder, then harder still as he twisted and tugged on Sev's nipples, working the nubs as Sev's gasping pants for 'more' and 'harder' and 'oh, God pleaseplease' spurred his fingers and cock to give more, give it harder, and, oh God, please them both until their brains melted.

A sharp, pinching tug on Sev's nipples had Sev's inner muscles squeezing Laine's dick in the tightest, velvety vice that existed. When Sev let go of Laine's forearm so he could reach his prick and start jerking himself, Laine's hips lost their smooth rhythm. He began pounding into his lover, one hand releasing a nipple so Laine could lock his arm around Sev's stomach and hold the man in place. Hips snapping, the bones ramming into the supple flesh of Sev's ass, Laine could focus on nothing but the driving pleasure surging through his body.

Heat coiled, sweet and wild in his belly, in his balls, shooting out into his extremities and up his spine to burst in brilliant colours behind his eyes. Laine buried his face against Sev's neck to muffle his scream, lipping the silver chain out of the way so he could bite and suck. Wet heat splattered onto his arm as Sev's channel pulsed around Laine's cock. The scent of spunk filled his nostrils. Come boiled up from Laine's balls and shot out his cock.

Sev's yell wasn't muffled at all, and it fuelled Laine's mouth, his hand still working a turgid nipple, his dick swelling and filling the condom as his hips stilled, burying him so deep inside of Sev he could feel the man's heartbeat. Laine cupped his hand over Sev's abused nipple, palming it gently to ease them both down from the heights their orgasms had taken them to. His lover felt pliant and limp in his arms, fucked out in the best way. Laine didn't want to let him go, or free himself from the warm tunnel holding his dick, but the semen on his arm felt uncomfortably cool on his sweat-dried skin, and he couldn't imagine it was something Sev was enjoying either.

"Are you okay?"

"I think I need to sleep for a week. Damn, I'm gonna feel you tomorrow — be like having you inside me still, not as good, but just... damn."

Laine carefully eased out of Sev, holding the base of the condom since he was certain it was damn near filled to overflowing. He nudged Sev to lie down, then made his trembling legs move, scooting to the edge of the bed. Laine tied the condom off and stood, only stumbling once as he made his way to the bathroom.

There was a washcloth laying on the countertop and Laine felt a moment's gratitude that he didn't have to try to find one. The water warmed and Laine doused the cloth. He cleaned himself and rinsed the washcloth before padding back to the bed to wipe his lover down. Sev's eyes were drifting shut, though he pried them open and nearly melted Laine where he stood with that soft, warm gaze. He wiped Sev gently, pleased deep inside that his man allowed him to do such an intimate thing, then Laine leant down, bracing himself on one arm so that he could kiss Sev the way he was aching to.

A funny, tingly warmth was growing inside him, and it wasn't until he crawled in bed beside Sev that Laine realised what that warm feeling was. Happiness, peace — they blended together, forging something that had the potential to be strong and binding and could swiftly blossom into love. He hadn't thought he'd ever feel that way for another man again, but it was there, gathering under the surface of his skin and in his heart. Not that he was going to be saying *that* to this man any time soon, Laine reassured himself. But as he watched Sev sleeping, that dark head resting on Laine's shoulder and his body curled all over and around him, Laine knew something he almost wished he didn't. A soft sigh slipped from Sev's mouth, and Laine felt an answering sigh passing his own lips as he smacked into the knowledge that, as unbelieveable as it might seem, he was already dangerously close to giving his heart to the man in his arms.

Chapter Eight

A ray of morning sunlight slipped through the curtains, bathing Sev's face in warmth. Bright colours danced behind his lids, and a dull throb seemed to streak from his feet to the base of his spine. Memories of yesterday's terrifying events rushed into his head only to be chased away by the reality of the present. The heavy weight of an arm holding him tight, a furry leg tossed over his own, felt enlightening rather than oppressive. Sev would never have guessed that he could wake up with a man two mornings in a row and not feel caged, or worse, bored and needing to flee. No, what he felt was a sense of contentment deep inside, a slow spreading of want that tingled along the surface of his skin and burrowed into the dark places Sev tried to ignore.

Sev blinked his eyes open, the lids heavy enough that he considered giving in and going back to sleep. He turned his head and, even through sleep-blurred vision, or maybe because of it, Sev saw something soft flicker across Laine's eyes as he smiled lazily. That fleeting emotion was gone when Sev's vision cleared, replaced by a need that had his prick aching, a bead of moisture welling from the slit.

"Morning."

Laine's lips curled into a smile that looked more predatory than anything else. His thick cock rubbed against Sev's hip, searing a trail of liquid need over his skin. Sev felt disoriented, and realised the feeling causing him so much confusion was one of shyness, something he definitely wasn't familiar with. Yet, somehow, with this strong, demanding man watching him, seeing into places Sev was afraid himself to look, he felt vulnerable and nervous… and, God damn it, shy like a blushing virgin. Something else was going on between them, more than just fucking, and it knocked Sev off balance, tore down his usual footloose façade—and scared the shit out of him. He had to find a way back to safer ground.

Sev let his eyes drift nearly shut, willing everything down except the need to fuck. He could handle keeping this on a physical level. That was one thing he knew how to do, to work his body, focus on the pleasure he could give his lover and, in doing so, himself as well. Sharing *that* was familiar and he was damned good at it. Sev sent Laine a look intended to melt the man on the spot, to stop his brain and kick-start his long, lean body into high gear, backing up his message with a writhing move and greedy hands. Only…it didn't seem to work.

A low growl vibrated in Laine's chest, his lips curling down and his eyes narrowing with displeasure. Sev found his wrists gripped bruisingly in Laine's big hands, then jerked up and pinned together above his head. That Laine could subdue him so easily set something needy free in Sev even as it shook him, inside and out—and, God, he was now only using one hand to lock Sev's wrists in place.

One very big, calloused hand. Laine's other equally rough hand gripped Sev's jaw, fingers digging deep enough to fire off a pleasant ache.

"No games, baby. No hiding behind your little safety net, no locking me out and keeping me at a distance." Laine's eyes pinned Sev as surely as his hand did, the grey softening and heating to a silver that swirled with things Sev wanted but was terrified to reach for, to accept. Sev felt hypnotised by that molten colour, sucked in by the promises offered. His heartbeat sped up in a moment of panic, his breath skittering as Sev fought to find the familiar ground he'd always stood on—fucking because it felt good, because it was all any man had ever expected, too often all he thought he was good for.

Laine's hand tightened on his wrists, the grinding pain of bone on bone shattering Sev's attempt to gather his reserves. The hand gripping Sev's jaw tightened as well, Laine's wrist flicking so that Sev was forced to shake his head to give in to the pressure exerted by his lover's hand.

"I said *no*. No more, Severo. You're gonna look at me, see me and feel me. I'm not just another fuck." Laine leant down and caught Sev's lower lip between his teeth, tugging and nipping until Sev shook with desire, his body arching up and his mind unable to fully concentrate on formulating a plan to keep him safe.

Any last-second bid to seal some part of himself away failed as Laine bit hard enough to sting, making Sev's eyes pop wide open when he'd thought to hide behind his lids. The second those steely eyes locked onto his, every bit of the urge to protect himself died an instant death, and that warm, flickering *something* he'd seen in Laine's gaze moments ago seemed to slip into him and fill him, soaking into places Sev had refused to acknowledge, desires and hopes he'd shoved ruthlessly away.

"That's it, just like that." Laine's lips brushed softly against Sev's tormented ones, the words spoken into the swollen flesh. "I'm not demanding anything you don't want to give, baby. You just didn't know you wanted to give it—until now. To me."

Laine's tongue slicked over Sev's lips, the tip parting them for a languorous kiss that left him breathless, panting and wanting more. He didn't realise, until his back was bowing as his nipples were plucked, squeezed and tugged, sending spirals of heat straight to his balls, that his wrists had been released. Sev couldn't have held back his groan had his life depended on it. A sweet lethargy filled him, but he forced his arms up and embraced his lover. The feel of smooth, hard flesh, the rippling muscles of Laine's back under his hands dragged another needy sound from Sev.

Time seemed to stop as every part of Sev's body was licked, kissed, or caressed—sometimes all three. His body hummed with passion, his prick was painfully hard, and while all the foreplay had been extraordinary, he craved Laine inside him.

"Please, please Laine." It wasn't the first time those words had been dragged from Sev's lips this morning, so he added, "I need you." And Laine listened, opening a condom package and covering his cock before applying lube. He hitched Sev's legs up over his shoulders and slid his knees under Sev until his opening was kissing the tip of Laine's cock. Without being told, Sev kept his eyes locked with Laine's as Laine pressed in and filled him slowly. He watched the emotions flicker across Laine's face, darken the grey of the man's eyes until they looked like tarnished silver, and knew this was something other than the two of them fucking, scratching an itch, just as last night had been different. As Laine lowered himself over Sev, Sev's breath hitched as he pushed away the remaining fear of *this*—giving himself over, trusting *this* man to keep him safe in every way.

Sev offered his lips to his lover and moaned as his mouth was plundered, devastated and owned. Sev gave it up, his control and fears, everything he'd held back and everything he'd hidden from. The kiss gentled and thrusts of tongue were matched by Laine's hips as Sev clung to his lover, hands holding on to Laine's broad back despite the sweat slicking his skin. It was beautiful, tender and sweet, but Sev needed more. His balls were nearly cramping, his prick steadily leaking. He needed to come.

As if he knew Sev's thoughts, Laine's kiss again turned nearly brutal, the sting of teeth on Sev's bottom lip felt so perfect. Laine tightened his arms around Sev and buried his face in Sev's neck, sucking strongly as his hips began pumping a frantic beat. Sev tried to meet Laine's thrusts, but the bigger man's weight held him down, forcing Sev to submit to Laine's rhythm. Frustrated, aching, Sev turned his head and bit Laine's jaw at the same time he dug his fingers into his lover's back.

Laine got the message. His hands clutched at the backs of Sev's shoulders, his teeth tugged at the skin where shoulder and neck met, and his cock... Sev didn't bother trying to muffle his yell as Laine pounded into him, his heavy balls slapping against Sev's ass almost continually as he worked Sev's hole. Sev couldn't do anything but try to breathe and hold on for the ride, his body heating and tingling, a feeling that surpassed any ecstasy Sev had ever thought he'd known filling him. Laine's furry, hard abs rubbed over Sev's prick *just right,* and Sev thought he might have yelled again, might have babbled a string of words and promises as his release ripped through him. Then Laine pushed himself up, his head thrown back as he buried his cock to the hilt. Sev opened his eyes, vision clearing just in time to take in the strained, corded muscles of Laine's neck and shoulders, the convulsive bobbing of the man's Adam's apple as he pressed even farther into Sev.

In that moment, as Sev stared at his lover caught in his release, a shudder racked Sev. It felt like he was being shattered into a million pieces, his fears and doubts dispersed as he was put back together and cocooned in the warmth of emotion blooming for this one man. It felt safe, sacred, and Sev didn't want to fight it any more. As Laine trembled above him, in him, Sev's eyes burnt with the intensity of this newly acknowledged feeling, and he swore to himself that he wouldn't run, wouldn't let this man go.

* * * *

Laine sat across the table from Sev, their uneaten breakfast pushed aside as they discussed the prior day's events. There was a soft look in Sev's eyes that had been there since their early morning love-making that Laine wanted to ask about, but fear of his lover's reaction kept Laine on the subject of who had broken into his home yesterday. Between the fear of chasing away that look and fear for Sev's safety, Laine found himself feeling oddly vulnerable, and he didn't like it.

Worries about his job, the reaction of people in the small town of McKinton just didn't seem that important, not when compared to the fact he could have lost Sev yesterday—could still lose him if Laine couldn't find and stop the man who seemed fixated on him. After what he'd found on his sheets yesterday once he and Zeke had made their way into the bedroom, Laine had no doubt he was the object of some sick fuck's obsession.

Sev leant back in his chair and crossed his arms over his chest, rubbing agitatedly at his biceps. "So, you're saying this guy left… He, uh, jerked off on your side of the bed and…"

"Yeah." Laine couldn't do much more than grunt the word as his throat tightened in anger. The 'and' that Sev had trailed off after saying was the worst part. When Zeke and Laine had found the sticky mess on his sheets, that had been a vulgar violation. But seeing the side of the bed where Sev had laid only moments before, slashed into bits of springs and material… The threat seemed pretty clear. It made Laine wonder if what had happened to Conner three years prior hadn't been a random act, if, just maybe, Conner had been targeted because he'd been Laine's lover. Was that what Conner was trying to tell him, why he knew someone was coming after Laine?

Maybe the police—himself included—had been wrong all along, and the sick fuck who'd killed Conner had had three long years to brood about Laine escaping, years in which he planned and honed the need for revenge. The thought was almost too painful to consider, because if it was true, then inadvertently or not, Laine had been responsible for Conner's death. But it felt right, as if Laine had found the piece missing from a hellish jigsaw puzzle. The pain of that realisation hit him as a physical sensation, his stomach cramping so hard Laine gasped and doubled over, vision dimming as he wrapped his arms around his middle as if to squeeze the feeling out.

He didn't hear Sev's chair slide back or the padding of feet as his lover ran to him. There was simply, suddenly, strong arms around his neck, and Sev was kneeling on the floor in front of Laine, trying to wedge himself in between Laine's knees.

"Laine, no, no. No, baby, don't do this." The words were breathed against Laine's ear, soft lips pressing to comfort and console from his ear to his forehead, then kisses were placed on his eyelids and finally his lips. "It wasn't your fault, he doesn't blame you."

Laine's eyes burned and he kept them sealed tight, refusing to break down. The sound of the kitchen door slamming open, of booted feet hurrying across to the table registered faintly, then Laine felt two more pairs of arms embrace him—and that soft, sweet scent that meant Zeke's mama had decided to pop in. Laine had a second's clarity to wonder why all the drama had suddenly kicked in, then Sev repeated the last part of his sentence and the wounded animal sound that filled the room came from Laine, was torn from him in an almost violent fit as he finally broke.

Three years of pain and anguish poured from him, of mourning he'd held in because he couldn't let it show, rushing to the surface and demanding acknowledgement. It tore at his guts, leaving trails of scalding anger and guilt, and later, Laine would think the only thing that had held him together, kept him from exploding and his mind from splintering, was the three men who held him as he fell apart, and maybe, the soft breeze that kept swirling over him as he struggled through this nightmare.

Sev held on to Laine after he stopped shuddering, after the awful sounds had ceased and Zeke and Brendon had quietly slipped away. Sev had seen the understanding flare in Laine's eyes, knew the moment his lover realised that, more than likely, the psycho who had broken in yesterday was the same man who had killed Conner. And he'd known the exact second when Laine had tried and convicted himself, condemning himself for Conner's death. But Conner didn't blame him. Laine hadn't known, any more than Conner had before the sick fuck torturing had told him, that Laine was the man's target, his obsession—just *his*.

Even then, Conner had blamed no one other than his killer, but he'd known what it would do to Laine to discover the truth. He'd known, and for that reason, Conner had done his best to hang around, so to speak. Conner just hadn't been able to make contact with Laine, not until recently, and Sev suspected it was due to Laine acknowledging Zeke's motherly ghost that had made it possible for Laine to be receptive to other spirits. Namely Conner's.

Laine's breaths were steady when Sev leant back and waited for his lover to meet his eyes. The pain in that silvery gaze would have brought Sev to his knees had he not already been on them.

"I meant it, you know; *he* meant it. Conner has never blamed you and didn't want you to blame yourself. That's why he couldn't go to…wherever it is souls go." Sev had to take a steadying breath himself before he continued. "That, and…he didn't want you hurt. He didn't want his murderer to kill you, too. Conner loved you, Laine." It hurt Sev to say it, but it was the truth, and Laine needed to know it, remember it. Believe it.

The fact that this strong, good man was looking at Sev with such a need to believe those words buried the pain it caused Sev to speak them. He would do anything to take away the guilt and anguish his lover felt, and, while Sev might be new to the whole concept of possibly loving a man instead of just fucking around, he was surprised he didn't feel threatened by the knowledge that Laine had loved Conner and vice versa. Laine had done nothing to make Sev feel like he was second best.

Sev brought one hand to Laine's cheek and cupped it, drawing his lover closer for a kiss. The soft press of hard lips, the warmth of Laine's breath as he opened and allowed Sev's tongue to slip inside, nearly undid Sev right then and there. If he'd had any doubt about how Laine felt for him, that kiss would have eradicated it instantly, but Sev didn't doubt, nor did he doubt himself. When the kiss ended, Sev felt a tingling that went from his head clear to his toes. He wanted nothing more than to take his man back to bed, but doubted it was possible.

"Do you have to go in today?" He tried not to plead when he asked, but didn't think he'd been very successful. Laine's eyes seemed a little less pain-filled, though, and that gave Sev hope that his lover would not let himself be buried in guilt.

"I do." Laine's voice was scratchy and rough, as though it hadn't been used in years. "I have to talk to Deputy Nixon since I called him over to the scene, see if he sent off the evidence we gathered, and..." Laine's lips tipped down and Sev started to ask what was wrong, well, what *else* was wrong, when Laine continued. "I'm pretty sure he figured out that you and I...that I'm gay. It may be okay with him, might not, but there will be other people who have a problem with it."

Somehow, Sev had managed not to think about that, but the reality of the complications for Laine started manifesting themselves in Sev's head. It wasn't pretty, and it would be much worse for Laine than for him. Sev scrambled for a solution.

"We can say that I didn't have anywhere else to go, that you slept on the couch or in the guest room, or — "

Laine clamped a big hand over Sev's mouth. "No. I am not ashamed of who I am. Maybe I was afraid of what would happen before you came along," Laine's hand moved to stroke down Sev's cheek and his neck, resting at the top of Sev's shoulder. "And I didn't have any reason to let anyone know besides Zeke and Brendon, but I won't hide. I did that with Conner, we both did." Laine shook his head, his eyes never leaving Sev's. "Never again. Not for my job, not to make some bigoted people happy, not for anyone or anything. We clear?"

Sev thought his heart would burst with happiness even as his head tried to argue. "But you will probably lose your job at the very least, and—"

A hard kiss cut him off. "And nothing. I was voted in to this position, and, unless it's legal to do a recall election, I can't be fired easily. No matter what happens, the decision on how to handle it is mine. People can accept me or not, I will deal with them accordingly." Another kiss, this one only marginally gentler. "Now, I need to get ready for work. You stay with Zeke and Brendon, and I mean *with* them. I don't want you alone any more than is absolutely necessary, okay?"

Now Sev felt happy and mushy, and he was pretty sure there was a sappy-ass smile on his face as well, and he didn't mind at all. "Yeah, okay."

Chapter Nine

To say he felt raw inside would have been an understatement, but Laine didn't let it interfere with his job, or the reality that he would be facing within moments of walking into his office. Even though Deputy Nixon had been the only other person called to the scene at Laine's house, and Laine doubted Nixon would talk, word would get around. It always did, as if it were carried in the wind to the biggest and most vindictive of gossips. He would deal with it, if need be, after he made another call to Detective Montoya.

Doreen was at her desk and greeted Laine with her usual enthusiasm. She handed Laine a stack of messages as he walked by on the way to his office and promised to bring him his morning coffee. He'd learnt there was no use protesting it. Doreen would snap his head off if he dared to get his own coffee. Laine sat at his desk and found the paper with Detective Montoya's number on it fluttering across his desk. He snatched it up and felt an absurd urge to grin.

"Yeah, yeah, I was doing that right now."

Doreen walked in his office with his cup of coffee in her hand and looked around. "Who are you talking to and what were you going to do?"

"Myself, obviously. Nobody else is here, now, are they?" Laine gestured for his coffee and Doreen stepped up to his desk, placing the cup in front of him.

"Well, I was going to ask if you were okay, what with the big hullabaloo at your place yesterday, but you seem just fine to —" Doreen's eyes shot wide open as Laine's tin star popped off and landed on the desk, spinning like a dervish. Laine was a bit surprised himself; the star had always landed on the floor despite his best efforts to stop it. If he had to guess, he'd say someone was sending him a message to make the call, especially since Detective Montoya's message was now spinning around on his desk, too.

"What... *what?*" Doreen's mouth was doing a fine imitation of a goldfish, and Laine knew if he let out so much as a snicker she would lay into him once she recovered herself. He wasn't going to be able to hold out much longer though, not with her arms flapping in the air and that look on her face. Laine reached out and snagged the paper, surprised that, for once, the object he was trying to grab didn't spin away. Maybe he could grab the star, too... It skidded off the desk and resumed spinning on the floor.

"Damn." Laine bit his lip hard enough that he tasted blood, but it stopped him from laughing. "Doreen, I really need to make a phone call or I'll never get that back." He gestured to the silver blur on the floor. "If you'll excuse me?"

Doreen's mouth snapped shut and she went from being astounded to sarcastic just as quickly. "Well, if you ask me, you need to call an exorcist or those guys who hunt down ghosts on TV." She nodded once then turned smartly on her heel and left.

"You about done now that you freaked out Doreen?" The star stopped spinning immediately. "Cute. Conner..." Laine closed his eyes and tried to picture the man he'd loved. "I am sorry. And I hope it's, that you... I guess I'm wanting to say that I hope it's okay with you, about Severo, because I think that—" Was it stupid to admit such a thing to your former lover? No, to your deceased lover's ghost? Probably, Laine decided, but what the hell. This whole thing was crazy. "I think that I can love the guy, you know? Maybe I've already started to. You and me, we tried to keep it quiet. We couldn't, or wouldn't, risk stepping out of the closet for each other, but we should have. We should have loved each other that much, right?"

What felt like the brush of a hand across his cheek, followed by the lightest touch of lips was the response. Laine kept his eyes closed, thinking over what those two things meant and decided it had to be good. Then his hat was tipped back on his head and Laine got the message. Enough mushy crap, make the damn call. Laine opened his eyes and picked up the phone.

"Gotcha, buddy, doing it right now."

Montoya didn't answer his work phone so Laine tried his cell, unsurprised when the detective answered on the second ring, still as annoyingly perky in the morning as he had been when Laine was partnered with him.

"Hey, Laine, how's everything going?"

"Well, to tell you—"

"Must be going to shit since this is the third call from you in about as many days, right? After not hearing from you for a couple of years?"

"Shit." Which was pretty much how Laine felt. He closed his eyes and pinched the bridge of his nose between his thumb and forefinger. And the man *still* sounded perky. "Rich, I couldn't stay there after... It was just too..."

"Too much to find your lover dead?" That comment got Laine's eyes opened back up. He shouldn't have been surprised that his former partner knew, but Montoya had never said a word—and Laine had left without explaining, unable to pretend Conner hadn't been more than a friend, and unable, or unwilling, to step up and say just what Conner had been to him.

Whatever it was that had kept Laine silent years ago no longer bound him. "Yes. Too much, and I think...I think it may be happening again."

At first, he thought Montoya had hung up on him, but Laine began hearing background noises, the sound of a car door slamming shut, then a slow exhalation from his former partner. "You're going to have to explain that to me, Laine. We need to sit down and have a serious talk."

"Rich, I know I should have—" Laine stopped as an obnoxious beeping sounded in his ear. Did Rich hang up, or had he hit a spot where he got bad reception? Laine started to call him back but stopped when someone knocked on his door. "Come in."

Deputy Matt Nixon opened the door and stepped in, pushing the door shut behind him. "Sheriff, I sent off everything like you asked, but..." Nixon pulled a chair closer to Laine's desk and sat, looking at his hands where they rested folded between his knees. When he looked up at Laine, the understanding in his blue eyes sent a trickle of adrenaline-laced sweat down Laine's spine. "I didn't exactly explain the situation, you know? I mean, I didn't lie, or do anything that would jeopardise the case once we catch this guy and he goes to trial. I just didn't *say* anything or put anything in the report that could, you know."

Laine did know. "Matt... I'm not going to keep this a secret. I did that before, when I was with Houston PD, and it was—" It was what? How could he describe it? Laine shook his head. "It was fucked up, okay? I won't do it again."

Matt narrowed his eyes as he studied Laine. "You know that there'll be some people that will want you out of office, and I have no desire to fill your position. Are you ready to deal with the fallout from this?"

"'From this?'" Anger speared through Laine as he pushed away from the desk and stood. He slapped his palms down on the desk and leant towards Nixon as he spoke. "Why the hell should I have to make a choice here? I know about reality, and I know that the last time I kept everything quiet and hidden away, it didn't make a damn bit of difference! Someone knew, and that person killed my lover!" Laine leant closer, forcing out the words that were twisting his insides. "And I have to live with the fact that maybe, *maybe* if I hadn't been too much of a coward to speak up and stop hiding who I was, Conner would still be alive today. I won't do that again, not for this job, not for my pride, not for any reason. If you have a problem with that, then you can—"

The door flew open and a voice cut Laine off. "Now, come on, Laine, don't say something you might regret."

Laine looked up and Nixon whipped his head around to stare at the man standing in the doorway.

"Who the fu—" Nixon was already rising from his seat in a show of aggression that Laine had never seen before, but didn't bode well for the shorter, dark-haired man smirking as he leant against the doorframe.

"Matt! Sit down." Laine smiled and wondered that his nerves weren't fried at this point. "This is my former partner from Houston PD, Detective Richard Montoya. I *think* he's here to help."

Nixon stopped in his tracks but didn't return to his seat. Instead, he stood glaring at Montoya. The tension between the two men was so thick Laine wouldn't have been surprised if they'd both pulled out their dicks and compared sizes. He started to say as much when Doreen appeared behind Montoya.

"I swear," Doreen didn't speak so much as almost cluck the words as she glared from Montoya to Matt, "I can't even step into the ladies room without a bunch of preening peacocks popping up—though I might just shorten the word peacock if you two don't stop acting like some chest-thumping Neanderthals."

Laine laughed before he caught himself, startled by Doreen's threat to call the men dicks, or cocks, rather, and earned Doreen's flinty glare.

"I'm sorry, Doreen." He wasn't stupid, and Nixon normally wasn't either, so why the man didn't speak up was beyond Laine. As far as Montoya, he didn't know Doreen would verbally annihilate him if he didn't conform to her wishes, but he was a quick study, always had been. Montoya turned to Doreen and offered his hand.

"I apologise as well. Richard Montoya." Laine would just bet the man was flashing his knee-melting smile. Laine had seen that smile work its magic on dozens of women, and Doreen didn't appear to be an exception.

"Well. All right then." Doreen shook Montoya's hand. "Doreen Crews. Don't let that big guy glaring daggers at you bother you, he's just protective of his friends, isn't that right Matt?" A grunt was the only answer Nixon made. "However, if you do happen to do anything that causes Sheriff Stenley any problems, Matt here'll be the least of your problems." Doreen's smile widened in a way that was predatory rather than friendly. "You do that, and that pretty smile you gave me won't save your butt, you hear me, boy?"

Maybe Rich is losing his touch. "Doreen—"

"I know, you need more coffee." Doreen slipped in the room and walked over to grab Laine's cup. She turned back to face Matt and Rich. "Now, I'm thinking I'll fetch you two a cup of coffee as well, if y'all can behave." Doreen shrugged, a physical 'what can you do?' "If you boys can't play nice, far be it from me to hype you up with caffeine."

"Fine," Matt muttered as he returned to his seat. "I promise to behave."

Rich laughed from the doorway and gave Doreen an innocent look as he waved a Styrofoam container at her. "What? I came prepared—and I *always* behave." At Doreen's snort, Rich winked at her then proceeded to walk right up to Laine's desk and sit on the edge, his back to Matt in such a way that Matt was blocked from Laine's view.

Laine sat back in his chair and tried not to be amused at the childish behaviour. The two men were acting out of character, or at least Matt was. Laine wasn't sure he knew Rich any more. Regardless, this needed to stop right now. Laine nudged Rich's hip, hard, pushing him off the desk, and glared at Matt in such a way that the man didn't dare to laugh.

"I've about had enough of this shit. You," Laine pointed at Matt, ignoring the small bit of satisfaction he felt when the man flinched, "stop acting like an ass or I'll send you out to Mrs. Hawkins' place to take her report about a prowler."

"Sheriff," Matt leant forward, a panicked look in his eyes. "Last time I went out there, she was... She wanted... God!" A shudder ripped through him. Laine couldn't blame him; Mrs. Hawkins was a few decades older than either of them and had always been, from what everyone told him, persistent and horny, two things that would frighten the bravest of men when it came to her.

"And you," Laine's finger swung to point at Rich, who was barely keeping in his laughter, "I will toss your ass in jail if you provoke my deputy. Got it?" Laine watched the laughter seep out of his former partner as the man realised he wasn't joking. "I've got enough shit going on that I don't need this from either of you. You want to help, stay. You want to goad each other and irritate me in the process, get out right now. Are we clear?" Two nods and a 'yes, sir' from Matt and Laine let go of his mad.

"All right then. Rich," Laine gestured to the chair beside Matt, "what are you doing here?"

Rich pulled the chair right up to Laine's desk just as Matt had done earlier. "Would you believe me if I told you I'm here because I needed to be?"

Laine and Rich both ignored the noise Matt made at that. Laine tipped his head. "Yeah, surprisingly, I would." Rich's smile turned his face from attractive to drop-dead gorgeous.

"Good, because that's the only reason I can figure that I requested two weeks off and drove up here. I thought maybe..." Rich glanced over at Matt, then back at Laine, who nodded once again, letting Rich know he was free to say whatever he needed to. "I thought maybe it'd help us both, and I'll admit, Laine, that I've missed you, okay? I kinda got used to you being my partner, and then you just left. I understand why—" Rich put up his hand when Laine started to speak. "I do, and I can't say I wouldn't have done the same thing, but it... Well, and I have some ideas that I didn't want to share over the phone."

That got Matt's attention as well as Laine's. Rich tapped the desk and his stomach growled. "You think we could maybe go grab a bite after we talk? I kinda skipped dinner last night."

"I can do you one better. Still like your eggs sunny side up?" At Rich's confirmation, Laine buzzed Doreen. "Doreen, would you call Virginia's and have her send over breakfast for all of us, yourself included? Yes, thank you, Doreen." Laine gave her their order and thanked Doreen again before disconnecting.

"Now, let's get down to business." Laine stood and hung his Stetson on the hat rack before returning to his seat. He nodded at Matt. "I need to fill you in on what happened three years ago, then we're going to eat and listen to what brought Rich to McKinton—without being dicks, you got it? Because your egos don't mean shit, and I want this fucker caught."

* * * *

"So..."

Zeke leant against one of the posts on the porch, a booted foot lifted to rest on a planter filled with ivy as he studied Sev. Brendon was watching him as well from where he was perched beside his lover. Neither of them looked particularly happy. Was this where he got grilled on his intentions towards Laine again? Judging by the frowns on both men's faces, Sev kind of thought it must be. His stomach felt fluttery as he tried to think of how he would answer such questions. Sev squirmed in his chair before he could stop himself and twisted the silver necklace with his fingers. God, he wished one of them would just speak! He sent a pleading look to Brendon — the softer looking of the two men who were visually pinning him in his seat.

Brendon tapped the railing then nodded. "Okay. I feel like my dad grilling one of my dates here, but…" That brought a smile to the man's lips and eased a little of the tension coiling in Sev. "I guess we just want to know if you're worth Laine risking everything, because he is, and if you're planning on hanging around…" Brendon shrugged, Zeke's frown deepened, and Sev felt a burst of anger that had him rising out of his seat.

"What? Do I have 'good time only' stamped on my head? Or maybe a relationship expiration date on me that I don't know about?" Sev realised he was gesturing wildly, his arms and hands trying to work out his anger. "Or maybe you think I'm having such a 'good time'," Sev curled his fingers in the air as he said the last two words, surprised at how much he hated them. "Nearly freezing to death, running from a sociopath, and worrying about whether I will get taken out by a smalltown lynch mob, and *those* are the reasons I'm hanging around?"

"Hey —" Zeke's foot dropped to the porch floor as Sev came closer. Brendon put a hand on Zeke's chest, to hold him back or reassure him, Sev didn't know and didn't care.

"I just meant —"

"I know what you meant, Brendon!" Sev was so angry now that his chest hurt with it. "You meant y'all are worried that I'm just a fuck and Laine is the poor sucker who's going to end up with his heart broken and lose his job and... What are you saying about him? That he's an idiot being led around by his dick?" The idea made Sev laugh, although it was a bitter sound in his own ears. "You should know your friend better than that. So you don't know me, and okay, I haven't had any serious relationships." That took some of his anger away, drained it out as quickly as it had overtaken him. "That doesn't mean that I don't want one, that I won't do everything I can to make it work."

Sev turned away and walked to the door, pulling it open before he glanced over his shoulder at the two men watching him steadily. "That just means I hadn't found anyone worth giving my...my heart to before. I'm not a fool. I know what I've got. I may not have the words to explain it to you two, but I don't need to. The only one who needs to know, to understand, is Laine." Sev left them there and went into the house, letting the screen door bounce shut behind him.

The truth of his words spun in his head as he stumbled to the guest room, and that buzzing sound in his brain wasn't helping him at all. Knowing he wouldn't have any peace until he listened, Sev flopped onto his back on the bed and stared up at the ceiling fan, watching it spin lazily in its attempt to disperse the heat. *That's what I feel like inside, all blown apart and scattered. Scared I'll fuck this up, which is why I lost my temper when Laine's friends were just trying to look out for him.* Sev groaned and closed his eyes, adding a forearm across them in an attempt to hide from his own fears swirling around in his head. The buzzing grew louder and Sev cursed. Conner wasn't going to leave him alone.

"Fine! Say whatever you want to say!" Sev opened his mind and gasped when he heard the voice that wasn't

Conner's after all, the message both reassuring and scaring him. He listened though, and the words seemed to firm up all the bits of him that felt fragile and broken. When the voice stopped, Sev smiled and quit trying to hide behind his arm. He pushed up on the bed, scooting until his back was against the headboard and grinned as Zeke came thundering down the hall and through the door, not bothering to knock.

Sev waved a hand at him before he could get a word out. "I'm sorry for overreacting; you have every right to be concerned about your friend. Just... I guess I'm a little touchy about the way people see me."

Zeke sat on the edge of the bed and studied Sev for several seconds before speaking. "I don't think Brendon or I saw you as some kind of slut, Sev. Sure, we were wanting to know that Laine wasn't gonna get his heart broken or anything, and maybe the way we went about it was kind of... Well, it's not something we've had to worry about before, ya know? But I think—" Zeke leant forward and tipped Sev's chin up, encouraging Sev to meet his gaze, frowning at whatever it was he saw in Sev's eyes. "I think you're the one who doesn't believe you aren't anything more than a quick fuck. Or didn't, before Laine, huh?" Zeke removed his hand and looked almost as uncomfortable as Sev felt.

The words were disconcertingly close to the truth, but Sev wouldn't deny or confirm them. He had, in the past few days, become very aware of the fact that he had some issues he'd previously ignored. That didn't mean he wanted to discuss them. "All I can tell you is, I have no intention of hurting Laine, okay? Anything else, that's really between me and him, not me, him, and you two."

Zeke nodded, his cheeks darkening the slightest bit. Sev grinned and decided to pass along the message he'd just gotten. "So, your mama says you two can be asses sometimes, but you mean well and she loves you both — and that you both better appreciate her giving Brendon more than just that one nudge in the hall the night you had your little tantrum, Zeke."

Movement from the doorway caught Sev's eye. Brendon stood behind Zeke, a silly grin on his face. Zeke had paled slightly and looked torn between suspicion and hope. Brendon came into the room and looped an arm around Zeke's waist and planted a noisy kiss on his cheek.

"You're mama loves me, you gotta keep me," Brendon teased, and Zeke finally broke into a smile himself as he looked at his lover.

"Yeah, I guess I do, don't I?" Zeke pulled Brendon into his arms. "Was planning on it anyway." Zeke kissed Brendon so tenderly that Sev felt a pang of jealousy. He wanted that with Laine, and being jealous was stupid, because he knew they could have it. Zeke looked at him and nodded. "Thank you, Severo."

Sev felt his skin heat with a flush, but his smile didn't dim in the least. "You're welcome."

Brendon pulled out of Zeke's embrace enough to offer his hand to Sev. "Come on. Let's go talk about this whole ghost-thing. You can explain to us how you do it."

Sev took Brendon's hand and accepted the gesture and words as the peace offering they were. "Okay, but I really don't know the answer to that. Maybe we can figure it out, huh?" And maybe Sev could figure out how to tell Laine the things he needed to while he was at it.

Chapter Ten

Rich pushed aside the empty container that had held his breakfast and patted his stomach. "Despite that sour-faced bitch who delivered our food, that was pretty good."

Matt and Laine nodded in agreement.

"Yeah, that was Virginia's niece Irma. She has a bit of a problem, not a very tolerant person, and I suspect she's a vindictive woman who would love to see me out of office," Laine explained.

"That's not gonna happen. I heard about her snit over you helping Zeke the other day, and while there may be other people who are as hateful as she is, most of the folks in this town learnt their lesson when Zeke's sister tried to kill him—and Irma is not well liked by anyone. That nasty temperament is applied liberally in many, many places on many, many topics." Matt leant back and stretched his legs, crossing them at the ankle. "I bet even the bigots wouldn't side with her. She's alienated just about everyone."

"Great. Maybe we should have checked our food before we ate it." Rich looked like he might be sick, and Laine wondered if his friend was thinking about some of the nasty food-tampering horror stories police officers loved to pass around. God knew Laine was.

"I did." Laine and Matt proclaimed together, laughing at Rich's irritated look.

"Well, you could have warned me!"

"Ah, now, I looked when you opened your food up. Everything was fine, and I didn't want you to starve yourself, so I didn't mention it before now."

Rich snorted and glared at Laine. "Thanks. It's much better that I puke after, huh?"

"I'd laugh," Matt offered, earning him two glares. "What? It woulda been funny."

"Behave." Laine stood and gathered the empty containers then dumped them in the trash before taking his seat. "So what do you have, Rich?"

"Well, you might say it's speculation, but my gut—" Rich shrugged, and for once, Matt didn't toss out a sarcastic comment. Good cops learnt to trust their instincts, and Laine knew Rich was a very good cop.

Laine rested his elbows on the desk and steepled his fingers in front of him. "Go on."

"You know we never found so much as a lead on Conner's killer, and you left right after, didn't tell anyone except, I'm guessing, the Chief, where you went?"

"I didn't tell him where I was going because I wasn't sure, but once I hit McKinton and decided to apply for a position as deputy, I had to tell him."

"But no one else?" Rich's dark blue eyes had a shine to them that told Laine his former partner definitely had a hunch that was burning to get out.

"No, no one, and I haven't set foot in Houston since I left."

"You could have called me." Rich grimaced and shook his head. "Sorry. Now isn't the time, I know, but after this is done…"

Matt let an agitated sigh slip from his lips. "Back on track, maybe?"

"Sorry to inconvenience you." Rich rolled his eyes, something Laine had always found humourous when they were partners but he knew had the potential to set Matt off right now. Luckily, Matt didn't rise to the bait. "We never closed the case on Conner, and there were never any more murders like his, so the general thinking was it was a one-time thing, maybe some serial killer passing through. God knows Houston has several of them, but there wasn't any similar to his. Odd, but not unheard of. I kept digging through the reports, even up to last month, and I'd swear I have the damned things memorised, but I kept thinking I was missing something. Then you called out of the blue, asking me for info on your little ghost whispering guy—"

"Ghost whispering?" Matt made those two words sound like a contagious disease. "Are you serious?"

"Matt, let him finish."

"No, hang on." Rich got up and walked out of the office, returning a few minutes later with a briefcase and an apologetic shrug for Laine. "Here." Rich tossed a file at Matt. "The file on Severo Adulio Robledo. And before you get all pissed off, Laine, let me just say that it's better if Matt is with us on this than not, okay?"

Laine wanted to snatch the file away from Matt and beat the crap out of Rich while he was at it, but Rich was right. Laine clasped his hands together tightly, the knuckles going white to keep himself from taking the file. "Okay, but one smart ass comment, Matt, and you'll be at Mrs. Hawkins every damn day you're on shift."

The smile vanished from Matt's face. "Yes, sir."

Rich studied Matt. "Huh. I might just have to meet this Mrs. Hawkins. Anyway, you look through that file, and you'll see that Mr. Robledo has consulted with several police departments and helped solve quite a few cases by doing what he does—and I don't doubt that he does it. I've seen too many things that can't be explained in this world to not believe something like this that's backed up with solid proof. Now." Rich flicked a hand at Laine. "The fact that Mr. Robledo came to McKinton could be a coincidence, but I doubt it. And the man is, I take it, your lover—which, in case you're wondering, isn't the way he usually works a case. Those records go on and on about how professional he is, so again, I'm deducing that you two are the real deal."

Laine nodded. "He's it, okay?" He felt Matt's eyes on him but kept his gaze locked with Rich's. "I loved Conner, but both of us… Neither of us were willing to step out, so maybe we didn't love each other enough, I don't know. But I won't make the same mistake with Severo. If it costs me my job, so be it." Laine let that sink in before continuing, making sure both men understood how serious he was about his lover. "And no, Sev showing up here wasn't a coincidence. He stopped in Houston, and basically felt compelled to come here. He told me he knew he had to pass along a message to someone, but until he…saw me—" *Here's where I see just how much these two believe.* "Saw that Conner was trying to communicate with me, Sev didn't know who the message was for, or what the message was. I kind of flipped when he asked me who Conner Sutherland was." Laine's cheeks heated with the memory of how he'd fled, leaving Sev covered in spunk like a cheap trick.

Rich apparently still knew Laine as well as he had years ago. He laughed and shook his head while Matt looked on curiously. "Judging by the way your cheeks are flaming, that must have been a very, er, interesting disclosure."

If you only knew. God, don't let him figure it out! "Yeah, you could say that."

"How exactly was Conner trying to communicate with you?"

As if on cue, Rich's hair ruffled and the papers flew out of his briefcase. He looked terrified for all of half a minute before he burst out laughing. Matt had eased his chair a few inches farther from Rich and looked more than a little creeped out.

"Uh, Sheriff?" Matt had an almost pleading expression on his face.

"Sorry, but that would be Conner. I didn't know until Sev told me." Laine nodded at the papers Rich was gathering up. "If you help him out, we can continue here."

Matt screwed up his courage and helped Rich out, too rattled to mouth off. They sat back in their seats, Rich grinning like a loon and Matt's lips disappearing into a thin line.

"That's kind of cool, but kind of creepy, too. I won't even ask for specifics—"

"You wouldn't get them anyway." Laine cut Rich off. "Conner's message was that someone was coming after me, and he did. He broke into my house while Sev was there asleep in my bed. Sev said that Conner woke him up and warned him, otherwise..." The image of his desecrated bed flashed before Laine's eyes and he couldn't quite suppress his shudder. "Matt took photos of the crime scene; we don't have a forensic unit out here—or, rather, we *are* the forensic unit, us and the two deputies that work the night shift. Here." Laine pulled the file from his desk drawer and handed it to Rich. "Everything's in there."

"Everything?" Rich's eyebrows drew together as he tapped the file on the edge of the desk.

"I wrote up most of that." Matt tipped his chin towards the file. "I tried to keep the sheriff's personal life out of it, and I didn't know about Conner then, but…"

"But," Laine slipped a hard edge into his voice as he looked at Matt, "I want every bit of information in that file, nothing left out, no matter how minute, because it could be important. Which means—"

"Which means," Matt's sigh sounded much put upon and not as cowed by Laine's attempt at intimidation as Laine had hoped, "that I have to go back and rewrite the damned reports, I know. I'll do it when we finish up here."

Laine noticed Rich was looking at Matt as if the deputy was barely a step above pond scum. "What's the problem, Montoya?"

Rich arched his brows as he met Matt's gaze, then he seemed to shake off his attitude as he turned back to Laine. "Not a thing. Getting back on track, I caught a murder case a few days before you called, rape and strangulation of a dark-haired gay man. He was kind of similar to you in build, Laine, reminded me of you even though I hadn't seen you in years. The guy could have been your brother, and then you called. It seemed like too much of a coincidence, I guess, and I started digging around and found that there've been three other murders similar to my case. No one either cared enough to connect them, or just didn't realise it. Personally, as much as I hate to admit it, I'm thinking that no one cared."

"That's fucked up." Matt's voice dripped with disgust. "I'd think a big city like Houston, it's gotta have a lot of gays. Surely people are more tolerant."

Rich shrugged one shoulder. "It's like most places, depends on who you talk to. We do have a large gay population, and a lot of people accept it, some even embrace it. But there's always going to be those people who hate anyone and anything that differs from their idea of the norm.

"The three other men were also raped and strangled, no DNA evidence though there was proof that he'd used condoms, and all of them were obviously similar in body type, build and looks. There were small differences, like eye colour, or an inch or two in height, things like that, but every one of them reminded me of you, Laine. And that made me wonder. The day you called, there was another detective in the pen. Do you remember who the responding officers were that showed up when you called in Conner's murder?"

There wasn't anything about that day that Laine thought he'd ever forget, no matter how much he might wish to. "Yeah, McAlister and Juarez were the first to arrive, why?"

"You ever been talking to one person and someone close by is listening intently but trying not to be obvious? I mean, you just *know* they're straining to hear every word?" Rich's eyes were gleaming, his excitement at having a suspect making him fidget enough that Laine started to feel twitchy as well.

"I think so," Matt finally offered when Laine only nodded.

He thought he knew where Rich was going with this, and the idea that the man could be right made it impossible for Laine to force words past the knot in his throat.

"That's how I felt the whole time I was talking to you, Laine. It was bad enough that I swear every hair on my body was damn near standing on end. I wrote down the information you gave me, and when we were done I asked Detective McAlister if he had any idea who I was on the phone with." Rich shuddered, his eyes darting around the room before meeting Laine's gaze. "You remember James McAlister? Well, he said he didn't know who I was talking to, but he *did*; and he had that look, so carefully blank but his eyes just... I always said it was a dead look, like there wasn't a soul behind those eyes, you remember, Laine?"

Laine didn't answer, his stomach had pitched as soon as Rich had said the other detective's name, and now, though neither of the two men in front of him had noticed yet, there was a distinct chill to the room. Laine knew that look, though, and he had no problem picturing Detective McAlister; the man was easily as big as Laine was, with pale skin and dark blond hair.

"I remember thinking he used to watch me, but I was pretty paranoid." Laine had worried that the man knew his secret, and that was why he watched Laine. "I worried he'd found out, and was going to say something. I wish he had, God damn it! I wish that was all he'd done." So many thoughts and emotions were pulsing through him that Laine couldn't seem to focus on any one. He was vaguely aware of the two men across from him muttering and rubbing their arms against the dropping temperature. "You going to tell me that McAlister is still in Houston?"

Rich scrubbed his arms harder and shook his head. "Nope. I came back later that day we first talked, and my notepad was gone, and McAlister's desk looked too neat and clean. Asked around the next day when the guy didn't show up for work, turns out he took an emergency leave of absence. That set off the rest of the alarms in my head. And with that file there that Matt gets to rewrite, I'm betting, though I wished to God I was wrong, that the son of a bitch has already found you — and Severo."

Laine had his cell phone out and was already punching in Zeke's number before Rich finished. He needed to let him know that they were all in danger now.

"Is it just me, or is it freezing in here?" Rich directed the question to Matt while Laine spoke in low, urgent tones on the phone.

Matt looked around the room, his eyes widening with a sudden insight. "Shit! This is what happened to Severo in his hotel room! Uh..." Matt felt the flush crawl up his neck. "Conner? Could you maybe back off a bit? We can't go after this fucker if we're Popsicles."

Rich started to say something snarky, Matt could see it in the man's expression. Then he noticed that the room had warmed, and he *still* said something snarky. "Well, lookie there, McKinton's got its own homegrown ghost whisperer. Maybe you'll get a show on SyFy."

Matt wanted to knock the jackass's teeth down his throat, or maybe ask Conner to freeze Montoya's balls at the very least, but Laine finished his call and smacked a hand on the desk. That was the *only* reason, Matt told himself, that he didn't kick Mr. Houston PD's stuck-up ass.

"Let's get moving. Matt, hurry up and fix that report. Call me as soon as it's done. We've got to get McAlister before he hurts anyone else."

It was on the tip of Matt's tongue to tell the sheriff the report could wait, but he saw that determined look in the man's eyes and nodded. He'd get the damned report fixed in record time. He had a feeling catching this son of a bitch was going to be harder than any of them suspected.

* * * *

He watched through binoculars as Detective Montoya walked out of the Sheriff's Department with Laine and felt a fury rising up inside that threatened to make him act rashly. Discovering Laine had a lover had nearly tipped him over the edge, but he was, in retrospect, glad he hadn't hurt the little fag—he wasn't the type to be savoured. When that burst of anger had died down, his path had seemed so clear. Let Laine worry that his lover was in danger. That would be a distraction that would make Laine vulnerable.

He wouldn't make the same mistake he had years ago, though. Laine's lover was safe, for now at least. This time, no one but Laine would do. And his former partner wasn't going to be able to do a thing to stop it.

So, Montoya thinks he's come to save the day. Not gonna happen, asshole. The Houston detective may have figured out who and what he was, but there was no proof, he'd made sure of that. Nothing incriminating would be found if his home or office was searched, no trophies or mementos from past conquests. He'd been meticulous when the need to satisfy his hunger had to be met. Three years he'd waited, finding poor substitutes for the man he really wanted, but he'd finally have Laine, and he'd take his time. When Laine Stenley gasped his last breath, he'd know without a doubt who he belonged to, who had stolen his soul and mastered his body.

I've learnt so much more in the past three years, and oh, Laine, I'm going to enjoy showing you the ways I can bring you so close to death and then pull you back. It will be good for me, and so bad for you – and it will be very soon, I promise.

Chapter Eleven

Sev tried not to hover as Zeke talked to Laine on the phone, but with every grunt from Zeke's lips, and the way the man's shoulders were tensing up, his frown deepening, Sev found himself drawn closer, though he tried not to be obvious about it. Brendon didn't even try to be subtle. He walked over to his partner and tipped his head towards the phone, his face scrunched up as he tried to hear what Laine was saying. Zeke reached for Brendon and pulled him close, rubbing Brendon's back as Zeke listened intently. Sev would have thought it sweet if he wasn't certain that the news Laine was imparting was bad, as in *deadly, dangerous bad.* It was hard to think happy thoughts when there was a psycho after you—or your lover. Zeke grunted again, then held the phone out to Sev.

"Here. He wants to talk to you." The twitch of Zeke's lips warned Sev the man was planning on doing some eavesdropping of his own. Well, it wasn't like they were going to have phone sex—not this time, anyway.

"Hey, Laine, are you okay?" Sev closed his eyes. God, he sounded like a wuss.

"Yeah, I just wanted to make sure everything was fine there." Laine's voice was a deep rumble that had Sev's cock twitching despite the worry pressing down on him.

"And what else? What's going on?"

"My former partner from Houston PD showed up. He thinks he knows who killed Conner, and why."

Sev's eyes popped open and he turned his back on the two men watching him. "You're not going to try to find him, are you? You're going to call for backup or whatever it is you do, right?"

A weary sigh drifted through the phone. "We don't have any proof, Sev, just Rich's gut feeling and some…things that have happened that seem like more than coincidences. Those aren't things we can turn in as evidence."

"What things have happened? What is it that you don't want to tell me?"

"Sev, you don't need to know the sick things this guy has been doing—"

Sev squeezed the phone so hard he was surprised it didn't break. "You listen to me, Laine. I am *not* your little woman! I don't need to be protected or coddled or any of that shit! If you think that son of a bitch is here, then you better tell me what's going on, or I will walk out of this house and—" Sev jerked the phone away from his ear, smiling as he did so. Laine could roar like a damn lion all he wanted, and cuss until he was blue in the face, but Sev wasn't giving, not on this. Zeke started to grab for the phone but Sev spun away and pointed a finger at him.

"You touch this phone before I'm done, and you will regret it, Zeke." Sev kept his finger aimed at Zeke until he took two steps back, then he brought the phone back to his ear. "Are you done throwing a fit now? Ready to act like an adult?"

"Sev, I swear, if you don't stop goading me…"

"What? You'll yell some more? Keep it up and I'll yell back, and then we'll be in a hell of a mess, won't we?"

Sev could hear Laine whispering to someone else, heard a muffled reply before Laine spoke to the other man again. Guess he had to get the okay from his partner to speak. The idea pissed Sev off.

"Did you get permission to speak?" Sev practically purred the question, feeling provoked and hurt that Laine didn't trust him. Maybe he was the only one who felt like this was *more* between them, that this was *it*. The Big One. The Only One. Maybe he hadn't seen what he'd thought he had in Laine's eyes, felt it in his touch—

"I wasn't getting permission, I was getting my ass chewed for being a—

"Boneheaded dipshit."

Sev could make out the words clearly. Laine's former partner had a very sexy voice that carried well, and he enunciated the words with a dramatic flair that made Sev smile despite his pique.

"Yeah. That. What Rich said." Laine's amusement died as fast as it flared. "There have been four murders in Houston, gay men that Rich says resemble me enough that they could be related. He—and I agree—doesn't think it's a coincidence, and neither is the fact that one of the police officers I worked with in Houston, the first to arrive on the scene of Conner's death, took emergency leave right after I called Rich."

Sev felt like he'd swallowed dry ice, his body chilled and burning at the same time. "A cop? You think the killer is a cop?" He couldn't say why that scared him so much more than if the guy were just some clerk or janitor, but it did.

"Maybe he really did have a family emergency; maybe his grandma died or—"

"Sev. No. It fits, okay? The guy used to watch me all the time, but I thought he was suspicious about my…me being gay. The fact that he took off after I called Rich fits, too, and when you add in all the times Conner's sent my star into a spinning frenzy… He was trying to tell me all along."

"Jesus Christ." It did fit, all of it. Sev could feel it in his bones as surely as he felt that he and Laine fit. The comparison was too close to a bastardisation of what Sev knew was in his heart for Laine, and he pushed it away. "I see it. What are you going to do?"

"Matt—Deputy Nixon—is going to finish up the report from yesterday, then he'll meet Rich and me at the scene from yesterday. We're going to walk it, try to figure out exactly how McAlister managed to get away, then see where to go from there. We might not learn anything new, but it'll be good for Rich to get a look at the crime scene. I also told Matt to fax a picture of McAlister over to Zeke so y'all would know what he looks like. I want you to study that picture until you're sure you would know him no matter how he might try to disguise himself, okay?"

Sev had never been so afraid in his life, but he buried it, unwilling to add to Laine's burdens. "I will, I promise. And tonight, when you get back, I'm going to—"

A strangled sound from across the room shut Sev up. Ears burning with the heat of his embarrassment, he found Brendon and Zeke both smirking at him. Brendon started making gestures, bringing his hand to his mouth repeatedly like he was—

"You're going to what?" Laine's voice was barely a whisper, but Sev had no desire to entertain Zeke, Brendon, or Rich. What he had to say was for Laine's ears alone.

"I, ah, forgot I had an audience," Sev admitted, smiling despite himself when Laine laughed. "I think one of said audience wants you to bring Rich—"

Brendon bobbed his head and held up three fingers. Sev looked at him with his best 'what the hell' expression.

"Matt. Tell him to bring Deputy Nixon, too," Brendon clarified. Sev made a note not to ever play charades with the man; he sucked at nonverbal messages—well, except for the sexual ones.

"And Deputy Nixon. He wants to invite them over for dinner." *And then I'll get you alone and tell you how I'm going to rock your world, baby.* Sev's prick was all for that idea, trying to fill up and embarrass him even more in front of Zeke and Brendon. Sev turned his back on the men again.

Laine's laughter brought Sev's prick to attention. "That should be, uhm, entertaining, to say the least, but tell him I'll bring them even if I have to cuff 'em and drag 'em in."

"Entertaining?" Sev felt his forehead scrunch as he thought about what Laine meant. "Do they not get along or something?"

"Or something." Laine laughed again and murmured something to Rich. "We'll be there after we finish at my place and get Rich a room. You be careful, all right?"

The way Laine's voice had went warm and low there at the end had Sev feeling like he'd drunk a bottle of champagne. Light and bubbly, and a little woozy as well.

"I will. You, too." Sev disconnected the call and peered over his shoulder at Zeke and Brendon. He wasn't going to turn around until his erection was under control; as hard as he was, that could take a while.

"Here." Sev tossed the phone to Brendon and, in what he considered a very mature manner, ignored the laughter from the two men. "I think I'll just go lay down for a while."

Their laughter echoed down the hall as Sev headed to the guest room, tempting him to laugh at himself, too. Then he thought of Laine, and the police officer who had stalked him, obsessed about him for years, and Sev discovered that he didn't need to go wait for his hard on to abate. It withered immediately as fear chased off his good mood.

* * * *

Once Rich had stowed his bags in the hotel room, Laine led the way to Zeke and Brendon's, Rich behind him in his sporty little car — Laine had warned him that car might get beat to pieces, but Rich insisted on driving himself — and Matt pulling up the rear in his truck behind them both. He wasn't surprised that they hadn't found anything new today, other than what they thought was McAlister's escape route. It could have been a deer trail. Tracking wasn't one of Laine's talents, and Rich and Matt didn't fare any better at it, either. McAlister had either covered his tracks with a skill Laine lacked, or he'd taken a different path away from the house.

A conversation he'd had with Rich before Matt had shown up kept niggling at Laine's brain. It was a little thing, and didn't have anything to do with McAlister, but it puzzled Laine nonetheless. He'd wondered about something Rich had said and finally worked up the nerve to ask him about it.

"How'd you know?"

Rich looked up at Laine's question, puzzled since it came out of nowhere.

"How'd I know… what?"

"You said you knew about me and Conner before he was murdered." Laine watched Rich's cheeks darken, his gaze turning from Laine to stare off in the direction of a clump of scrub. Rich tucked his hands into the pockets of his slacks and studied the ground, toeing a rock like a nervous kid before finally answering.

"I just did. I saw y'all out once, at a Rockets game." Rich shook his head. "There wasn't anything obvious, really, I just knew. And when Conner... Jesus, Laine, I'd have had to be blind to miss the pain in your eyes. I never heard a whisper of a rumour, but I knew." Rich turned, and Laine wished he could read the man as well as Rich had read him. "I wish you had told me. You could have, you know."

The conversation seemed almost surreal, and it bothered Laine that he felt like he was missing something there. He thought about Rich's expression, the look in his eyes and felt a flicker of guilt. Rich was trying to tell him something, and Laine wasn't sure he wanted to hear it.

Or maybe he was letting his imagination run away with him. Laine puzzled over it until he pulled into the bumpy drive leading to Zeke's place. As soon as he saw Sev standing on the porch, sandwiched between the two bigger men, everything else faded into the background. He'd worried that he'd feel awkward with Rich and Matt being around his lover for the first time, worried that he might not be able to keep from reverting to the stoic, private man he had been.

Yet as soon as Laine saw Sev, he knew Sev was the most important thing in his life, and he wouldn't be able to pretend otherwise, ever. The smile on his lover's face was enough to do that, and the sweet look in his big, beautiful eyes had Laine's heart filling to overflowing. Laine got out of his truck and hadn't taken two steps before he had one sexy, hard man leaping at him, arms wrapped around his neck and lips pressed to Laine's. Nothing had ever felt so perfect before, and Laine knew he'd fight with everything in him to keep this feeling and this man for the rest of his days.

* * * *

"That was...an experience." Sev stood on the porch with Laine, Zeke and Brendon having gone back inside after Rich and Matt left. Saying dinner was an experience was being polite. Rich and Matt had bickered and sniped at each other throughout their meal. Once, Sev had thought they would come to blows when Rich made a comment about Matt tampering with reports, but Laine had calmly and authoritatively shut both men down. Sev had been sporting a decent hard on ever since.

Laine's gaze seemed to be riveted to the taillights of the departing vehicles. "Yup. Those two remind me of a couple of tomcats chunked in a pillowcase together. Guess they just rub each other the wrong way." Laine paused, one big hand massaging the small of Sev's back. "I'll admit, I was worried about how they'd handle seeing you, knowing..." He shrugged and chuckled softly. "Other than a few curious looks, Rich and Matt didn't seem to care. Gives me hope that maybe me being gay won't be so hard for everyone else to accept."

"Mmm." Sev was afraid it wouldn't be that easy, but the other two men had seemed happy for Laine more than anything else. "Maybe, though I suspect there will be some people who aren't quite so open-minded." Sev slid his hand around to the back of Laine's belt and fingered the spot where Laine's handcuffs had been dangling earlier. He'd had all day to plan, but now he had Laine alone, Sev couldn't quell the fear that he might be overstepping his boundaries with this man. Or blowing those boundaries into a million pieces. He stepped in front of Laine and pressed up against him, writhing before he could stop himself. Laine's attention shifted from the taillights to Sev, arms wrapping around Sev's lower back. His eyes dilated rapidly so that only a fine ring of silver showed as he focused on Sev.

"Do you trust me?" Sev breathed the words against Laine's lips, the fingers of one hand still toying with the back of Laine's belt. Laine stilled, his big body tensing as he looked down at Sev. A trickle of fear slithered up Sev's spine; maybe he shouldn't have asked. He might not like the answer. *Don't ask questions you might not want to hear the answer to, remember that in the future.*

The edges of Laine's lips tipped up and he nudged his cock against Sev's belly. "Yes."

One word, three letters, yet it held so much power and promise. Sev cupped the back of Laine's neck with one hand and pulled him down for the kiss Sev needed more than his next breath. He licked Laine's lips, slipping his tongue inside when Laine opened for him, just opened, handing over control of the kiss to Sev. A shudder shook them both as Sev's tongue stroked over the roof of Laine's mouth, then twined and slid against Laine's. Sev explored every inch of his lover's mouth, every tooth and hollow as he pressed into Laine. Laine's arms tightened around him, lifting and holding him so close Sev could feel Laine's heartbeat, the pulse of his cock. Sev gentled the kiss and nipped Laine's lower lip before turning his head away just enough to speak.

"Let me?" Sev didn't want to explain what he wanted, or why he needed Laine's agreement without an explanation. He hoped, yet still was surprised when Laine didn't hesitate.

"Yes." There it was again, that one, small, powerful word. Sev pushed and Laine loosened his grip, allowing Sev to take one of his thick wrists and lead them both inside. He thought Zeke and Brendon might have said something as they walked by the living room, but Sev didn't notice. Right now, he couldn't think about anything other than Laine's implicit trust and what, exactly, it could mean that Laine didn't hesitate to hand over control to him.

Once they were in the guest room, Sev positioned Laine beside the bed then walked back to shut and lock their door. He turned and met Laine's gaze, the need and trust in those dark eyes nearly knocking Sev on his butt. How could a look make him weak, yet fill him with a rush of power at the same time?

Sev tucked his hands behind his back and leant against the door, soaking in every detail of his lover. From the tips of his booted feet to the top of his thick dark hair, the man was pure perfection. Long, muscled legs, lean hips, tight, taut abs and chiselled chest—and broad, strong shoulders that could carry responsibilities too many other people would shirk.

By the time Sev watched the pulse pounding in his lover's corded neck, his hands were itching to touch. He strode over to Laine and tugged on the hem of Laine's t-shirt, humming his approval when Laine reached for the edge and pulled the shirt off, tossing it aside. Sev ran his hands over the expanse of bare skin, revelling in the hard muscles and light smattering of hair that tickled his palms. It seemed that everywhere he stroked was followed by a twitch of the flesh under his hands as Laine's breaths became shaky.

Sev flicked his tongue over a taut nipple, grunting and pushing Laine's hands away when he would have held

Sev to him. Laine let his hands drop to his sides as Sev sucked the hard bud into his mouth, his teeth scraping over the tasty bit again and again. Sev licked his way to the other nipple, bringing a hand up to continue the sensual onslaught he'd begun on the first nipple. The shudder that ripped through Laine almost dislodged Sev from the nub of flesh he was tonguing, so he bit down, pinching the other nipple with his fingers, rolling it hard between his thumb and forefinger.

A raspy groan was torn from Laine, his hips thrusting to grind against Sev in a display of need that filled him with a sense of power. That he could do this to his big strong lover, could reduce him to a shuddering, moaning mass of need with a few touches, was a heady realisation that threatened to demolish Sev's plans in favour of finding immediate release.

And that would *not* do. Laine may very well trust him—Sev was almost certain he did—but Sev was smart enough to know that control was vital to Laine and not something he'd hand over with any sort of regularity. If he didn't act on Laine's capitulation now, he might not get another chance for a long while.

Sev stepped back, admiring the saliva-slicked nipples, so hard and dark from Sev's attentions. He trailed a finger down the soft fuzz bisecting Laine's abs, smiling when Laine sucked in a breath as though the slight touch carried an electrical current. When his finger brushed over the button at Laine's waistband, Sev popped the button open then shoved Laine back on the bed.

The big man went down without a fight, flopping fully onto his back with a bounce that sent the springs to squeaking. Sev knelt and removed Laine's boots and socks, setting them off to the side. He let his fingers linger over one foot, then the other, tracing the high arch before cupping the heel and rubbing his cheek against Laine's denim clad calf. Sev had an urge to rub all over the man, which struck him as funny once he realised he wanted to leave his scent on his lover like some wild animal marking its territory.

Sev reached up and unzipped Laine's jeans, tapping his thigh so Laine lifted his hips. The jeans and boxer briefs were tossed to the floor, and Sev's kneeling position gave him a view that had his prick leaking precome. Sev pushed Laine's thighs farther apart, then stared at the fat cock and heavy balls that were only inches from his face. The dark, wrinkled skin of Laine's sac kept drawing Sev's gaze; he finally braced his hands on Laine's upper thighs and leant forward, tonguing the furry globes.

The musky scent of his lover filled Sev, and Laine's moans spurred him on. Sev sucked one nut into his mouth, pulling gently and rolling his tongue over the orb. Laine's thighs trembled then tightened under his hands and Sev hummed, knowing the vibrations would send bursts of heat throughout his lover's body. Laine bucked, his ass rising off the bed as he moaned, fists twisting in the sheets.

"Sev, shit!"

It was more of a gasp than a plea, but Sev would get him there. Sev gave Laine's balls a last lick then pushed himself up. He took a minute to appreciate the beautiful display of Laine spread out before him, his big cockhead glistening with moisture, a string of precome bridging the gap from crown to stomach. Laine's hands were clenched tightly around fistfuls of sheets, the veins in his arms and neck standing out. Breath coming in pants, Laine lips were parted, his eyes almost closed as he stared back at Sev.

Sev scrubbed the heel of his hand over his prick, aching with the need to gorge on his lover. He forced himself to take a step back, then another.

"Move to the centere of the bed." Sev freed his prick with a flick of his fingers. "Put your arms over your head and grab the headboard." He waited until Laine complied, enjoying the smooth glide of muscles as the man followed Sev's orders. Once Laine was in place, Sev removed his own clothes then walked over to the dresser, feeling Laine's gaze on him, and picked up Laine's handcuffs before turning back to face his lover.

Laine's eyes flared open as a flush spread over his chest and up to his cheeks. The sound he made as he sucked in air went straight to Sev's balls and he arched a brow in surprise. He'd thought Laine was just giving him this, maybe as a way to prove that he did trust Sev. Looking at Laine, watching him tremble, his chest rising and falling with rapid breaths, his cock bobbing and his eyes blazing, Sev realised that this was more than just something Laine was doing for him. Laine wanted this, maybe even needed it—and he was for damn sure getting off on it.

Sev reached down and squeezed the base of his cock, afraid he'd shoot before he ever got the cuffs on Laine. The move wasn't lost on the bigger man, his lips curling up on one side in a heart-stopping grin. Sev gave him a narrow-eyed look, then let go of his prick and sauntered back to the bed, smiling himself when Laine's grin faltered, his gaze locking on to Sev's cock.

"Damn, Sheriff, you look so fucking sexy." Sev crawled onto the bed and straddled Laine's hips, moaning when he leant forward and their cocks brushed together. He made himself focus on his plan rather than the desire to grind against Laine as he reached above Laine's head for his wrists. Sev couldn't resist the offer of those parted lips, though, and stopped shimmying up the hard body underneath him to devour Laine's mouth, claiming him with tongue and teeth. Laine's fingers buried in his hair snapped Sev out of the kiss and he sat up, slapping a cuff around the offending wrist and pulling it back up above Laine's head.

"I don't think so." Sev meant to sound firm, but it came out more of a purr that flooded Laine's eyes with need. Sev wound the empty cuff and chain through the slat in the headboard, then snapped it around Laine's other wrist. He stroked his hands down Laine's forearms to his biceps, then over his shoulders.

"Look at you, Laine. God, you have no idea..." *Sev* certainly hadn't had any idea, but the image of his lover cuffed to the bed was giving him thousands now.

Laine arched his back and squirmed, his legs shifting behind Sev. "Sev—"

Sev scooted back until Laine's cock was rubbing against his hole. At first contact of his thick cock head against Sev's opening, Laine's arms jerked, rattling the headboard.

"Sev—"

Sev rocked against the hard flesh, the copious amount of precome making a slick path in the crease of his ass.

"Sev." Laine's voice was strained, strung tight. "I need-"

"I know what you need." Sev slithered farther down Laine's body, then sucked his cock down deep as Laine bucked and yelled, thrusting into Sev's throat. One hand circled the base of Laine's cock, the other held his balls, tugging them away from Laine's body. Sev wanted to tease, to slick a finger and slide it into Laine's tight hole, but they were both too on edge. He bobbed his head, tongue swirling around the shaft in his mouth, teasing the underside of the crown as the handcuffs rattled and the headboard jostled and thunked the wall. He glanced up to see the cuffs biting hard into Laine's wrists, his lover straining as he writhed on the bed. Sev pulled off Laine's cock with a lascivious slurping sound, releasing his grasp with his hands as well.

"Laine, you're going to hurt yourself." Sev's stomach pitched as he saw the deep red marks on his lover's wrists. He'd intended to play, not hurt the man! "Let me get the key before—"

"No!" Laine's harsh command stopped Sev before he got off the bed. "You fucking finish this, Sev. Now!"

"But—" Sev shut up when he flicked a glance at Laine; there was no sign of pain, only the same clawing need that Sev felt. The fact that Laine had just snatched back the control with his snarled demand didn't bother Sev once he realised Laine was hurting in the best way possible. Sev leant across to the nightstand and grabbed the lube and a condom. He popped the top open on the lube and slicked a light coating over Laine's cock before ripping open the condom package and rolling it down the hard length. Another dollop of lube, spread over the condom, then Sev coated the fingers of both hands. One trailed down, over Laine's balls and lower still until he traced the wrinkled ring of Laine's hole.

He checked and saw Laine sucking on his lower lip, the flush still high on his chest and cheeks. Sev teased the puckered opening, pressing and rubbing until the tip of his finger slipped in. Laine drew his legs up, bending them at the knee until his heels rested by his ass cheeks. Taking the move for the request that it was, Sev spread his own knees and reached behind himself, working two fingers into his hole as he penetrated Laine deeper with his other hand.

The sounds coming from Laine were twisting Sev's guts with the need to fuck; the tight clench of Laine's ring around his finger was stealing Sev's ability to think. Sev pumped his fingers into his own ass as he carefully pushed another digit into Laine. The resultant yell from Laine as well as an ominous popping sound from the headboard told Sev it was enough, yet not. He slipped his fingers free from Laine first, then himself, and pushed Laine's legs down.

"Sev, please..." God, could Laine's voice sound any more raw?

"Just sit back, I've got you." Sev lined Laine's cock up to his hole and bore down, his back arching as he took the big cock into his ass. Sev ran his hands over his chest, pinching his nipples, knowing the image would drive Laine wild, shatter his control, and that's what Sev wanted.

Knees spread, Sev rode Laine slowly, his inner muscles clamping down, trying to keep Laine's thick length buried deep inside. Pleasure coursed from Sev's channel to his balls, then coiled in his stomach as he slid back down, the crinkly hairs surrounding Laine's cock rubbing against Sev's ass. He kept the rhythm deep and easy, almost rocking until Laine whimpered. The sound shot straight to Sev's prick which spurted out a warning.

"Now." Sev arched his neck, pushing down to take that big cock inside again.

"Yesss." Laine hissed the word as Sev's ass swallowed Laine's dick. Laine pulled against the cuffs, his own neck arching until only his shoulders and the crown of his head rested on the pillows. "Sev, God, please..."

Sev hadn't known how much he wanted to hear Laine beg until it happened. With a throaty groan, he fell forward, arms braced on Laine's shoulders, and began riding his lover hard and fast. Sweat slicked their skin, making for a slippery ride as Sev's hands lost their grip more than once. Laine bent his legs, the position providing him with the ability to thrust harder. Sev's eyes rolled back in his head as Laine's hip bones slammed against Sev's ass, driving Laine's cock in deep. It was unlike anything he'd ever imagined, raw and rough—and perfect.

Thighs burning from the strain, Sev took Laine again and again, fuelled by his lover's coarse words and breaths, his own burning need. His passage rippled around Laine's length, squeezing and clamping so tight Sev couldn't move as come spewed from his prick. The sight of the first creamy rope on Laine's neck short-circuited Sev's brain. All he could do was *feel* the pulsing in his ass, the swelling of Laine's cock as his lover shouted, eyes wide instead of closing. Another burst of spunk hit Laine's chest, an answering throb from Laine's dick inside Sev, and Sev felt his vision dim. It seemed that he came and came, each jet of seed matched by the shaft in his body, and when it finally stopped, Sev found himself collapsed on Laine's chest, his body trembling as he gasped for air.

The rattle of metal on wood registered in the recesses of Sev's mind, and he pushed himself up on shaky arms. Laine's eyes were closed, his chest heaving and his lips parted—

"Oh God. Laine, your wrists... " Sev was up and moving, at least having enough forethought to grab the base of the condom before he dismounted from Laine's cock. He pulled the condom off, tied it and tossed it in the small trashcan by the dresser. Sev found the key for the cuffs and hurried back to the bed, his hands shaking when he saw the red marks on Laine's wrists.

"Laine, I didn't mean for you to be hurt. Fuck." Sev's throat tightened until the last word came out as a squeak. He unlocked the cuffs and reached for Laine's arms and quickly found himself on his back, held tight as Laine stole whatever words Sev had intended to speak with a bruising kiss. Something hot and wet tickled his temples, but it wasn't until Laine drew back and pressed soft kisses from the corners of his eyes, tracing the wet paths there, that Sev realised what had happened. He squeezed his eyes shut, mortified at being such a pussy, wishing he'd never cuffed Laine in the first place. What was he trying to prove, anyway?

"Hey, Sev." Laine nudged Sev, rubbing his cheek against Sev's before raising his head. "Open your eyes."

Feeling ten kinds of a fool, Sev pried his eyes open, the tender expression from Laine greeting him.

"You stop feeling bad, okay? There's no call for it."

Sev tried to turn, tried to get a look at either of Laine's wrists, only to have Laine's hands frame his face and force him to meet his lover's eyes. "I...I didn't think, should have padded the cuffs or something, not used the damned things to be—"

Laine's laughter cut Sev off. "Oh honey, you didn't do anything wrong, though I'll concede that maybe next time we should wrap my wrists first."

Next time? Holy fuck! And honey? Sev's mind spun with the promise of a next time and the endearment as Laine continued.

"You did everything exactly right, blew my damn mind. I can promise you, I did not feel the least bit of pain while you were fucking my brains out—or when you were doing anything else to torment me before you finally let me into your tight ass."

Sev's eyes nearly bugged out as he watched Laine's mouth speaking those words. It was as if the bit of bondage had freed something inside his lover, and the words the man was speaking were sending Sev's blood flow back to his prick as Laine's verbal seduction, intentional or not, stroked over Sev.

"And when you did seat yourself on my dick and ride me, I swear to God, I felt it from the tip of my cock to my toes and the top of my head, and everywhere in between. I've never—" Laine leant down and planted a series of kisses along Sev's cheek, "ever, felt anything like that before. So, there's some marks on my wrists, and every time I see them, you know what's gonna happen?'

"I... Maybe?"

"You do, I can tell by the way your prick is hard and pressing into me, and by the way your skin is heating, darkening on your cheeks." Laine's grin was doing all sorts of things to Sev, burning him in ways he couldn't begin to describe. "So tell me."

The press of a thick cock against inner thigh prodded Sev to answer. "You're going to get hard." Laine's hips pumped and he pressed the head of his cock to Sev's hole. "You're going to think about fucking me, fast and hard, me riding you until you scream."

Laine closed his eyes and groaned, his head of his prick spreading Sev, pushing but not quite entering fully. Sev could feel the heat of Laine's cock, wanted to feel every bulge, every vein—

"Laine." God, Sev didn't want to say anything, wanted to feel every bit of his lover, feel him shoot deep inside. "Laine, condom?"

"Mmm." Laine stilled, not pushing any farther. Sev was glad Laine had the sense to stop. He wouldn't have been able to say no if Laine had wanted to fuck him raw. "Let's take this to the shower. You grab those." He gestured to the nightstand where the condoms and lube were kept. "I can tell you I'm negative, and I told you earlier that I trust you."

Laine pushed himself up and crawled over Sev to the edge of the bed. He stood and smiled down at Sev. "Come on, let's get wet." Then he turned and headed to the guest bathroom, leaving Sev to wonder if that had been an offer or what.

While he had always practiced safe sex, and he believed Laine, Sev would never take a chance of hurting his lover again. He might be inexperienced at relationships, but even he knew you don't want to put the man you love at risk. Sev grabbed a condom and the lube, wondering at how easy it was to let oneself love the right person, and padded after Laine.

Chapter Twelve

Laine slipped out of bed, careful not to disturb Sev as he did so. The man was curled on his side, one hand tucked under his chin, the other clutching a pillow to his chest. He was tempted to wake him, to spend hours making love until they were both too exhausted to move, but, more than he wanted to sate them both, Laine wanted Sev safe. Thinking about finding Sev's body butchered and violated as Conner's had been was unbearable. It might very well kill him; it would definitely crush his soul.

The strength of what he felt for Sev was awe-inspiring, and he knew it for the precious gift it was. Laine quietly gathered his clothes and boots, along with his gear and, with a last look at the man he loved, opened the door and stepped into the hallway. He dressed quickly, uncaring of the fact that Zeke or Brendon might find him, but needing to find McAlister and put the man away. Laine had just buckled his belt and was tugging on a boot when Zeke appeared in the hallway.

"You sneaking out or something?"

Laine finished putting on his boots and gestured for Zeke to follow him into the living room before he answered. "Or something. Sev doesn't need to be worrying, and he will. Better to let him sleep."

Zeke looked at him like he was an oar short of a pair. "Don't you think he ought to be able to decide that for himself? Brendon would be pissed if I did what you're doing."

"Brendon would kick your ass, babe." The man himself stepped into the room and pointed at Laine. "And I will help Sev kick yours, if he needs my help, when you get back."

Laine nodded. "Okay. As long as he's safe, and I get back, he can do whatever he wants."

Zeke looked Brendon with astonishment. "You're taking his side? Even though if I did it—"

Brendon shushed him with a hand gesture. "But it's not you, and I *know* why Laine feels he has to do this. Why he has to keep Sev safe." Brendon pinned Laine with his big brown eyes, and Laine nodded again. Brendon got it. Laine picked up his Stetson from the hutch and put it on.

"So what makes it okay, then?" Zeke sounded confused, and a little exasperated.

"I'll check in off and on," Laine informed them as he opened the door.

"You do that," came from Zeke, with Brendon chiming in, "Of course you will."

"Now, Zeke, how would you feel if a psycho had killed your lover years ago, and was back, and you'd just found the love of your life?" Laine heard Brendon explain as he shut the door.

Yep, Brendon got it.

* * * *

Matt snagged his cell phone out of its belt clip as he pulled into his usual parking spot, not even checking the number, knowing intuitively it would be his boss.

"Morning Sheriff."

"Yeah. Matt, where are you?"

"In the parking lot at work, why? Something wrong?" No one was late yet…

"I don't know. I can't get hold of Rich, his cell is going straight to voicemail and no one is answering the phone in his room. Might be nothing, he could be at the café, or… Shit. Can you go check? You can get there before me."

An icy dread had settled over Matt. He tried to tell himself he was a melodramatic idiot, but he couldn't shake it as he shifted into reverse and turned around, heading for the hotel. "Well, he's a city boy, maybe he— I just passed the café, his car isn't there." And that bad feeling was growing, weighing on Matt until he wondered how he could breathe.

"Shit. Matt, I don't like this. No matter what you think, Rich is a smart cop. He wouldn't turn his phone off or let the battery die, and he wouldn't do anything else irresponsible. You two may hate each other, but he's—"

Matt's gut clenched hard as he pulled in at the hotel. "I know, I do. We're just different. Fuck, Laine," Matt dropped the title, propriety be damned. "His car isn't here, either." Matt unbuckled and opened the door, shutting it quietly behind him.

"You stay right there. I'll be there in under ten minutes. I'm going to hang up and keep trying Rich's cell. You try the room number. I'll text it to you."

"I got it. I followed Rich back last night and made sure he had my numbers and yours, and vice versa." He hadn't wanted to admit doing so. It might give Laine the wrong idea, like that Matt and Rich would ever get along. They wouldn't. Matt had only followed Rich back because it occurred to him, belatedly, that they should have one another's cell numbers in case of an emergency. That was all there had been to it.

"Good, that's good. Wait for me there—and don't go near his room."

Matt grunted and hung up, one hand raised to bang on Rich's door. Well, he was already here before he was told any different, so...what the heck. Maybe he'd wake Rich up, and they'd laugh about it later.

The door whipped open and Matt was jerked inside. The door was kicked closed and his arm wrenched around his back. He was spun and his face slammed into the door with enough force that he saw a brilliant explosion of stars. He realised that his gun had been stripped away, then his face met the door again, knocking the colours away and filling his vision with a dimming grey. Before he could even hope to orient himself, Matt was turned around again to face his attacker. A sharp pain ripped through his stomach, up towards his chest, and he tried to scream through the hand clamped over his mouth.

"Shut up, you God damned pussy, you won't die from that...yet."

Matt blinked, trying to clear his vision, then wished he hadn't. *McAlister. Oh God, Rich!* The face peering at him was devoid of emotion, and the eyes... Matt wanted to look away, look anywhere but at this man, but the hand clamped over his mouth kept him from turning away.

"Now, I know that Sheriff Stenley is on his way, you were loud enough to wake the dead." McAlister laughed and brought a hand covered in Matt's blood to Matt's cheek. "You're going to give him a message for me."

Those dead eyes drilled into Matt's. "You tell him I've had hours to play with his former partner."

Matt started to gag, feeling the bile rise up. He'd seen the pictures of Conner. If McAlister really did have Rich, the man would surely be dead — or wishing he were.

"You tell him he's got fifteen minutes to get to where he needs to be, and if he doesn't make it… Well, Rich is still alive. He's got more fight in him than I would have thought. But if Laine is one second late, or brings anyone else, I will put Rich out of his misery. Who knows…" McAlister leant forward, his hand slipping from Matt's face to cup his chin in a bruising hold. "I might just kill the fucker anyway." He bit Matt's bottom lip, tugging until the skin gave and blood gushed down Matt's chin.

"Good boy." McAlister tossed Matt to the floor, smiling as he threw a hard kick into the knife wound he'd given Matt. Matt curled up into himself as much as he could, fighting the agonising pain that ripped through him as he moved. He heard the door open and close and tried to focus, his thoughts a swarming mass of fear for Rich and himself. Laine's anger would be justified. Matt knew he'd been stupid, had walked right into McAlister's hands. He fumbled for his phone, one hand clutched to his stomach, trying not to panic over the blood he could feel seeping out steadily.

If he died, it would be his own fault for being such a cocky son of a bitch, but he couldn't let that sick fucker kill Laine, and maybe, if he hurried, Rich might make it. Matt got the menu open and hit Laine's number, grimacing at the busy signal. Laine must have been dialing out at the same time. Matt disconnected and tried again, hoping he could stay conscious long enough to warn him.

Laine hit the end button on his cell phone and nearly dropped it when it rang immediately. He saw Matt's number and felt a moment's hope that Rich had shown up at the hotel.

"Is Rich there?"

A pain-filled moan had Laine's hand tightening on the steering wheel. "Matt? What's wrong?"

The answer turned Laine's blood to ice. "He has Rich, said he's had hours to play with him—"

"God damn it!" Laine's stomach clenched and he laid the gas petal to the floorboard. "Matt! Matt!"

"Said you have fifteen minutes to…" Matt grunted, then groaned. A bolt of panic shot through Laine, followed by an eerie sense of calm as the star popped off of his shirt. "Get to where you need to be, alone. Or Rich dies. You gotta…"

Laine didn't have a doubt where McAlister meant, and knowing the sick bastard had been going at Rich for hours, in Laine's house… "Matt. What did he do to you? What happened?"

Harsh breathing was the only answer he received for several seconds before he heard the faint reply. Knowing his deputy was lying in an empty hotel room, bleeding out from a stab wound chased the ice out of Laine's blood and replaced it with a burning anger. He would kill McAlister—fuck the man ever going to trial.

"Matt, I'm going to hang up and call nine-one-one. You just stay calm. I'll get Rich out alive, I promise." *Or die trying. And if I go, I'm taking that fucker with me straight to Hell.* Laine didn't wait for Matt's agreement, hanging up and placing the emergency call immediately instead. He finished that call and tossed his phone down on the seat, watching from his peripheral vision as the tin star continued to spin.

"What good is that doing, Conner?" Laine snapped, tired of the senseless game, and feeling strangely bereft when the star stilled, then slid to the floorboard. "He has Rich, Conner, and Matt is… God, Matt may die, and you're spinning that damn star! *I know who it is now!*"

Laine took the turn to his house so fast that his truck nearly flipped. If McAlister had left the hotel right before Matt called, then Laine couldn't be too far behind him. Sure enough, once the dust cleared, Laine saw a man getting out of an SUV in his drive. Rich's little car was pulled off to the side, the tires flat.

McAlister ran up the steps into the house. Laine had a fleeting thought of ploughing his truck into the house and running McAlister down but put it aside to the foolish notion that it was. He roared down the drive, braking hard and sideswiping McAlister's SUV in the process. Then Laine threw the gear in park, shut the engine off, got out and tossed his keys into the scrub. If he didn't make it out, he'd be damned if McAlister would have an easy escape. Laine's truck had the SUV pinned in neatly, and his keys wouldn't be easy for anyone else to find.

The kitchen door swung open before Laine had even stepped away from his truck. McAlister stood in the doorway, gun trained on Laine's chest as he tipped his head towards the vehicles.

"Well, aren't you smart? Toss your gun."

Laine did, seeing no alternative, then McAlister fired and pain ripped through Laine's shoulder, and he wondered if he should have pinned that damned star back on as he stumbled and his knees hit the ground. *Shit! I didn't see that coming!*

"I figured you had all that righteous indignation behind you, you know." McAlister shrugged one shoulder. "Since I killed Conner and gutted him like a hog. And Rich, well, that boy's a mess, let me tell you. Your deputy, though, he might make it, if he gets help fast enough." He aimed the gun at Laine's head and nodded. "Now, get the fuck up. That didn't do anything other than hurt you. If you don't get your ass in this house in the next minute, I'll put a bullet between your eyes, then make sure Rich dies as painfully as possible."

* * * *

Sev heard the phone ring and the low rumble of Brendon's voice as he answered, then he was yelling for Zeke and Sev. Sev ran from the kitchen, Zeke hard on his heels, nearly toppling them both when Sev skidded to a halt in front of Brendon. The man's brown eyes looked haunted, his skin pale and worry etched into his handsome features.

"That was Matt," Brendon began before Sev or Zeke could ask. "McAlister has Rich, has had him for hours, if I heard right."

"What do you mean, if you heard right?"

Brendon darted a glance at Sev before answering his partner. "Matt was…in and out of consciousness. He said McAlister had stabbed him, and told him to tell Laine to meet him, but Matt didn't know where." Brendon and Zeke both turned to Sev as a sweet scent filled the air.

Sev ignored the presence, racking his brain, trying to figure out where McAlister would want Laine to meet him. He could only think of one place.

"His house, has to be. How long ago was that?" Sev was already heading for the door, only to find himself jerked back when Zeke grabbed his arm. "What the fuck? Let's go!"

"You need to stay here with Brendon while —"

Brendon slapped a hand to Zeke's chest and shoved. "I don't think so! This lunatic has taken out a detective and a deputy, and now he may very well have Laine! There's no way you're going alone, so forget that!"

"But—" Zeke sighed and pointed to the gun cabinet. "Grab a weapon and let's go. Sev, you know how to shoot?"

Sev nearly rolled his eyes as he followed Brendon to grab a gun. "I'm a native Texan, don't we all?" Hopefully, he still remembered how. It had been years, but if Laine's life depended on it—or any of their friends' lives depended on it—Sev knew he'd do whatever was necessary. He chose his rifle, taking the box of shells Brendon handed him. "Let's go."

* * * *

Laine pushed up from the ground and stumbled through the door, one hand pressed to the wound on his shoulder, the other clenched into a tight fist. He wondered how he'd worked around McAlister and never noticed the blank look in the man's eyes.

"Where's Rich?"

McAlister shook his head and waved the gun towards the bedroom. "Keep moving, Laine. I've waited for you for years."

"Why me, McAlister? What the—" The gun stilled in McAlister's hand, aimed at Laine's heart and making him reconsider his words. He couldn't let McAlister kill him, not before he got Rich out of here, but he was beginning to lose hope of either of them surviving this.

"Who knows, why you, Laine. Not me. It just was—is." McAlister surprised him by answering. "At least, this time, I left your lover alone. Why you'd go from a big, attractive man like Conner to a little pretty boy like that is beyond me. Maybe that's all you could get out here in bumfuck, Texas, huh?"

Laine refused to rise to the bait, seething at being so close to Conner's killer and unable to do anything. As he passed the spare bedroom, McAlister pointed inside the room.

"There's Detective Montoya, alive and... I wouldn't say *well*, but he is alive, for a little while longer. Probably wishes he were dead, though."

He saw Rich tied to the bed, naked but covered in so much blood that very little skin showed. Laine stumbled, turning for the door. McAlister waved the gun.

"I don't think so, Laine. You'll just have to take my word for it." He laughed, the sound high pitched and psychotic. Laine grabbed the doorframe and met McAlister's gaze.

"If he's dead, I will kill you, no matter how many bullets you put into me." He saw something shift in McAlister's gaze, a nervous flicker that belied the man's calm appearance.

"Brave talk, Laine. I doubt you'd recover from having your brains splattered all over the hallway. Somehow, I'm not worried."

Laine turned to watch Rich. He saw the man's chest rise, a slight movement that gave Laine back the hope that had started to slip away. A sudden insight flared in Laine's mind—McAlister had done this, hurt so many people, killed people, just to have *him*. He wouldn't be satisfied with a simple bullet. His smile when he faced McAlister again was tight, a bare thinning of lips.

"That would ruin all your fun, now, wouldn't it? To hunt me for all these years, then end it in a split second. I don't think you'd do that." Laine pushed away from the doorframe, knowing he was right, seeing it in the surprise on McAlister's face. He lunged for the gun, gripping

McAlister's wrist and smashing it into the wooden trim. The gun went off, a bullet ripping into the wall as they struggled. Laine dug his fingers in deep, twisting and slamming McAlister's arm against the hard wood again.

The gun fell to the floor, but before Laine could reach for it, McAlister looped an arm around Laine's neck and began choking him, dragging Laine down the hallway as Laine tried to free himself. Desperation speared through Laine as his vision dimmed, and he bit, tearing at the flesh as he brought a hand up and squeezed McAlister's balls. An agonised scream pierced the air and Laine was shoved down to the floor, a sharp kick catching him in the ribs, then another landed to his kidneys. Laine tried to work through the pain, dodging another kick as he scrambled across the hall, trying to grab onto the wall, anything to pull himself up.

McAlister delivered another kick, this one under Laine's arm, right to the armpit, and Laine went down hard. An explosion of sound ricocheted in the house, quickly followed by another, then a third, and McAlister was falling, blood spraying in an arc, turning the hall into a crimson-coloured hell.

Laine tried to roll over, his hand slipping in blood, then Sev was there, his face wet with tears, kneeling beside him. Sev's hands raced over him, and Laine tried to hear the words his lover was speaking, but nothing made sense. His head was spinning, other hands were grabbing at him, pulling him up. Brendon and Zeke, he realised, then they saw Rich and there was a blur of movement, raised voices. Sev's arms tightened around Laine, holding him up as his knees gave out, the smaller man taking his weight.

"Come on, baby, you're going to be fine."

Laine's ears stopped ringing and Sev's words finally penetrated the grey wall of unconsciousness that was threatening.

"Sev..." Laine tried to grab Sev's arm as Sev laid him on the couch, kneeling beside Laine so he could apply pressure to the shoulder wound. Fiery fingers of pain speared out from Laine's shoulder as Sev pressed harder, and Laine gasped, trying to buck Sev off even though he knew better. Sev leant down and brushed a kiss across Laine's lips, the salty flavour of his tears finding Laine's tongue. Sirens wailed in the distance, the sound rapidly growing closer.

"Sev, need to tell you..." Laine fumbled for the words, his world tilting and rapidly growing dark.

Sev smiled tremulously, his eyes shining. "I know, Laine, I know. Me too."

Those words eased the pain and followed Laine into the dark well that swept over him, freeing him from everything but the love of, and for, this one man.

Epilogue

Laine stood beside Rich's hospital bed, watching the slow rise and fall of his friend's chest. Machines beeped and whirred, pumping oxygen and fluids into Rich's body. Sev stood beside Laine, an arm wound around Laine's waist. Laine's arm rested on Sev's shoulders, snugging the man tight to his side. He could feel the strain in Sev's body, the smaller man almost vibrating as he worked to fend off voices he didn't want to hear. It would have been easier on him, and Laine would have understood, if Sev had stayed at Brendon and Zeke's while Laine visited Rich. As it was, Laine had left the hospital well before Doctor Hunter wanted him to. He couldn't bear to see Sev struggling to maintain the walls he'd erected in his mind to keep out the ghosts.

And he'd rather have Sev playing nurse for him any day than the sour-faced guy who'd been prodding at Laine here in the hospital. Matt tapped on the door then made his way over to the bed. He'd been released three days earlier, but as far as Laine could tell, the man hadn't left the hospital much at all. He seemed to feel personally responsible for Rich's survival.

"Any changes?"

Laine shook his head. "No, but that isn't necessarily a bad thing. He's not getting any worse. Dr. Hunter says it could take a few more days, and considering…"

Matt nodded in agreement. Considering all the blood Rich had lost, the multiple stab wounds that had taken hours in surgery to repair, and the near miss to Rich's jugular from the gaping gash to his neck, the man was lucky to be alive.

"But he will wake up; he'll be okay." Matt's voice rang with a surety that Laine wished he felt. Rich was so still, except for the steady breaths. He hadn't flicked so much as a finger since he'd been laid on a gurney and wheeled from Laine's house.

"He will be." Sev squeezed Laine's waist before stroking his hand over Laine's hip. "Rich will wake up soon."

There was that surety that, once again, Laine wished he could feel. "Matt, call me if—the second he wakes, okay?"

"Yeah, I'll do that. You get everything straightened out at work?"

Laine shrugged and grimaced, the move pulling at his wound. "Wasn't as many people screaming for a recall vote as I, or the mayor, thought there'd be. Irma was the loudest, and I think she scared off most the other people who weren't happy with me being gay. Or maybe the people of McKinton are tired of violence and hatred. Everything's okay for now."

"Laine," Sev's voice carried a hint of reproach, "I think you misjudged the people of McKinton. There are a few narrow-minded bigots, sure, but you'll find those people anywhere. Think about all the flowers and cards and visitors you've had, and Doreen tearing into anyone who dares to speak ill of you. The support has really been overwhelmingly in your favour."

Thinking about it made Laine's cheeks heat with embarrassment. "I guess so, though Deputy Sparks doesn't seem to be able to even look me in the eye. I keep hoping he'll come around, but..." Laine didn't think it would happen. It had hurt, having a man he'd worked with and known for years look at him like that, disapproval clear in his eyes.

"Sparks is an asshole, Laine, seriously. If he is gonna be a dumbshit, then I hope he does quit. I personally can't stand the guy, anyway." Matt's gaze darted away, and Laine wondered what had happened between the two men to make Matt feel that way.

"You never said anything before."

This time it was Matt who shrugged, blowing off the unasked question.

"Well, guess he'll do whatever he'll do. Worrying isn't gonna make a difference." Laine looked at Rich, willing the man to wake, to smile and make a snarky comment to Matt, or bitch at Laine for not staying in touch. Anything. He'd settle for a nervous tic, but Rich remained as he'd been for days, silent and unmoving.

"Yeah," Matt rested his hands on the bedrail. "But I'm sorry he's being a prick."

Sev tapped Laine's hip and Laine took it for the signal it was. He touched Matt's shoulder then let Sev lead him out of the room. They left the hospital and, after a short debate, decided to have lunch at Virginia's café.

Laine parked his truck in front of the café and fingered the keys as he considered what he wanted to say. He could feel Sev watching him, and it made him more nervous, terrified he would bumble the words that were so important to him.

"Laine, you're making me nervous," Sev teased, trailing a hand up Laine's thigh. "Just spit it out already."

That's my romantic little lover. All poetry and flowers. And he was stalling. Laine raised his eyes to Sev's and held his hand where it pressed against Laine's thigh.

"Okay. I'm not good with words, but there's some things I need to say." He felt the tips of his ears burning and wondered if he couldn't have found a card to say it for him. A distinctive thump to the back of his head knocked the idea away. *Guess that would be Conner's version of 'no'.*

Sev looked worried now, his brows knitting together, and Laine realised he'd been quiet too long. He was fucking this up.

"I... You haven't said if you're planning on staying, and—" Sev didn't look worried anymore. He looked pissed, and Laine hurried to finish before that frown on his lover turned more severe. "We've been staying with Zeke and Brendon, I can't go back to that house, can't live where Rich almost died, I just can't." A quick check told Laine Sev had softened somewhat, but the man still wasn't happy. "If I... We could, maybe, we could get a different place? If you want to stay here, stay with me?" *Say the words, you idiot!* Laine would have sworn that wasn't his voice he heard rattling between his ears. And Sev still didn't look happy.

"Laine, why do you think I'm not planning to stay around, as you put it? Do you think I'm not capable of being serious, of loving one person, loving you?" Sev's voice hitched with hurt. "I thought... I thought you—"

Laine was stuck on the 'loving you' part of Sev's speech. He smacked the seatbelt release and jerked Sev into his lap, grunting at the pain in his shoulder, and not giving a damn who was watching or if he made a fool of himself any more.

"Because I love you, and I'm scared. I haven't ever felt like this, Sev, and you didn't say anything… Ah, what you said when I was shot, well, you were emotional and—ow!" Laine didn't know if the second thump to the back of his head or Sev's strong fingers pinching his thigh hurt more. "Christ, Sev!"

"*I* was emotional? *You* were the one trying to say it first!" Sev's chin tipped up at a stubborn angle that had Laine's cock growing hard in a heartbeat.

"Yeah, but—"

"But what? You didn't mean it?"

Shit! "I meant it, Sev. I did, I do, but I wouldn't hold you to it under the circumstances, that's all I was trying to say."

And it still wasn't the right time, Laine thought, until Sev's glower turned into the smile Laine loved so much.

"Now I know why Brendon calls you a dumbass, Laine. I meant it then, I mean it now. Quit doubting me—and yourself, okay?" Sev brushed the tips of his fingers over Laine's lips. "I'd love to kiss you, strip you naked and show you just how much I love you, but—"

Laine was pushing Sev from his lap, back over into his own seat before Sev finished. "But nothing. You love me, I love you, we're out of here. Lunch can wait."

Sev's laughter warmed Laine's heart as his hand started warming other parts of Laine's body. For the first time in days, Laine knew everything was going to be better than okay. He had the man he loved, and the freedom to be himself, and if there was the occasional spinning star or head thumping, that was fine, too. He'd take it all, and love every minute of it.

About the Author

A native Texan, Bailey spends her days spinning stories around in her head, which has contributed to more than one incident of tripping over her own feet. Evenings are reserved for pounding away at the keyboard, as are early morning hours. Sleep? Doesn't happen much. Writing is too much fun, and there are too many characters bouncing about, tapping on Bailey's brain demanding to be let out.

Caffeine and chocolate are permanent fixtures in Bailey's office and are never far from hand at any given time. Removing either of those necessities from Bailey's presence can result in what is know as A Very, Very Scary Bailey and is not advised under any circumstances.

Bailey Bradford loves to hear from readers. You can find her contact information, website details and author profile page at http://www.total-e-bound.com.

Total-E-Bound Publishing

www.total-e-bound.com

Take a look at our exciting range of literagasmic™
erotic romance titles and discover pure quality
at Total-E-Bound.

Made in the USA
Lexington, KY
20 November 2010